A Lady's Guide to London

FAYE DELACOUR

sourcebooks
casablanca

Copyright © 2025 by Faye Delacour
Cover and internal design © 2025 by Sourcebooks
Cover design by Alan Ayers/Lott Reps
Hand lettering by Sarah Brody/Sourcebooks

Sourcebooks and the colophon are registered trademarks of Sourcebooks.

Published by Sourcebooks Casablanca, an imprint of Sourcebooks
P.O. Box 4410, Naperville, Illinois 60567-4410
(630) 961-3900
sourcebooks.com

Cataloging-in-Publication Data is on file with the Library of Congress.

Printed and bound in the United States of America.
SB 10 9 8 7 6 5 4 3 2 1

To my husband,
for his unfailing support and patience.
I could not have written this book without you.

One

London, 1842

"WE NEED TO HIRE MORE ATTRACTIVE STAFF." CORDELIA DANBY made this suggestion from the safety of the offices of their gaming house, where there was no risk of any of their thoroughly average-looking staff overhearing her. The place was nearly deserted at this time of day. Their real work began in the evenings, when their rooms would be packed with women coming to gamble away their pin money.

The small but fashionably located building they'd rented on Piccadilly had once belonged to a chocolate house that went out of business when its owner passed. Taking the opportunity as serendipity—for what better start could there be for a gambling club modeled after White's than a chocolate house?—they'd maintained the vocation, but converted the upstairs smoking and retiring rooms to card rooms. The sign out front read MRS. BISHOP'S CHOCOLATE EMPORIUM, and beneath, in slightly smaller print, LADIES ONLY. There was no Mrs. Bishop, of course. The name had been chosen in honor of Della's friend and business partner, who had ceased to be a Bishop on her wedding day and was now Jane Williams.

"Pardon?" Jane looked up from the ledger in confusion. She hadn't heard a word—a frequent occurrence of late. She had her infant daughter, Gloria, tucked in the crook of one arm and was rocking her gently while she used her only free hand to tally their accounts. Her eyes were bleary and her hair was askew.

"The dealers," Della repeated. "The only good-looking one in the whole lot was Frederick. Now that he's gone, there's no one to entice our clientele."

"Frederick was stealing money from the pot, you will recall." Jane's husband, Eli, set aside the bills he'd been organizing to join in their conversation. He, too, sported shadows beneath his eyes and a look of perpetual fatigue. It was hard to say whether the club or their baby was the cause. Both of them were needy little creatures, though rewarding in their own ways. "I should think that's more important than his looks."

"Maybe I didn't express myself properly," Della amended. Other people often needed a certain amount of coaxing before they appreciated the value of her ideas, even when those ideas seemed perfectly obvious to her. "What I *meant* to say is, there's no one handsome enough to tempt the ladies into staying all night and spending more money than they ought. It's not frivolous; it's just good business."

Not that I'd object to a little diversion. If she was going to spend nearly every evening supervising play now that Jane was busy with her newborn, she should really have someone to flirt with. It had been ages since she'd had time for a paramour.

"Anyway, I want to be the one to do the hiring next time."

Eli shot a glance to Jane, who merely shrugged. "She's right about our members staying longer at Frederick's table."

There we are. Once Jane had come round to her way of thinking, the matter was settled.

"We should do something about the decor, too," Della added. She might as well press home her advantage while she had their attention. "A few more paintings would do wonders."

The main gaming room was looking much brighter since they repapered it with something from this decade, but the walls were still so *bare.* They couldn't attract a wealthy set if they looked shabby.

"This is starting to sound expensive." Jane frowned. "You can hire one more dealer and an extra waiter. If we're adding a roulette table like we talked about, we'll need them anyway. But we don't have a budget for any more than that, and we certainly can't afford paintings."

Jane worried too much. They were doing quite well, else Della wouldn't have pushed for new expenses. Things had been shaky in their first few years of operation. What profit they made from the games had gone straight to fixing up the premises and hiring their first staff, little more than a skeleton crew. Della had loaned their establishment rent money more than once. But now that they'd amassed a steady base of members and a small nest egg, it was time to aim a little higher.

Of course, she understood why Jane and Eli were more cautious. The club's income was their entire livelihood, whereas Della could go home and live comfortably on her parents' largesse, should she choose not to aspire to any more in life than what was handed to her. That was certainly what everyone *expected* her to do.

No matter. With a little ingenuity, she could accomplish her goal without causing any financial stress, as she usually did.

"I could borrow a piece or two from my parents' collection until we find a more permanent solution." She cast a hopeful glance to the others. "Perhaps your families could loan us a few forgotten treasures of their own? If we pool our efforts, we'll fill the walls without spending a shilling."

"I suppose." Eli seemed to consider this a moment. "My mother and Hannah are coming up from Devon to visit next week. I can write to ask if they'll bring a few decorations with them, but we won't have much say over their choice."

"Thank you!" Della nearly squealed with glee. "You'll be happy once you see how nice it looks."

"I'll be happy if it really brings in more members," Jane muttered.

"I have another suggestion for that," Della began. "And it won't cost a thing. Wait until I tell you."

Jane didn't always approve of Della's plans, but *this* one was sure to impress. It involved very little effort and would bring in new clients for years to come. She'd outdone herself.

But alas, Gloria chose that moment to turn her tiny face from side to side, fitful mewls escaping her mouth.

"Not again." Jane looked as though she might join her daughter in tears soon. "She only slept twenty minutes. How can she be awake already?"

"Let me take her," Eli offered. "I'll walk her around the hall so you can finish what you need to, and then let's go home so you can get some rest."

Jane looked at her husband regretfully. "I think she's hungry. Turn around so I can feed her first."

"*I* should turn around?" He laughed, with a look toward Della.

"It's different at home. And anyway, I want to hear Della's idea." Eli shook his head, but turned away as he'd been bid. As soon as her husband's back was to them, Jane unlaced the front of her gown and began nursing the infant, who quieted immediately. She turned her attention back to Della. "I'm sorry. She never seems happy unless I'm holding her or feeding her. Maybe I should just hire a wet nurse so that I could finally get these accounts up to date, but it seems such a needless expense. What were you going to tell me?"

"Have you heard of this book?" Della lifted a small, leather-bound volume from the desk, holding it up so that Jane could see without having to reach. *The Discerning Gentleman's Guide to London*, read the gold-leaf lettering across the front.

"No."

"It would really be better if Eli could see it." He was far more likely to fall within the book's readership. "Can't he look for just a moment?"

"I promise it won't shock me," Eli piped in.

"Very well," Jane relented, a note of fatigue in her voice.

Eli turned back around and Della passed him the book.

"Oh, yes. My brother has a copy." He thumbed through the pages for a moment before setting it back down on the desk.

"Mine does too. Many men use it to decide where to spend their time and money, particularly those who only come to town for the season." Della turned her attention back to Jane. "It has all sorts of recommendations. Public houses, baths, theaters, and gentleman's clubs."

Jane frowned at the little book. "What does that have to do with us?"

"Well, if White's is in there, why shouldn't we be? Just *think* how many people would read it and come here."

Della folded her hands on her lap and awaited the praise she so richly deserved. Unfortunately, Jane proved stingy with her compliments this morning.

"At the risk of stating the obvious, we run a *ladies'* club. This is a guide for gentlemen."

"Gentlemen have wives and sisters, don't they?" Della motioned vaguely at Eli, but instead of coming to her aid, he chose this moment to turn his back again and let the two friends sort it out. So much for any support there. "It's only addressed to gentlemen because they can go anywhere they please, but plenty of the attractions are for *both* sexes. I'm sure I'm not the only woman who consults it."

"I suppose..." Jane's reluctance was merely a step away from approval. Reluctance was her natural state.

She'll thank me when we're rich.

"I wrote to the publisher to ask how we might go about making a suggestion to the author for a future inclusion, and they told me he's working on a second edition *right now*." Della clapped her hands, startling Gloria, who began to wail. "Oops! Sorry... All we have to do is persuade him to include us and we'll have free publicity for years to come. I'm going to meet with him tomorrow."

"Meet with him?" Jane echoed. Though she'd been distracted trying to get the baby settled again, this shocked her back to attention, and she raised her voice to carry over the cries. "Have you been introduced to this man? Where will you find him?"

"His publisher forwarded him my letter and we've been corresponding. I used my initials, so he's going to be surprised to see that I'm a woman, but there you are."

He might have some reservations at first, but once they were face-to-face, Della knew she could convince him. She had a knack for this sort of thing. And it was perfect—a mention in his book would grant them the stamp of approval they'd been after for years. Recognition that they weren't a passing fancy, but an established fixture of London.

Then Jane might finally be able to stop fretting over money, and it would be all thanks to her. Everyone would finally see that Della wasn't just a pampered socialite who'd joined her friend's endeavor on a whim; she was a proper businesswoman with valuable ideas to contribute.

But Jane only frowned, oblivious to her genius. "Della, really, this is a bit much. Will you talk some sense into her?"

"I'm sure I can't," Eli replied. *Good man.* He and Della had grown to know each other well enough over the past three years that he could see when he was outmatched. He came over to her side to look at the book once more. "Lyman E. Price, Viscount Ashton," he read. "The name sounds familiar, but I don't believe I know him. Shall I take Gloria now?"

"Yes, please. I'm certain I just heard her say 'papa'; she must be calling you."

"At only three months! What a remarkable baby."

They both chuckled at the joke, which seemed to mean something more to them than Della understood. There had once been a time when she knew all of Jane's secrets, but lately they seemed to be out of step.

You missed some things during her confinement, that's all. It will be better now that she's coming back to the club again.

Eli leaned down to gingerly lift his daughter into his arms. Though she still fussed, the noise subsided as he began pacing the room with her, bouncing lightly on each step.

"Why should a viscount want to publish a guidebook of popular attractions, anyway?" Jane asked, her attention back on Della.

"Perhaps it makes him feel fashionable."

Lord Ashton certainly wouldn't be the only aristocrat with a vanity project. At least his guide was something useful. Della had never understood why most members of her class should be content to pass their time without any challenge to occupy them, as if life was just one long afternoon tea. She couldn't stand to be at loose ends. Maybe the viscount would share her outlook on life, and they would become fast friends. He seemed very gentlemanlike in his letters.

"It's reckless to meet a strange man in public." Jane clucked her

tongue. "But I know you'll do it anyway, so good luck. I suppose it's
no worse than the time you snuck into Mrs. Berry's autumn harvest
party without a chaperone. Will you still be done in time to supervise
here afterward? I really can't get away. Gloria gets colicky at night."

"Of course. Don't think of it."

Jane had put in her share of long hours before her confinement
and delivery. And she'd scarcely had time to recover before she
resumed her practice of handling the bookkeeping every morning,
while Eli still returned most evenings to help supervise and deal at
the main table. Della couldn't ask for more. They deserved to have
what little rest she could give them.

"Oh!" Jane exclaimed. "And if Mrs. Muller comes in, you have
to tell her we're cutting off her credit and canceling her membership
unless she settles her debts." With a wince, she added, "Sorry. I know
it's not very pleasant, but please don't forget."

"I won't," Della assured her, blushing. She wished she had Jane's
ability to store every detail in her head, but she'd been known to
misplace a page from the betting books or forget to place their champagne order on time. When things got busy and the noise of the
crowd overpowered her, it sometimes felt like she was trying to juggle
more balls than she had hands to catch with.

No matter. If Jane could do it, so could she.

Her friend slid the leather-bound ledger across the table. "I book-
marked the page with her account for you."

Della tried not to let her reluctance show as she flipped it open
and glanced at the tally. A hundred and twenty pounds. Cold as it
might seem to turn Mrs. Muller out, it had to be done. They had a
strict policy on such matters. Warnings given if the debt reached a
hundred pounds, and swift action if one failed to settle up promptly.
Better to cut off the ladies who didn't know when to stop than to let
them ruin their households.

They differed from White's in that respect.

"I'll be fine," Della assured her. She would have to be. Jane couldn't handle *everything* herself, and they were partners, weren't they? Partners shared things. "Go home and get some sleep. I'll take care of everything here while you're gone, from intemperate gamblers to handsome dealers to gentleman authors."

"Thank you." Jane's sigh of relief was gratifying. "I don't know what I'd do without you."

"I want the next one named after me."

Two

LYMAN PRICE WAS SEATED BEFORE A LARGE WINDOW IN VEREY'S café, overlooking Regent Street. It was a small but expensive establishment in Mayfair that catered primarily to ladies' luncheons at this hour of the day, though gentlemen could find good French cookery and wines for supper in the evenings. Not a place Lyman would have chosen for a meeting, but it hadn't been his suggestion. At least it wouldn't be difficult to find Mr. Danby, even if he had no idea what the man looked like.

Lyman had described himself in his last letter (*I'll be the one with dark hair, wearing spectacles and a brown coat*), but Mr. Danby hadn't seen fit to return the gesture. He might be any of the gentlemen who passed by the window.

Why am I even here?

He needed to get his revisions finished and turn his draft over to his publisher so that he could return to work on his guide to Bath. The sooner he was done, the sooner he'd get his money. Mr. Danby probably didn't even have anything new to tell him. Half the time, when someone wrote about some perceived omission from the guide, it was only a neighborhood pub with stale bread and warm beer, unworthy of mention.

But there had been something compelling about Danby's letters—an engaging wit that made him think his correspondent's ideas might be worth his time—and Danby had insisted that it would be simpler to explain the attraction in person. Better to take a half hour from his day than to miss something his publisher might chide him over later.

A feminine voice interrupted his thoughts, her tone too cheery.

"Excuse me, are you Viscount Ashton?" He looked up to find a lady of his own class standing before his table.

She was small and plump, and exceptionally pretty, with a round face and large, dark eyes. Her honey-brown curls were pinned up beneath a wide-brimmed straw bonnet with a ribbon that perfectly matched her blue gingham morning gown, trimmed with French lace. She looked rather like an expensive doll, right down to the healthy flush of pink that dusted her cheeks.

"I'm Cordelia Danby. I wrote to you."

Cordelia. The C was for Cordelia. Not Charles or Colin or Christopher.

Lyman blinked, as if the sight before him might transform itself if he only refreshed his eyes.

"I'm not what you expected," she said, mischief warming her smile. It was a look designed to charm, and it was working. "I apologize. But I wasn't sure you'd come if you realized you were corresponding with a woman."

I wouldn't have. There was no brother or husband with her, nor any lady's companion. What could she mean by this?

"You aren't very talkative, are you?" That same smile again, quite devilish. "Would you mind if we walked over to Hanover Square? I would sit, but..."

Evidently she had no objection to meeting him alone, but dining together was a bridge too far.

"Forgive me," Lyman said, rising to his feet. He should've stood earlier. "You surprised me, Miss Danby. That's all."

Was she a miss? He didn't see a ring, and she didn't correct him, so she must be. Besides, if she had a husband, he wouldn't let her wander about town meeting strange men.

"A walk would be lovely," he added, setting a tuppence on the table for his tea and offering his arm as they exited Verey's. She took it, settling neatly against his side.

She smelled nice; slightly lemony. A tart, bright scent that seemed to match her carefree manner.

He had no idea who this woman was, or what gossip he might be fueling if they were seen together, but Lyman wasn't going to show more concern for her reputation than she did. She'd arranged this meeting, after all.

"I'm the co-owner of Bishop's," she began, the moment they crossed the street. "Perhaps you've heard of us?"

"I regret to say I have not."

"We're a chocolate house, exclusively for ladies. We have all the amusements one could traditionally find at a gentlemen's chocolate house, such as White's, for example."

"Ah." *A gaming hell for ladies. Whatever next?*

He studied Miss Danby as they reached Hanover Square, where they set down the small path that encircled a little patch of garden before the church. The sun's rays had lightened her eyes to a rich shade of toffee that contrasted with the darker hue of her thick lashes and straight brows. Her skin was smooth and flawless.

She didn't look like a hellcat; she looked like any other young lady of means, remarkable only in how pretty she was. But if he'd thought her daring or foolhardy for meeting him like this, it paled in comparison to her other activities. How did someone in her position end up running a gambling club?

With a growing sense of unease, Lyman pondered what her business had to do with him.

Surely not.

But Miss Danby continued talking, confirming his fears. "We're a unique venture, the only one of its kind in London, and I daresay the whole country. I think we'd make an excellent choice for a mention in your book."

What presumption! Best to end this quickly, before she could get carried away. "Thank you for the suggestion, Miss Danby, but I don't intend to add any more gaming establishments in the next edition."

"But why not?" Her playful manner faded, leaving real confusion in its wake. The lady wore her sentiments so openly that Lyman could read her thoughts before she gave them voice. "If there's something new and interesting, you must include it. That's the whole point of releasing new editions, isn't it?"

Lyman held his tongue as another couple approached them. The man's gaze lingered a touch too long. Though Lyman couldn't place him, there'd been a hint of recognition on his face before he turned to murmur something in the ear of his companion. Had they recognized him? He waited until they'd gone a little further down the path before he spoke again, lest they tell all their friends they'd seen the Viscount Ashton discussing gambling clubs in the company of an unmarried lady.

"Miss Danby, with all due respect, it's a *gentleman's* guide. Why would I include a ladies' club?"

"Some gentlemen have wives."

"Only the unhappy ones," Lyman replied, before he could think better of it.

"What a terrible thing to say." Miss Danby's generous lips parted in shock, though he wouldn't have taken her for an innocent. "If you're unmarried, it's very conceited of you to issue a blanket condemnation of something of which you have no firsthand knowledge. And if you *are* married, it's quite cruel of you to speak that way about your wife, who would be heartbroken to hear you, I'm sure."

She raised one dark eyebrow, challenging him to deny the assessment.

He might have said nothing. The opportunity was there, and Lyman's instinct was to take it. Better to avoid such an unpleasant conversation with a woman he barely knew.

But that's not the real reason you don't want to tell her, is it? As with all things, it came back to his own selfish pleasure. There was temptation in the way Miss Danby's gaze lingered on him as they spoke, in the teasing note in her voice, and the ever-present spark in her large, dark eyes.

She was very pretty, and she was trying to charm him. And Lyman—bastard that he was—enjoyed it.

This wasn't a mature widow, in a position to take risks with her reputation. Miss Danby was young—in her mid-twenties, he would guess—and unmarried. In spite of her unconventional pastime of running a den of sin and ruin, she struck him as guileless. There was a certain childlike optimism in her speech and manners that warned him away.

He would drain every ounce of goodness from her spirit if given the chance, just as he had with Ellen. Better to stamp out this spark before it could burn her.

So he forced himself to say what he did next: "I'm afraid you're mistaken on both counts, Miss Danby. I *do* have firsthand knowledge of the subject, for I am married, and I assure you it has made me miserable. As for Lady Ashton, there is no need to worry about my breaking her heart. I accomplished the task years ago. If we were still on speaking terms, I'm sure she would be the first to tell you that no sane person should enter the yoke of matrimony."

The result of this speech was exactly as expected. Miss Danby stared at him as if he'd just dipped a kitten into a cup of tea and eaten it whole.

Monster, her eyes said. *Scoundrel.*

All true. And now that she knew it, Miss Danby would clutch her skirts and run back to wherever she'd come from. Her mischievous smile would never entice him again.

But she didn't run. She drew a long breath and studied the scenery while Lyman tried not to dwell on the sensation of her hand upon his arm or her lemon-tart scent.

"Well," she said finally. "I suppose when you put our club in your book, we can't count on your wife's patronage then."

A bark of laughter escaped him, quite against his will. *Who is this woman?*

"Miss Danby, I admire your tenacity, but my answer is still no."

A gambling club for ladies.

If she ran any other sort of establishment, he would have been tempted to give in, if only to reward her persistence. But this was out of the question. It was bad enough that the men of this country brought their families to the brink of starvation and ruin on a roll of the dice. He wouldn't help Miss Danby infect the remaining half of the population with the same affliction. He knew the toll it took all too well.

"Come and see it for yourself," she invited. "I'll give you a tour of the premises, then you can judge if it's worthy of a mention alongside White's or Brooks's. You won't be disappointed."

Lyman stiffened. The promise of a personal tour from a beautiful woman might have tempted him in other circumstances, but not here. She couldn't know how unwelcome her offer was.

He searched for a polite excuse. "I wouldn't want to frighten away all your guests. It can't be much of a ladies' club if you let me in."

She flashed that smile again. An impish glimpse of white between the pink of her lips that promised something more wicked yet to come. "I'd be more worried for you than for them, to be quite honest. Our members are known to get a bit rowdy without their husbands and fathers around, and you'd grant them a tempting diversion. But if things *did* get out of hand, we have a six-foot-tall reformed pirate handling our security who could quiet things down rather quickly." At Lyman's stunned chuckle, she added, "None of that was a joke."

It seemed Miss Danby had an answer to everything, but he wouldn't drag this out any further. What she asked of him was impossible.

"Let me be as clear as I can. I won't attend your club under any circumstances."

She withdrew her arm from his and squared her shoulders.

"I urge you to reconsider. I would much rather be your friend than your enemy, Lord Ashton."

My enemy? Of all the absurdities that had escaped her mouth in the past quarter hour, that had to take the cake. Standing in a patch of sunlight that fell across her face, dressed in her fine clothes and barely coming to his shoulder, Miss Danby couldn't have looked any less threatening. A pampered tabby who thought herself a tiger. Yet the firm set of her jaw betrayed how serious she was.

"I regret that I cannot." He almost meant it. This short acquaintance had proven Miss Danby to be an unconventional lady, one that he would have liked to know better. But that path held more danger than he could afford.

He needed to finish the revisions to his book as soon as possible—with *real* attractions, not the thinly veiled temptation this woman offered—and collect his money. He had debts to pay. Too many to count.

"Very well," she finally conceded. "But you're making a mistake."

With that ominous warning, Miss Danby took her leave. Lyman watched her until she was out of sight, unable to shake the feeling she had only been a strange dream.

The club was busy that evening. So much so that Della should have quickly forgotten her rejection from Viscount Ashton. Eli hadn't arrived yet, which meant it fell to her to keep an eye on any suspicious play, nip extravagant bets in the bud, circle the room to make sure their guests were happy, and monitor that the service of refreshments was neither stingy nor intemperate. It was a lot to handle, and Della had begun to wonder if their profits were at a point where they might hire a manager to oversee such practicalities for them.

Jane will say no. Della sighed as she slipped into the kitchen to inform the waitstaff to stop serving champagne to Mrs. Fairfield before she had to be rolled into her carriage.

Her friend could be too spendthrift sometimes. But Jane has also been indefatigable, prior to meeting her match in the form of an eight-pound, squalling tyrant. When *she'd* been the one managing the club in the evenings, there had never been a need for more help.

If she could handle it, why can't I?

No matter how Della tried, she never achieved the same level of competence. Jane never got distracted, and she had a no-nonsense tone that made people fall in line. One arch of her brow and debts were paid, overly boisterous ladies hushed their voices, and servants whisked away empty glasses and plates. No one took Della half so seriously.

Just look at Lord Ashton. She'd used every tool at her disposal. She'd been charming, then she'd tried reason, then finally threats. None of it had made the slightest difference.

At best, he'd thought her silly: a reckless young lady who'd bitten off more than she could chew with this endeavor. He was hardly the first to draw such a conclusion. Most men scoffed at her club—if not to her face, then certainly behind her back. Della had learned not to pay any mind what they thought of her, but the condemnation in the viscount's eyes was more difficult to shrug off.

It's because he was so handsome.

What a disappointing reason! Della wished she were above such thoughts—particularly given that she'd approached Lord Ashton purely for matters of business—but she had a terrible weakness for handsome men, and the viscount was exactly her type. Although, to be fair, "her type" was a broad category that could encompass some variety in the male figure. In this case, the gentleman was of trim build and very neat in his personal appearance, his jaw cleanly shaven and his hair combed back. He was taller than her (although this wasn't difficult to accomplish), but not so large as to be imposing. The sprinkling of gray at his temples hinted he might be a touch too old for her, or perhaps that impression came from his stern gaze.

I wonder if he likes to take charge in the bedroom. She did love a man with a sense of authority.

"Sorry I'm late." Eli interrupted her reverie, his cravat askew. "Where do you need me?"

Oh dear. She should be minding her own business—quite literally—not indulging in speculation about Lord Ashton's sexual prowess. Besides, hadn't he said he was married? She couldn't tell if that part was real or only his attempt at dark humor. The circumstances of the revelation had been so strange.

Why can't you ever focus?

"We're running low on champagne. You might run over to the wine seller's and buy a few more bottles."

"Already? We've just restocked."

"We've been busy," Della replied. "It's a good thing. Speaking of which, the games are overcrowded. There isn't enough space for everyone who wants to play. Do you think you could manage to squeeze another card table over by the sideboard and get one of the waiters to sit as an extra dealer? Only pick something simple, like faro."

"Champagne first, though?" Eli looked to her for confirmation.

"I suppose so?" Della wasn't sure who she was asking. Jane, probably. But Jane was gone, and it was up to her to make these decisions now. "Yes," she repeated, more firmly. The trick was to pretend she was sure of herself, so it looked like she knew what she was doing. "Champagne first. Ten bottles should keep us safe for tonight. Then the extra table once you're back."

She would have liked Eli's help managing the floor, but he should go where he was most needed. Della sized up the crowd, trying to decide where *she* was most needed. Lady Eleanor Grosvenor was at baccarat. As one of their more influential members, she always required a degree of attention. But Della also spotted Miss Chatterjee and Mrs. Duff circling one another at the edges of a vingt-et-un table like sharks on the scent of blood. Everyone knew they'd had a falling-out which had something to do with Mr. Duff's wandering eye. Oh, and there was Mrs. Muller, about to lose a heap of chips at whist! Della had promised to cut off her credit tonight. But she could hardly do it *now*, with everyone watching. She would have to get her alone first, which would mean abandoning her other tasks.

There were simply too many things to attend to and not enough of her to do it all.

Mrs. Duff had just said something that made Miss Chatterjee's brows draw together. *Oh dear.* They were the most urgent priority then, before someone came to blows and set their club's reputation tumbling down to the level of a common public house. She would deal with the rest after.

Della drew a deep breath and strode into their midst. Between the two of them, Reva Chatterjee was the one she was closest to. They'd been good friends for years, though they hadn't seen one another as often this season as they used to. Better to start with her than with Mrs. Duff. "Reva, how are you? We could use another player at the baccarat table. Won't you let me accompany you there?"

"Good riddance," Mrs. Duff muttered as they withdrew, not nearly softly enough to escape their hearing.

"Ugh." Reva rolled her eyes, once her back was safely turned. "*She's* the one who came up to *my* table."

"What happened between you two, anyway? I thought you used to get on."

"We *did*, until her awful husband started going on and on about what beautiful eyes I have at their rout last month. Now she's convinced herself that I'm trying to steal his attention, when I don't even like the man!" Reva's nostrils flared in indignation. "If she keeps this up, she'll ruin my reputation."

"Don't worry; everyone knows what he's like," Della reassured her. "I dined at their house once and he stared at my chest the whole night, even though my parents were right beside me. I think he's that way with everyone."

Reva made a face. "I hope so. Not that he should be a lecher, I mean, but I hope everyone knows it wasn't me who led him on. We're expecting Mr. Bhattacharya to propose soon, and I don't want him hearing any rumors about me."

"I'll have a word with Mrs. Duff as soon as things quiet down," Della promised. "And that's wonderful news about Mr. Bhattacharya! Are you excited?"

Reva's expression transformed to a bright smile, revealing a row of white teeth. "He's terribly handsome, and our families get along well. I think we'd make a good match."

Della wanted to ask Reva more about her courtship, but they'd already arrived at the baccarat table. She needed to make sure Lady Eleanor was properly attended to or she would feel slighted, and then there was still Mrs. Muller to talk to, and now Mrs. Duff as well.

"I need to get back to work, but why don't you stop in again tomorrow and we'll catch up properly?" she suggested. "Come a bit earlier, before the crush is in full force."

"I tried to call on you a few weeks ago," Reva revealed, biting her lip, "but you weren't at home and you never returned my call..." Her tone didn't carry any accusation, only a measure of doubt. As if she weren't quite sure if she'd been snubbed.

Oh dear. That's right, she'd seen Reva's card among the others and meant to do something about it, but that had been the same day that she'd first thought of her plan to get Bishop's put in *The Discerning Gentleman's Guide to London.* She'd been so excited with the idea that she'd forgotten everything else.

"I'm sorry." She squeezed Reva's hands between her own. "I've just been so busy at the club since Jane's confinement that I haven't had time to keep up with my friends as I ought. But if you come back another night, you're sure to catch me!"

Wait a minute, why should she stop there? Reva used to deal for them when they were shorthanded, back when the club was an informal group of ladies who played vingt-et-un in Della's drawing room on Monday evenings. And Della was certainly shorthanded now.

"What if you helped out again, the way you used to in the old days?" It would be wonderful to have a friend by her side in the evenings again. Eli did his best, of course, but Della missed having another woman to talk to. "We've got hired dealers now, but we could always use another lady to play hostess, if you want to earn some extra pin money."

"Er...thank you, Della." Reva's gaze slid away, toward the other players clustered around the baccarat table, who gave a whoop of victory as the next card was turned up. "It's always great fun here, but..." She shrugged helplessly as she met Della's eye once more. "I think I'm getting a bit old for this sort of thing. As I said, I wouldn't want Mr. Bhattacharya to hear any rumors about me."

"Oh." Della slumped a little as her fantasy went up in smoke. It would have been so perfect! But she could hardly blame Reva for having other plans for her own life, so she forced a smile and said, "I understand. Let's call on one another soon."

Once she'd said her goodbyes, she went directly to Lady Eleanor's side and was informed that her guest longed for nothing so much as a watercress sandwich, but the last one had been eaten by none other than Mrs. Muller (who had no doubt done it *on purpose*), which sent Della scrambling to the kitchen to persuade Cook to prepare another batch before Lady Eleanor expired from hunger.

The rest of the evening passed in a blur. Eli came back at some point to keep the champagne flowing, though Della scarcely saw him. She moved from table to table, smoothing away any troubles that might mar the thrill of the game. Jane's cousin, Lady Cecily Kerr, showed up around one in the morning and immediately made a hash of her play at vingt-et-un, leaving Della to intervene before anyone mistook her natural inability to recall the rules for an attempt to cheat. Some people really couldn't be trusted with a deck of cards.

Oh! Mrs. Muller!

Della had meant to find her hours ago. Where had she got to? A quick scan of the room revealed nothing. At this hour of the morning, only a few last hedonists remained at their games, their faces flushed with excitement and drink. Della went over to the whist dealer, who was packing away the chips.

"Good evening, Mr. Parekh. Did Mrs. Muller already leave, do you know? I thought I saw her here earlier."

"You just missed her, miss. She left about a quarter hour ago."

Drat! How had she forgotten? Della was loath to ask the question that weighed on her spirits, but she had to know. "Did she...um, lose very much?"

"Hmm." Parekh looked up from his count just long enough to bob his head in a noncommittal fashion. He pointed to the ledger for his table, letting the numbers speak for him. Twelve pounds, and that was on top of what she already owed them.

Della raised her eyes to the heavens and suppressed a groan. *Jane is going to kill me.*

"What's the matter?" Eli had finally found her again, now that his own table was empty.

"I forgot to cut off Mrs. Muller. I meant to do it earlier, but there was always something more urgent and it got away from me."

"Don't be too hard on yourself. We had our hands full the whole night. No one could have done more."

That wasn't strictly true, and they both knew it.

"Jane did more," Della said with a touch of regret.

Eli sighed, his expression turning wistful at the mention of his wife. "Jane is a singular woman. Not everyone can store the smallest details in their brain as she can, but we each have our own strengths. There's no point in comparing yourself to her. And as for Mrs. Muller, you'll get another chance."

"I suppose." Eli was probably right; there was no sense in worrying about what she couldn't change. But Della had a nagging feeling that she might have made Mrs. Muller her first priority if she hadn't found the prospect of catching up with Reva Chatterjee to be infinitely more appealing than the difficult conversation that was still in store for her.

"Anyway, I have good news," Eli continued. "I found someone for the new dealer's post. An old friend of mine from the navy."

What?

"I said *I* wanted to do the hiring, remember?"

Eli couldn't be trusted to judge the subtleties of male beauty the way she could. And handsome dealers were an essential part of her business plan!

"I know, I know." Eli winced. "But he's just been dishonorably discharged, and he has nowhere else to go. I can't abandon him."

"*Dishonorably.*" Della cocked an eyebrow.

"It was all a misunderstanding. Give him a chance before you say no, won't you? He's coming to London in two weeks. You can judge for yourself if he's handsome enough to be a dealer."

"Oh, is that how you're choosing staff now?" Parekh murmured. He fixed them both with a cool gaze, evidently having heard his fill.

Oh dear. When had he finished tallying his chips?

"Don't pay Mr. Williams any mind," Della blurted out. "That's just a little joke of his."

The dealer latched the box that held his chips and cards, then carried the whole lot over to the gaming cabinet, shaking his head as he went.

Eli turned back to Della. "I never had a chance to ask you: How did your meeting with that author fellow go this morning?"

"Terribly." She felt like pouting, if she weren't far too old for it. "He was so stubborn. He wouldn't even give me the courtesy of *pretending* to consider my request. Please don't tell Jane she was right; I would prefer to maintain an illusion of infallibility."

Eli chuckled. "I'll tell her that you thought better of meeting a gentleman alone, took her sage advice, and canceled the whole plan, shall I? Then she'll be very pleased with you."

"No." Della sighed regretfully. "She'll know we're lying. Let's tell her something believable, like a kitchen fire destroyed our meeting place and prevented me from speaking with the viscount, so we'll never know what he might have decided."

"That's much better," Eli agreed, laughter still lighting his eyes. He turned his attention away for a moment to see a group of stragglers out, leaving Della to ruminate on her failure.

She could picture Lord Ashton now, looking very disapprovingly at her from behind those adorable wire spectacles of his. She loved men with spectacles.

Miss Danby, with all due respect, it's a gentleman's guide. Why would I include a ladies' club?

It echoed the dismissal she faced every time a new acquaintance learned of her endeavor. *Why should ladies want to gamble? Aren't you worried about your reputations?* Everyone thought she should be encouraging virtues, not vices. As if her sex made it physically impossible to enjoy a little fun.

Well, she thumbed her nose at all of them every day that Bishop's kept its doors open. Why shouldn't she thumb her nose at the Viscount Ashton as well?

He wasn't the sole arbiter of entertainment. No one had vested him with any superior taste or authority; he'd merely claimed his status by being born with a title and then writing a book. And not even a real book, with a plot and characters, and intriguing twists, that might require some creativity. No. His guide was nothing more than a list of things he liked, with the sort of idle commentary any number of gentlemen might exchange when deciding how they should spend their evening.

In short, anyone could do it.

I could do it.

The realization struck her with such force, Della could scarcely contain herself. She *could* do it! Why shouldn't she? Heedless of the last few ladies trickling out into the night, she grabbed the club's guest book, flipped to an empty page at the back, and began scribbling.

She would scrap the public houses, of course, and any other place ladies couldn't be seen. What could serve instead? There weren't many shops in Lord Ashton's book, only a few tailors and cobblers. That was his most glaring omission. Women came to London to see and be seen, not to drink. Milliners and dressmakers should occupy the opening chapters...

"What are you doing?" Eli had returned to squint at her messy scrawl.

"Writing down some ideas," she said impatiently, not looking up. "I've decided to publish a lady's guide to London."

Three

It was the first of the month. The day that Lyman normally paid his landlady, Ellen's family, and all his other creditors, in that order. But today he rose early, shaved, and dressed himself before the sun was up, and tiptoed down the stairs. He took care to hop over the second step, which creaked. Mrs. Hirsch had the watchfulness of a barn cat, but she couldn't ask after the rent money if he was gone before she woke.

His account balance had been dwindling for months, every new expense bringing him closer to ruin. Again. Poverty was never far behind him. If Lyman forgot it for a moment, it would pop up in the fraying end of his coat sleeve or a hole in his shoe. He would taste it in his supper of bread and beans at the local public house, while the other diners ate meat. It had made itself a home in his debts, gobbling up his meager repayments so quickly they seemed little more than air.

But today, things were different. Once Lyman gingerly shut the back door behind him and stepped out into the safety of the gray morning, he walked with a lighter step. He had tucked a large parcel wrapped in brown paper under one arm, thick and heavy with the promise of financial security. His revisions were done, and he would turn his manuscript in to his publisher today, just as soon as the clock struck a decent hour. That meant fresh money.

Once the deposit had cleared, he could pay Mrs. Hirsch, and Michael, and all the rest, and then he would breathe easy. At least until the funds got low and the whole wretched cycle started over.

He would try to work quickly on the Bath guide.

Lyman desperately needed a strong cup of tea, but everything on this street was closed for another few hours. He decided to walk to his publisher's office in the hopes of finding a hotel tearoom along the way. It would help kill the time until the start of business, in any case. It was well over an hour on foot from his little boardinghouse in Pimlico to the booksellers of Paternoster Row.

The fastest route was to take Rochester, but that path led straight into the Devil's Acre, where half a dozen thieves would be all too happy to relieve him of what few valuables he had left, even at this hour of the morning. Lyman headed north, instead, to pass Buckingham Palace and take Piccadilly. It would add time to his stroll, but it was far safer.

After about twenty minutes, the change in the quality of the neighborhood became evident. Signs in windows proclaiming "Comfortable lodgings!" became less frequent, then vanished altogether. They were replaced by the brass plaques of doctors' and dentists' offices for a short time, until those, too, gave way to white-washed row houses of the finest caliber.

Lyman had lived here once. It felt like eons ago. If he kept walking north into the heart of Mayfair, he might pass his old town house. Instead, he pulled up his coat lapels to shield his face from the wind and hurried on. No good came of dwelling on the past. That life was lost to him and he had no one to blame but himself.

He had just passed the Green Park when he saw it. He'd still been looking for a tearoom, and instead had fallen upon another sort of amusement. Similar, yet entirely different.

MRS. BISHOP'S CHOCOLATE EMPORIUM, the sign proclaimed. And underneath, just in case Lyman had forgotten, LADIES ONLY. So, this was Miss Danby's gaming hell. He hadn't quite been able to scrub their brief encounter from his mind. In spite of himself, he wondered what such an establishment would look like. Its owner must be quite fearless. Lyman crossed the street to get a better view.

He was almost disappointed by how normal it seemed. It was a small, unassuming storefront bordered tightly by its neighbors. The plaster was freshly painted in sky blue, with a little flower box on either side of the door. As fashionable as anything you would expect to see on Piccadilly, but nothing exceptional. Certainly no chasm threatened to pull the place down to hell before his eyes. The windows were shuttered, leaving Lyman to guess what it might look like inside.

You don't want to see the inside, he reminded himself. There was curiosity, and then there was self-destruction. Everything about Miss Danby promised the latter.

Lyman hurried his steps on toward Paternoster, but his destination was still far off, and now his thoughts were fixed on the gaming hell and its beautiful proprietress.

How pleasant it might have been to reciprocate her flirtation—for she had flirted with him, he was sure, at least at first. He might've taken the opportunity to laugh with her for a moment, to do something charitable like agree to put her business in his book and bask in the light of her attention a little longer, forgetting his problems. His current mode of living hadn't allowed him to keep up his friendships with the wealthier set he'd once frequented. It would have been nice to talk to someone new.

But for Ellen.

She always weighed heavy on his conscience.

They hadn't spoken in nine years and he'd long since pawned his ring, but his wife still lived. What little opportunity he had for feminine companionship was strictly limited to people in similar situations. Widows and ladies who'd separated from their husbands and wished to engage in a discreet affaire. He would never be free of the bonds of his marriage, which meant he had to steer clear of eligible young ladies like Miss Danby, whose prospects might be harmed by an association with him.

He wouldn't think of her any longer. She was like any other attractive woman who might cross his path—occasionally tempting, yet always out of reach. It did no good to imagine what might have been. She was meant for a better life than his.

No worse than what you deserve. The voice in his head sounded suspiciously like his father's.

But when Lyman finally arrived at his publisher's office and rapped on the door, he found Miss Danby sitting inside the receiving room as if summoned by his thoughts, calmly sipping the cup of tea he'd not yet managed to procure. A slim young lady was at her side; her companion, perhaps.

Lyman was so surprised, he couldn't even greet her. *What is she doing here?*

"Oh! Good morning, Lord Ashton." She set her tea down upon a little side table covered in card-stock advertisements for various texts. "Allow me to present my sister, Miss Annabelle Danby."

He recovered enough to blurt out a hasty, "Good morning, Miss Danby. Miss Annabelle." There wasn't much of a resemblance between them, except for the honey-brown hair. Where Miss Danby had a round face and generous curves, Annabelle was narrow and angular, almost sharp. But she had a watchfulness in her eyes that somehow called to mind her older sister's quick wit.

"Er, your hat." Miss Danby motioned toward his head. He'd

forgotten to remove it. She always seemed to set him stumbling one step behind.

As he fumbled to hang it on the coat rack, the secretary returned, pausing only a moment to take in Lyman's presence before he announced, "Mr. Armstrong will see you now."

Lyman strode forward automatically, but Miss Danby cleared her throat and rose to her feet.

"Excuse me, my lord, but I have an appointment."

An appointment. With *his* editor. What was happening?

This was about her club; it had to be. The timing was too suspicious to be anything else, and hadn't she warned him that she would be his enemy? It appeared the threat was more than a fit of pique. Perhaps she'd come here to complain about him, or to go over his head and persuade Armstrong directly.

Either way, Lyman wouldn't have it.

"I'll accompany you then," he said swiftly. "I have something for him, in any case."

We'll see how far she gets when I'm there to set things straight.

Miss Danby had the decency to look flustered at this. "That's really not necessary—"

But Lyman walked ahead, leaving her to either follow or cede her appointment. She chose to follow, her sister scurrying behind her. At least she'd brought a chaperone this time.

When they reached John Armstrong's office, the man looked up in surprise, "Lord Ashton! I didn't expect to see you here this morning." He motioned them all in, pulling out a chair for Miss Danby, then for her sister. Lyman had to stand. "Does this mean you've all reached an understanding then?"

"No," Lyman replied. What lies had she spun to secure this meeting? "I'm not sure what Miss Danby has told you, but I won't include her ladies' club in my book."

Armstrong puckered his graying brows in confusion. "What club?"

"My lord, if I may." Miss Danby turned in her chair to face him. "We have moved on to other projects, and you're quite behind the times. Would you allow me a chance to explain?"

She said it politely, a sweet-as-a-lemon-drop smile on her face, but Lyman bristled at the condescension. Armstrong, on the other hand, appeared utterly smitten. He was grinning like a schoolboy half his age.

What Miss Danby said next did nothing to improve Lyman's mood.

"I perfectly understand why you refused to include ladies' entertainments in your book. You're right; it's not the proper place for them. That's why I've proposed to Mr. Armstrong that I write my own guide to London, intended for the fairer sex."

"A lady's guide to London?" *What's the point of such a thing?* "But you can't attend hotels and public houses unescorted, and all the things you might wish to do with a husband are already in the gentleman's guide. What's left to write about?"

What were they even doing here? This woman was wasting everyone's time. But instead of showing her the door, Armstrong was fawning over her. His secretary even returned to offer the ladies pastries, though Lyman *never* received baked goods when he visited.

"Do you think we women do nothing at all while you lot are out drinking at your clubs all day?" Miss Danby shot him a scathing look. "It would include all the best shops, for everything from hats to furniture, bakeries, charities, theaters—"

"Theaters are already in my book."

"I don't believe you own the concept of theaters, my lord."

"To be sure," Armstrong cut in, "it would be a smaller volume.

Less to cover. But it's an interesting idea, to capture all the readers left out by the first book. A companion piece, so to speak."

"Exactly." Miss Danby gave Armstrong a winning smile, which seemed to overset the man entirely.

"My guide is a complete document," Lyman protested. "It doesn't need a companion piece."

Had he misjudged things? The ground felt suddenly unsteady beneath his feet. He wasn't sure if *all* of his readers were men. If their wives did the shopping, they might well decide they preferred a ladies' guide and leave his volume lying on the shelves. He couldn't afford a drop in sales.

I should've put her damned club in the book when I still had the chance. It would've caused less headache.

Mr. Armstrong addressed Lyman as though he hadn't spoken. "I was hoping you could help her write it. We wouldn't want her name attached to it publicly, to protect Miss Danby's reputation."

It was all Lyman could do not to let his shock show plainly. "You want me to write a lady's guide for her? She's only doing this because I wouldn't put her business in my book."

"Please don't speak about me as though I'm not sitting right here," Miss Danby cut in. Had he thought her flirtatious at the café? Seeing her expression now, it was clear those days were long behind them. "Mr. Armstrong, I don't need anyone to write the guide for me. I'm well acquainted with all the attractions of London, and I assure you that my parents have provided me with a thorough education. I'm quite capable of writing it myself."

"Have you ever written a book before?" Lyman asked, suspecting he knew the answer. For Armstrong's benefit he added, "If everyone who aspired to be a lady novelist actually published something, we would all be drowning in paper. It's much easier to plan than to accomplish."

"I shall prove you wrong," she said coolly.

"We seem to be getting off on the wrong foot," Armstrong intervened. "Lord Ashton, even if there's no need for you to collaborate on
the text, Miss Danby might benefit from your advice and guidance,
as a sort of mentor, to produce a document of quality."

Impossible. He wasn't going to keep company with the owner of
a gaming den. He'd fought to sever ties with anyone involved in that
world. He wouldn't be pulled back in.

Armstrong continued. "I could pay you a stipend for your contribution, of course."

"Pay?" Lyman turned to him with a hawk's focus. That changed
things.

"Shall we say twenty pounds upon submission of an acceptable
finished draft?"

Miss Danby cleared her throat delicately. "Could we please clarify
whether this is to be deducted from money that would otherwise be
mine?"

"Well, yes, Miss Danby," Armstrong replied with an affectionate
chuckle. "If we buy your book, a portion of the price we agree upon will
go toward Lord Ashton. Unless you'd prefer to publish on commission?"

Miss Danby's lovely brown eyes widened as she looked from
Armstrong to Lyman. She was obviously lost.

"She doesn't," Lyman said firmly. Publishing on commission was
a risky venture that put the majority of both profits *and* losses in the
hands of the author. For an unknown writer like Miss Danby, it was
far safer to sell her copyright for a lump sum and let the publisher
take on the risk.

"Wait." Miss Danby looked at him in suspicion. "I didn't agree to
that. What's the difference?"

She didn't even appreciate the fact that he'd just saved her from
a crushing error.

"If you publish on commission, you'll have to repay any losses if the book sells poorly," Lyman explained patiently. "You don't want that."

Why am I helping this woman? She obviously didn't know the first thing about publishing. She had no business coming here. But twenty pounds was twenty pounds. Even if Lyman wasn't persuaded this idea had real merit, there was no need for him to spend more time with Miss Danby than was strictly necessary. She'd said that she could write it herself, so let her try. He would take some tea in her sitting room a few times to tell her what she was doing wrong, and she could sort it out as she liked. It would only cost him a few hours of his time. Well worth the rewards Armstrong had promised.

"As far as I'm concerned, you have a deal," he said to his editor.

"I'm not sure I like the idea of sharing the monies from my own work," Miss Danby protested.

"You've come here selling me an idea, Miss Danby," Armstrong explained. "It has potential, but you're unknown to our readers. If the viscount attaches his name to the project, it will go a long way to helping me justify the investment to my superiors. His books are very successful. I'm sure his assistance will prove worthy of a share of the price."

Lyman finally found the good humor to favor Miss Danby with a smile.

"Well...if this is the only way." She pulled a card from her reticule, handing it over to Lyman with a trace of reluctance. "You may call on me on Monday to work out the details."

She spoke as though his assent was assured.

"I have a standing engagement on Mondays and Wednesdays," he said, with a certain satisfaction.

Those were the days he tutored several young gentlemen in

composition and decorum to supplement his income, though he wouldn't reveal the depths of his poverty by sharing this information with Miss Danby.

"And I'm needed in the House of Lords at the end of the week." He couldn't find the time to attend every sitting, but he made a point to go when the business was something important.

"Tuesday then." She pushed the card in his direction once more, and he finally took it. One glance at the address told him everything he needed to know about her family's place in the world. She was waiting for him to return the gesture, her hand still outstretched. There was no avoiding it. Lyman fumbled in his breast pocket and produced his own card. Miss Danby frowned as she read it. "But this only has your publisher's address."

"Yes, I prefer my mail to be sent here. It saves any overeager readers from turning up at my door. In any case, there's no need for you to call on me. I'll come to you."

Mercifully, Miss Danby didn't question the explanation. She merely tucked his card away and took a bite of her pastry, which seemed to signal that the discussion was complete. Her sister hadn't said a word the whole time. What sort of family had Miss Danby come from, to turn out so bold? It didn't seem to be a shared trait.

Well, he would soon have the opportunity to see them up close.

"I almost forgot," Lyman said. "I've finished my revisions." He pulled the parcel from the crook of his arm and presented it to Mr. Armstrong, who took it with a smile.

"Ah, wonderful. I wasn't expecting these until next week."

"I made it a priority."

"Very well, very well. Please see Bradshaw on your way out, and we'll make an appointment to go over this with me next month. You can let me know then how things are progressing with Miss Danby's book."

"Might I attend, if the meeting is to concern me?" Miss Danby batted her eyes very fetchingly at Armstrong. "I'm sure I could learn a great deal by observing your work."

She knows exactly how to get what she wants, that one. Lyman really was being made to pay for his initial refusal. If it weren't so intrusive, he might almost have admired Miss Danby's cunning.

"Of course," Armstrong agreed, without missing a beat. "We'll draw up a contract for you and Lord Ashton to sign then. Please bring your father with you. I trust you'll want him to look over the terms."

There was finally a reaction from Miss Annabelle, who hid a smirk behind her gloved hand. Her elder sister shot her a furious look before she replied to Armstrong. "I'll...bring my brother."

Why not the father? They couldn't be orphans, or her sister wouldn't have smiled that way. Perhaps their parents didn't approve of Miss Danby's more risqué endeavors. *Interesting.* Lyman made a mental note to use that to his advantage, should the need arise.

He might not have chosen this situation, but he could still come out on top, one way or another.

Lyman took his leave of Armstrong and the Danby sisters, plucked a pastry from the tray, and went to go see about his advance.

Whatever else might have gone wrong today, he'd made a bit of money, with the promise of more to follow if Miss Danby could be made to produce her manuscript in good time. That was all he could afford to care about now.

"Peter, I need your help with something." Della began this conversation with no preamble, finding her brother alone in his study at three in the afternoon with a glass of brandy or two behind him already.

Like Della, Peter had brown eyes, light brown hair, and a figure that tended toward plumpness. He was two years her junior, but he had the irritating habit of behaving as though he were somehow her intellectual superior on account of his sex. This wouldn't have been so bad if Peter had distinguished himself in any way, but as he had thus far done nothing at all with his life, Della detested the conceit.

"What's this?" He looked up from a puzzle box he'd been toying with and blinked at her entrance. Della didn't often intrude upon his time.

"I need a male relative to approve a legal matter for me in a few weeks. It won't require much on your part. Just wear something smart and say 'I thoroughly agree' once or twice, and then we can go home. Only let's not bother Papa with it; it's hardly worthy of mention."

"This isn't to do with your club, is it?" Peter narrowed his eyes. He had never been impressed by Della's business, though he spent enough of his own time lounging around Brooks's to have paid for an additional wing by now.

"No," she said curtly. "It's another matter entirely."

"If you want my help, you're going to have to tell me what."

Drat. Della should have known there would be no avoiding it. She straightened her shoulders and tried to adopt a nonchalant tone, as if this were a perfectly ordinary project. "I've reached a tentative agreement with a publisher to produce a lady's guide to the sights of—"

She made it no further before Peter's groan drowned out her words. "It's bad enough you run a gambling club. Now you want to write a book, as well? Why can't you be a normal sister, and spend your time at charities? It's embarrassing, Della."

"It's to be published anonymously," she protested. "So it won't cause you any more embarrassment than you currently suffer."

"Which is *considerable.*" Peter shot her a dirty look and helped himself to another brandy. "And anyway, do you really think *you'll* be able to write a book?" He cast her such a doubtful look that she was tempted to smack him.

"Why wouldn't I be able to? I'm perfectly literate."

"Yes, but you must admit, you aren't the most organized person. And you have a tendency not to finish your projects. Remember when you decided to learn Italian? That lasted all of three weeks."

"I learned some very useful phrases," she retorted. "For example, mio fratello è uno stupido."

The nerve of him. True, her papers were perpetually out of order and she could never find two shoes that matched without help from her maid, but that had nothing to do with whether she could write up a few comments on attractions she knew like the back of her hand! Once she really put her mind to something, she could accomplish it. After all, she was the only one in the family who'd built up a profitable business from nothing. That should have earned her some respect.

"Or the time you insisted you were going to be a harpist and begged Father to buy you a harp," Peter continued. Once he was on a subject that made him feel superior, he could keep talking all day. "Whatever happened to that? Gathering dust in the attic, isn't it?"

"I'm a passionate person; I won't apologize for sampling what life has to offer," Della snapped. "Anyway, let's not dwell on the past. I've stuck with Bishop's for three years now. That should count for something."

"Don't be silly. Everyone knows your friend did all the work."

Murder. I shall murder this sad excuse for a Danby, just as soon as I've gotten what I need from him.

"Mrs. Williams didn't do *all* the work." Della had to force the words through her clenched jaw. "In fact, I'm practically running the place alone since her confinement." That might have been an exaggeration, but Jane would forgive the fib if she knew Della's character was under attack.

But it didn't persuade Peter, who merely snorted. "I fear for its solvency then."

Oh, to be an only child!

Weren't siblings supposed to be kind and helpful? She had yet to meet any that fit the bill.

"Will you agree to meet the publisher with me or won't you? If I have to trouble Papa, I'll be sure to mention you refused to do it."

It wasn't that Della *couldn't* ask her father if it came to that. It was only that he spent most of his time sampling cigars with his friends or out on hunting trips. She was likely to seek him out on the appointed date of her meeting only to find he'd departed for the countryside and forgotten all about her. It wouldn't be the first time.

"Fine, fine," Peter relented. "For my usual fee."

A bottle of good champagne, which she got from Bishop's at wholesale price (or for free, as far as Peter was concerned).

"Agreed."

"Annabelle and I would never get away with half the things you do," he muttered darkly.

This was only true if one considered the things Della did were frequently odd endeavors, and neither of her siblings endeavored much of anything. But if one counted every scandalous mishap, regardless of its nature, there was certainly a family resemblance.

Never mind. Peter had agreed to what she wanted. She wouldn't prolong her own suffering by dragging this conversation out.

"Just so it doesn't surprise you, there will be a gentleman author present as well, the Viscount Ashton—"

"The one who wrote the guidebook?" Peter interrupted. "I consult it regularly! How did you meet him?"

"If you would let me finish a sentence, I was getting to that." Della narrowed her eyes. "He's mentoring me for the book. It's going to be a companion guide for ladies."

"Why on earth didn't you tell me from the start? I'd love to meet him! I have so many suggestions for the section on public houses."

Of course. When *she* had a project, it was embarrassing and absurd, but when Viscount Ashton did the same, he was an authority to be respected—nay, swooned over.

"I think it's too late to make suggestions now. Please don't embarrass me by insisting."

"It would serve you right to be embarrassed for once." But Peter couldn't maintain his arch tone for more than a minute before it gave way to awe once more. "What's Lord Ashton like? I expect he's quite fashionable. Did he say what haunts are favored this season?"

"I didn't ask." Della glanced at the clock, eager to be on her way. "As to what he's like, the best description I can find is 'appallingly condescending.' The two of you should get along famously."

Four

Miss Danby lived in a very well-to-do house on Baker Street, just north of Portman Square. Before he even rapped on the knocker, Lyman had judged her to be excessively wealthy, but a glimpse inside confirmed it. The marble-tiled floor at the entry echoed each click of his shoes. Above him, an enormous chandelier cast light and shadow over the hall. It reminded him of the one that had hung in his old country house.

Don't think of the house now. But it was too late. The thought had popped into his head, and once it did, it would follow him all day like a bad penny. His first meeting with Miss Danby hadn't even begun and he already regretted it.

He was shown into a sunny pink drawing room where Miss Danby and her sister awaited him. The mysterious parents and brother were nowhere to be seen.

"Don't mind me," Miss Annabelle said, after their obligatory greetings. "I'm just here to make this whole endeavor more, er... proper. I won't interfere with your work one bit." With that, she returned to her seat, opened a book, and began to read.

"Don't be fooled, my lord," Miss Danby said, taking a place next to her sister on the divan. "She's thrilled to join us this morning."

Miss Annabelle pursed her lips, but refused to rise to her older sister's bait.

Lyman took the armchair across from them. This room was as opulent as the rest of the house, boasting large windows overlooking their courtyard, a Persian carpet, and a smattering of paintings on the walls. They weren't the amateurish product of a family member, either. He recognized a Fuseli among them.

"Would you care for some tea?"

"Thank you."

Miss Danby rose to ring for the maid. Lyman studied her as she moved, though he couldn't have said whether the instinct was born from a desire to regain the upper hand on the woman who'd outmaneuvered him recently or from a more licentious motive.

It was impossible not to notice how attractive she was. The sway of her generous hips drew his gaze as she walked away from him, despite Lyman's best efforts not to be distracted. When she'd tugged the cord on the wall and returned to her seat, he was struck by that flawless face. Full, pink lips, always parted in a smile. The healthy flush of excitement on her round, smooth cheeks. And the most arresting part of her—eyes dark and full of mischief that was half challenge, half promise.

No good can come of this.

There was no denying Miss Danby's beauty. Judging from her house, the family had money. Such a woman could have found herself a good match, if she put away her scandalous pastimes and applied herself to the task. Why hadn't she? She must have been out for many years already.

"Do your parents know what you're doing?" he asked. He'd never been one to mince words. Before his fall from grace, no one would have dared to remonstrate a wealthy and titled gentleman. The habit had lingered, even now that his status was diminished.

"Of course." Miss Danby spoke as if it were obvious. Seeing his skepticism, she added, "They trust my judgment."

No doubt this went a long way toward explaining how she found herself co-owner of a gaming hell and aspiring author of a book of ladies' amusements. A bit more parental oversight might have done her some good.

The maid came in with their tea. Miss Danby looked at him expectantly. "Where shall we start, my lord?"

Was he meant to plan things out for her?

"It's your project," he pointed out. "You were adamant you could do it yourself."

"And you were adamant you deserved twenty pounds of *my* profits, in exchange for a contribution that has not yet been revealed to me."

"Would you prefer I left?"

Perhaps she would say yes and save them both some trouble. Then he could return to his own work, free of the unwelcome temptation she represented.

"No." *Damn.* But then, he'd never been lucky. "If you're going to take your cut, I would prefer that you earn it. Your experience must give you *something* to contribute. Maybe you can start by being a bit less critical. You did volunteer for this, you know."

Miss Danby took a long sip of her tea while Lyman tried to ignore the way her upper lip formed a perfect Cupid's bow as she brought it to the rim of her cup.

She wasn't wrong. That was the most infuriating part. With a heavy sigh, Lyman replied, "I apologize, Miss Danby. I'm anxious to finish up my own work, and I'm afraid it's coming through in my deportment. But you're right, I agreed to help you and I'm being compensated for it, so I will try to show you greater civility from now on."

There was no sense bickering with her every week. The time would pass faster if they got on.

His confession seemed to surprise Miss Danby, but her tone was warmer as she replied, "Thank you."

"Why don't we start by agreeing to some terms for my contribution that we both consider fair." It was important to keep their expectations in step. "I can make time to meet with you once a week, for a half hour, to answer any questions you might have and to see how you're progressing. In turn, you should aim to complete an initial draft in the next four to six weeks."

There. No one could say he hadn't given her a chance. He would educate Miss Danby as best he could. But there would be a limit, to prevent this obligation from entwining them without any end.

"That doesn't sound like enough time." She bit her lower lip as she considered, and Lyman's eyes were stuck to the sight. This would be much easier if she were plain. Or if he hadn't been quite so long without feminine companionship. That must be why she kept drawing him in so effortlessly. "I attend my chocolate house nearly every evening to supervise. My days are quite full."

Her chocolate house. If he forgot himself in her presence for a moment, there it was to remind him.

He was tempting fate by forming any connection to such a woman. Hadn't he learned his lesson?

"For you to decide if you have the energy to take on another commitment then," he said briskly. "But I thought we agreed it would be a small volume. And you're free to copy anything you need from my book for the overlapping subjects. There's no need to spend months on something you're only using as a tool to promote your other venture."

"The idea may have started with Bishop's, but if I'm going to do this, then I'll do it properly. Could we compromise and say two months?"

"Very well." At least she was industrious. Maybe she really would write the book.

"Excellent. Now, I was wondering how you compile your list of attractions. Have you selected every place in your guide from personal experience, or do you rely on the recommendations of friends?" She was watching him with such effortless trust that it made Lyman uncomfortable. Miss Danby presumed him to be wise, when he could barely hold his own life together. She must not have heard the stories. She would never look at him that way if she had. "I wouldn't want to cut corners, but if I'm going to include shops, I can hardly go out and buy something everywhere to compare."

"I could help you shop." It was Miss Annabelle who spoke, her voice hopeful, but at her sister's look she sighed and returned to her reading.

"I've been to every place I mentioned," Lyman explained. "But I confer with friends as well, to make sure my experience matches theirs."

"You can't have been to *every* place," she insisted. "You've included both White's and Brooks's, but surely you don't have memberships to both."

And they were back to gambling clubs again. They couldn't seem to escape the topic for more than a minute.

"*Nearly* every one," he corrected.

"Which is your club?"

Was this how she sized men up? She probably thought of little else. A woman didn't build her own club unless she's been seduced by the game.

"Neither."

"Beg pardon?" Miss Danby seemed not to believe what she'd heard.

Perhaps they'd best get this out of the way.

"I object to gambling."

"Oh." Understanding came over her face. "Is *that* why you dislike me?"

"I don't dislike you," Lyman replied, startled. She was so unguarded. Not merely plainspoken, as he was. It was as though she were incapable of shielding her heart from the slights of others.

He had a horrible premonition he would hurt her before this was over, if he hadn't done so already. She seemed determined to seek out her own ruination, and what man was more apt to bring it about than him?

The room suddenly seemed not to have enough air.

"Yes, you do." Miss Danby tried to laugh, but it rang hollow. Her tone was carefully light as she continued. "I must say I don't care for it."

No, she wouldn't. She was in every way pleasing—her looks, her spirit, her wit. She probably had a collection of admirers. He should offer her some compliment to reassure her of her virtues and set their conversation back to right. But the words wouldn't come.

"You make me uneasy," he admitted. "That's not the same thing."

Her sister was watching them with something like shock in her eyes, but when Lyman spotted her, they darted back down to her book.

"Do you feel the same way about male gamblers, or is it because I'm a woman?"

"The same way about all gamblers."

"You must avoid half of London then. And here I'd assumed the author of such a book must be a bon vivant."

His father had used those words to describe him, once.

"We're getting off track." Lyman cleaned his spectacles on his handkerchief, mostly to give himself somewhere else to look. It was hard to meet her eye, suddenly. "This meeting is supposed to be about your book. If you don't have anything more important to ask me, perhaps I should be on my way."

Miss Danby exchanged a glance with her sister, as if looking for assistance. Lyman rose to his feet before she could find it. "It was a pleasure to see you again, Miss Annabelle. Thank you for having me, Miss Danby. It would perhaps be helpful if you could prepare something for us to look over next week. An outline, or a first chapter, to keep our work focused."

He bowed, donned his hat, and turned his back on Miss Danby and everything she represented.

"Well, that went poorly," Annabelle said, the moment Lord Ashton had gone.

Della would have liked to argue, but it would be pointless. It *had* gone poorly.

"The worst part is, I *do* have an outline we could have looked at, if he'd asked me first instead of assuming I'd done nothing and rushing off." Maybe she should have led with that. It was just that she grew so flustered under his scrutiny that she forgot what she'd planned. The viscount seemed determined to think the worst of her without giving her a chance to explain. But then, he was hardly unique in that respect. Even her own brother didn't believe she could write a book. No one took her seriously. "Do you think it was rude of me to ask what club he belonged to? That's not a personal question, is it?"

He'd been almost civil for a moment, until she'd asked about that.

"I think you've met someone who's immune to your charms, and you don't know what to do with him," Annabelle replied, quite amused.

"That's horrid. I'm not trying to win over Lord Ashton, nor do I charm every man I meet."

"You don't have to. They find you charming all on their own." Annabelle closed her book without marking the page. She probably hadn't read a word the whole time, the little busybody. "But not this one. So how do you intend to make him fall in love with you?"

"He's married." Only a second after this pronouncement, Della paused to revisit the memory of their first meeting. "At least, I think he is."

"You don't know?" Annabelle wrinkled her nose. "Didn't it occur to you that it might be a good idea to clarify whether or not the gentleman you agreed to meet with every week is married already?"

"He said he had a wife. But he also said that they hadn't spoken in years and that no one should ever wed, so I'm not sure if it was supposed to be an attempt at dark humor."

"Why would that be a joke?"

"I don't know. You had to be there. It was all very strange." Della perused her memories of the two meetings that had preceded this morning's catastrophe, searching for some clue that might tell her where she'd gone so wrong. "I'm not sure if he'd explain himself even if I asked. He seems terribly private. His card didn't even have his own address on it! Isn't that odd?"

She'd known gentlemen to put their club's address on their card before, but that was always someone down on his luck, who didn't want his friends knowing he couldn't afford a town house in the West End. If the Viscount Ashton wanted to hide his residence, she could only conclude he must be too snobbish to want the riffraff knowing where he lived.

"Shall we consult Debrett's?" Without waiting for her answer, Anabelle rose and left the room.

"Oh, let's not." Della scurried after her, down the hall to the library. "It doesn't signify anything."

It wasn't as though she was hoping Lord Ashton was eligible. He was standoffish and arrogant and frequently rude.

No matter that she still found those spectacles adorable; that was just a personal weakness of hers.

Annabelle had already cracked the tome open and was flipping through pages by the time Della entered the room. "Ashton, Ashton... Ah, here we are. Oh look, he's got a stag on his coat of arms. How dashing. Married 1830. Lady Mary Ellen de Villiers, second daughter of the ninth Earl of Eastmeath." She looked up to favor her sister with a smug expression. "Looks like he wasn't joking then."

"If he is married, they can't be very fond of each other," she reasoned aloud. After all, couples didn't live separately for years if there was any affection left. "He's not really bound by it in the same way as if his wife were under the same roof."

"Not bound by it how?" The judgment in Annabelle's tone intensified. "Do you mean, would it still be bigamy if he married you? Because *yes*, it would."

"Don't be ridiculous," Della scoffed. "Who said anything about marriage? You know I'm not in any rush to settle down."

Having a fortune to her name already and more than enough to keep her days occupied, Della was in no hurry to wed. When her time came, she would no doubt be swept off her feet by a true romantic. A poet, perhaps. Or a diplomat with a seductive accent who would show her the continent in style. She'd always wanted to travel the world.

In short, she was saving marriage for a passionate soul like herself, which Viscount Ashton certainly was not.

A kiss, though.

She might like to kiss him, though she knew she shouldn't. He'd done nothing at all to make himself agreeable to her. He and his friend Mr. Armstrong behaved as though he was doing her an enormous favor by deigning to visit her home, when he hadn't even lasted ten minutes before storming back out. He was probably sitting in a town house the size of a small palace right now, judging her. Aristocrats were so insufferably superior.

Maybe that was why Della thought about kissing him. It would represent a victory; an admission that he'd been wrong to doubt her, and that she was worthy of his notice.

Oh dear. Annabelle might be right about my needing everyone to like me.

But a wife was still a wife. Unless she knew they'd both abandoned their marriage vows, she was wrong to fantasize about him.

"I wonder why they haven't spoken in so long," Della mused.

"Maybe she got tired of sitting at home alone while he sampled every amusement in the country, including the disreputable kind."

"What do you mean, the 'disreputable kind'?"

"Haven't you read his book? There's a part about where to find prostitutes."

"There is *not*." Della rummaged through her reticule, where she'd been keeping her brother's copy permanently at the ready. She'd read it, of course, but her attention may have wandered during some of the longer chapters. There were thirty whole pages on the House of Lords, which she simply could *not* make herself care about, though not for lack of trying. Her eyes must have darted over certain sections a dozen times without committing anything to memory. "Show me."

Annabelle flipped through the pages at a snail's pace, no doubt enjoying the chance to have her older sister at her mercy. Finally, she turned the volume back toward Della, index finger poised on the offending passage. It was in the section on "Nocturnal Amusements," which covered music halls, dancing rooms, and casinos.

> Where it was once the custom for those seeking fast company in London to attend the Theatre Royal and stroll the houses of ill fame in the neighboring slums between acts, the fashion is now for casinos and dancing halls. Laurent's Casino is the most recent addition, where licentiousness and other entertainments beyond the musical variety reign unchecked from half past eight until midnight for the entrance fee of a shilling. These vices, to rival anything found in Paris, exist within full sight of the law, which does nothing at all to stop them.

"He did say he had *personal* experience with everything in the guide," Annabelle reminded her.

"That...might be about something else." Della wasn't entirely convinced by her own theory.

Goodness. She couldn't imagine the straitlaced Lord Ashton in the embrace of a lady of pleasure. The very idea of pleasure seemed antithetical to him. Besides which, he'd condemned her for gambling. Surely adultery was worse, in the eyes of a moralist?

She read the passage again. She'd heard of the places he'd listed, but ladies didn't go there, and the few gentlemen who spoke of them in her company only talked of seeing plays and listening to music. Even their brother, Peter, frequented Laurent's Casino. Was this what he'd really been doing when he went out with his friends?

It was disgusting, really. Not the indulgence in carnal pleasure, of course. She could forgive that, for who among them had never been tempted?

But the *lying*. Behaving as though she engaged in the worst kind of depravity by allowing the ladies at her club to drink a little champagne and play games of chance in the company of their friends, when half the gentlemen in London were doing much worse every night of the week!

If there was one thing Della abhorred more than uselessness, it was hypocrisy.

"Why must men prove so disappointing when I wish them to be admirable?" she lamented. They always started off well. One could enjoy a new lover's looks, his wit, his kind attentions as the connection was forged. But they rarely measured up to her ideals as time wore on.

At least Jane found her storybook ending. That proved there must be at least a few decent ones left.

"As I've been telling you for years, women are superior in every respect," replied Annabelle smugly.

Five

UNLIKE LYMAN, WHO HAD PLUMMETED TO HIS CURRENT SITU-
ation from loftier heights, the two men who rented out the other
rooms above the Hirsches' house were of modest birth, looking to
climb up. They were both apprenticed to Mr. Hirsch, the solicitor
who lived downstairs.

Joseph Clarkson was the son of a tradesman. Though he was a
decade younger than Lyman, he had a good head on his shoulders
and the two had become fast friends.

James Wood was the son of a tenant farmer, come to London to
pursue a career he hoped would advance his station. He took a sour
view on nearly everything about life in town and resented having to
live under the same roof as two men whom he considered beneath
the sort of society he aspired to, Lyman's title notwithstanding. As
he prided himself on his good manners, he never said this directly,
but let it be known in a thousand veiled comments.

"I noticed one of you finished the last of the tobacco the other
day," Wood mentioned offhandedly as they sat down to the breakfast
of kippers and toast Mrs. Hirsch had prepared for them. "I don't

mind, of course, but perhaps it would be a good idea if whoever keeps using it so quickly could buy the next bag."

The person who used it up so quickly was, without any doubt, Mr. Wood himself. He could rarely be found without a lit pipe in his hand.

"I don't smoke," Lyman reminded him. He'd given the habit up years ago to save money.

"I took a pinch," Clarkson admitted, "but I believe I bought it last time."

"Did you?" Wood's tone betrayed some doubt, though Clarkson had never given them reason to suspect him of dishonesty. "Well, if you *insist* it's my turn, I suppose I'll have to find time to get to the tobacconist today. We have that lecture on estates at the Law Society this afternoon and I can't stand to miss it. Do you think I should run over there now, before work? It will be such a bother." He looked at the clock, then back to Clarkson, as if expecting him to give way.

Clarkson kept his eyes pointedly on his meal. The ticking of the seconds counted off their silent battle.

Mrs. Hirsch broke the tension by bringing in tea, something she only did when in a good mood. Lyman's rent payment yesterday had probably put him back in her good graces. She even offered him cream, which he graciously accepted.

"I almost forgot that some mail came for you, my lord. I'll go and fetch it, shall I?"

Once she'd left on this errand, Wood folded his napkin and rose from his place, still looking pointedly at Clarkson. When the awkwardness had nearly become unbearable, he donned his hat and set out.

"He is insufferable," Clarkson murmured the moment the door had shut on Wood's back. "I never get more than one puff of that tobacco before he smokes the whole sack, and he knows it."

"You could each buy your own," Lyman suggested, "as we had to do for the stationery."

"It's so miserly," Clarkson said with a sigh. "Three grown men should be able to share a few common comforts without bickering."

"Here you are, then." Mrs. Hirsch returned with Lyman's mail in hand.

It was a slim, light envelope addressed not to him, but to his publisher. Their address had been crossed out, and Mrs. Hirsch's written beside it in Armstrong's neat hand. A note at the bottom read:

This came for you at our office.

—J.A.

Lyman flicked his gaze to the sender's address to see who had written him, expecting some unknown reader to fill the space. Like his first letter from Miss Danby. Instead, Michael's name hit him like a slap in the face.

He scrambled to open it with shaking hands.

Ashton,

There's an important matter we need to discuss. Write me back to say where you can be found now. Don't come by the house.

—Villiers

Lyman had to read it twice, as if more information would present itself upon further scrutiny. Not a word of concern from his brother-in-law after years of silence, nor even a salutation. Well, it was too much to hope that Michael's hatred would cool with time. But what was the important matter they needed to discuss? Had something happened to Ellen?

Once their deed of separation had settled the terms of their living arrangements, she'd told him never to contact her again. He'd tried to respect her request. It seemed the only courtesy still in his power to grant. Why would her brother reach out now, when he'd had no word for so long?

"Is something the matter?" Clarkson's smooth baritone broke the silence. "Bad news?"

"My brother-in-law wrote me." Lyman wished it was in his power to say more than that, but he had no idea what to add. It could be anything.

"I thought you said you two weren't on speaking terms." Though his fellow boarders had been too polite to ask Lyman directly how he found himself in accommodations like these, he had given Clarkson a general outline of his story once they'd become friends. Wood had no doubt picked up the information from rumors.

"We aren't," Lyman replied. "I haven't heard from him in years. He says there's something important to discuss, but he doesn't say what."

"If it was anything terrible, he would have told you directly," Clarkson assured him.

He was probably right. If Ellen was ill or dying, Michael could have said so in a letter rather than calling for a personal meeting. And if he was hiding something serious, any of their mutual acquaintances would have let him know. A number of them had cut ties with Lyman after the disastrous breakdown of his marriage, but he still had a few friends who would get word back to him if anything drastic happened.

Michael probably just wanted more money.

Lyman was worrying over nothing; at least, nothing he had the power to change.

"I suppose so."

"I should head downstairs soon." A trace of regret pinched Clarkson's brow. "Are you all right?"

"Of course, of course. Don't let me stop you." Lyman stood, though his plate was still half-full. He hated to waste good food, but his appetite was ruined. "I have somewhere to be soon, anyway." It was somehow Tuesday again, and he was due at the Danby residence in an hour. His misgivings about their meetings only seemed to have made the week go by that much faster.

"I'll see you this evening then. Take care." Clarkson fetched his hat from the stand near the door and gave a final nod before he set out for his day, leaving Lyman alone with his troubles.

The truth is, dear reader, there are many things men ~~hide from us~~ *do not share with us, should the subject be deemed unsuitable for the gentler sex. We ladies must often rely on one another for* ~~guidance~~ *knowledge. I hope, then, that this humble volume shall be a friend to you,* ~~telling you~~ *imparting the secrets—*

"How is your book coming?"

Della looked up from her notes to find her sister standing in the doorway, craning her skinny neck as if to spy the pages from there.

"It *was* going perfectly well, until you interrupted me midsentence. I thought I asked you to leave me alone for the next hour."

"I *have* left you alone for an hour." Annabelle looked as though she'd eaten a lemon, so unpleasant was this order. "Lord Ashton should be here any minute. Aren't you going to fix your hair before he arrives? You can hardly convince him to commit bigamy with you if you look shabby."

"Will you *please* stop teasing me?" Della glanced up at the clock. "And it's been nowhere near an hour. It's only half eleven. I still have plenty of time."

She intended to finish a proper opening chapter today to show Lord Ashton when he arrived, and she still had heaps to do before she reached her goal. She'd meant to start writing first thing after breakfast, but then she'd noticed how messy her desk was and judged it best to organize her papers first. She'd been halfway through *that* task when the butler had announced Miss Chatterjee had come to call on her, and she couldn't very well turn her out after she'd just promised her friend a proper visit. As it happened, Reva had plenty of suggestions as to which shops Della should include in her book, so it practically counted as working.

After *that*, Annabelle had insisted on playing her new accordion at the loudest possible volume until Della had chased her out of doors and exacted a promise not to return for an hour upon pain of dismemberment. She'd finally sat down to concentrate, and for a few blissful minutes the words had been pouring onto the page as fast as her hand could write them until her sister came right back in to bother her, little demon that she was.

"It's not half eleven." Annabelle walked over to the clock that stood on Della's mantel and picked it up to inspect it. "The clock in the hall reads past noon. When was the last time you wound this up?"

"You're joking!" Della tore the clock from Annabelle's grasp and held it to her ear. Sure enough, there was nary a tick to be heard. She'd forgotten to wind it before bed last night. "I haven't finished anything I intended, and Lord Ashton will be here any second!"

"That's what I've been telling you. You're welcome, by the way."

"Out! Out! I have to change. Could you fetch Fanny for me? Quickly, if you please."

But before anyone could send for Della's maid, they heard a knock from downstairs and the heavy tread of their butler moving to answer it.

"Too late." Annabelle didn't even try to look sympathetic. "I suppose if Lord Ashton's heart is pure, he'll love you no matter what you look like. Unless he's comparing you to his ladies of pleasure. They must always be done up well."

"Enough!" Della snatched a crumpled page from her desk (there were quite a lot of them to spare, the casualties of her changeable ideas), and hurled it at her sister. Annabelle batted it away easily, laughing.

There was no time for this. Lord Ashton was already downstairs, and she still had ink-stained fingers. Della hurried to the basin to wash her hands and assess her appearance in the mirror. Her hair had been freshly arranged before her morning call, but she'd been winding one curl around her finger as she worked (a horrid habit) and it now hung looser than all the others. *Would* he think her shabby? No, it would be worse if she kept him waiting to try to fix it. He was here for her book, not to admire her hair. She shouldn't even care about such things.

Della came back to the desk, stuffed the pages she wanted under one arm and grabbed her sister with the other. "Come down and greet our guest, won't you? Unless you'd rather leave us some privacy, for once."

There was no need for a chaperone, really. She was six-and-twenty, not sixteen. And no one would know that Annabelle had left them alone unless she told.

But her sister adopted a solemn tone as she replied, "And risk a scandal? You know how seriously I take propriety."

"You seem to take *my* propriety far more seriously than your own," Della muttered, recollecting a half dozen of Annabelle's misadventures. "Never mind, let's just go."

She could already hear their butler's footfalls on the stairs, coming to announce Lord Ashton's arrival.

They found the viscount waiting in the drawing room, in the same chair he'd occupied last week. He rose to greet the ladies when they entered, but came straight to business the moment they were seated again.

"How is the book coming along?"

"I'm off to a good start."

Lord Ashton was as crisp and put-together as always—not a hair out of place—though Della recognized his toffee-colored morning coat as the same one he'd be wearing that first day she'd met him in the café on Regent Street. And she thought the cuff links might be the same too. A family crest in plain gold. As he reached for the tea the maid brought in, she could barely make out the stag.

Odd. Most of the wealthy men she knew didn't repeat their wardrobe between calls. But then, perhaps he didn't rate their meetings highly enough to keep track of such things. Or perhaps when one was a viscount, one was permitted such eccentricities as standing by an old favorite.

"Do you have an outline for us to go over today?"

Oh dear. She'd had the outline ready last week, but half her papers were out of order from her race downstairs and she had no idea where it had got to.

"I do, if you'll just give me a moment..."

Beside her, Anabelle radiated smugness. The grandfather clock chose that moment to chime the half hour. No one had forgotten to wind *this* one, it seemed.

Why, oh why, hadn't any of the maids seen to the one in her room and saved her from this upset? Oh, that's right. She'd asked them not to tidy her things because she could never find her papers afterward.

Maybe she should amend her instructions to include an exception for clocks.

"Aha!" Della held up the page triumphantly. Although it looked less impressive in the light of day than it had when she'd written it at two in the morning in a fit of inspiration. The margins were smudged where she'd scribbled too quickly, and she'd already changed her mind about half of it.

Nevertheless, it was all she had to show for her work thus far, and she would turn it over to Lord Ashton with her head held high.

He adjusted his spectacles as he read and Della was seized by the wish that her penmanship were a bit neater. She'd never managed to produce the round, bubbly script most ladies seemed to turn out effortlessly. Her old governess once said her writing looked more like a boy's—careless and rushed.

She studied Lord Ashton as the silence stretched on. He truly was handsome, in an understated way. He had a strong, square jaw and high cheekbones. His nose was unremarkable, neither too small nor too large, and the same could be said of his mouth. There was nothing flashy about his looks, but the final effect was one of quiet elegance. It had as much to do with the way he carried himself as anything else.

Why isn't he saying anything?

Della cleared her throat. "I know it says the opening chapters should be about shops, but since then I've decided it should have an introduction first to explain my intentions."

He finally looked up, giving Della a better view of his eyes.

Green. Not the true green of new grass or an emerald. Nothing poetic. It was the muddy green of moss on an ancient tree; mottled into brown and easily overlooked. It suited his personality.

"I thought I might write the introduction. To link the two volumes together."

That might have been intended as a kindness or an

imposition—Della couldn't tell. She wasn't entirely sure she wanted to hand any more control over to the viscount, particularly after what Annabelle had shown her after their last meeting. How could she trust the judgment of a hypocrite?

"I've already started working on it," she said.

This didn't seem to deter him. "I can include anything you'd like. What did you have in mind?"

How was she supposed to expose her ideas, tender as fresh shoots, when Lord Ashton might trample them underfoot? But he was waiting, so she had to say something. "I thought it would be nice to invite the reader in." No, that sounded silly; why had she worded it that way? "I wanted to adopt a confidential tone," she amended, "to make it feel like you're getting advice from a trusted friend when you consult it."

"I'm sure I could sound perfectly friendly." Lord Ashton hadn't understood her meaning, it was plain.

"I'm afraid it wouldn't be the same. A lady doesn't let her guard down around a gentleman the way she would around another lady."

"Quite true," her sister chimed in.

"Thank you, Annabelle." Turning back to their guest, Della continued, "Maybe we could write two introductions." That was the solution! Then they could both have everything they wanted.

"Two introductions?" Lord Ashton removed his spectacles and pinched the bridge of his nose, his expression one of utter fatigue. He seemed more careworn than usual today. Unsettled. Was something else troubling him, or was he simply tiring of her already? "Surely one would be sufficient. I've never seen a book with two in my life. If you want this project to be a success, you must learn to work with others."

There was that chiding tone again. It made Della want to push back, but she also had to admit that there was something oddly attractive about it. She liked a man who took charge, even if she wasn't willing to give way. And his eyes seemed to linger on her a bit longer than was strictly necessary. As if he couldn't bring himself to look away, despite his skepticism.

"I work with others every day," Della retorted. She had her share of flaws, but that wasn't one of them. "The problem is that I don't know you well enough to trust you yet."

"We don't need to be friends. This is a business arrangement."

"But I like to know my business partners too." In fact, all her business partners *were* her friends, though she sensed that Lord Ashton wouldn't approve if she tried to explain this. But wasn't friendship a natural consequence of spending any length of time with another person, unless one was ill-tempered?

That was probably Lord Ashton's problem.

Indeed, he was shaking his head right now, his disapproval plain. It made her want to ruffle his hair and loosen his cravat. Why *couldn't* they be friends? He was so staid, and yet he must have a more adventurous side, else he would never have been able to visit half the establishments in his book. What could make him put aside his reserve and open up to her?

"How old are you?" she asked. She should have thought to look in Debrett's when Annabelle had it out last week, but she hadn't, and she didn't much feel like waiting until he was gone to check again now.

"Is this relevant to your book, somehow?"

"I have my book quite under control, and I'm not asking you to stay beyond our agreed-upon thirty minutes," Della assured him, "so it shouldn't matter to you what we talk about at our meetings."

There were probably only ten minutes left at this point, but as long as the clock hadn't sounded, she wouldn't let that stop her.

"It matters to me whether we ever finish this project." He put the spectacles back on, and she was struck once again by how endearing they were.

She shouldn't be fantasizing about him like this. It was probably hopeless, and entirely inappropriate. This conclusion did nothing to rein in her mind, which had always tended to rebel against constraint. The more impossible something seemed, the more she found her thoughts fixed upon it.

Lord Ashton was no exception.

"I've already made a good start on the section on shops, which will be the longest," Della informed him. "I'll do my best to finish my draft in two months, as we agreed."

"Seven weeks, now."

"Yes, yes." Della waved this away. Seven weeks was still heaps of time. "But as to how much say you should have in the final text, that depends on whether you can reassure me."

"Reassure you of what?" Lord Ashton still sounded tired. She wished she knew how to resolve this debate in a manner that would please both of them.

"That your advice will be useful to me. That your intention to help is sincere." Thus far, he'd opposed her far more than he'd encouraged her. Not the best beginning for their imminent friendship. "That you can be trusted."

If Ashton had seemed preoccupied at the outset of this conversation, something about that last part caught his attention. He looked up at her sharply, his indifference vanished.

"Unfortunately, I can't be."

His expression was so intense that she suffered a *frisson*. He wasn't joking, unless it was his odd, grim humor again. There was something in his manner that reminded her of what he'd said about his wife. Like then, Della wasn't sure how to interpret it.

After a beat, he continued in a more measured tone, "You said so yourself. You don't know anything about me."

"But that's exactly why we should take some time to become acquainted," she protested. "I'm not comfortable letting a stranger have any say over something I'll be working so hard on, particularly when you only warmed to the idea after you bargained your way into a share of my money. It's not enough to know that you've written a successful book. I want to know your character before I share any control over my work."

"Thirty-five," he answered with the grim tone of one getting an unpleasant task over with. It took Della a few seconds to remember her earlier question. "And I haven't written one successful book; I've written three. There are also guides to Brighton and Dublin, and I'm working on Bath next."

Only nine years between them then. She would have guessed he was older. But perhaps it was the gray in his hair that aged him.

"What else do you want to know?"

"About your wife..."

His face hardened immediately. "There are limits to my willingness to indulge you, Miss Danby."

"I have no wish to pry into the details of your private life," Della began (a blatant lie), "but you *are* the one who brought it up at our first meeting and seemed to imply you've been living separately for years. May I ask whether you've both concluded that reconciliation is out of the question?"

"Why should this be of any interest to you?"

"I suppose I'm trying to judge whether I'm risking my reputation by meeting with you. I'm an unmarried woman, after all, and you are...a married man who doesn't seem to be bound to his wife any longer. It might make a difference in how things appear to others."

Annabelle cleared her throat.

Oh, be quiet, Annabelle. It took all Della's self-control not to kick her sister in the shins.

"Reconciliation is out of the question, and it's safe to assume that you're risking your reputation, yes." Ashton delivered these facts much as the ladies at Bishop's laid winning cards on the table. The emotion fell somewhere between triumph and fatalism. "But I would think that ship sailed long ago."

Was he referring to her club, to the way she'd shown up at Verey's café to meet him without a chaperone, or to her behavior at this meeting? Regardless, his words had the appearance of an insult, and they loosened her tongue accordingly. (Something she hardly needed help with today.)

"Did you and your wife part ways because you frequent houses of ill-repute?"

Lord Ashton choked on his tea. By the time he was done coughing and could finally speak, his voice was reduced to a thin rasp. "What?"

"I read the portion of your book on dancing halls."

"I don't that's not—" He paused to compose himself, mopping his cravat furiously with a handkerchief. "Just because I made mention of a well-known location doesn't mean that I engaged the services there."

Annabelle put her book away, all pretense abandoned.

Della continued on, following her thoughts down whatever path they took, as she usually did. "Is there an equivalent for ladies?"

"I'm not sure I understand you."

"I'd never really thought about it before now, but surely if bordellos exist for men, they could exist for ladies too. I'm asking you for research purposes, by the way, so you can count this as working on my book again."

"Perhaps this could be your next business venture," Lord Ashton suggested, sarcasm lending an edge to his tone. "Not *everything* has to exist for both sexes, you know."

"They must," Della concluded, growing more sure of herself. The more she thought about it, the more sense it made. "All it would take are a few adventurous ladies or lonely widows who are willing to engage such a service. If there's money to be made at something, *somebody* will prove willing to offer it. I feel very silly for having never thought of this before."

"I can't believe we're talking about this in front of your sister." He turned to Annabelle, who had been glued to the exchange. "How old are you?"

"Nineteen."

"I'm sorry to have been a participant in your corruption, Miss Annabelle, even if an unwilling one."

"Oh, it's nothing I'm not used to," Annabelle said.

"I'm beginning to see that."

"Please don't behave as though *I'm* a bad influence." Della drew herself up, offended. They had no business ganging up on her this way! "I assure you, Lord Ashton, if you knew my sister better, you would realize the key difference between us lies not in any moral superiority, but in a greater inclination to *act* the innocent."

"I have no idea what you mean." Annabelle sat primly in her chair, her voice clear and childlike.

"There, you see those doe eyes? A performance worthy of Drury Lane."

Annabelle's expression soured.

"Go back to your reading, please," Della instructed. "It will save you from hearing anything scandalous and allow us to return to business."

"I question your use of the word 'return,'" said Ashton dryly.

"All of this is business," Della insisted. "I'm trying to decide whether I should have a section on brothels in my book too."

"Please don't."

"*You* did."

"It's different for men."

Did he think that would hold water with her?

"My lord, if you please. I know we're nearly strangers, but even a short acquaintance should have taught you that I refuse to accept that excuse. If ladies want my guidebook to tell them about things they couldn't ask anyone else, we must meet their demand."

The clock chimed the hour, but Lord Ashton seemed not to hear it. Della flushed with pleasure at the realization that she'd finally captured his full attention.

And they were discussing a matter of real importance: namely, what subjects her book should include. Lord Ashton might have something valuable to contribute if he would only set aside his misgivings for a moment and have a discussion that wasn't clouded by scorn. It was such a narrow-minded, pointless emotion.

"How can you have so little concern for decorum?"

"It's to be published anonymously," she reminded him. "So my only concern should be what readers will pay for. And I assure you that when no one is watching, ladies enjoy a little titillation as much as anyone, particularly from the safety of a book."

Ashton opened his mouth, then closed it again, at a loss.

"Do you suppose I must visit a bordello myself before I have the authority to write of it?" Della continued. "I wouldn't need to actually engage the services there, but I should at least take a look around and make some inquiries as to its quality, or I would have nothing to write about. Could you help me find one?"

He studied her a long moment before he finally replied. "Come now, admit it. You've been joking with me this whole time. You wanted to see if you could shock me, and you've succeeded."

His theory brought him such evident comfort that Della was almost reluctant to break the spell. But while she hesitated, Annabelle stepped in. "You really don't know her, if you think that."

"Hush," she said firmly.

"Good Lord." Ashton buried his face in his hands. "I did *not* agree to find you a ladies' bordello to put in your ladies' guide that was supposed to be a way to promote your ladies' chocolate house. This book is barely started, and it's already become a parody of itself."

"What about a show, then?" She wouldn't abandon the bordello idea, if further information presented itself, but there was no point in terrorizing her straitlaced viscount any further. She'd been too long without the sort of diversion a well-built gentleman could provide, but she wasn't yet at the point of needing to pay for it. Not when there was another source of amusement right before her. "You wrote about the entertainments at Laurent's Casino. I might like to see them for myself."

"The shows aren't for ladies." His patience seemed to have worn down to its last thread, pulled taut and about to snap. "And before you ask: *no*, I don't know of an equivalent for you."

"I wasn't *going* to ask." Though she had been thinking about the possibility of putting on a show at Bishop's, if Jane could be persuaded. Nothing too scandalous, of course. But what if they had an attractive musician sing in a sultry baritone every Friday? Maybe with his collar unbuttoned and his sleeves rolled up. That might be enough of a draw without crossing the line into indecency.

A little research might inspire her.

"Whether they are for me or not, I should like to see a show. Do you think they would refuse me admission if I presented myself? Is there no mixed company at all?"

"The company is always mixed," Ashton replied easily. "But the women who attend are not of your class, and they come in hopes of finding a wealthy gentleman willing to part with his coin to join them after the show, without exception."

"I see." On the bright side, this meant she could attend without any danger of being seen by her friends. Oh, but if a gentleman she knew should spot her there, what then? "I could disguise myself," she thought aloud.

"This isn't a masked ball. Will you entrust your reputation to the concealment of a gaudy wig?"

"What if I borrowed one of my father's suits and attended as a gentleman? With a hat on top, in a darkened room, no one will look closely enough to tell."

"You." He raked her up and down with his eyes, with an intensity that was not unpleasant. "Dressed as a man. You wouldn't fool anyone for a second."

Admittedly, her figure had a few too many curves to be transformed into rigid lines from shoulder to hip, but she wasn't ready to give up yet.

"You shouldn't dismiss the effort before you've even seen it."

"I have absolutely no desire to see it."

"Have you no sense of adventure?" There was something about the stern set of his chin that pushed Della to capture his attention. To break through his strict control. "That's a shame. I'm going to be attending with or without you, but I'd feel much safer with company."

"Have you ever considered that you might get some sort of thrill from taking these risks, much like an opium eater, and that it's entirely unhealthy?"

There was a thought. She didn't care for it much.

"I prefer the view that society is unfairly constraining and that I'm doing my part to thumb my nose at it."

A long silence followed, in which Della and Lord Ashton locked eyes. He had such a commanding expression; it made her feel like a misbehaving child. She shivered at the energy in his gaze, but she wouldn't be the first to back down.

It was Annabelle who spoke and broke the moment. "If you're

going, I suppose I have no choice but to go with you, to make sure you come through it safely."

Though her voice was meant to convey great reluctance, Della wasn't fooled.

"Ha! You see, my lord? She's every bit as bad as me." Turning to Annabelle, she added, "I'm sorry, but you're too young to attend. You're staying home."

"What if something happens to you?"

Never mind. She should use this to her advantage.

"Lord Ashton, won't you put my sister's mind at ease and tell her you'll accompany me? I hardly see how it could be a hardship for you. You can even cancel next week's meeting to make up for your lost time. Surely you'd rather spend an evening looking at beautiful women than a morning sniping at me over my book?"

He was silent for so long that Della's heart began to hammer in her ears. Goodness, she was actually nervous.

When he finally spoke, those mossy eyes of his bored into her without mercy. "If your disguise is shoddy, I'm canceling the whole thing without any further discussion."

He drew to his feet immediately, placing his hat back atop his head.

"It's a deal." She hopped to her feet as well, before he could escape. "It will have to be on Monday, when my club is closed. Every other night I'm there. Let's shake on it."

He blinked at her outstretched hand, then clasped it and shook, as he might have with a gentleman. But his warm, firm grip didn't make her think of a professional agreement. She was shamelessly imagining what else he might do with his hands.

Well, she would do her utmost to find out, or humiliate herself trying.

Six

"I WISH YOU GIRLS WOULD COME WITH US," MRS. DANBY remarked next Monday evening as her maid curled her hair. Her daughters were peering into her room, trying to look as though they weren't counting the minutes until she left. Della needed time to prepare her disguise before she was to meet Lord Ashton, and her work couldn't begin until her parents were safely out of the house. "Ever since you started that club, you spend all your time there."

Della had used Bishop's as an excuse to escape the fête the rest of the family was attending this evening. Even though the club was closed on Mondays (and had been for the three years it had existed), her mother hadn't noticed.

If Mrs. Danby objected to Bishop's, it was only in an abstract sort of way. Not really an objection so much as confusion. She had never understood why her eldest daughter should want to tie herself down in such an endeavor when she could be socializing instead.

"Annabelle could come with you," Della volunteered.

"I can't," her sister replied without missing a beat. "I have heaps of reading to catch up on."

They exchanged a simmering glance.

There would be a row over it once they were alone, but Della would be damned if she would let her sister ruin this for her.

She *never* had time to do something for herself these days. Della intended to make the most of her evening out with Lord Ashton, and that didn't include fending off Annabelle's barbs.

Mrs. Danby sighed, pinching her cheeks in the mirror of her vanity. With her rich, chestnut hair and full lips, she was still a beautiful woman, even in her mid-forties. "For you to manage your own lives then."

If their mother's childrearing style had a motto, something to be stitched above the nursery in petit point, this would be it: *For you to manage your own lives.*

The Danby siblings had been managing their own lives for decades. With great success, as far as Della was concerned.

"Have a good time, Mama. Give my regards to Mrs. Hayward."

Their parents went out nearly every evening, leaving the children free to do as they wished without any consequence until one or two in the morning. Peter occasionally posed a problem, for though he was as reprobate as any of them, he expected his sisters to hold higher standards. But as he was accompanying their parents this evening, they were quite safe. The moment the front door clicked shut in the latch, Della raced to construct her disguise.

"If you're going, I'm coming too." Annabelle hollered after her.

Not if I leave without you.

But this proved easier thought than done. Della had given her maid the night off (her usual reward in exchange for continued silence about everything Della got up to) and now she had to dress herself. Most of her gowns were a bit complicated. Besides which, she still wasn't sure which one would be least recognizable if they crossed paths with a man she knew.

Annabelle popped into her room without knocking, pausing to stare at the sight of Della in her shift.

"Are you not coming with us? I can accompany your viscount all on my own if you like. He'll be quite safe with me."

Annabelle had already donned her disguise in the time that Della had been assessing her options. She was dressed in a gentleman's suit and top hat, her hair pinned up carefully beneath.

She stole my idea, the little cheat. She looked the part very well, being so slim that she had no figure to hide and so young that her hairless face passed as boyish. Her suit draped perfectly from her narrow shoulders, forcing Della to conclude that she'd had it tailor-made for the occasion. Their father's and brother's clothes would have been far too large for her. Where had she found a tailor willing to indulge this scheme?

"You've wasted your money on that getup. I've already told you, you're not coming."

"Then I'll tell." Annabelle stuck out her chin defiantly. This was an empty threat, and they both knew it. There could be no appeal to their parents before ten or eleven tomorrow morning. And if Annabelle wanted to betray her secrets, they each had a list a mile long they could use against each other. No one wanted to open that Pandora's box.

"Don't be childish. Just let me have my fun for one evening."

"You can have your fun with that stuffy old hypocrite all you like, just so long as you let me come too."

Della narrowed her eyes, irritated. She secretly hoped she might kiss Lord Ashton tonight, if the opportunity arose. Annabelle would ruin everything.

"Be honest," she said. "You aren't really worried about me. You just want to see the dancers." Without anyone else here, there was no need to pretend.

"Fine," Annabelle conceded. "I just want to see the dancers. When else will I have a chance like this one?"

"The ballet."

"You and I both know it's not the same thing."

That was true enough. Della felt her resistance giving way. At times, she and her sister had much in common.

Sensing her advantage, Annabelle pressed home. "And anyway, I have more reason to want to go than you. You don't even like women. This might sustain my dreams for weeks."

Far be it from me to force conformity on anyone.

"Fine, fine." Della cast her hands up in defeat. "But help me get ready, at least. Your disguise looks quite well on you. Do you think I should try that?"

Annabelle beamed at the praise. Once they'd pilfered some clothes from Peter's closet, it became apparent that Della couldn't transform herself with quite the same ease. Her breasts and hips were simply too full to be hidden by an evening coat.

"It would help balance you out if you padded your middle," Annabelle observed.

"Absolutely not."

"Which is more important, your vanity or passing undetected?"

"My vanity," Della replied without hesitation.

Annabelle heaved a great sigh and rolled her eyes. "It's back to disguising you as a light-skirt then."

"Won't it be obvious my clothes are too fine? I can't find anything suitable."

"Maybe you're a wealthy gentleman's mistress," Annabelle replied, obviously enjoying this. "Lord Ashton's, perhaps. Just pick whichever gown has the lowest neckline."

Della would have liked to issue a cutting retort, but the fact of the matter was that she would do exactly as her sister suggested. She picked a scarlet gown with an off-the-shoulder neckline that dipped in the front of the bodice to close in a wide vee with a trail of silk roses at the center. It was designed to draw the eye down.

She hadn't worn it in years, and it was a bit too snug on her now. Once Della had squeezed herself into it, she looked downright indecent.

"Do you have a gaudy wig, as your viscount suggested?"

In fact, Della *did* have a wig, but she'd been reluctant to try it on, remembering his scorn. With some assistance, she managed to pin her real hair beneath the false, and she was a blond.

Annabelle clucked her tongue. "Your eyebrows don't match *at all.*"

"It's dark out!"

They found a large fan to complete her disguise, so that Della might shield her face if she needed to.

Another ten minutes, and they slipped outside to meet Lord Ashton without the servants seeing.

"Both of you?" He raised his eyebrows at Annabelle's clothes, but didn't comment on them. "Does Miss Annabelle fear to leave us alone together even though this whole scheme is your idea?"

"Yes," Annabelle said firmly, before Della could answer. Only her fidgeting hands betrayed her excitement at the sights that awaited them.

"I was hoping you might have changed your mind," Ashton continued. He was dressed in sleek black evening wear, as if he were on his way to the opera. It made their outing seem more significant. "Don't either of you care about what will happen if you're recognized?"

"No one will even look at us. They'll all be watching the show," Della said. The brim of Lord Ashton's top hat cast a large shadow beneath the gas streetlight, hiding his face from view, but Della could feel his eyes roaming over her. She drew in a breath. "We'll be sitting in the dark the whole time and we won't say a word to anyone. In and out."

"And if you're mistaken, what then?" He shook his head. "I'll be the one accused of corrupting you, while you behave as though nothing bad could happen in your charmed life."

"I'm not ignorant of the dangers of anything I do, my lord. But I won't live in fear, pretending I don't want to experience anything London has to offer because of what someone else would think of me. None of us know how long we are for this world. I'd rather enjoy my life while I can, even if I should pay for it one day."

His voice softened, though only slightly. "Very well, but see that you stick to your word. Stay in the shadows and don't talk to anyone. You stay by my side the whole night, and you follow my instructions."

A shiver crept over Della's spine. He couldn't possibly know how attractive she found this speech, particularly the last part.

"Thank you," she murmured, hoping he could hear the feeling in her voice. "We appreciate this."

"Thank me when the evening is over, if we all escape unnoticed. Not before."

They set out to find a hansom cab and were soon on their way.

Laurent's Casino was located in the Adelaide Gallery on the north end of the Lowther Arcade, on the Strand. It was only a short drive east of Mayfair, though the streets were clogged enough to slow them down.

Della kept peering out the window to catch a glimpse of their surroundings, while Lord Ashton reminded her to stay out of sight and not speak to anyone every few minutes, looking very stern all the while.

The poor man. If the carriage ride over had him this worked up, how would he survive an evening of debauchery?

She couldn't wait to find out.

Lord Ashton paid the coachman and handed Della down from the carriage. Was it her imagination, or did his fingers linger on hers for the barest moment? He moved as if about to assist Annabelle, then quickly turned away, remembering she was supposed to be a gentleman.

The building was quite large and stately, as were those on either side. Della had been here back when the building used to house the Royal Gallery of Practical Science. It had been a popular attraction for children and families until it closed and was replaced by the present casino, which was said to be far more profitable.

There was a marked difference between the gallery of her memory and its current circumstances. Lively music was punctuated by the occasional whoops and cheers of the revelers inside. A number of ladies were gathered in the shelter of the Italianate columns before the door, laughing together and without any man to accompany them. They were as well dressed as she was, and Della might have mistaken them for members of the upper class, had not one turned to a passing gentleman just then and leered at him invitingly.

Why, I needn't have worried about my gown at all! They looked just like anyone else.

"Remember not to talk to anyone," Lord Ashton said for the hundredth time, as they approached the entrance. "Keep your head down."

Della lifted her fan to conceal her face. Ashton drew a deep breath and turned over six shillings to the doorman, receiving three tin tokens in exchange.

The entrance opened into a large, carpeted room, furnished as handsomely as anything one might see in a Mayfair town house. Gas jets lit the glittering chandeliers above them, making Della rather conscious that the place was not so dark as she might have hoped.

Lord Ashton must have shared the same concern, for he led them directly upstairs to the first floor. Della lingered at the bottom of the steps, striving to take in as much as she could before she was whisked away. The majority of the ground floor, which had once held exhibits on the functioning of steam engines or the application of laughing gas, had been stripped bare and converted for dancing. What little space was not occupied by the dance floor belonged to the liquor counters, which were doing a brisk trade. Della had no time to observe any more, for Lord Ashton hissed, *"Come here!"* and jerked his head toward the stairs.

She followed him up to a balcony, where the difference in class immediately became evident. The dancers below, still visible to Della through the railing, were mainly dressed in the style of clerks and tradesmen. Upstairs, the gentlemen wore full evening attire like Lord Ashton. The ladies were all in silks, with long trains and heavy jewelry. She could have mistaken them for her social equals, until a blonde called out for more "fizz" and lit herself a cigarette.

The band was situated on the opposite gallery, above the dancers. They were a larger number than she would have expected, perhaps forty or fifty all told, and very skillful. She understood the conductor to be Laurent himself, who was said to be the best in all of London.

"This way," Lord Ashton said, and led them to an alcove that was tucked away from view, just beyond the bar. It was fitted with paintings on all sides: Leda in the embrace of the swan; Europa riding the white bull.

"My, there certainly is a common theme to these."

"Hmm?" Lord Ashton followed her gaze. "Oh, I hadn't noticed."

"I hope this doesn't reflect on the evening's entertainment."

He paused to consider the paintings for a moment before responding, "I expect all the performers to be human."

He said it so seriously that she had to laugh.

"Don't do that," Lord Ashton looked to either side of them, as if fearing eavesdroppers. "It attracts attention."

Della doubted the risk was as great as he thought. The casino wasn't too crowded (perhaps because it was ten in the evening on a Monday), and those who had come were concentrated on the dance floor.

But Lord Ashton was only trying to protect her in his own way, so she whispered, "I'll do my best." It seemed to reassure him.

"We can't see anything from back here," Annabelle complained. "I'm going to move closer to the railing."

"Don't." Lord Ashton must be the sort of man who was used to bringing others in line with a look, but his powers of glowering were wasted on Annabelle, who stood and marched herself to the edge of the balcony.

"I'm going to go too," Della whispered. "Just for a minute."

"Why did you bother asking me to accompany you if you had no intention of listening to a word I say?" he ground out through clenched teeth.

"Only a minute!" Della hurried to follow her sister.

"Is that Lord Palmerston?" Annabelle tipped her chin toward a clean-shaven man in his fifties, who was seated on a plush velvet sofa some distance from them, flanked by two ladies several decades his junior.

"It could be," Lord Ashton replied. He'd crept up on Della's other side, startling her with his nearness. He smelled clean—like freshly laundered sheets and something warmer just beneath it. Sandalwood, maybe? She couldn't tell if it was a very mild cologne or just the natural scent of him. "This place is popular among men from all ranks of life."

Della took in the scene below with eyes wide enough to capture every detail. There were some sixty-odd couples on the floor, and their dance was at once familiar and unlike that of any ballroom she had attended. They repeated movements she knew, but without any of the ordered unity she expected. One couple danced a waltz, another a polka, with no regard for their neighbors. Miraculously, no one crashed into anyone else. They all seemed to be having the time of their lives. Though their dance might be unconventional, Della noted there was no rough behavior from anyone. Where there weren't enough partners for all, a pair of ladies even danced together, and no one seemed to pay them much mind.

Della nudged Annabelle, who nudged her a bit harder in return, as if to say, Yes, yes, I already saw.

When the dance ended, gentlemen flocked to the liquor counters and purchased glasses of what looked to be beer and gin, often turning these over to their dance partners, who drank without restraint. Della couldn't stop staring. Ladies could do whatever they wanted here! Why hadn't she discovered this place sooner?

A few of the couples made their way back upstairs to rest after the song and Lord Ashton grew nervous again. "That's enough, let's go back to the alcove. It's darker there."

Della had seen enough to have satisfied her curiosity and moved to obey, though Annabelle ignored them.

"Leave her a little longer," Della murmured. "She looks well enough like a boy in her suit. No one will give her a second glance."

Lord Ashton frowned but said nothing, which she took for agreement.

"Might we have something to drink?" she ventured to ask. Her fan wasn't as effective combating the heat as she'd hoped. "What's that icy thing those people have got?"

"Sherry cobbler. It's an American cocktail. I'll buy one for you if you like. They aren't too strong. Only you must give me your word you won't wander astray while I'm gone."

"You speak as if I were a cat rather than a person," Della noted.

"You're certainly as ungovernable as one," he muttered, though there was a reluctant twitch at the corner of his lips. This seemed a victory.

Lord Ashton withdrew to the adjacent liquor counter and returned a moment later with two sherry cobblers. When he reclaimed his spot on the divan, he set the second one before Annabelle's vacant seat rather than his own.

"Thank you. Don't you want anything?"

"I don't drink," he said simply.

Della was so astounded, he might have knocked her over with a feather. *Everyone* drank, save the teetotalers. The question was only whether a gentleman drank in moderation or to excess.

Goodness, was Lord Ashton a teetotaler?

How did such a man write a guidebook full of amusements?

Della tried not to let her shock show plainly, though she wasn't sure she succeeded. She took a sip of her drink to give her face something to do besides make unwanted expressions. The sherry cobbler was both sweet and tart, but she refrained from telling Lord Ashton how much she enjoyed it, given his most recent revelation. Best to find a safer subject of conversation.

"Have you been here often?"

"Only once or twice," Ashton replied. "I needed to see what all the fuss was about once it opened, but I can't waste my time here every night." After a small pause, he added, "Though I'll own the music is excellent."

He was right about that. There was nothing like music to unite a group of strangers in common feeling. Della's thoughts were already leaping to plans for Bishop's. They couldn't fit anywhere near this many musicians on their premises, of course, but perhaps a string quartet would elevate the atmosphere...

Oh dear, she was neglecting their conversation to follow her own train of thought. And just when Lord Ashton had dropped some of his usual reserve. She could almost imagine they were old friends catching up.

"What sort of place do you prefer to frequent?" Della asked hastily. He didn't gamble. He didn't drink. He didn't attend casinos or dancing halls. What was his pleasure, then? "How do you like to spend your time when you aren't working on your books?"

When Lord Ashton replied, his tone was crisp and businesslike once more. Perhaps she'd lost her moment. "I don't leave myself much time to be idle. I devote my days to my writing, and I sit in the House of Lords when the debate is important. I make time to visit a few close friends, but I don't see the point of drinking and dancing all night."

Della shouldn't have been surprised by this, but somehow she was.

"You mean to say you don't even attend house parties here in town?" She'd wondered why she'd never seen him before their first meeting at Verey's, for she used to attend all the major events of the season before she'd begun devoting herself to Bishop's. She'd presumed that a peer might run in a more exclusive circle than hers, even if the Danby family's wealth was enough to make them welcome in most houses. "Not even a country ball?"

"I don't have time for such things." Those lovely green eyes of his had grown guarded. She'd touched a sore spot somehow, without meaning to. If only Lord Ashton would let her understand him, it might be easier to navigate his moods.

"It doesn't sound as if you leave yourself any time for fun," she observed.

"Fun?" He said the word as if he harbored great suspicion for it.

"Yes. It's something people do to enjoy their lives and replenish their energy."

"In my experience, the selfish pursuit of pleasure only leads to heartbreak. Men gamble away their fortunes, or drink to excess and make fools of themselves, betray their wives, or even get themselves killed at racing or dueling on occasion. Far from replenishing their energy, self-indulgence makes them useless for anything but further self-indulgence."

"What an unforgiving view you take of your fellow man."

"Come, Miss Danby." He leaned back in his seat and cocked his head, studying her. "You run a business that you've told me you attend every night of the week except Mondays. You now aspire to write a book, as well. Our acquaintance has been brief, but you strike me as a woman who likes to keep herself occupied. Surely you can't tell me you find time to keep pace with the events of the social season on top of all this?"

"Well..." Della's face grew hot, as if she'd been caught out in a fib. "I suppose I have been forced to decline a number of invitations since we opened our doors." She thought of how long it had been since she'd seen Miss Chatterjee, or any of her old friends. It was hard to maintain connections when she missed so many of the routs and balls they attended while she was at Bishop's. "But I still make my morning calls whenever I can, and besides, missing a dinner party or two doesn't mean I don't have fun. All my endeavors are things that I love. So I'm always enjoying myself."

He smiled at this. It was his first real smile of the evening.

"I've no doubt that you do."

Might she be winning him over, at least a little? He seemed more relaxed in her presence than he had been at their Tuesday meetings. Perhaps the change in setting did him some good, notwithstanding his proclaimed aversion to fun.

Della still wasn't persuaded he was being completely honest with her—or with himself, more likely. No one could live without some joy in their days.

"Don't you love writing?" she asked. She took another sip of sherry cobbler and savored the feeling of citrus at the back of her cheeks. "You must, to have produced three books and be working on a fourth. And you must love seeing new places, or you wouldn't have chosen the subject."

Lord Ashton seemed to need a moment to consider his reply. His lips parted the barest touch, without forming words. When he spoke, Della wasn't sure if he was talking to her or to himself. "I suppose I did love traveling when I was younger. Discovering new places, as you say. But I'm not sure if I can say that I *love* writing. More that it's something I'm good at, and it seemed a way to make myself useful when I needed that."

There was something like a confession in the way he presented this information, though Della felt as though she didn't quite understand him. Why should a viscount need a hobby to feel useful? In her experience, peers usually considered themselves useful simply by virtue of being born.

And then there was the more pressing question: "But how can you spend so much time on something unless you love it?"

"I just sit down and apply myself to the task." Ashton shrugged, as though this were perfectly ordinary and not a feat approaching sorcery.

"For three entire books? I can't imagine working that long on something unless I feel a passion for it."

"You're a more passionate person than I am, perhaps." He said the words almost affectionately. Or was that only wishful thinking on her part? She would swear that she'd caught his eyes skimming appreciatively over her gown just now.

I could teach this man a thing or two about passion if I had the chance, Della mused, eyeing him in the darkened room. She liked the way he was speaking to her this evening. His voice had a naturally commanding quality to it. Though this had annoyed her at their first meeting, she'd soon come to enjoy it, particularly when any coldness in his tone was chased away by good humor. The gaslight above them made the gray at Lord Ashton's temples shine with silver and set his features into stark relief. Though she had always admired his looks, he was at a particular advantage tonight. The lighting lent him an air of mystery, or perhaps that was the result of their conversation, which had begun to feel rather intimate. His perfectly tailored clothes skimmed the planes of the firm body beneath. She wanted very much to reach out and touch him. To feel the heat of his skin beneath her own.

You really shouldn't. The more reasonable part of Della's mind often adopted a tone that was very similar to Jane's. *You still have most of a book to write. How will you manage that if he rejects you and you're too embarrassed to show your face again?*

But the less reasonable (and far stronger) part of Della's mind had its counterargument ready: First, she was perfectly capable of writing her guidebook without Lord Ashton's help. If he stopped calling on her, she would simply manage on her own as she'd intended from the start. Second, it was apparent that Lord Ashton was far too proper to make any advance toward her, even if he did feel an attraction. The only way she could be sure how he felt was to signal her interest too clearly to be ignored. And third (here was the most important part), she wanted very, very much to make her cold, aloof viscount melt into a helpless puddle of desire at her feet.

In fact, she could think of nothing that would please her better this evening. The matter was decided.

Seven

THE BAND'S SONG REACHED A CRESCENDO AND FADED INTO silence, the last hum of the instruments soon replaced by applause. A few more people filed upstairs, and Lyman eyed them nervously. How long would it be before they encountered someone who knew him? Miss Danby's disguise wouldn't fool anyone who looked too closely.

Lyman wasn't sure why he'd agreed to come here.

He also wasn't sure why he hadn't called Miss Annabelle back from the balcony railing, which was far too conspicuous a vantage point, except that Miss Danby had been distracting him all evening. It was altogether too easy to lose track of himself in her company.

He should call her sister back now. Before he came to regret it.

Lyman opened his mouth, then realized they hadn't agreed on a false name for the girl beforehand. He couldn't very well shout out "Miss Annabelle," nor even the more masculine "Danby," lest someone recognize it. Before he could rise from his seat to collect her in person, the conductor turned to address the crowd below in a booming voice.

"And now," he cried, raising his arms up high, "we present to you, Madame Wharton and her tableau vivant!"

Oh no.

Lyman hadn't thought to check the playbill for the evening. The last time he'd been here, in the first weeks of the casino's opening, it had only been music and dancing. They must be expanding their attractions to compete with all the imitators that had sprung up to steal a share of their success.

He turned to murmur in Miss Danby's ear and found her so close to him that he froze. Their knees were touching. "We should go," he said.

"But I love tableaux vivants. Annabelle and I did one at our parents' May Day party." She didn't seem conscious of how alluring she was in that gown. It was a struggle to keep himself from staring.

"Not like this, you didn't," he warned her. "I strongly suspect Madame Wharton won't be wearing much."

"Oh!" Her eyes lit up—not with shock, but with joy. "How exciting. We must stay a little longer then. We can go after."

Lyman ran a hand through his hair. He wouldn't be surprised if he went entirely gray before the night was done.

On the opposite balcony, a white canvas curtain had dropped from the ceiling before the band and conductor, shielding them from view. It was painted with an image of a town. A cobblestone street with white plaster houses and a blue sky above. From one house, a man's face could be seen in the window, peeping out. The band began to play again from their hiding place, the flutes and oboe lilting out a gentle melody. No one dared to dance to it. They were all transfixed by the scene on the balcony above.

A wooden horse was led slowly before the curtain by a woman who must have been assisted by some unseen mechanism, for it looked far too heavy for her. It had been carved and painted with attention to realism, then fitted with a bridle and saddle. The woman was dressed austerely, in the plain, dark clothes of a servant with an old-fashioned veil around her head.

"You told me there wouldn't be any animals!" Miss Danby reminded him, her voice full of laughter. "It doesn't look large enough to be the siege of Troy. Did Zeus ever seduce a lady disguised as a horse? He tricked so many women I can hardly keep track."

"I think it's to be Lady Godiva."

"Oh, of course!" She was smiling brightly, her toffee-colored eyes as eager as a child awaiting a present. How did she maintain such enthusiasm for everything?

All my endeavors are things that I love, she'd said. *So I'm always enjoying myself.*

She'd seemed to mean it. Lyman couldn't imagine what it must feel like to go through life that way. He would have said he was envious of her, but that wasn't the right word for this feeling. Envy made one petty and resentful. He wouldn't wish for Miss Danby to lose this flame, even if he longed for a spark of his own.

What he wanted might have been to bask in her light a little longer. A foolish, dangerous desire.

Another woman entered the scene, apparently nude, though Lyman considered it likely she was wearing fleshings. It was hard to tell from a distance. Regardless, it was a very convincing approximation of nudity, and the crowd murmured their appreciation. She had long blond hair that cascaded down her back, and *only* her back.

"They don't seem terribly concerned with faithfulness to the story," Lyman observed wryly. "I thought she used her hair to hide her nakedness."

Miss Danby laughed at this, though she quickly suppressed it. He almost regretted scolding her earlier; it was a beautiful sound.

A laugh isn't worth being found out over. You should have left already.

He glanced back to the balcony. Lady Godiva had mounted the horse with the aid of a step cleverly carved into its curved leg and hoof, and now assumed her pose, fearlessly braving the streets of Coventry. She and the serving woman held perfectly still for a long minute. Like statues.

Before them, Miss Annabelle was likewise frozen. The poor child was probably so shocked she didn't know what to do with herself.

"We should really—"

Lyman's words died in his throat as a hand crept over his knee, coming to rest midway up his thigh. *Miss Danby's* hand. Her touch was hot even through the wool of his trousers.

Lyman went as still as the actors onstage, too stunned to react.

It was suddenly far too warm in here, with the acrid smoke of a dozen cigars mingling into the noise and heat of all these people. He couldn't think clearly before the sight of a naked woman posing for all the room to see, while a much more inviting reality sat at his side.

Now he understood. This was why he'd agreed to come tonight, despite his better judgment. This was why he'd allowed Miss Danby to lead him about without any regard for her own safety. Some unacknowledged part of him had hoped (perhaps even known) that this would happen. That she was willing, and he was badly wanting.

Her thumb brushed a slow line across his thigh, and Lyman's cock stiffened in response. She was playing him effortlessly, and he needed to stop it before things went too far. He clamped his hand down atop hers, fully intending to push her away.

But he didn't.

He stalled there, locked in place, unable to make himself end this. *You can't have her. You know you can't.*

Lyman's throat had gone dry. He finally turned to look at Miss Danby and saw exactly what he expected on her face. The promise of mischief that always lurked in her impish grin, finally made good.

I'm not going to stop her. The realization settled over him with a terrifying gravity. *I'm going to take anything I can, and damn the consequences.* He would ruin her if she asked him to.

Lyman had tried to stay strictly within the limits he set for himself these past few years, and for a time he'd fooled himself into thinking he'd truly changed. But all it took was a few weeks of playful teasing and a gentle touch, and he abandoned all his pretensions to honor. No, even sooner than that. He'd begun to slip the moment Miss Danby met him at the café, when he'd suffered an instinctive wish to make himself sound better than he was. She'd made him laugh even while he was trying to warn her away. That was when the cracks began to appear in his mask.

So Lyman sat there, his hand upon hers, unable to break the point of contact between them. He sat there for another five minutes. His mind darted through a range of lurid possibilities, trying to find a reason not to give in.

There was no reason. None strong enough to subdue the rush of desire pumping in his blood. He no longer worried over what threat he posed to Miss Danby's innocence, for it was clear by now that she had none. She wanted to seek out her pleasure in life? Well, he could provide her with several hours of pleasure, if he could only get her alone.

"Let's leave now," he whispered hoarsely. "You must be ready for something else."

She smiled knowingly at this, and the sight heated his blood to an intolerable degree.

Miss Annabelle protested when they went to collect her, her voice pitched lower to maintain her disguise as she argued that they hadn't seen how it would end yet.

"She's going to sit on a horse looking exactly as she does now for the next two hours while everyone else keeps dancing," Lyman snapped, exasperated. "At the end they abolish taxes."

And here he'd thought she would be shocked! Maybe Miss Danby had been telling the truth about her sister's character. They were two of a kind.

He tried not to look at Miss Danby as he led their group outside and into one of the many hansom cabs lounging near the entrance, but it was impossible. She drew his attention like a brilliant red flame in the darkness of the London streets. Whenever she caught him staring, she smiled her encouragement, her eyes full of promise. *Stop doing that,* he wanted to scold her. She was too lovely. Someone would take a second look and realize she was wrapped up in an ill-fitting costume.

It was a relief to finally motion her into the carriage and shut the door on the outside world. He felt a stab of regret at the thought of all the expenses of the night adding up—the ride here and back, plus their admission, which he had too much pride to admit he could ill afford—but he was too distracted to dwell on it.

"You see?" she said triumphantly. "It all went very well."

Lyman leaned his head back against the leather seat, willing his heart to stop pounding. He couldn't say how much stemmed from the fear of discovery, as opposed to the memory of her hand upon his thigh. "Promise me you'll never attempt anything this foolhardy again."

"What can you mean? No one suspected a thing."

He didn't answer, still struggling to regain his self-control. What would happen when they arrived? She hadn't touched him that way only to say good night, surely.

The carriage stopped before their mansion of a town house, and Lyman descended first to pay the coachman before he could get a good look at either of his companions.

"Aren't you continuing on to your house?" Annabelle asked, confused.

"I'll walk the rest of the way. It's not far," he lied.

"Go on inside, Annabelle," her sister commanded over the clopping of hooves on stone as the coachman drove his team on. "I'll be up in a moment."

What would happen in that moment?

Miss Annabelle gave them both a disapproving look, but trudged up to the front door all the same. Whatever bargain her sister had struck with her, Lyman was grateful for it.

When she was gone, Miss Danby turned her attention back to Lyman, winding her hand around his neck with languid amusement. "It seems we're quite alone, my lord."

He needed no further invitation. He bent his head to kiss her, desperate with pent-up desire. He would have liked to be gentler, but his body refused to obey him, and he claimed her lips roughly, a groan escaping him.

She took it in stride, opening her mouth to him eagerly. She tasted faintly of the sherry and lemon she'd drunk back at the casino. He explored her with his tongue, his blood pumping faster at her eager response. This woman was no stranger to pleasure. He should have known it would be like this. She snaked a hand down his chest and around his waist, to find the small of his back and pull him tight to her hips. At the evidence of his significant arousal, she chuckled, the sound low and husky.

Good Lord, she was going to drive him mad.

He'd had no idea how badly he'd needed this. How he'd been aching for an affectionate touch. Her hands set his skin alight.

Miss Danby broke off their kiss to trace the line of his jaw with her mouth, feigning surprise as she whispered. "Oh my. What do you plan to do to me, hmm?"

Lyman struggled to rein himself in. Her hot breath against his ear threatened to send him over the edge.

Privacy. He needed to get her alone somewhere.

"Come back to my rooms," he murmured. He couldn't even summon an ounce of shame that she might see how poorly he lived. It was a hovel compared to her house, but it had a bed, and no meddling family to discover them in it. That was the important thing.

"I can't." There was a note of regret in her tone that gave him hope. "My sister might look the other way for a short time, but she'll make a fuss if I'm gone for hours."

In spite of this refusal, she began nibbling on his ear. He was going to lose his mind.

"Take pity on me, Miss Danby." Lyman was not above begging, at this point.

"You may call me Della," she breathed. "I think we're past formality now, don't you?"

She kissed him again, and he slid his hands down to cup her rear and pull them still tighter together. His cock was aching for release.

"Someone will see us," he warned. "There must be someplace else we can go."

It was late enough that no one would be out walking the street, but there was nothing to protect them from a carriage returning from a neighbor's fête or, worse, her family.

"Follow me." She took him by the hand and led him around the side of her town house, to a gate that opened upon a narrow alleyway, barely three feet across. It led to a shared courtyard, enclosed on all sides by the other houses. She stopped just short of the exit and leaned back against the rough brick wall. Apparently this was the full extent of her plan. A darkened alley. "No one will see us here," she explained. Lyman had to accept it, for he could barely see her himself, though he still clutched her hand.

He released his grip and placed an arm on either side of Miss Danby—Della, now—penning her in. He'd barely begun to kiss her again when her hand found his trousers, working at buttons that seemed to take an hour to yield.

"What are you doing?" he groaned, though he knew full well. He just wanted to hear her say it.

"Taking pity on you." He could hear the smile in her voice as the first button gave way.

Good God. He couldn't talk after that. Couldn't summon the strength to do anything except gasp for breath as she slid her hand inside and began to stroke. It took all his self-control to keep from spending himself the second her soft, warm skin made contact.

"Do you like that?" she murmured, in a voice thick and heavy with excitement.

"You have no idea," he gasped. Her hand was like silk, her movements sure and knowing. She wasn't a woman who hesitated to go after what she wanted, nor who felt any need to feign virginal innocence. He liked that about her.

She increased the pace of her attention, bringing him perilously close to climax already. Every nerve in his body was begging for more. He had to stop this before he lost control. "Enough," he gasped, catching her hand in his own. "Give me a moment."

He thought of Laurent's Casino and how he'd craved her touch too badly to push her hand away when he'd meant to. It was much the same now, except that Della obeyed his request and slid her fingers gently back out of his falls. He shuddered.

"Even when you're making love to a woman you have a hard time enjoying yourself, don't you?"

"I'm enjoying myself," he assured her. "Far too much."

In truth, he couldn't remember the last time he'd been so happy. The last time he let himself savor an experience without worrying about the expense or the work he should be finishing instead.

He kissed Della again, eager to show her the truth in his

declaration. She melted into him, running her hands roughly up and down his chest, now grabbing the end of his cravat to tug him closer. How could she be so uninhibited? So unbothered by what he or anyone else might think?

He'd never known anyone like her. It made him feel alive.

He needed to make her feel it too. Lyman began hiking up her skirts; a considerable task, as they were numerous.

"Someone might see us," she hissed into his ear.

"This is no truer now than it was ten minutes ago," he noted.

"Yes, but I'm not concerned about *your* modesty." She chuckled, the sound dying abruptly as he found the slit in her drawers.

She was wet already, and Lyman slipped a finger inside her, thrilling at the hitch in her breath. She didn't tense or grow nervous at his incursion. She groaned and relaxed into it, making no attempt to conceal her pleasure.

"Show me how you like to be touched," he invited, even as he deepened his attentions to find that silken part of her that needed him.

She didn't hesitate. "Harder." With one hand, she found the back of his neck and pulled him down to meet her kiss. With the other, she guided his movements to a rougher pace before she released him to manage on his own.

He fell into a hypnotic rhythm, his tongue parting her lips above, his fingers parting her lips below, in time to the music of her rapid breath. With his free hand, Lyman cupped Della's breast, tracing the tight peak of her nipple with his thumb.

"Your gown is downright indecent," he accused her. "Do you know what you're doing to me?"

"You scarcely looked at me all night!" she protested.

"Because I was worried that if I did, I wouldn't be able to stop staring." He let his lips roam down her throat, then lightly traced the top of her breasts. With greater focus than he'd thought remained to him, Lyman reached around her back to undo the top few buttons of her gown, which fell open to expose her shift below. He pushed the thin muslin aside, exposing her to the night air. Della shivered as he bent his head to suck and tease at her nipple.

"Oh," she groaned as she squirmed on his fingers. "Keep doing that. Exactly like that."

"You are the most arousing woman I've ever met," he breathed, the confession drawn from him without any forethought. It was true. He'd never known anyone who lived life so freely as she did, and even as it frightened him, it also transfixed him.

"And here I worried you didn't like me." Her words came out broken, stumbling over halting gasps.

"I like you," he assured her. "See how much?"

She kissed him deeply as he focused all his attention on bringing her to climax. It wasn't difficult. She was eager for him, and after another moment she cried out (a touch more loudly than was prudent), bucking against his hand until her pleasure had passed and left her shaking in its wake.

Lyman slid his fingers free and gently settled her skirts back into place.

"You should hurry back inside," he said. "Someone might come to see what that noise was."

She laughed, the sound as pure and joyful as birdsong. "I'm sorry. I tried to be quiet. But what about you?" Della glanced at the bulge in his trousers, a smile teasing her lips. "Don't you want to continue?"

Yes. More than I want air.

Lyman shook his head. "Not now."

He didn't know why he refused when he'd been so excited only a moment before, except that a sudden foreboding had crept over him. A premotion that, if he should take his own pleasure instead of merely giving it, he might hurt Miss Danby.

She was happy with him now. She thought him attractive and considerate, and she was grateful for a successful evening.

Let it end this way, before he could ruin things.

"Next time then," she promised. What possibility lived in those words. "Why don't you come by the house tomorrow? I know we said we'd cancel our meeting, but I'd love to see you again. Maybe I can find some way to get rid of Annabelle."

"All right."

"Or..." She took three steps backwards, her eyes still warming Lyman with their heat, then stopped short of the entrance to the alleyway.

She pointed up.

"Do you see that window?"

It was almost impossible to make out anything in these shadows, but he could almost detect the glint of a reflection on glass, one story above them.

"I think so."

"That's my room. I'll leave it open tomorrow night, if you'd rather continue this in a more private setting."

How in the hell he was supposed to climb to the second story without the aid of a ladder, Lyman didn't know. Was there a trellis around here somewhere? Never mind; he would think of something.

"Aren't you worried we might be discovered?"

"My parents are never at home and the servants are well compensated for their continued ignorance. As for Annabelle, I'll handle her."

With that, Della blew him a kiss and disappeared from sight, leaving only the empty frame of the gate before him.

Eight

DELLA OPENED THE DOOR, DEPOSITED HER CLOAK, AND TIP-
toed up the stairs without taking in any of it. She felt as if she were
drunk, though Lord Ashton had been telling the truth when he'd said
those sherry cobblers didn't have much kick to them. No, Della was
drunk on victory—a far sweeter refreshment.

She had driven away her nemesis, the stern-faced aristocrat who
underestimated her at every turn and never gave fair consideration
to her efforts. *He* was the one who'd refused to put her club in his
book and scoffed at the idea that she could write one herself. And
now Della had replaced him with a slightly less stern-faced aristocrat
who kissed her as sinfully as the devil himself.

What a fantastic trade!

She hadn't expected Ashton to be a good kisser. She'd mostly
wanted to do it because she found him so handsome (even though
she *knew* handsome men were often the worst kissers, as they tended
to be selfish), or perhaps it had only been to see if he would finally
warm to her. But that hadn't been warm, it had been...feverish. The
way he'd touched her and the things he'd said to her! *This* was a man

she could believe had visited all the places in his books, a man who knew how to live.

This version of the viscount would be a pleasure to work with. He wouldn't sigh and run his hands through his hair at the suggestion that they each write their own introduction. He would smile and say, "That's a capital idea, Della. How thoughtful of you to have found a compromise for us."

She opened the door to her room and floated inside. They were going to get along so much better now that—

Della screamed at the sight of a shadowy figure on her bed. A prowler, come to kill her! No, it was only the housekeeper, come to ask her where she'd been all evening and demand a shilling to keep quiet about it. Scarcely better, as Della hated being extorted.

But a closer inspection in the lamplight proved that it was neither of these things. The intruder was only Annabelle.

"You terrified me! I nearly dropped the lamp and set us both ablaze."

Such a reaction didn't bode well for Lord Ashton's future rendezvous with her bedroom window. She would try to keep from screaming if he appeared so suddenly.

Unless she was screaming for another reason, of course.

"You've been outside for nearly an hour," her sister said flatly.

"So? You didn't need to wait up. Go back to your own room and go to bed, please."

"*Someone* should keep an eye on you!" Annabelle whispered, furious. "What if Lord Ashton took advantage, and no one heard you cry for help?"

"I promise you, I took advantage of him and not the other way round."

"He's *married*, Della."

"His wife left him years ago, and they haven't spoken since. Surely you don't think she can object if he seeks out companionship now? I doubt she's been living as a nun."

"What's between them is between them," Annabelle conceded, "but you don't need to get mixed up in it. There's no future with such a man."

"Who says I want a future?" Della asked belligerently. "I'm enjoying the present, that's all." And what enjoyment! It was even better than she'd dared to hope, having the stern Viscount Ashton moaning and at her mercy. He was more attentive than she'd expected. Most men only thought about their own climax, but he'd *wanted* to please her. And he'd done a very good job of it. She couldn't remember the last time she'd felt so content.

"I should tell Mama and Papa about this and save you from yourself." Annabelle narrowed her eyes to feline slits. The similarity didn't end there, for her air of superiority and ever-watchful manner had always reminded Della of a cat.

"Do we really want to start down this road, dear?" Della pulled off the too-tight gown, eager to shed her disguise. She'd grown uncomfortable hours ago. "I don't think I need to remind you of all the occasions I've saved your neck."

There was the time Peter had gone fishing, to find Annabelle and her latest paramour swimming naked in the lake at their country house. Della had to persuade him this was a perfectly innocent adventure for two young ladies, which he should never mention to either set of parents. Then there was the time Annabelle stole a bottle from the wine cellar to hole up in her room with her lady's maid, and nearly got the footman sacked for theft. Della had discreetly purchased a replacement and "found" the missing bottle behind a cabinet to save the poor fellow.

There was a distinct theme to Annabelle's misadventures.

Honestly, I'm a saint.

"You haven't done anything for me recently," Annabelle observed. "Whereas *I'm* forced to sit through your flirtation with Lord Ashton every week just to make sure you don't get yourself into more trouble than usual."

"I let you come to the casino with me tonight," Della snapped back, indignant. "That should count for something."

"That bought you my silence. You were going anyway, so it was your caper, not mine."

Ah, now we come to it.

"And what do you have planned that you need my help for?"

"I don't know what you mean." Annabelle plucked a loose thread from her wrap. For some reason, she maintained the absurd fiction that she was the better behaved one even when they were alone. It probably came from being the youngest child. All she'd had to do was feign innocence for their governess when she wanted to get Della or Peter into trouble. "But..." She sighed as though she were struggling to think of some possible solution. "I suppose if you want to repay me for my kindness, you *could* let me into your club tomorrow night."

"Never." Della didn't even need to consider. "We've been over this. Family aren't allowed to play the tables. People will think we're cheating them when you win, and you'll expect us to forgive the debts when you lose. It's bad business either way."

"I don't even want to play much," Annabelle whined. "I just want to attend. Why must you be so mean?"

"You said my club was a foolish venture bound to fail," Della reminded her. The taunt had been issued nearly three years ago, but she could hold a grudge when it counted. "Why should you want to attend now?"

"Fine. I'm sorry I said that. Are you satisfied?" When Della didn't budge, her sister groaned and buried her hands in her face. "All right, all right, it's to impress a girl."

Della perked up instantly. "A matter of the heart! Why didn't you say so? Of *course* you can come."

This changed everything. While Della might enjoy antagonizing her sister on occasion (strictly to even the score), she would never sabotage anyone's chance at happiness. Besides, Annabelle was much more fun to tease when she was in love.

"Whose heart have you captured this time?"

"It's none of your business."

"I'm going to find out anyway, so you may as well tell me."

Della wasn't quite sure how her sister managed to seduce anyone—gangly, charmless hoyden that she was—but somehow she always seemed to be in pursuit of one debutant or another. Many of her dalliances were entirely one-sided and ended with nothing to show for her efforts, the object of her affection proving unable or unwilling to entertain that sort of connection with another lady. But every now and again she succeeded in winning one of them over and would spend weeks or months doing adorable, ridiculous things such as writing her paramour a dozen sonnets or sending her coded messages through flowers, until eventually the flame burned out or someone's parents grew too suspicious.

Annabelle rolled her eyes, but accepted the inevitable. "Eliza Greenwood. But I haven't captured her heart yet. That's what this outing is for."

"Oooh, a worthy challenge." Miss Greenwood was uncommonly pretty, recently out, and highly sought after this season. In truth, Annabelle probably didn't have much of a chance with her. As far as Della knew, Miss Greenwood seemed as interested in the gentlemen who filled her dance card as any other young lady. No wonder Annabelle wanted her help. An invitation to Bishop's would lend her a certain cachet she sorely needed.

It almost made Della wish she hadn't invited Lord Ashton to sneak into her bedroom tomorrow evening.

"I'm afraid I won't get to see how it turns out for you, as I have another engagement." She would call on Eli and Jane in the morning to make sure they could manage Bishop's without her. She didn't often ask for a night off, but it would be the first time in months, and the chance to seduce Lord Ashton was too good to pass up. "So whatever you do, don't make a mess you can't clean up on your own."

"You think I need *your* help?" Annabelle looked so offended, Della might almost have believed the emotion was justified. "You'd only embarrass me. That's why I'm bringing Miss Greenwood when you're not there."

Wait.

"Beg pardon?" Della wondered if it was too late to rescind her invitation. "How did you know I'd be seeing the viscount tomorrow? Were you eavesdropping on me?" The insufferable snoop! She'd probably cracked a window open the second she'd got in the house.

"Not at all." Annabelle laughed, pouncing to her feet and making for the exit. "It was an easy guess, and you just confirmed it."

She slammed the door just before Della flung her slipper.

Lyman walked back to Pimlico from Miss Danby's doorstep. The brisk night air would do him good. Besides which, he couldn't justify the cost of another carriage ride when he was perfectly capable of walking. It wasn't that those few coins would make any difference in the grand scheme of things; it was the principle of it. How could he permit himself unnecessary luxuries when he should be sending every penny toward Michael and Ellen?

Tonight was a luxury, but that didn't stop you from wasting your evening at the invitation of Miss Danby.

Della.

Lyman walked a bit quicker, the clack of his shoes on the cobblestones echoing back at him as if he were being pursued. His heart was still pounding at the thrill of what she'd given him so freely. It had been ages since he'd gone out for an evening. Far longer since he'd had a woman in his arms. The last one had been Mrs. Chatham, a widow several years his elder. She hadn't expected too much from Lyman. Not love, certainly, nor a second marriage. She'd known about his situation before they began their dalliance. He suspected she suffered more from boredom than from loneliness and had judged him just scandalous enough to provide a spark of excitement to her evenings. He wasn't sure if he'd lived up to her expectations of a rakehell, but she'd liked what he did with his hands, at any rate.

Della had liked it too.

But Della wasn't a widow, in a position to risk a discreet liaison. What did she expect of him? Lyman would feel better about this if she were a bit older and less full of that thoughtless enthusiasm that made her throw herself into every idea that caught her fancy. Her gambling club, this ladies' guidebook, and now him. Had she really thought about the consequences of any of it?

I'm not ignorant of the dangers of anything I do, my lord, she'd declared a few hours ago. *But I won't live in fear.*

It had the appearance of bravery, but Lyman wasn't persuaded she truly understood. Anyone could *believe* they were prepared to risk everything. Until you lost what was dearest to you, you didn't know how you would bear it.

Lyman wished he could shut out the fears that tarnished his evening. Why should he feel guilty if he did want to see her again? Was that so terrible? They weren't hurting anyone, and he'd been honest with her from the start about the fact that he wasn't free to remarry. Whatever this was, it wouldn't last. A month or two, perhaps, until she finished her book and they parted ways. Any connection between them promised to be so insignificant that Lyman shouldn't have minded what happened.

But he did mind. He could still feel the silk of her skin beneath his hands and the citrus scent of her in his lungs. Could still hear the sounds she'd made when he brought her to climax. That unchecked cry of pure bliss that had wrapped itself around his whole being. She'd ensnared him completely.

When he reached the Hirsches' house and let himself into the second-floor apartments that were reserved for the boarders, he found Clarkson still awake and at the table in the common dining room. He was reading a heavy, leather-bound volume by the light of a cheap tallow candle that leaked an acrid plume of smoke into the air.

"Good evening," his friend greeted him. "You're up late."

"I could say the same to you."

"Mr. Hirsch has me searching for a precedent in a particularly tricky case." If Clarkson was tired, he didn't show it. He slipped a bookmark into his text and closed it with a heavy thud. "Did your friend enjoy her clandestine view of Laurent's?"

Lyman wouldn't risk Miss Danby's reputation by telling anyone else what she'd been up to, but he'd trusted Clarkson well enough to confide the general situation without revealing her name. He wasn't the sort to pry or gossip, unlike Mr. Wood. But Wood's door was shut and there was no sound from within, so he must be asleep already. Lyman was careful to keep his voice down. If their conversation disturbed the other lodger's rest, they would never hear the end of it.

"She did." Lyman hesitated, unsure of what he wanted to say next. Finally he added, "Something happened tonight."

"Were you discovered?" Clarkson's brows drew together in mild concern.

"No, no, nothing like that. She kissed me."

"Ah."

"That's all you're going to say?"

"What should I say?" Clarkson shrugged, his voice mild. "Are you looking for advice?"

"I suppose I am," Lyman admitted, though he'd only realized it in that moment. "She's made it clear she's interested in continuing things where we left off, but I'm worried the risk might be too great. What would you do?"

"*I'd* never go near her again." Clarkson didn't hesitate. "But that's because I know her father wouldn't be likely to bother with a duel before murdering an apprentice solicitor who laid a hand on his daughter. The question you're really asking is, what would I do if I were a viscount?" He made a little show of considering this, leaning back and stroking his chin. "That depends on how much you like this lady, and whether you think her father is likely to call out his social superior. Is he a good shot with a pistol?"

"This is an extremely sobering discussion," Lyman replied. "I'm hoping he never learns I exist."

It wasn't as though the Danbys kept their children under close watch. As far as Lyman could tell, they'd never been at home when he'd called. The only person who knew or cared about their meetings was Miss Annabelle, and Della seemed confident that she could be managed.

"I hope so too, for your sake," Clarkson said. "And for mine. I don't want Mrs. Hirsch to have to replace you with another Mr. Wood."

Lyman chuckled at this. What an unbearable prospect.

"Does this table seem different to you?" Clarkson asked abruptly, craning his neck back to assess the ceiling. "I swear it used to be nearer the window. I think Wood's gone and moved it to have more space on his side at breakfast, but now my elbows keep hitting the wall."

Lyman took a moment to assess the furniture. Sure enough, the dining table looked to be about eight inches further away than it had been this morning. "I think you're right."

Clarkson rose to his feet with a frown and wrapped his hands around either side. Seeing his intent, Lyman took the other end and helped him lift the table back into its former position. Once they were done, they both stood silent, listening to see if the noise had awoken Mr. Wood. They were safe for the moment.

Clarkson's face took on a more serious air as he sat back down. "Be careful with this woman, though. Truly. Wealthy young ladies aren't to be trifled with unless you're prepared to compensate them with your life, one way or another."

"And I'm not in a position to offer her my life in matrimony," Lyman finished the thought for him.

"Precisely."

Nine

DELLA WAS TOO EXCITED TO WORK ON HER BOOK BEFORE LORD Ashton's call the next morning, even though she knew she should. Today marked their third meeting, which meant she was nearly halfway through the two-month deadline he'd imposed for her first draft.

She wasn't quite sure where the time had gone, but she wouldn't despair yet. If she put everything else aside for a whole week and devoted herself to the task, she would *have* to catch up. That was exactly what she'd do, just as soon as Lord Ashton's visit was over. Then she would feel better about everything.

But Miss Chatterjee called shortly before her rival-turned-mentor-turned-paramour could arrive.

"I'm so happy you came, but I must warn you I have an engagement at eleven," Della explained as she showed her into the sunny drawing room. "I'm expecting a gentleman."

Della must have been vibrating at a high frequency (probably owing to the four cups of tea she'd already drunk that morning to calm herself), for Reva was quick to jump to conclusions.

"A gentleman? I didn't realize you had a new suitor!"

"I wouldn't call him that," Della added quickly. "We're friends. He's mentoring me for that guidebook I told you about."

"Oh." Reva looked watchful, gauging the situation before she replied. "Are you sure there's no particular attachment there? You seemed excited just now."

"I'm sure." Della spoke firmly enough to hide the question in her heart. "I'll admit that he intrigues me, but we wouldn't suit. For many reasons."

She didn't know what stopped her from pouring the whole story out to Reva. Her friend would keep her secrets, and she'd been longing to confide in someone. But Della couldn't shake the nagging suspicion that if she revealed Lord Ashton had an estranged wife out there somewhere and she'd kissed him anyway (in an alleyway, no less!), Reva's opinion would be set against him. Jane would react the same way, no doubt. Which meant she couldn't tell anyone about her budding affaire with Lord Ashton unless she wanted a concerned lecture on the subject, which she certainly did not.

I already have one Annabelle in my life.

"It's been so long since you mentioned anyone who interested you. Have you given up on the season altogether?"

"No, no, of course not," Della assured her. "I'm just focusing on the club these days. But forget about me. How are matters progressing with Mr. Bhattacharya? Have you received a proposal yet?"

Reva didn't answer, but pursed her lips and dropped her eyes in a knowing manner.

"*Reva!*" Della shrieked.

"Shh, there's nothing final yet. His family are going to call on my parents on Friday to settle the details and choose a wedding date. After that we can make an announcement."

"I'm so happy for you!" Judging by her smile, Reva was happy too.

Della swept her friend into a tight embrace. "Tell me all about him. Is he very handsome?"

"I find him handsome. He's tall, with a kind smile. He loves poetry as much as I do, and he's studying to become a barrister." She was blushing as she spoke. "He's very clever."

Lord Ashton is clever too, Della couldn't help but think. It was a good quality in a man. And Reva was the sort of lady to need a husband she could really talk to, not someone who would stick to his own sphere of interest and ignore her.

"I'm happy for you," Della repeated. "I can't wait for your wedding."

Though her joy was quite real, she couldn't help but wonder if this would mean that Reva would be busy with a baby of her own in a year or two, just like Jane. It seemed most of her friends had settled down now. She hadn't noticed it happening; they just slid away one by one until before she knew it, she'd clipped out a wedding announcement for everyone except herself.

She was glad they were happy, of course—with the exception of a few who weren't—but it made Della uneasy to see how her friends changed afterward. They retired to the countryside; they stopped coming by the club when they were in town; they started throwing dinner parties made up entirely of married couples to have a "balanced table." By the time a baby came along, the gap between their lives and Della's had often widened into a chasm. Even if she might follow them into matrimony one day, she would never abandon her old life that way.

Why were they all in such a hurry to stop having fun?

"You must promise you won't be too busy for me once you're a married woman." Della squeezed Reva's hands. "I shall still come and visit you, and you must do likewise. You're staying in London, I trust?" If her future husband was to be a barrister, there was a good chance he would work in town.

"Yes," Reva confirmed.

"Wonderful." Della breathed a sigh of relief. Whatever else might come, at least her friend wasn't disappearing to some forgotten corner of the countryside like so many others had. "Let's make sure to have some fun together before you get too busy preparing for your wedding. I need to tour some attractions in London for my book soon, if you'd care to join me."

"Oh, where are you going?"

"The shops, the botanical gardens, the theater, any place interesting we can think of, really. It's been ages since I visited most of them, and I need to make sure my descriptions are up to date."

Before Reva could answer, a knock at the door indicated Lord Ashton had arrived. Reva cast a questioning look at Della as she rose to her feet. "You aren't going to rush me off before I can even see the man, are you? I need to judge if you *wouldn't suit* as much as you claim."

Della smiled at her friend's teasing. "Very well, but you must promise not to make a fuss. I meant it when I said he wasn't a match for me." She was trying to look stern, but as usual, it proved beyond the abilities of her face. Reva didn't seem mollified in the least.

The butler showed Lord Ashton in, and he halted his step mid-stride when he saw them. "Forgive me, I didn't realize you had company."

"I was just leaving," Reva explained.

"Miss Chatterjee, please allow me to present the Viscount Ashton, who's been kind enough to help me with my book."

Reva curtsied gracefully. "How do you do?"

"A pleasure to make your acquaintance, Miss Chatterjee," Lord Ashton said as he bowed in return.

He looked particularly handsome today, dressed in a crisp fawn morning coat and a green silk cravat that brought out the color of his eyes. Or perhaps it was only that Della saw him in a new light now that they had breached the walls between them. Belatedly, she realized that she was smiling at him too warmly, her eyes lingering too long, and that Reva had probably noticed all of it.

She flushed, which did nothing to help matters.

"Miss Danby was just telling me about her plans to tour every attraction in London! I hope you aren't keeping her too busy, my lord."

Reva said the words with a friendly smile, but Della caught a flash of panic in Ashton's eye. What was wrong? Oh, but he must think that she'd said something about their trip to Laurent's Casino last night.

"The decision to see all the shops and theaters again was my own, not Lord Ashton's," Della cut in smoothly, hoping the words would convey her discretion. "You know I don't like to do things in half measures."

"True," Reva agreed with a little laugh. "You're nothing if not ambitious." With another little curtsy to Lord Ashton, she said, "I won't keep you from your work any longer. I'm sure you have lots to discuss."

Della invited Ashton to make himself comfortable while she saw Reva to the door. Once they were in the foyer and safely out of earshot, Reva whispered excitedly, "You didn't say he was a *viscount!*"

Della decided her best course was to feign innocence. "I thought you knew. Didn't I tell you he was the author of that guidebook for gentlemen?"

"I've never read it," Reva replied with an apologetic look. "Are you very sure you don't suit? Just think, you could be the next Lady Ashton."

Except that there's already a Lady Ashton. The woman might have separated from her husband, but she would always retain her position in life. And if Reva should trouble herself to search through Debrett's or ask after him, she would learn the truth quickly enough.

"Very sure." Della managed to force a little smile, as though none of this troubled her. It really wasn't her concern. She and Ashton were just having some harmless fun until they went their separate ways. There was nothing wrong with that, as long as they kept things quiet.

"What a pity." Reva deflated a little. "We might have been married right after one another. Ah, well. I hope your writing goes smoothly."

Once Reva was gone, Della took a deep breath.

It was only natural for Reva to have such hopes for her. Most ladies her age wished to marry as well as they could, and a viscount would be a fine catch for anyone of her station. More than fine.

But most ladies had neither the money nor the daring to live precisely as they liked, much less a profitable business to fall back on. Della *was* ambitious. And right now, her goal was to make the most of her present situation before the opportunity was gone.

She returned to the drawing room with a quick step. A maid had whisked away Miss Chatterjee's tea and brought in a fresh cup for Lord Ashton in the brief time she'd been away, but there was no sign of her now. Della and her guest were quite alone. She shut the door softly behind her, wondering how long she had before Annabelle realized that she was late to her chaperoning duties. Not more than a few minutes, probably. She would use them well.

"I'm sorry to have kept you waiting," she murmured with a warm smile.

Ashton rose to his feet politely at her entrance. "It's quite all right."

They stared at each other for a long moment, neither one of them quite sure how to behave after the way they'd parted. Della made no move to sit, and the viscount was too well mannered to take his own seat first. He watched her expectantly. His expression was always so intense, but this time Della was finally sure she was the cause of the emotion there.

She relished the feel of his eyes on her body.

Della crossed the room and wrapped her hands around Ashton's neck without a word. His swift intake of breath betrayed his surprise, but he didn't resist as Della stood on her tiptoes and tugged his head down to meet her embrace. He kissed her hungrily, as if it had been far longer than a few hours since their last encounter. "Sit on the divan," she breathed, giving his chest a firm nudge in the direction she wanted him.

Lord Ashton obeyed—for a bossy aristocrat, he seemed willing enough to listen to her instructions when it mattered—and slid his hands lower to grip her waist as he sat down. Della followed quickly after him, hiking her skirts up to straddle his legs and rest her weight upon him.

"What if someone sees us like this?" His eyes were wide with shock at her boldness, their muddy green shade growing brighter in the light of the morning sun streaming through the windows. The shrubbery outside and the lace curtains obscured them from the view of anyone approaching the house, but their actions weren't without some risk. Della judged the reward to be worth it. As she eased herself down to press against Ashton's growing arousal, his protest died off in a low groan.

"They won't." Della reassured him, rocking her hips slowly as his breath grew quick. "We'll stop in just a minute. I only wanted to greet you properly while I still had the chance."

Unless you beg me not to stop.

Ashton's hand clenched against her lower back, as if he were thinking the same thing.

It was far more comfortable to kiss him at this angle, where their difference in height was reduced. Della ran a hand through Ashton's hair and down the back of his neck, pausing to anchor herself on the firm base of his shoulder as she pressed herself against him.

"Della." He gasped her name like a plea. "You're driving me mad."

"Good." She felt merciless. That was exactly what she wanted.

After the way he'd left her last night without ever taking his own pleasure, Della wanted to know that she could break that self-control. That she could make him so desperate to have her he wouldn't be able to resist. She bit his lower lip—half by accident in her haste to drink her fill of him before they were interrupted, half on purpose.

His hand slid lower to cup her rear and pull her tight against him. "We shouldn't," he murmured, even as his own actions betrayed him. "Anyone could walk in."

As if summoned by this observation, a set of light footsteps sounded overhead, drawing toward them.

Annabelle.

Della leaned over to whisper into Lord Ashton's ear. "I want you thinking of this all day, until you can come back to me this evening and finish what we've started."

With that promise, she rose to her feet and smoothed down her skirts, selecting a seat several feet away. Ashton swayed forward as she retreated, as if he intended to pull her right back against him, but he slumped back against the divan a moment later, breathing deeply. His eyes bored into her with such heat that it took all her willpower to maintain a distance between them.

He adjusted himself to hide the obvious evidence of his arousal, but nothing could hide his tousled hair and flushed cheeks, a sharp contrast to his normally immaculate appearance. Della had no doubt she looked much the same, if the hammering of her heart was any indication.

Annabelle would guess what they'd been up to, no doubt. But she smoothed her hair into place all the same. It was important to keep up appearances.

If it were possible to die of sexual frustration, Lyman would already be six feet underground.

The woman behaved as though she'd been raised in a brothel rather than the drawing rooms of Mayfair. The way she'd spread her legs over him without a trace of hesitation! Yet somehow, she managed to look perfectly innocent and rosy-cheeked—not an ounce of shame in her body—when her sister entered the room a moment later.

It was infuriating.

It was extremely arousing.

He'd never known anyone like her. During his marriage to Ellen, Lyman had been entirely in the dark. Whether she was too demure to tell him what she wanted, or whether she truly wanted nothing at all, Lyman couldn't have said. All he knew was that they'd been like two icebergs bobbing hopelessly around each other. Their only options were a collision course or complete indifference. When he'd finally allowed himself the satisfaction of a discreet affaire, long after Ellen had banished him from her life, it had been a shock to realize how different it could be. What mutual passion could look like between a man and a woman. But even then, he'd never met anyone quite so lively as Della. She was unmatched in that respect.

"When did Miss Chatterjee leave?" Annabelle asked in an accusatory tone. "You should have called me if you were alone."

She was watching Lyman with an extra dose of suspicion this morning. This didn't bode well for his plan to avoid any duels. He cleared his throat and tried to look unconcerned.

"Only a moment ago," Della replied. "Honestly, there's no need to fuss."

He should say something. More specifically, he should say something ordinary and reassuring. A question about Della's book, or even the weather—anything but the fact that she'd been straddling his lap five minutes ago.

I want you thinking of this all day, she had said, her breath hot in his ear. Well, she'd achieved what she set out to. He hoped she didn't regret the loss of his opinion on whatever it was they were supposed to be talking about.

Lyman sipped his tea and tried to focus on the bitter heat washing over his tongue, rather than the very different sort of heat coiling low in his stomach.

Della, in contrast, didn't seem the least bit distracted. Her smile was so dazzling that Lyman was certain it threw a reflection on his spectacles as she addressed him. "I hoped we could talk about some ideas I had last night."

Lyman swallowed hard, his mind flooding with images of their evening, until she continued.

"There are some important subjects missing from your book, and I wanted your thoughts on whether I should add them to mine."

"Oh." Of course she meant her book. He should be grateful she was focusing on the business at hand, for once. Although Lyman bristled a little at the suggestion he'd left anything out. "I endeavored to be quite thorough."

"I've no doubt you did," she replied with a knowing smile. Next to her, Miss Annabelle rolled her eyes, killing any thought he'd had of forming a flirtatious reply.

This was damnably awkward.

"I wanted to add a section on views," Della continued.

"Views?" He struggled to follow her proposal through the host of other thoughts swimming around his brain.

"Yes! Think of it—the people who come to London from the countryside for the first time want to see the whole city laid out before them." Della grew more animated as she spoke, spreading her hands wide as if to paint him an image of the Tower and Westminster and all the other landmarks looming above the water. "I think you likened it to ancient Babylon somewhere in your guidebook, didn't you?" He had, in the opening chapter. He was pleased that she remembered. "I wouldn't want to see Babylon and never look at the whole thing from a nice hillside somewhere. So, which vantage point do you think is best to take in the city?"

She'd conjured a notebook and pencil from somewhere, but Lyman had nothing to help her fill it. "I've never given it much thought," he admitted.

"Never?" Della set her pencil down, looking at him incredulously. "When you come back to town after a long absence, aren't you ever struck by the vastness of it?"

"I live in town year-round."

"You don't return to your country house?"

"Not in years."

"Oh, of course. Forgive me." Della blushed. Her assumption was evident—that he must have left his country house to the use of his estranged wife and taken up the town house as his residence. He should correct her, but he didn't.

She's going to find out eventually, a hateful voice whispered in his mind. *And once she does, she'll never look at you the same way again.*

"I felt the purpose of my guide was to enable people to seek out establishments of quality and avoid those that would fleece them and offer little in return," he said, ignoring the oppressive feeling that weighed on him. They were having a lovely morning. He wouldn't ruin it. "I hadn't considered the views important."

"Do you think it would be silly of me to include them?" Della's rich brown eyes were wide and earnest, her lips parting slightly as she drew a breath. Lyman was all too conscious that he might crush her enthusiasm with a careless word, though she should never have given him that kind of power.

He'd been dismissive of her at the beginning, he knew. He'd

refused to put her club in his book, then scoffed at her plans to write one of her own. But it wasn't too late to remedy that.

"I don't think it would be silly in the least." Lyman offered her a faint smile. "I only wish I'd thought of it first."

The burst of joy upon Della's face was more gratifying than he'd expected. Like the sun breaking through a patch of rain to dispel a chill.

"Shall we go and search for the best ones, then?"

"Now?" Lyman was knocked off his feet once more, struggling to keep up with her changeable impulses.

He couldn't afford to spend the day gallivanting around London with her on a whim. He'd already lost the time he normally allotted to his writing this morning by rising late, and then there was tonight's rendezvous to think of. He couldn't seem to tear himself away from Della, despite his better judgment.

"Why not?" Her bright smile promised that it would be a great adventure, as all things in her life were, it seemed. "I need to determine which vantage points to include, and you could stand to have your sense of wonder renewed."

"My sense of wonder." Surprise tugged a laugh from Lyman's chest. "Isn't that normally reserved for children?"

"Why should it be?"

He had no answer for her, and Della took his silence for assent. Perhaps it was. "Where shall we start? We might try Fleet Street, looking toward St. Paul's."

Lyman took a moment to consider. "That's not bad. You can see St. Martin Ludgate from there as well, and the architecture contrasts nicely."

"It's settled then. I'll ask the footman to ready a carriage for us."

"I'm coming too," Annabelle immediately proclaimed.

"You are *not*."

"You can't be alone in a closed carriage." She wore a smug little smile as she spoke. "And Peter already took the phaeton."

Della made a noise of supreme frustration. "Why can't you find a hobby?"

"You should be grateful I'm helping you! Besides, I know all sorts of spots with lovely views, if you'd bothered to ask me."

"Thank you, Miss Annabelle." Lyman intervened before Della could vent her spleen any further. "We'd love to hear your ideas."

Much as he would have relished the chance to get Della alone again, it wasn't likely to happen. And they would do better not to cross anyone who knew as much about them as Annabelle did.

His encouragement took the girl by surprise, but she quickly recovered. "The Waterloo Bridge," she said matter-of-factly. "Toward the Surrey side. You can see everything from there. It's a lovely place to take anyone who's new to town that you might want to impress."

Lyman managed not to raise an eyebrow at this, though it cost him some effort. It was none of his business whom Miss Annabelle was impressing. Turning to her sister (who suffered no such compunction about making a dubious face), Lyman asked, "Shall we start with the bridge then?"

"Very well." Della rang for a servant and relayed her instructions. After the ladies had gathered their things, their party was off.

True to Miss Annabelle's word, the view from the Waterloo Bridge was a pretty sight. At this hour of the morning, the sun was high in the sky and cast silver reflections across the curve of the Thames below. Any direction they turned offered something interesting to look at. With the South Bank at their backs, the pristine white facade of Somerset House stood before them. To the east, church spires broke through the skyline between the array of town houses and theaters and parks. The familiar dome of St. Paul's Cathedral was among them. To the west, a little further off, they could glimpse Westminster. At this distance, the people walking on the streets before it were featureless silhouettes. As anonymous as only London could make them.

Della had been right. He should have thought to put this in his book.

"You see?" Annabelle watched her sister expectantly.

"I suppose it is quite pretty," Della admitted. "Thank you for the suggestion."

Annabelle beamed at this praise.

Della turned to Lyman, her face full of the sense of wonder she'd promised him. "It really is something to see the whole town laid out at once. To think how many people built all this and keep the cogs turning each day."

"One point nine million, at the last census," Lyman offered helpfully.

Della laughed, the sound high and clear. "Of course you would know that."

"I could hardly expect people to buy my guidebook if I didn't," he explained. "If I'm holding myself out as an authority, the least I can do is provide accurate information."

"I quite agree. That's exactly why I want to see all the sights I intend to write about."

Yes, her friend Miss Chatterjee had said something like that back at the house.

"You've set yourself quite the task if you intend to visit everything in the time we have," he said. "Shall we head back to the carriage and start on something else?"

Her coachman was waiting for them just past the entrance to the bridge, as they'd wanted to take the pedestrian path to examine the view at their leisure.

You should turn back home and tend to your own work. The warning crept into Lyman's thoughts, but he couldn't seem to summon the willpower to cut their interlude short.

Della paused for a moment and turned to look out over the water again. Her lips parted slightly, animated by an almost imperceptible movement, as if she were whispering her thoughts to herself as she struggled to memorize the skyline. The sight was so unguarded it felt almost too intimate, but Lyman didn't turn away. Perhaps he, too, was trying to memorize the sight of something bright and lovely.

"Very well. Let's head over to Fleet Street next. Then I can try to write up the chapter on views later today. As you say, I need to work quickly if I'm to manage everything."

He offered an arm to each sister as they turned back toward the carriage, though Miss Annabelle declined, preferring to stride a few paces ahead of them than to walk demurely at his side. He was beginning to see what Della had meant when she'd claimed that her younger sibling wasn't as innocent as she seemed.

They'd come some distance to reach the archway she'd identified as having the best angle on the whole city, so retracing their footsteps took several minutes. Della was uncharacteristically silent. When Lyman glanced down, he found her watching him so intently that he grew uneasy.

"What are you thinking?" he asked.

"Only that you're proving much more fun than I expected," she replied with a smile.

He inclined his head. "In that case, I hope I don't disappoint you again."

"I realized last night that I feel as though I've met two of you: the strict and proper Lord Ashton who looked down his nose at me when I wanted to put my club in his book and the fun-loving Lord Ashton who can appreciate life's pleasures."

"I didn't look down my nose at you," he protested. Her assessment made him more uncomfortable than he cared to let on. "And the strict and proper Lord Ashton sounds more like my father than myself. He used to consider me rather irresponsible."

Della raised an eyebrow, as if she might have challenged this, but she only said, "You were young when you inherited the title, weren't you?"

He nearly missed his step.

"Have you been asking others about me?"

"We looked you up in Debrett's," Annabelle volunteered helpfully. Even four paces ahead, she appeared to be listening to their every word. *How lovely.*

Still, the explanation brought Lyman a measure of relief. Debrett's recorded essential facts, not rumor. "I was twenty-four. My father's health had begun to decline the previous year, and before I knew it, he was gone and I was the new viscount."

"I'm sorry." Della seemed to mull over his words for a moment before she continued. "So you were a carefree youth when you went to all the places in your book, but then you inherited the title and you felt an obligation to become serious and respectable. Is that it?" She wrinkled her nose, her opinion of respectability plain.

Lyman shivered. It felt as if someone had walked over his grave.

"Something like that," he murmured.

"It needn't be one or the other, you know," Della continued, oblivious to the sense of foreboding that had come over him. "You can fulfill your responsibilities and still enjoy yourself from time to time."

"You seem to manage it very well," he replied with a tip of his hat, "but I'm not certain I can follow your example. I find a strict prohibition easier to maintain than moderation."

Lyman was pointedly ignoring the fact that his time with Della didn't fit neatly in either category. He'd broken his own rules for himself when he kissed her last night, and she didn't seem to be the sort of woman he might confine into "moderation." She threw herself into everything with full abandon.

"To be perfectly honest, I'm not sure I manage it as well as it seems," Della said with a self-conscious laugh. "Though my fault is in the opposite direction from yours. I try to do everything I wish, both in business and pleasure, but there never seems to be enough time in a day to meet all my obligations."

"Why did you set yourself the task of writing this book then?" Lyman tried to ask the question without any judgment.

"The book isn't the problem. I'm enjoying seeing all the sights of London again. Why, if it weren't for the book, I would never have thought to sneak into Laurent's with you last night or come here to take in the view this morning." Her bright smile was all the evidence he needed that she was grateful for both. "The club is what takes most of my time," she continued, "I feel I can scarcely keep up lately."

"I thought you said you were a co-owner," Lyman said, recalling their first meeting. "Who are your partners?"

"My friend, Mrs. Williams. She used to do most of the work, but she's in her confinement, even though she still stops by as often as she can to handle our bookkeeping. Her husband handles a great deal of the finances as well, as we needed a man to open our bank account, and he places orders with those of our suppliers who prefer not to deal with a woman."

Lyman frowned to himself. "Why don't you hire someone for any of those things?"

"We haven't been in business very long. This is our third year of operation, but the profits were rather unsteady for the first two. I think Mrs. Williams is wary of bringing on more staff in case we run low on funds again." Della bit her lip. Lyman's eyes fixated on the sight, though he'd been listening attentively until then. He'd never given much thought to the hazards of running a business, particularly a gaming hell. He would have assumed they were flush with cash. But then, perhaps their female clientele didn't have the same access to funds that the men of White's and Brooks's did.

He would have liked to turn the subject away from gambling clubs, but he couldn't think how to go about it without wounding Della. If she felt easy enough in his company to share her troubles, he didn't want to rebuff the opening.

Miss Annabelle proved happy to fill the gap in their conversation. "The problem is that you and Mrs. Williams don't trust anyone but yourselves," she called over her shoulder. "I'd be willing to help you for a pinch of your profits."

"You're nineteen," Della said flatly. "Get one glass of champagne into you and you're liable to forget how to count."

"You see?" Miss Annabelle cast a pointed look to Lyman. "She doesn't trust her own sister."

Perhaps it was time to jump back into this discussion. "Regardless of whom you might select, it sounds like you do need some assistance. You told me earlier you attend every night except Monday?"

"Sunday and Monday," Della amended. "We're closed both evenings, although we often use those nights to restock and make other adjustments that can't be done with our members around."

"So you attend nearly every night, and you've also set yourself the goal of touring the whole town for your book in the next few weeks." Lyman recalled how only last night she'd reluctantly admitted that she had precious little time to keep up with the social calls that were expected of most ladies of her station. "You'll wear yourself out if you continue on this way."

"Oh no!" Della protested. "I've given you the wrong idea. I'm happy to do it, really. I don't want you thinking that my friends have put too much on me."

That was exactly what Lyman was thinking, but it was plain that Della wouldn't want to hear it.

"Anyway, it's for me to manage my own life, isn't it?" Della asked. "I like to keep myself busy. I know it might look a bit like chaos from the outside, but I always manage to get everything done."

Though Lyman had his doubts, this seemed to mark an end to the conversation. They'd arrived at her carriage.

Ten

ONCE SHE'D PARTED WAYS WITH LORD ASHTON, DELLA requested the coachman drop her off at Jane's town house on the way to take Annabelle home. This was no hardship, as they lived on the same street and popped in on each other unannounced most mornings. Or at least, they'd used to. As the carriage approached their destination, Della was startled by the realization that she hadn't been here in weeks.

Nor had Jane called on her. Since Gloria was born, it sometimes felt like they only saw each other at the club.

Don't be silly. She's at Bishop's nearly every day. It was normal to have less free time when one had a new baby. Besides, Della had been so busy with her book these past three weeks, she'd scarcely had time to call anyway.

Even now, her outing with Lord Ashton this morning had set her arrival back hours later than she'd planned. She hadn't seen the time go by. He was so *different* with her now that she'd broken through his initial reserve. He talked to her without his former hesitation, offering glimpses of his true thoughts and feelings where there had once been only clipped reproofs. He treated her as an equal, despite the obvious advantage his peerage and experience bestowed. If they continued on this way, she might yet call him a friend.

And if Jane and Eli could do without her tonight at Bishop's, she intended to show Lord Ashton just how friendly she could be.

The carriage lurched to a halt, and she bid goodbye to Annabelle. The maid of all work answered her rap on the front door and showed Della into the receiving room. When this house still belonged to Jane's uncle, he'd kept a butler, but Jane had slashed her household expenses to devote all her resources to the club.

If my book brings in new members, maybe she'll be able to afford to live a bit more comfortably again.

It was Eli's sister, Hannah Williams, who finally came in to welcome her. The wailing from upstairs indicated Jane was occupied.

Della rose to return her greeting. Miss Williams was closer in age to Annabelle than to herself, but she was a sensible, good-natured sort of girl. She couldn't be called pretty, exactly, though she shared her brother's expressive face. Her nose was a touch too long, and she carried herself awkwardly, as if forever unsure where to put her body. Hopefully she would grow into some confidence soon.

"When did you get into town?" Della asked her.

"Only yesterday. And we've brought you some paintings for your club like Eli asked. Come and see!" Miss Williams led Della to the corner of the room, where two framed canvases had been tucked into the space between the sideboard and the wall. "I helped pick them," she announced proudly. "Mama wanted to give you an old portrait of some dead ancestor none of us could remember, but I said you needed something more colorful."

The pieces she'd chosen were a still life of some exotic fruits and a painting of the Durdle Door at sunset. Della rather liked the pinks in the sky.

"Thank you. These are perfect."

"I could help you decide where to hang them," Miss Williams continued eagerly. "I should *love* to see what the club looks like. Eli told us how much you've done to fix it up since you moved in."

"Absolutely not." It was Jane who interrupted them. She'd materialized in the doorway while they were distracted, as if summoned by the threat of mischief. "You know your mother will kill me if I let you set foot in Bishop's."

"She doesn't need to know!" Miss Williams dropped her voice to a stage whisper. "I didn't come all the way to London just to be dragged to her friends' house parties every evening."

"She's only trying to protect your reputation."

"You and Miss Danby built a whole gambling club by yourselves, and it didn't hurt *your* reputations!" Miss Williams was so indignant, her cheeks had grown red.

"That depends on whom you ask." Jane finally came over to greet Della properly, and they all sat down together. The maid returned with some tea and sandwiches a moment later, which Jane fell upon as though she hadn't eaten all day. Perhaps she hadn't.

"How are you?" Della asked, after she'd given her friend a moment to chew and swallow.

"Quite out of sorts, to be honest," Jane replied. "Gloria has a fever and hasn't stopped crying all morning. The doctor thinks it's only colic again, but she won't settle for anyone but me when she'd like this." She massaged her temples. "I don't think I'm going to be able to make it to the club tonight, but I hate to ask you to handle things all alone again..."

Oh dear. Della could hardly reply that she'd come here to ask for the evening off, with Jane looked so worn out. And what was she supposed to tell her—that she'd invited a strange man to sneak into her bedroom window this evening for a few hours of bawdy amusement?

Della heaved a regretful sigh. Taking care of a sick infant trumped an indecent liaison. She would just have to write Lord Ashton a note asking him to postpone.

"It's no trouble at all," Della said. "You should be with Gloria."

"Are you sure? You've been taking on so much extra work lately. I hope it isn't an imposition."

"Don't think of it." True, she'd had to decline more invitations this season than she'd ever done before, and a few of her old friends had probably forgotten what she looked like by now, but Jane was the dearest friend of them all. That counted for something. And Gloria wouldn't be a newborn forever. If they could just make it through this patch, things would get easier.

"I could help," Miss Williams chimed in. Seeing Jane had parted her lips to object, she hurried on. "I wouldn't wager any large sums! And I could do anything you need, just so long as I can have one evening without Mama watching over me."

It wasn't clear whether the girl's plea was addressed more to Della or to Jane, for her dark eyes entreated them each in turn, but it was her sister-in-law who answered firmly. "I'm sorry, Hannah, but you know we can't."

"You're as bad as she is!" Miss Williams leapt to her feet. "She'll marry me off to some old man just to be rid of me, and you'll all stand by and watch." With that, she fled the room, leaving Jane to slump on the divan in defeat.

Was I that dramatic when I was younger? Della wondered. She could vaguely remember sobbing into her pillow for three days when the first gentleman she'd fancied proposed to Miss O'Hara, though she'd been sixteen at the time. Hannah was already twentysomething, if memory served. Shouldn't she have grown out of this stage?

"I feel badly for her," Jane confessed, unprompted, "but what am

I supposed to do? Her mother is determined to see her married and thinks gambling will ruin her prospects."

"Your uncle used to think the same thing about you," Della reminded her friend. "And we didn't let that stop us. Would it do any harm to let her attend for one night?"

It wasn't only a sense of feminine solidarity that moved Della to speak in the girl's defense. She recalled Lord Ashton's comment that she would wear herself out, followed by Annabelle's accusation that the problem was a lack of trust. Though she hadn't wanted to admit it when they were united against her, she *was* tired. And Miss Williams seemed a more reliable choice than Annabelle. If she was serious in her offer to do anything, they could always find a task for willing hands.

It would finally give Della the chance to have a night off now and then for indecent liaisons or even—dare she hope—to make some real progress on her book.

"I can't afford a row with Mrs. Williams right now." Jane was massaging her temples again. She looked as though she had a headache. "She already thinks my house is too messy because we only have one maid, and that my baby is colicky because I didn't hire a wet nurse. I don't want to be accused of corrupting her only daughter as well."

Della took a long sip of her tea to prevent herself from saying something uncharitable about Jane's mother-in-law. Once her temper had cooled, she managed a more diplomatic suggestion. "Perhaps the elder Mrs. Williams would like to go back to her country house and leave her daughter here alone?"

That would solve everything, wouldn't it?

"I don't think she's in any hurry to go back home. If anything, she might like to stay with Hannah to help her set up her own household, if she succeeds in finding her a husband this year. She's a bit overprotective." After a moment, the strain on Jane's face eased. "I shouldn't criticize. She truly *means* well. It's just that she has such a narrow view of what a woman's life should be. It can be...suffocating. Particularly for Hannah."

"What if I took her out to show her the town once in a while?" Della suggested, struck by inspiration. At Jane's look, she added, "Not to the club, of course. But I've been meaning to visit a few attractions for a project I'm working on, and it might give the poor girl a respite from matchmaking if I bring her with me. You could come along and we'll make an outing of it!"

"Oh, yes, Eli said you were planning to write a guidebook to London?" Though she was good enough not to say anything critical, Jane's eyebrows nevertheless conveyed a measure of doubt. "When did that happen?"

"It's a recent endeavor. Remember that gentleman author we talked about, the Viscount Ashton? I couldn't persuade him to put our club in his book, so I decided to write my own and now he's helping me."

Jane blinked. "You do manage to make the most unexpected things happen."

"You know I like a little variety to my days," Della returned. "In any event, I'd love to get your opinion on my opening chapters if you have the time for it." She rummaged through her reticule, looking for the notes she'd brought, just in case. "We couldn't agree on the introduction. Lord Ashton wants to write it himself, to bridge the two volumes together, but I'm not persuaded he understands the best tone—"

A knock at the door interrupted them before she could finish explaining. The elder Mrs. Williams crept in, an apologetic smile on her face and a fussing child in her arms. "I'm sorry to interrupt your call, girls, but I think this one is hungry again."

Jane rose with a resigned sigh, Della's story forgotten. "I really should get back to her. We'll catch up more next time, all right?"

"Of course. I still have five weeks to finish—" But Jane wasn't listening. She was already rocking Gloria gently upon her shoulder, focused on her cries. "Never mind, I'll explain it all to you later. Take care." Della stood awkwardly for a moment, then moved to show herself out.

"Oh!" Jane seemed to remember her again just as she neared the door, but it wasn't to do with her book. "Eli told me to remind you that his friend is coming by about the dealer post next week."

Oh yes, she'd nearly forgotten. Hopefully he would prove competent. She didn't want to spend hours training someone with no knowledge of the game.

"And if you see Mrs. Muller—"

"Yes, yes," Della assured her. "I'll be sure to catch her this time, don't you worry."

Lyman walked up the approach to his lodgings with a spring in his step. Despite himself, he'd enjoyed his morning. Though it was hardly the first time he went sightseeing, it usually felt like a chore. Something he did out of obligation to keep his book up to date. But Della's lively manner made everything look new again.

It made him forget all the troubles that weighed him down.

He walked up to the second floor and unlocked the door that divided the rented rooms from Mrs. Hirsch's home below. There were voices coming from the common dining area the three men shared, but he didn't hear Clarkson's smooth baritone. Wood must have company then.

There's a first time for everything.

He'd expected to be greeted by the sight of someone resembling Mr. Wood as he came inside—a cousin from the country who shared his doughy face and muttonchop sideburns, perhaps. But as his gaze fell upon their visitor, Lyman realized the man hadn't come for his fellow lodger at all.

It was Michael, sitting at their dining table as if he belonged there. Lyman's breath rushed out of him as swiftly as if he'd been punched in the gut.

"Hullo." Wood greeted him with a genuine smile—a rare occurrence. "I was just getting acquainted with your brother-in-law."

"Yes, I see that." How long had Michael been here? Why had he come to his lodgings?

Michael said nothing, but watched Lyman impassively. Though it had been years since Lyman had seen him, he looked the same as ever. He was a slender man with black hair that gained a smattering of red as it progressed down his cheeks to end in a pointed beard. His thin lips were pressed together in silent judgment.

"We were just having the most illuminating discussion about judicial reform," Wood continued. Judging by his enthusiasm, he hadn't picked up on the subtle signs of Michael's annoyance. "It's so rare to meet someone who understands the complexities of the courts. Most people think it's just like in *The Pickwick Papers*, which really doesn't paint a fair picture. But of course, Lord de Villiers understands everything so well I almost feel as though *he* could teach *me* a thing or two about the law."

Still, Michael didn't speak. He raised an eyebrow slowly, but his gaze remained cold. *What is this idiot on about?* he seemed to be asking.

It was jarring to witness his brother-in-law sitting next to Wood. Like watching a raven glide down among a chattering flutter of sparrows. He seemed to belong to a superior world, one that should never have intermingled with this one. Though Lyman had long since grown used to his diminished circumstances, now he saw it all through fresh eyes, as it must appear to Michael. The little cracks in the plaster walls; the way the curtains had faded in the sun; the creaks and groans that escaped the ancient wooden chairs whenever one of the men shifted his weight. Every detail painted a sad picture.

Lyman cleared his throat. "I hope you haven't been waiting long. If you'd told me you were coming, I would have been home to receive you."

"I wouldn't want to interfere with your plans." It was plain from his tone that Michael had already formed his own ideas of what Lyman's "plans" might have been, and he didn't think too highly of them.

Heat crept up the back of Lyman's neck. He felt as exposed as if Michael had been watching him all day, stalking his path from Della's house to the Waterloo Bridge to Fleet Street. As if he knew Lyman had spent the past twenty-four hours chasing after the promise of carnal pleasure with a woman who wasn't his wife.

"Would you like to come to my rooms?" Lyman asked. "We can speak privately there."

Michael rose to his feet and took his leave of Mr. Wood with polite indifference. They removed to Lyman's quarters and shut the door behind them. He had two adjacent rooms allotted to his use, one for writing and the other for his bed and clothes. There was a chair and desk near the window, as well as a threadbare settee in the corner. Lyman searched for a match and lit an oil lamp to brighten the space. When he turned back to Michael, he found his brother-in-law scanning absently through the notes spread on his desk.

Has he been reading through my draft?

"I'd proposed we meet at a public house," Lyman observed quietly.

"I didn't want to be seen with you."

Hell. Michael couldn't make anything easy, could he? Without Mr. Wood observing them, his careful manners had evaporated. He wrinkled his nose as he took in the state of the room. "I never thought you'd be caught dead in such a place." He jerked his head toward the door to indicate the room from which they'd just retreated. "A *solicitor,* Ashton?"

"It was economical," Lyman said simply. He didn't want to talk about the state of his lodgings with Michael. "Is Ellen well?"

"None of us are well, since you ruined our family."

Lyman winced, but forced himself onward. He had to know. "I mean, is she ill? When I saw your letter, I thought..."

"She's as well as can be expected, though you might do something to improve her situation."

"I've paid you the maintenance we agreed to each month," Lyman reminded him. "I know it's not much, but—"

"Not that," Michael cut him off with an impatient swipe of his hand. "She wants a divorce."

Lyman's heart skipped a beat. Whatever he'd been expecting, it wasn't that.

He didn't feel anything for Ellen, save the hot shame of his own failure. But he'd grown so used to the obligations that bound them that it was hard to imagine any other way of living. The terms of their separation gave her what independence it was within his power to grant. For nine years, she'd been satisfied with that. *Why now?*

"Has she met someone?"

"My sister is a moral woman," Michael snapped. "She would never betray her marriage vows."

Lyman held his tongue. Michael seemed not to expect any comment from him, as he continued speaking. "It isn't fair to keep her chained to you forever, when she might have the opportunity to meet

someone if she were free. She's still young enough. She should have
the chance to have a happy home, children...everything you denied
her."

Lyman's hands clenched into fists at his sides, his nails biting
into flesh. It wasn't Michael he wanted to hurt, though. "I agree
completely."

"Good." Michael crossed the narrow room to stand before the
door, as though their discussion were at an end. "I trust you'll coop-
erate when we bring the matter before Parliament. Only don't be
too eager—we don't want it to look like a case of collaboration. It's
probably best if you don't attend at all. Make it appear that you have
no interest whatsoever in the outcome."

"But how can you afford such a thing? You know I can't pay for it."

The proceedings would cost a small fortune, and no one in this
room had another fortune to spare. It was precisely why he'd thought
a divorce was impossible.

"A generous friend has offered to assist us. That part isn't your
concern."

A friend.

Ellen *had* met someone then. A gentleman wealthy enough to
shoulder the monumental burden of dissolving her prior vows. It
was no surprise that Michael would want to seize the opportunity.
They could only improve their circumstances by such an alliance.

"Money alone can't buy us a divorce," Lyman protested. "Ellen
hasn't been unfaithful to me."

Perhaps that was no longer true, but none of them were going to
admit otherwise before open Parliament, surely.

"We'll say you've been unfaithful to her," Michael replied easily,
disdain in his voice. "If you're willing to identify a woman or two who
could confirm the tale, it would help speed things along. If you won't
do it yourself, we'll find someone for you."

The frank assessment stunned Lyman into silence. He hadn't betrayed Ellen while they still shared a home—at least not in the way Michael meant. But there was no point in arguing. Not when he was willing to hire a witness to say otherwise.

"Here." Michael pulled some papers from inside his coat, unfolded them, and set them on Lyman's desk atop his writing. "It's a citation and libel for Consistory Court, to pave the way for Parliament. We have a hearing date next month. Our proctor assures me that if you don't contest the facts we should be able to move it through quickly."

He'd evidently put significant thought into this, but he'd missed the most essential detail.

"It won't be enough. I consulted my solicitor after she broke ties with me, you know. He said a man could divorce his wife for adultery, but a woman couldn't do the same. There's no way out of this, Michael."

No way that would leave Ellen's reputation intact, at least. And he wouldn't bring any more grief down on her head.

"You don't need to explain this to me." Michael's voice dripped with scorn. "You think we haven't spent enough time trying to figure out how we could be rid of you? She can divorce you if we show both adultery *and* intolerable cruelty, so that's what we'll do. It's all right there in the libel."

Intolerable cruelty? It was a description reserved for the worst type of men. The ones whose brutality nearly crossed the line into murder.

"I never raised a hand to Ellen," Lyman said. "I know I failed her, but I never hurt her. Not like that."

"You cost her everything, left her destitute, and you haven't lived under the same roof in nine years. If that isn't cruelty, I don't know what is." Michael let the accusation hang in the air a long moment before he continued. "The courts have shown some flexibility in their interpretation for exceptional circumstances. I think we can make a case, if the adultery is proven and you don't dispute any of it. We have a good proctor."

Lyman didn't get the chance to learn what he would have replied to that. Before he could imagine what it might mean for him, a knock at the door interrupted his thoughts.

"Lord Ashton?" Mr. Wood's voice called from the other side. Lyman hoped he hadn't been listening at the keyhole. "There's an errand boy here with a message for you. He says it's from a lady."

The look in Michael's eye was one of bitter triumph. *You see?* he seemed to say. *I know what you are.*

"It's not what you think," Lyman began, but his brother-in-law already had his hand on the doorknob.

"I hope you'll do the right thing," Michael said, with a faint motion toward the documents he'd left. "I'll be in touch."

Then he was gone, slipping past the obsequious platitudes of Mr. Wood and down the stairs with the silent tread of a jungle cat.

Lyman was scarcely aware of his path to the entryway to meet the errand boy, who stood breathless as if he'd run across town. He probably had. Lyman recognized him at once, for he'd often seen him scurrying around Armstrong's office.

"A footman brought it to the office, m'lord," the youth said, producing a rumpled envelope from his pocket. Lyman tore it open and read.

I'm sorry, but they need me at the club tonight and I won't be at home after all. You might meet me there after closing if you'd like. I should be free by 2 a.m.

—D.

A message from a lady, indeed. She'd actually dared to put her invitation in an envelope addressed to his publisher. What a foolish risk. She couldn't have known that Armstrong wouldn't snoop.

Lyman couldn't think of Della now without a creeping sense of dread, the thrill of the morning withered up by the astringent of Michael's visit.

She wanted him to come to her club, of all places. Of course she did. Gambling was her whole life. Hadn't she said as much this morning? Hadn't she shown him that plainly a hundred times over? And yet he insisted on seeing only what he wanted to see.

He'd let his desires guide him, and this was the result. Mixed up with the proprietress of a gaming hell. There could be no question what Michael and Ellen would think if they learned of it—they would assume he was running with the same fast crowd as before, still chasing his own ruination.

They'd be right.

He'd been lost in a fantasy today, but his brother-in-law's visit had brought him crashing back to earth. The idea of any romantic connection with Miss Danby was ludicrous. They were both flirting with disaster.

If they were caught together, they couldn't salvage her reputation with a hasty marriage. Even if Ellen succeeded in divorcing him, it would take months, maybe even years before he was free. And once he was, his name would be further tarnished by the stories Michael intended to spread to get what he wanted. No family with any affection for their daughter would want him darkening their door.

Della was completely exposed, with everything to lose and nothing to gain from their dalliance.

And he would fare no better. Even if his own reputation was already in tatters, there were other things Lyman could lose. His good judgment, for one.

As much as he feared he might destroy her, he was selfish enough to save the greater portion of fear for himself: that she would destroy him. He knew how it would begin—the nagging temptation to go and visit her club, just as she'd invited him to do tonight. And then he would grow nostalgic for the days when he'd spent his time at White's, in the company of all his old friends. He might get the urge to look in on them—just to say hello, of course, not to wager anything. Then perhaps it would just be one little wager, nothing too serious. And before he knew it, he would be spinning excuses and taking advantage of anyone foolish enough to place their trust in him, be it his friends, Della, or himself.

No. He couldn't risk this. He would put a stop to it now, before he was lost.

Lyman bid the errand boy to wait at the door and carry his reply back to Della's house for an extra tuppence. Fetching a scrap of paper from his writing desk, he jotted down a short line.

I regret that I cannot.

—A.

There was nothing else to say, at least nothing that he would trust to a letter that might fall into the wrong hands. He took her note back to his rooms once the boy had gone and burned it in the flame of his lamp, lest Mr. Wood or anyone else see such damning evidence of her indiscretion.

One day, this woman would get herself into some real trouble, but it wouldn't be with him.

Unbidden, his mind conjured an image of Della receiving his reply, a half hour or so from now. A footman would bring it in to her with more formality than its contents warranted. Her eyes would light with unbridled excitement as she tore the seal—the same spark that he'd seen a dozen times already when she spoke of a new idea for her book or tried to persuade him of the rightness of something she felt strongly about. That light would snuff out a moment later as she saw his curt refusal. The corners of her lips would fall, her smile extinguished. Anyone who looked at her would be able to spot the hurt in her eyes, the emotions she never managed to conceal.

Lyman could've done with a stiff drink, if he'd still indulged.

There's no sense in feeling guilty. It's for her own good.

He'd lost his head last night, but he was back in possession of his reason. He would do what needed to be done to keep them both safe. If that made him unfeeling, so be it.

Della was, in fact, put out by the rejection, but her temperament was such that she couldn't linger on it for too long. She allowed herself about an hour to mope before she put on a brave face and set out to pay a few quick calls she'd been neglecting before it grew too late in the day for them. She wanted to look in on Lady Eleanor and some other connections to make sure she stayed in their good graces. It was important to maintain friendships with the right people to keep everyone talking about her club—something she hadn't done enough of lately. After that, she jotted down some notes on the views she'd seen earlier while she ate a sandwich Cook had made for her and then got changed to go to Bishop's for the evening. She'd been hoping to finish a chapter today, but when all was said and done, there'd been barely half an hour left to scribble a few paragraphs.

Ah, well. I'll write twice as much tomorrow to make up for it. Though this wasn't the first time she'd made such a promise to herself, things were still quite manageable. Five weeks was plenty of time.

Della found her thoughts wandering back to Lord Ashton as she slipped through the last hours of daylight. Had he changed his mind about meeting her because of something she'd done? Had she been too forward with him in the drawing room this morning and frightened him off? *If I did, he wasn't worthy of me,* she reassured herself. There were plenty of men in the world. If the viscount didn't appreciate her as she was, then it was his loss.

Despite these encouraging thoughts, she couldn't entirely shake off a feeling of regret—or perhaps it was hope. The viscount had some originality to him, after all—an independence of thought that she admired. Shouldn't he be capable of defying convention? His reaction at the casino last night and in her drawing room this morning showed great promise.

This was enough to make Della consider the second possibility: that he had *not* run in fear of her wantonness, but actually had a good reason for not coming. One that was too personal to confide in a letter. After all, they hadn't had much time alone to talk about anything properly. Perhaps he'd been forced to cancel their plans due to an urgent obligation, just as she had, and would make it up to her later. Though she had her doubts, Della much preferred this explanation and made a conscious decision to adopt it until it was disproven. She was nothing if not an optimist.

Besides, she was far too busy to feel sad. She'd promised Jane she would handle the club by herself tonight. Best of all, Annabelle didn't yet know she would be there to observe what was sure to be an embarrassing evening for her. Bishop's didn't track wagers outside of card play, but if it did, Della would have offered five-to-one odds that Annabelle couldn't win over Miss Greenwood. Ten-to-one odds there would be sonnets involved.

I can't wait.

Tragically, she had no choice but to wait, for she arrived at the club to learn that the greengrocer's delivery hadn't come as planned and she had to spend the next hour adjusting the menu with their cook. Soon after that, the first group of ladies arrived, a cluster of regulars she knew well, and Della hurried out to greet them.

After another hour or so, Annabelle *finally* appeared with a pale siren on her arm. Della caught a glimpse of them from across the room and hung back, making her way slowly through the edges of the crowd to better trap her unsuspecting prey.

She eavesdropped shamelessly once she drew within earshot. After enduring Annabelle as a chaperone these past few weeks, it was the least she could do.

"...certain you'll love it. You have such a free spirit, you're meant for a place like this."

"It's much bigger than it looks from the outside." Miss Greenwood was taking in the club with something like awe. Della liked her already. "How long ago did you say your sister and her friend founded it?"

"Two years, more or less."

It was three years! Doesn't Annabelle know anything?

"And they couldn't have done it without me," she continued. "It takes a keen mind to get a business off the ground. Not everyone is up for the challenge."

Not even Della's curiosity could force her to hold her tongue at this outrage.

"Annabelle," Della exclaimed from behind her sister's back. "You made it!"

"What are *you* doing here?" Annabelle wore a look of utter horror as she whirled around.

"You do recall that I own the place?" She managed to keep the sarcasm from her tone.

"I–I thought you were meant to be at home tonight."

"Change of plans." Della smiled and turned her attention to the gorgeous blonde by Annabelle's side. "And you must be Miss Greenwood. I believe we were introduced at Ascot last year, weren't we? How do you do?"

"Very well, thank you. You have a lovely establishment."

"Why *thank you*. You're so sweet. I can see why Annabelle wanted to bring you here."

"I was just going to show Miss Greenwood the retiring room," Annabelle blurted out. "So, um, we'll go do that now."

"What's the hurry? I think you were just about to tell your friend all about your business skills, weren't you?" She arched one eyebrow, watching Annabelle squirm. *Ah, sweet justice.* "Would you like to tell the story of how we found the premises? I'm sure she'd love to hear that one. You remember it, don't you?"

Annabelle was giving her such a ferocious glare that she was liable to wrinkle that way. It was delightful.

Wait, who was that a few yards behind her sister at the faro table? Della craned her neck to get a better look, hoping her eyes deceived her. *Oh no.* She recognized the little woman with the pink gown and graying hair. Mrs. Muller had already placed a wager, though Della had been watching the door for her all night except for this one little break. Couldn't she torture Annabelle in peace for even a minute? Surely she'd earned the right!

"Will you two excuse me for a moment?" Della turned back to the girls. "I've seen someone I have to—"

But they were already gone, having escaped into the crowd the second Della's attention was elsewhere. *How dare she avoid my teasing, when I've dealt with her comments about Lord Ashton for weeks now!* Ah well, she'd had enough fun to make it worthwhile, at least.

It was time to face Mrs. Muller.

She crossed the room with a reluctant step, wishing Jane were here to handle this task. She always managed to deliver bad news without any hand-wringing, while Della *hated* making people upset with her.

That's a selfish wish. Jane shouldn't have to do all the unpleasant work herself. But as Della slipped through the crowd, her sense of dread only grew.

She had planned out the first part. She waited until Mrs. Muller had finished her play (another loss, for a sum that made Della wince), and then she invited her guest to provide her opinion on which of the paintings they should hang in the entryway. She had the two pieces Hannah Williams had brought with her from Devon in their office, along with a large china vase Della had pilfered from her own parents without their noticing. The art made the perfect excuse to get Mrs. Muller alone. It wouldn't do to embarrass a patron publicly.

But once they were safely ensconced in the office and Mrs. Muller had pronounced herself in favor of the still life with the pineapple, Della's orderly plan ran out. When she'd written herself a mental script for this moment, she'd never managed to find the right words to devastate Mrs. Muller. The other woman cut a timid figure, with her mournful eyes and a high voice that would've suited someone half her age.

She made Della feel like the villain of the story.

"Don't you like the still life, Miss Danby?" Mrs. Muller was watching her expectantly, unaware of the ax about to descend upon her neck.

"Yes, that's a lovely choice," Della took the painting from her arms and set it upon the desk, where they could both view it from a distance. "You have a good eye. Thank you."

"You're most welcome." She drew herself up, her eyes flitting to the exit. "Shall we go back out?"

Ugh, I wish someone would save me. Why didn't I ask Eli to do this? Oh, that's right. Because she hardly deserved the title of co-owner if she couldn't manage this task on her own. Jane had trusted her. Della girded herself and forged ahead. "Actually, Mrs. Muller, I'm afraid we need to discuss your outstanding debts."

The words had an immediate effect. Mrs. Muller stared at her hands, then at her shoes—anywhere to avoid Della's gaze. She tittered nervously, the sound catching in her throat. "I–I know I'm a bit tardy settling up, but I'll pay you straightaway once I get my pin money next month."

Next month would be perfectly fine. That was what Della wanted to say, so they might forget this whole unpleasant business. Anything to put an end to the ugly flush creeping up Mrs. Muller's neck.

But whatever her pin money might total, it wasn't likely to be enough to cover what she owed. The lady was no heiress.

"I understand. You've always been a loyal patron." Della felt so ashamed, she was blushing as well. "We appreciate your attendance, and we hope to see you with us again after your account is settled."

"What do you mean?" Mrs. Muller looked as if she'd put her foot out to climb a stair and found only empty air. "Are you revoking my membership?"

Yes. The word was on the tip of Della's tongue. Better for everyone that Mrs. Muller stop attending the club, before her losses could grow any larger. But then a tear snaked down the lady's cheek.

Oh no.

"Nothing so final as that." The reversal escaped Della's lips of its own volition. She couldn't abide crying. Not when *she* was responsible for it, at any rate. "I'm sure it will be of short duration. Just as soon as your pin money comes in and you've paid up in full, as you say."

Maybe Mrs. Muller would take her exit gracefully, while her dignity was still intact.

But Della was not so fortunate. "Please, Miss Danby. I've just had a little string of bad luck, that's all. There's no need to overreact. I've supported you from the very beginning. Is this how you treat your friends?"

The words were laced with accusation, striking hard on Della's conscience. It was true. She *had* been with them since the days when they were an intimate circle playing vingt-et-un in a drawing room. This seemed a poor reward for her loyalty.

"I'm sorry," she tried, though it did nothing to relieve her sense of guilt. "I really wish there were some other way. But we can't let your debts grow any higher."

"Please," Mrs. Muller repeated, rushing forward to clasp Della's hand. Her grip was clammy. The tears were spilling freely down her cheeks now, her words interrupted by her hiccups. "What will my friends think when I have to explain why I can't accompany them any longer? I can't bear to be the subject of gossip. Couldn't you make an exception? I promise I won't place any large bets. I'll just enjoy an evening out with the other ladies and play a few hands at the penny table. Then no one would have to know."

Della felt her resolve weakening. She hated to be cruel, and banning Mrs. Muller outright would humiliate the poor woman. But she couldn't let Jane down either.

"I want your word that you won't play for high stakes," Della relented. They had a "penny table," as Mrs. Muller had called it, for the less adventurous among their guests, though it didn't see much use compared to the other games. But if she was willing to stick to that, she couldn't do further damage to her account. "If I see you anywhere else, I'll have no choice but to cut you off."

She would slip a word to the staff to keep a close eye on Mrs. Muller, in case she tried to break the terms of their agreement. Then there would be no real danger.

"You have it." Mrs. Muller was still clutching her hand, and she shook on their deal with two rapid jerks, as if flinging the water from a dishcloth. "Oh, *thank* you, Miss Danby. This means the world to me." Della offered her companion a cup of tea to restore her composure before she saw her back out to the gaming rooms, feeling a bit better about the whole business. It was past midnight by now, and Annabelle and Miss Greenwood seemed to have disappeared. (Had they left together? She'd missed everything!) She found herself a glass of champagne and downed it in three large swallows.

That had been utterly horrid, but Della felt proud of the solution she'd found. A loyal patron would keep her dignity, and Bishop's would keep its accounts in good standing. It likely wasn't the option Jane would have chosen, but Jane wasn't always as diplomatic as she should be. The last thing they needed was for Mrs. Muller to spread talk of ill-treatment. Far better if they could reach a solution that harmed no one.

Eleven

LYMAN HAD NO FURTHER WORD FROM MICHAEL IN THE DAYS following his unexpected visit, although what he saw in the libel his brother-in-law had left behind made him dread their next encounter. They seemed to have drummed up anyone they could find who might say something damning about him, though the list was small and the accusations vague—an old friend he hadn't spoken to in years and a disgruntled former housemaid who were willing to pretend they'd seen him engaged in scandalous behavior. Lyman was less insulted by the fact that these people were willing to spin lies about him than by the fact that they were being so ham-fisted about it. He would never have been so indiscreet as what they described.

But the false allegations were nothing compared to the truth: The sections that detailed his every failing as a husband, the circumstances of the end of his marriage, and the fact that he hadn't spoken to Ellen in nine years. It was one thing to live with it on the back of his conscience; quite another to see it all laid out in black and white.

Lyman tucked the document into a desk drawer and tried not to dwell on it any longer.

Nor was there any news from Miss Danby. He'd half expected her to write him after he'd rebuffed her invitation, or worse, extract his address from Armstrong and show up at his door. She'd certainly proven herself daring enough for such a feat. Lyman couldn't keep himself from asking Mrs. Hirsch whether there had been any further mail for him at least twice a day, driving the poor woman mad with his persistence. But the only note addressed to him was a hasty scrawl from Mr. Wood left on the dining table, instructing whoever had come in late the other night to please keep his voice down in consideration of his fellow lodgers.

He couldn't put off their reunion indefinitely, however, for Friday was the date of the meeting they'd arranged with Mr. Armstrong to discuss the terms of her publishing contract. Lyman went early, to discuss his revisions to the second edition of his London guide first, but the time flew by so quickly that he'd barely started when the secretary announced that Miss Danby and Mr. Peter Danby had arrived.

Lyman had only a second to take in Miss Danby's expression, precious little time to gauge how they were to act with each other, before her brother was pumping his hand in the most exuberant manner imaginable and asking him something about beer.

"I beg your pardon?" Lyman extracted himself from the handshake as politely as he could. He hadn't heard a word the fellow had said.

He glanced to Miss Danby again, bracing himself for the anger or condemnation that would surely be written on her face. She always wore her emotions too openly, and Lyman doubted very much that ravishing her in an alley and then jilting her the next day had elevated him in her esteem.

But her brother positioned himself maddingly close to Lyman, blocking his view. "The Lamb and Flag. In Covent Garden. I wonder that you didn't include it, only Della tells me you're working on the second edition. I say, it would be a fine addition to the chapter on public houses."

There was a strong resemblance between the siblings. Both Miss Danby and her brother were quite plump, with round faces and rosy cheeks. They also shared the same brown hair shot with strands of bronze, dark eyes, and easy smile. Both had no reserve to their manners, launching into conversation as if every stranger was an old friend. But where Lyman had grown used to Miss Danby treating him like a confidante, on her brother he found the unearned intimacy jarring.

"I may have already added it, Mr. Danby; I'll have to look over my manuscript. Thank you for the suggestion."

He finally got a good look at the man's sister, who had been obliged to walk around his back to make herself noticed. She caught Lyman's eye and mouthed, *I'm so sorry.*

About their tryst or about something else? Inexplicably, this felt worse than her anger. It was the last thing Lyman had expected. He didn't like to think that he'd made her regret anything.

"Peter." She placed a hand lightly atop her brother's shoulder. "I'm sure Lord Ashton has his book well in hand. We're here to discuss *my* book, remember?"

Oh. She'd been apologizing for her brother. The relief Lyman felt was as swift as it was surprising.

"Come now." Peter Danby rolled his eyes at his sister's words, with a chuckle that made his reply sound more indulgent than quarrelsome. "The *Gentleman's Guide* is the real authority. Everyone knows that."

Lyman frowned, but said nothing. Did Mr. Danby realize he'd snubbed his own sister in front of the rest of them? He opened his mouth to say something, but shut it again quickly. Della was more than capable of standing up for herself. Better not to make a fuss in front of Armstrong if that wasn't what she wanted.

"Shall we go over the contract together?" Mr. Armstrong suggested, motioning them to sit. There were only two chairs, so Lyman insisted the Danbys take them while Armstrong sent an underling in search of a third. Armstrong passed several pages from his desk to Mr. Danby, then handed a second copy to Lyman. There was no copy for Della. "Here you are. It's all quite standard. I'll give you a moment to read through, shall I?"

Della was craning her neck to peer over her brother's shoulder—a difficult task, as she was at least five inches shorter than him. Lyman observed them for a moment, unnoticed. Now she tugged on Mr. Danby's arm to signal her difficulty, but he only waved her away, turning to the second page before she'd even glimpsed the first.

Lyman cleared his throat softly. "Miss Danby, would you like to share my copy?"

"Thank you." The flush that dusted her cheeks betrayed her annoyance. Lyman stepped nearer the large oak desk and set his copy of the contract where she could read it, bracing one hand on the back of her chair as he leaned forward to join her. Her lemon-drop scent filled his lungs as they bowed their head and read in unison. Before he could stop himself, Lyman had drawn a deep breath, savoring the sensation.

What in God's name are you doing?

It was too late for that. Though he tried to force his mind to the task at hand, his body had already stepped into the snare. At this angle, her gown displayed her breasts to a thrilling degree. The cut of her necklace would no doubt have been modest enough on a lady with less to show, or if they'd both been standing, or if Lyman hadn't spent the last three days wondering what pleasure would have been in store for him if he'd only gone to see her that night as planned. In the circumstances, it was enough to break his restraint. Now Miss Danby was biting her lip as she read, and all he could think of was how desperately he longed to kiss her again. Nothing too serious. Just a taste. Couldn't he let himself have that little glimpse of pleasure before he bid her goodbye and returned to his barren existence? Lord, he needed...*something*. Not more nothing. He'd had years and years of nothing, and it was crushing the life out of him.

The realization hitched Lyman's breath in his throat.

Armstrong's assistant finally returned with the extra chair, and Lyman took it gratefully. It was dangerous to keep leaning over Miss Danby this way.

She looked up just then and caught him staring at her instead of the contract. Her rich brown eyes were large and vulnerable, framed by thick lashes. She leaned closer to him.

"What does this part mean?" she whispered, so softly the others might not have heard it, even in the still room.

Lyman drew an unsteady breath, willing himself back to self-control. She needed him, but not as a lover. As a friend.

He read the passage where the tip of her finger had come to rest. Though couched in awkward legal language, it was only a provision that set out the same duration on copyright and renewal that was already in the Statute of Anne. No need to include it, really.

Lyman was selfish enough to inch closer and breathe his answer into Della's ear, instead of speaking aloud. "It only means they can apply to renew the copyright after it expires, but you likely don't need to worry about that. It lasts fourteen years, and a guidebook won't have any value after that long."

She shuddered against the caress of his voice, and it took every ounce of self-control to pull back before he ran his mouth down the small of her neck and tasted the heat of her skin. They weren't alone. Armstrong or her brother might look over at their whispering any minute. Lyman pulled back and turned away, looking to the painting on the far wall and struggling to get himself under control. He could read the contract later.

It was nothing. This was nothing. She hadn't wanted anyone to see that she didn't understand the words, and he'd whispered in her ear to protect her pride, that was all.

He had a great deal of practice with lying to himself.

They made it through the contract discussions somehow, Armstrong offering explanations to Miss Danby's brother, who did nothing more than nod and say, "I thoroughly agree," a few times.

"Would you like to wait and have your solicitor read it over?" Lyman suggested, fearing Miss Danby might be utterly without guidance, if this was the best she had.

"I'd rather have done with it than postpone things further. Tell me, do *you* think it's a sound deal, Lord Ashton?"

Lyman's heart began to race. There it was again, that thoughtless trust she had in him. Why should she put herself so completely in the care of a man she barely knew? And with the same confidence she did all things, sure in the knowledge that no one would ever want to harm her.

Because she believes you to be a good man, and you haven't had the decency to show her what you really are. The thought slithered into his mind unbidden, leaving a trail of slime in its wake.

Do better, then, he told himself, in a futile effort to chase the feeling away. *Do the best you can, at least.*

Lyman picked the contract back up and skimmed through, looking for any differences with his own agreement.

"You're only offering sixty pounds for the book?" he observed, raising his eyes to Armstrong. "After I take my share, that's only forty for Miss Danby. You gave me a hundred and ten for mine."

"Lord Ashton, surely you see that this book is more of a risk than your own. We were confident that readers would want the opinion of a viscount on fashionable life in London. While Miss Danby's idea has potential, we don't expect it will reach the same audience."

"Not the *same* audience." Lyman agreed. "But their money is the same, isn't it? I'm sure you can do a bit better than sixty."

In the end, Armstrong relented and they came out at eighty pounds. Once all had signed and the ink was dry, Lyman saw them out to their carriage, which awaited them on Paternoster.

"Thank you," Miss Danby's eyes lingered on him for a long moment. "I appreciate what you did."

"It was no more than you've a right to." He inclined his head, hoping his discomfort at the praise didn't show too plainly. He always chafed at compliments.

"Where is your carriage, my lord?" Mr. Danby asked, peering at every coach that happened by, as if one with the Ashton livery might materialize from the fog.

"I walk most everywhere I go," Lyman admitted, unwilling to lie in front of Miss Danby. Not when she had just placed her trust in him.

"Walk? In town?" Danby couldn't conceal his surprise at this. A moment later he recollected himself. "Well, I suppose it must come in useful for your books if you know every neighborhood."

Lyman murmured something like an assent, but Danby didn't really seem to be listening. He was already on to his next idea.

"It was so wonderful to meet you. Why don't you call on us sometime? Not for Della's little project, I mean, purely a social call. We'd love to get to know you better."

"Oh." Lyman shot a glance to Miss Danby, but she appeared as unprepared for this turn as he was, her dark eyes growing round. "I—"

"Our parents are having an intimate get-together the Friday after next," Danby continued, without seeming to realize that he'd just interrupted a viscount. "You should join us."

"I wouldn't want to impose." Miss Danby and her brother were too young to have run in the same circles as he had nine years ago, but their parents might recall his marriage to Ellen and its unsavory conclusion. He doubted he'd be as welcome as Peter Danby presumed.

"Nonsense. You'd be doing us a service. My parents are always trying to get *this* one to join us more often, instead of—" Danby cut himself off without finishing his sentence, a mild panic contorting his features.

"It's all right, Peter," Miss Danby said, in a tone of long-suffering patience. "Lord Ashton already knows about my club."

"Ah." Her brother drew a breath, his shoulders loosening. "Yes, of course. Well, as you can imagine, they do wish she'd attend the usual events a bit more often instead of frittering away all her time at that chocolate house."

"If they wanted me at the rout, they might have scheduled it on a Monday, when they know I'm free." Though her manner was easy, Miss Danby's eyes had lost their usual warmth.

"Who does anything on a Monday, though?"

"Thank you for the invitation," Lyman interjected. "It's very kind, but I—"

"Excellent! We'll see you on February 11. Come by for supper first, say around eight?"

Before Lyman could so much as blink, Peter Danby had pumped his hand twice, tipped his hat, and disappeared into his carriage without even thinking to hand his sister inside.

Lyman could do nothing but stare at Miss Danby, who seemed vaguely amused by the entire ordeal. "What just happened?" he murmured.

"I believe you've agreed to join us for dinner, though I can't promise I'll be there unless Mrs. Williams is free to mind the club. Have fun with my family, I suppose. I'm warning you now, I'm the most interesting one of the lot."

Her smile was full of humor, but it faded into an awkward silence as they stood alone before the carriage.

Della cleared her throat delicately.

"I'm sorry about the other night," Lyman murmured. "I wanted to come, but..."

She arched one dark brow. "But?"

Why had he said that? Now she expected something from him, some promise to try again, when he'd resolved to put an end to this. The words had slipped out of him without any forethought. It shouldn't be so damnably hard to extricate himself from the attentions of one plucky miss.

Peter Danby stuck his head out of their carriage. "Are you coming, Della?"

The coachman stood waiting for her at the door, watching them.

"Give us a moment, please," she called back. "We have important matters to discuss for my book." She inclined her head to indicate that they should walk a little farther down the road, to the relative privacy of the stoop of someone else's front door.

Lyman offered his arm and tried not to savor the way her soft curves fit so neatly against his side.

"Well?" she prodded, once they'd put a few yards between themselves and her brother.

Lyman bit the bullet. "I had a lovely time with you, but we can't carry on this way. The risk if we're found out is too great."

Della sighed and glanced away, pressing her lips together. "I must admit I'd hoped you might have more backbone."

"It isn't about backbone," he replied. Despite himself, the judgment stung. "I'm perfectly willing to risk my own reputation. It's not as though I'm a paragon of moral virtue anyway. But I won't risk yours."

Della gave a short, humorless laugh at this. "How noble of you! I'm lucky I have a viscount to make these decisions for me, or I might have to shoulder the difficult task of deciding for myself what risks to run." Lyman bit his tongue. He probably deserved that, but it didn't change his mind. If their union had been dangerous before, Michael's plans to drag him before Parliament would magnify it a hundredfold. He didn't want that on his conscience. Better to keep his distance than to bring his ruination to her doorstep.

"I'm sorry," he repeated. "I'm grateful for the pleasure of your company this past week. It meant a great deal to me." More than he could explain. He'd felt alive for the first time in years, but he should have known it wouldn't last.

Della was unmoved by this declaration. "I don't understand why you insist on denying yourself any joy in life, but I suppose you've decided your reasons are none of my concern, so I'll try to respect that." Her mouth was set in a firm line, while her eyes were soft with disappointment. "It seems the strict and proper Lord Ashton has vanquished the fun-loving Lord Ashton. I hope your choice brings you whatever it is you're looking for."

It brings me the taste of ash in my mouth and an empty bed each night. Lyman didn't give voice to the thought. It was the *right* choice, and that was all that mattered.

"It isn't about being strict or proper," Lyman tried to explain. "It's about maintaining a measure of order in my own life. What you call fun would be disastrous for me."

Her club, the risk of their affaire being discovered, and now Michael promising to destroy what little remained of his dignity. It was all too much. He worked too hard to regain control over his life. Over himself. It might not look like much to an outsider, but he found some satisfaction in his writing, and in the steady progression of each day that put him farther from the memory of his own mistakes without his having repeated them.

"And what you call order looks a good deal like cowardice to me," Della replied coolly. "But there's no point quibbling about it. Tell me, do you intend to cancel our visits?"

Lyman shifted uncomfortably. Whatever his feelings on their romantic entanglement, he didn't like to abandon her when she might need his help. "I'm still willing to continue our Tuesday calls if you wish, but it will be strictly a business arrangement. Or if you'd rather not see me, you can ask me any questions you might have by correspondence instead."

"No, you're perfectly welcome to come by the house as usual," Della replied. "I may be disappointed, but I'll get over it soon enough." Did she really feel so little at their rupture? Lyman wished he could be as impassive. But then, Della probably her choice of admirers, whereas the need for discretion had forced him to be more circumspect. He hadn't let himself care for a woman this way in some time. "Until next Tuesday, Lord Ashton. Farewell."

With that, she strode back to her carriage where her brother waited impatiently, without a second glance for Lyman or his misgivings.

The next morning, Della rose early, full of resolve to write an entire chapter even if it killed her. She was going to finish the section on shops today.

Signing that contract had made everything seem real, and not just because it was a binding legal document with a lot of unnecessarily obtuse wording that she'd only understood half of.

Besides that, there was Lord Ashton to think of. A few weeks ago, he would've been all barbs and scorn to see her out of her depths, but yesterday he'd been so thoughtful about the contract. Kind, even. Della didn't think she could bear it if she had to tell him she'd failed. Her heart had been pattering his name, right up until he'd cast her aside for some foolish idea of propriety.

What a disappointment.

The worst part was that she *knew* he was wrong, not only about her, but about himself. Lord Ashton had relished every minute of their too-brief time together. He'd brought her to climax effortlessly. He'd moaned and curled beneath her touch like a man in ecstasy.

Why deny them both such pleasure, unless he was the sort of person who only knew how to be miserable? And if so, why? Della wanted to argue with him until he saw reason, but her pride wouldn't allow it.

If he didn't want her, then she didn't want him. That was the end of it.

Their agreed-upon deadline for a draft manuscript was now only four weeks away, however, and Della would be damned if she let Lord Ashton know she had nothing more to show for her efforts than an outline and some notes on the view from Waterloo Bridge that she couldn't work into a proper text without a distinct feeling of regret.

Actually, the notes on the view were all she had to show. She'd lost the outline two days ago. Never mind. She remembered what most of it had said, and what she didn't remember could still be found. It had to be somewhere in her desk, she was sure. Perhaps she should take everything out again? It might have been in that bottom drawer with her petit point...

You're supposed to focus on writing your chapter today!

She could hunt down the outline later.

If she left straightaway, Della could use the next two hours to take an inventory of all the most fashionable places to spend one's money; then she would come straight home to write up her findings with *no distractions*; and finally she would eat a quick bite and change into evening attire before she went to Bishop's to supervise the rest of the night. She should have just enough time to manage it all. And once she did, she would set herself another goal for the next chapter, and so forth and so on, until she had an entire book.

She could do this. She only needed to be disciplined.

Della made it exactly as far as the landing when Annabelle found her.

"Where are you off to so early?" she asked, taking in her sister's burgundy walking dress and matching gloves. "If you're going to meet Lord Ashton, you have to bring me along."

"I'm not, so I don't." Della tried not to wince at the mention of his name.

"Did Peter scare him off yesterday?"

"Quite the opposite. He invited him to dine with us and attend Mama's rout the Friday after next, without so much as a by-your-leave from anyone, including Lord Ashton himself." Della was fuming just thinking of it. Peter hadn't even checked if she was free! What business did he have trying to steal her friends? Particularly when her relationship with the friend in question was so tenuous. "By the way, how did your tête-à-tête with Miss Greenwood go the other night? I was hurt you left without saying goodbye to me."

"Because you were *embarrassing* me," Annabelle moaned.

"Just as you've been embarrassing me with Lord Ashton every week? You reap what you sow, my dear." Della was not too mature to stick out her tongue at this juncture.

"You were worse," Annabelle insisted. "*You* tried to make me look foolish, whereas *I* merely enjoy watching you be foolish of your own volition. Anyway, where are you going?"

"To the shops, if you must know. For research for my book, not for buying things."

"May I come?"

"No."

"Don't be mean." Annabelle's lower lip was dangerously close to a pout, her eyes imploring. "I want to buy a present for Eliza. She likes all those frilly ribbony trimmings that you wear, which you know I could never select for myself. Anyway, you can hardly go alone. We can help each other."

Della let out a huge sigh to make it clear what an imposition this was, though she'd secretly decided to relent as soon as Miss Greenwood's name was mentioned. If their romance had already reached the gift-giving stage, she was going to have to reassess the odds she'd staked on Annabelle's failure. Things were getting interesting.

"*If* I let you come, you must let me set the itinerary and promise not to delay my progress. I'm on a strict schedule."

"You won't regret it! Let me just fetch my bonnet and gloves."

"And I wasn't going alone," Della called after her sister's back as she raced up the stairs. "Reva Chatterjee is meeting me there, and I was planning to invite Jane and Hannah Williams on the way over."

Twenty minutes later, Della was rolling along in her carriage, lamenting their late start and wondering if she would still be able to visit every place she intended before one o'clock, the time she'd planned to begin writing. Annabelle and Miss Williams sat across from her, gossiping about some girls their age that Della didn't know. She used to take note of each season's new round of debutants, but there was simply no time for it these days.

Jane had been napping after a sleepless night when Della had called, and hadn't joined them.

I don't understand why anyone should choose to have a baby, if they're this much work, Della reflected. Of course, she doubted her own mother had ever stayed up with her. They'd had nursemaids for that. Money did seem to make things easier. It was all the more reason to work hard and finish her book soon, so they could bring in more members and Jane could finally rest.

Della left a message with Eli just in case Jane decided to seek them out after she woke up. She'd been dearly hoping to have a real discussion with her friend about everything that had happened these past few weeks.

But it turned out that Miss Williams was an excellent listener, eagerly devouring Della's stories once they arrived at the first shop, the hatter's, where they found Reva waiting for them.

"Your life sounds so *exciting*." Miss Williams sighed. "How did you get a viscount to help you write a *book*? And what's he like?"

Della hesitated. She'd answered that same question easily when Peter had asked it a few weeks ago: "appallingly condescending." She blushed to think of it now, after how he'd touched her that night after the casino and then helped her yesterday. He'd been the only one in the room to think of her interests. All her impatience with his cold manner had evaporated after that.

Until he'd left her with nothing but frustrated desire and bruised pride.

"He's clever and a bit too proper," she finally replied. "But I don't think I can tell you much more than that. He's a difficult man to know."

"You forgot to mention handsome," Reva added teasingly.

"I don't find him handsome at all anymore," Della said quickly. "Our meetings are strictly a business arrangement." She was startled to hear Lord Ashton's own words escape her lips. She'd spoken without thinking, eager to snuff out speculation. Reva must have detected something in her tone, for she raised an eyebrow and dropped the subject.

Miss Williams chatted away, oblivious to their exchange. "Writing a guidebook to London, running a gambling club—how do you do it all without upsetting your parents?"

"Why should they object?"

"Aren't they worried it will hurt your reputation and prevent you from marrying?"

"Not really," Della said lightly. Her parents had never been particularly concerned with finding a match for any of their children. Of course they'd done all the customary things, like presenting Della and later Annabelle at Court for their comings out, but they'd never seemed to care much about what happened after that. It always made Della feel like the odd one out when her friends complained about their meddling parents, even if she *was* grateful for her freedom. "Mama always says that I'll know if I've met the right man, and I've decided he should have a sense of adventure."

Lord Ashton was sadly lacking in that respect, their interlude in the courtyard notwithstanding. His cold retreat had proven it.

"I wish I had your parents." Miss Williams seemed a good deal calmer than she had been at their last meeting—no doubt owing to the fact that Della had rescued her from her morning calls—but there was still a strong measure of emotion in her voice as she spoke. "I sometimes think I'd rather die than marry."

"Hannah!" Annabelle looked up from a selection of hats, shocked. "You mustn't say such an awful thing." After a long moment, she added, "Although trapping oneself in bondage to a man does sound perfectly odious, and I encourage you to do everything in your power to avoid it."

"That isn't helpful." Della scowled at Annabelle before turning her attention back to Miss Williams. "Please don't listen to her. She's a particular case. Don't you believe in love? Look how happy Jane and your brother are."

"They're happy because he's utterly devoted to her," Miss Williams said, "and lets her do whatever she wishes. No one else is half so kind."

"I used to be nervous at the thought of meeting my future husband," Reva put in tentatively. "But Mr. Bhattacharya and I turned out to have far more in common than I'd thought."

"I'm sure we could find you someone—" Della began, but the look on Miss Williams's face froze her tongue in place. That had evidently been the wrong thing to say.

"*Please* don't." Miss Williams looked as though she'd swallowed a slug. "If you want to help me, you should find a way to stop my mother from marrying me off. That's the only outcome I'm interested in."

"Excellent. We can be old maids together," Annabelle said happily, holding up a straw bonnet. "Does this one have too much ribbon on it? I think it has too much ribbon."

"It has precisely the right amount of ribbon," Della assured her. The blue would bring out Miss Greenwood's eyes.

"Couldn't I come to your club tonight?" Miss Williams asked, turning away from Annabelle's purchase. "I don't see why everyone should be allowed to attend but me! If I'm old enough to marry, aren't I old enough to decide how to spend my time?"

Oh dear. Della agreed with her in principle, of course, but she wasn't foolish enough to get in the middle of a row between Jane's in-laws.

"You'll have to talk to Jane about that," she replied diplomatically.

"So if she agrees, I can attend?"

"Of course." Though it didn't seem particularly likely, Della still hoped Jane might permit a bit of harmless rebellion. After all, they'd managed their club in relative secrecy for an entire season without their guardians knowing all of the details until they were ready. It wouldn't be right to hold Miss Williams to a higher standard. Besides which, she couldn't get into any trouble with Della there to keep an eye on her. "But don't be too hard on her if she says no. She's only trying to keep the peace with your mother, you know."

Miss Williams only gave a sullen grunt in response to this.

Annabelle purchased the bonnet and left instructions for it to be delivered to Miss Greenwood, then moved on to a glove shop next door, where she selected a pair in the finest kid leather and dispatched it likewise. Goodness, this was to be a full siege of the lady's defenses! It was nearing two o'clock by the time they left, which bumped Della off the schedule she'd planned. But she couldn't in good conscience say she'd toured the most important shops in London unless they went to see the new draper's that had just opened in Cavendish Square, so she was forced to extend their allotted time.

I'll just have to write quickly once I get home. I can still finish my chapter if I hurry.

They were still admiring the display in the windows when Della heard someone calling her name. A woman on the other side of the street raised a gloved hand and moved to cross. It was Jane! She must have come to find them after her nap. Della extracted herself from the crowd, eager to tell her friend all about her plans for her opening chapter, not to mention the solution she'd found to their problem with Mrs. Muller the other night.

But as she drew near, Della realized it wasn't Jane at all, but Lady Kerr. At a distance, they looked so alike as to be mistaken.

Cecily Kerr was Jane's cousin and sometimes rival. When Jane was present, Della would be the first to proclaim that Cecily was utterly self-obsessed and the most taxing person she'd ever encountered. The bonds of friendship commanded some loyalty, after all.

But as Jane was *not* present, Della was free to acknowledge—at least in the safety of her own thoughts—that she rather liked Cecily.

To start with, whenever she came to their club, she always spent her coin liberally, brought several friends, and made sure everyone around her was enjoying their evening. It was almost like having someone there to help them host, if the hostess also happened to be terrible at cards.

She also knew all the latest gossip and could be counted on to share it at the slightest invitation. Della had taken to asking her about the background of their newest members, just to make sure there were no surprises before they allowed a lady to buy a subscription. In short, Cecily was very useful if you knew how to harness her talents properly.

Oh, but this is perfect!

Della was surprised she hadn't thought of it sooner. If there was any information to be had about Lord Ashton, Cecily was sure to know. All she had to do was ask, and she might finally learn something that would explain his vexing behavior.

"Cecily, how are you?"

"Wonderful, darling. You aren't shopping *there*, are you?" Cecily pointed to the draper's. "They'll tell you everything is the latest fashion from France but half their stock is just cotton from Nottingham."

Della made a mental note of this for her book. Cecily was proving useful already!

"I'm so glad to see you," she began.

There was a flash of surprise in Cecily's eye before she recovered herself with a laugh. "Of course you are! I'm heaps of fun."

"Tell me, do you know anything about Viscount Ashton, the author of those guidebooks?"

"Hmm?" Cecily's brows arched at the name. "Oh yes, I should say *everyone* knows about him. I bought his book for Sir Thomas on his birthday last year, but I suppose you're more interested in the man than the book, are you?"

Success!

This was sure to be interesting, but Della held herself back before she could blurt out every question that weighed on her. Things such as: "Why didn't he want to come to visit my bedroom when I invited him?" and "Have I made a terrible mistake by kissing him?"

One had to tread carefully with Cecily. Gossip could cut both ways.

"A friend of mine offered to introduce us," Della lied, thinking quickly, "as she knows I have a number of artistic sorts in my set, but I didn't want to agree to it until I'd asked your opinion. You always know who qualifies as good society and who doesn't."

There. That was a passable fib. Although she felt comfortable telling her closest friends about her book, there wouldn't be much point in publishing it anonymously if she gave Cecily the opportunity to tell the whole world about it. Far safer to cover the more risqué subjects such as the entertainment at Laurent's Casino from behind a silk screen.

Cecily practically glowed at the praise. "You did quite well to come to me first, for I can assure you he does *not* qualify. I'd decline the introduction, were I you."

"Oh?" Della hadn't been expecting that. She'd thought Cecily would answer with a resounding "yes" and then plunge into a detailed history of Lord Ashton's entire life for her benefit. Surely no one would refuse the acquaintance of a peer, especially someone as concerned with appearances as Cecily.

Was it because he'd separated from his wife? He was hardly the only man to do so, even if people didn't tend to speak of such things openly.

"Haven't you heard about him?" Cecily asked. There was no helping it; Della was on pins and needles. Annabelle had abandoned all interest in some lace she'd been eyeing through the window and wandered closer to listen once she realized whom they were talking about. Reva and Miss Williams weren't far behind. Cecily seemed to speak even more slowly under the sway of all the attention. "He separated from his wife nine years ago. She was from a very good family. Ellen de Villiers, I believe was her maiden name. The daughter of the Earl of Eastmeath. The two of them used to run in the very best circles until their rupture. And then he ruined her completely; left her destitute. It was all anyone talked about when it happened. All the fuss spoiled my debut year, as you can imagine."

"How do you mean, he *ruined* her?" Who on earth cared about Cecily's debut? She was deliberately saving the juicy details for last. Della's fingers were twitching with impatience.

"It's the most horrid thing you can imagine." Cecily widened her eyes in shock, as if the story were fresh instead of nearly a decade in the past.

What does that mean? Adultery? Cruelty?

Neither of these possibilities sounded like the subdued gentleman who'd bent his head close to hers to share his copy of the contract yesterday.

Cecily cast a wary glance around the circle of ladies hooked on her tale. "I don't know if I should say it in front of everyone. It might be unpleasant for you to hear, on account of your club."

"Cecily, *please* tell me. You have me dying of curiosity." It was quite true, though hopefully she would ascribe Della's emotion to her own expert storytelling and not any particular concern for the viscount.

"Very well." Cecily leaned in, dropping her voice to a stage whisper. "He gambled away his family's *entire* fortune. The country house, his wife's dowry, *everything*. He left the poor woman destitute."

Twelve

DELLA DIDN'T KNOW HOW TO BEHAVE AFTER CECILY'S REVELA-
tion. She had no further word from Lord Ashton, and her bedroom
window stood unassailed and lonely. Or at least, she presumed it did.
She was always at Bishop's in the evenings.

How would she face him on Tuesday? She couldn't look at him
the same way now.

Perhaps Cecily was wrong, or at least exaggerating the tale.
Perhaps there was something she didn't know. But after a few well-
placed inquiries among her friends, Della couldn't deny the truth.
Lord Ashton was known for precisely two things: his series of guidebooks and losing his country house in a wager to the Earl of Carlisle
at White's nine years ago.

How could the upright, disapproving man she knew have taken
such a risk? It seemed entirely out of character. Was it a youthful folly
that had taught him a painful lesson? It would explain why he hated
gambling so much.

His poor wife, though. She had to live with the consequences of
his actions forever. No wonder they'd parted ways.

Maybe I should have listened to Annabelle and stayed well enough away from him. What a depressing thought.

But whatever her feelings for Lord Ashton, Della wasn't going to abandon her book. She scribbled down passages whenever things were slow at the club and managed to cobble together most of her chapter on shops, even if it took far longer than the day she'd originally planned.

When the fateful Tuesday finally arrived, she was so nervous there was no danger of forgetting to wind the clock and missing the appointed time. She paced the drawing room in wait, too preoccupied to set herself to any other task.

When Lord Ashton finally joined Della and Annabelle, she saw everything about him in another light. If she looked closely, she noticed how the cuffs of his jacket had grown threadbare. Where she'd thought his tendency to repeat certain clothes was an eccentricity, she now understood it was more likely a necessity. He'd gambled away everything, Cecily had said. No wonder that he couldn't maintain a style of living befitting his station. Was that why he'd given her a card without his address on it? If he'd lost his estate, it was unlikely he could still afford rent in Mayfair. He must live in a low neighborhood. And here she'd thought he was being snobbish.

"Good morning, Miss Danby," Ashton removed his hat and greeted them with a bow. "Miss Annabelle."

"Good morning."

He looked at her hesitantly as he took his seat. Lord Ashton seemed as standoffish as she felt. Hopefully he would attribute any distance in her manners to their recent rupture, and not to the revelation of his secret. As much as she longed to know more, she didn't dare to broach the subject.

"How is your writing coming along?" he asked.

I should probably have written half the text by now, but all I've

finished is one chapter, half an introduction you intend to replace with
something of your own, and some notes on a lovely day we shared taking
in the views before you decided you didn't like me anymore.

"I finished the chapter on shops recently." Della put some sun-
shine into her voice to banish the shadows in her thoughts. "I could
share it with you if you like, but it's mostly about things that will
appeal to ladies—modistes and milliners and such."

"I don't mind," Lord Ashton replied. "I'd be looking it over to see
how the language flows, not to critique your assessment of a subject
on which I have no knowledge. But I wouldn't want to take up all our
time today reading if you have any questions for me. Why don't you
give me your pages? I'll make some notes at home and bring them
back next week."

"Oh, I wouldn't want to take more of your time than we agreed
to," Della said quickly. "I'm sure you need to focus on getting your
next book out soon."

He blinked at her. Had that been a strange thing to say? She was
normally so preoccupied with her own projects, she hadn't given
much thought to the impact she had on Lord Ashton's life. Maybe
she'd been selfish. She hadn't *meant* to be, but she'd thought his writing was an interesting hobby he might take a break from whenever
he pleased. Now Della understood it must be his livelihood.

"Never mind," she amended, flipping through the pile of papers
she'd brought downstairs to set the chapter on shops in some sem-
blance of order. It gave her somewhere else to look. "It's very kind of
you to read them over, if you can afford to spare the time. I mean, of
course you can afford to spare the time. You're a viscount. I'm sure
you can do whatever you like." Della ended her rambling speech
in a sudden cough. Goodness, why couldn't she keep herself from
acting this way?

Lord Ashton watched her for a long moment before he spoke

again. When he did, his voice was measured and precise—almost regretful. "Someone told you."

"Told me what?" The response was instinctive. Della wasn't trying to deceive him. But she hated to admit to what she'd heard, on the slim chance they weren't thinking of the same thing.

Lord Ashton saved her the trouble. He dropped his gaze to his teacup as he replied, "That I gambled away my country house."

"Oh!" Annabelle gasped so loudly she might have been a stage actress discovering a murder in the final act.

Won't she ever stop making a nuisance of herself?

"Annabelle, could you please give us a moment of privacy?"

"Leave you unchaperoned?" Her sister placed a hand to her breast in a poor imitation of horror. "I couldn't possibly. I'm sure Mama and Papa would never forgive me."

"*Privacy,*" she repeated. "Or Mama and Papa will learn who really took that bottle of wine they thought Thomson had stolen, which you *never paid me* for replacing."

With a glare to ignite the house, Annabelle rose to her feet and exited the room.

Finally.

Della turned back to Lord Ashton, feeling suddenly shy. Trying to resume the path of their conversation was like stepping into a pair of ill-fitting shoes. She wasn't quite sure how to move forward without tripping. "Yes, I heard the rumor." She paused here, in case he wished to dispute it, but he held his tongue. The weight of the silence grew oppressive, between the soft clicking of the grandfather clock. "I know it's...none of my business," she said softly. "I didn't mean to pry."

"It wouldn't matter if you pried; the story would have reached you sooner or later. It always does." He offered her a joyless smile, his eyes shadowed. "My deepest shame is never far behind me."

He looked so hopeless under the weight of this confession that it moved Della to pity. She wanted to take him in her arms and reassure him, despite what he'd done.

"I don't think any less of you for it," she assured him.

"Miss Danby." His tone sharpened, grazing across her name like a whetstone. "You *must* think less of me for it. I think less of myself for it, and I would be disappointed in you if you did otherwise."

Della didn't know what to say to that, so she said nothing. She had no idea how she should behave in such circumstances.

A moment later, Lord Ashton sighed. "I'm sorry. I shouldn't have spoken to you harshly. You were trying to be kind, but I'm afraid I can't tolerate much kindness in this matter."

Della hardly knew what to do with herself. *What happened?* she wanted to ask. *What made you lose your reason so completely?* But any answer he could give would only add to his humiliation. If he were insensibly drunk when he'd done it, or if he were goaded on by his friends, would that make it any better?

"That's why you dislike gambling," she finally ventured.

He confirmed this with a sharp nod. "I haven't set foot in a gaming house since that day. Nor shall I, for as long as I live."

Della's face grew hot with the memory of how she'd behaved at their meetings. That note she'd sent him last week inviting him to meet her at Bishop's. *Was that why he changed his mind about me?*

"I'm so sorry. I must have seemed like I was provoking you. I never would have tried to persuade you that you should visit my club, or argued with you about your views on gambling, if I'd had any idea—"

"Don't think of it," Ashton said quickly, as if her remorse, too, were difficult for him. "If I were to be angry with you, I should be angry with half of Britain. Card play is only rivaled in its popularity by horse racing and dice."

What must it be like to be hounded by reminders of your folly wherever you went? Della couldn't imagine. Thus far, she'd been remarkably successful at keeping the consequences of her own follies at bay.

"You will perhaps want to call an end to our meetings, now that you know what I'm capable of." Was that regret in his tone? "I would understand if you did."

"Nonsense." Della didn't even need to consider her reply. "You told me at the outset I was risking my reputation, and it never stopped me. Why should I turn back now? I've rather grown to like you."

Lord Ashton watched her for a long moment, his green eyes suddenly gentle. That *was* regret, and she hadn't imagined it. "I've grown to like you too," he said softly.

It was such a modest declaration, said in that measured way of his. Yet it was enough to make her heart do a little somersault.

"But your opinion of me shouldn't be your only guide." He still wore a grim expression. "There's something else I should tell you. I had a visit from my wife's brother last week. She wants a divorce."

Oh my. If Della had been without a map for the first half of this conversation, now she was utterly lost. He could be free. Not for her, of course. But for *someone.* Himself, perhaps. Would it be rude to express hopeful sentiments?

"Are you… Do you want a divorce?"

"It promises to ruin my life."

Yes, it would definitely be rude.

Della bit her lip and waited.

"I thought there wasn't much left to ruin, but they've filed proceedings before Consistory Court, and they're planning to go before Parliament for a private bill as soon as they have their judgment in hand. They'll have to prove adultery and intolerable cruelty to succeed. Do you understand what's in store? Every witness they can drum up to testify will have their words printed in the papers, and I'll be lucky if I'm not the most hated man in London by the time the year is out." He held her gaze for a long time. "That friend of yours, Miss Chatterjee, saw us together the other day. Not to mention anyone who might have been in the crowd at the Waterloo Bridge. You should end your association with me if you don't want to be caught up in the talk."

Lyman watched the spark in Miss Danby's eyes dim as he laid out the future that awaited him. His name would be spoken in hushed whispers at dinner parties, as a warning of the lows to which a man could fall. It wasn't as though he had much of a place in high society as it stood now, with his means so reduced. But this would put him in another category entirely. People might not want to buy his books anymore. The wealthy families who hired him to tutor their sons might not want him in their homes. How was he to support himself?

"Whatever passed between you and your wife, I'm sure you aren't capable of that." She had such trust in her voice that it made Lyman ashamed. He didn't deserve it.

"Which part, the adultery or the intolerable cruelty?"

"I wouldn't want to speculate on your romantic entanglements. You may tell me if you wish, and I will take you at your word, for you've been very frank with me about your failings thus far. Were you unfaithful to Lady Ashton?"

It was an indecorous question. A few weeks ago, he might have reacted with shock. But they'd moved past formality now, the exchange between them passing into the sort of openness Lyman might have shared with a close friend. So he answered her honestly.

"Not while we still lived in the same house. After we separated, and it became clear I could never atone for what I'd done, I formed a few connections over the years. But I was always careful that no one should be harmed by it."

"I don't think anyone could blame you, once your wife had made it clear reconciliation was impossible." Miss Danby's tone was matter-of-fact, as if they were discussing nothing more shocking than the weather. "And as for cruelty, I'm sure you aren't guilty of that. It would seem you have little to worry about. They won't be able to make their case."

"I cost her everything. Her chance to marry a better man and start a family, the house where we lived, even her dowry, which should have been settled on our future children. What else would you call it? You don't know me well enough to judge my character, Miss Danby."

"I know you aren't a violent man, which must be the primary concern in a case of divorce," she persisted. "I've certainly annoyed you enough in our brief acquaintance that I should have seen some sign of it by now, if you were."

Lyman smiled, in spite of himself. "You haven't annoyed me. You simply have a penchant for taking risks which make me uneasy. But very well, I'll own that I'm not a violent man. Does that mean I haven't been cruel through my own recklessness, even if I regret it?"

But Miss Danby refused to concede any ground. "Not *intolerably* so."

A laugh escaped his lips. Bless her stubbornness.

"I'll call you as a witness, shall I? To prove that there is at least one person in all of London who considers me tolerable."

"I would be happy to attest as much." The smile on her lips fell away slowly. "Truly, if there is something I can do, will you tell me? There must be some way you can defend yourself."

She was on his side. There was no rational reason she should be, now that she knew of his worst mistake, but she was.

Would her loyalty endure once his name was splashed across the front page for days on end, alongside the details of Ellen's devastation and whatever lurid stories of adultery they would contrive? It almost made Lyman regret what he had to say next.

"No. I won't fight their claims. After everything I've done to that family, the least I can do is to let them try to get their divorce, however they think best."

"You can't mean it!" At last, Miss Danby showed some sign she was angry with him, though it was aimed at the wrong part of his actions. "Not defend yourself? You'll let them say whatever they wish about you, even if it isn't true?"

"I owe her that much."

He could never repay his debts to Ellen. Never restore what he'd cost her. The money he sent every month was a pittance, like throwing pennies down a yawning black well to wish for a chance to live his life over again. If she ruined what was left of his good name to find her own freedom, maybe it would finally feel like he'd made amends.

Miss Danby held her tongue, though her expression betrayed furious disagreement.

"You can get away while there's still time," he continued. "Sever your connection with me before I become infamous."

"Lord Ashton," she admonished, "I am the proprietress of a gambling house. If I were to cut ties with you for your history engaging in the same activity I'm peddling, I should be nothing but a hypocrite." Her tone cooled as she added, "I detest hypocrites."

She was clear and resolute, without a trace of hesitation. Should he have expected anything less? He'd seen it from the very first day they met; she lived as she saw fit and made no apologies for it. It made him wish that he could accept her support.

She was admirable, in her own way. But she'd never been made to pay a price for her actions. With her indulgent parents, and her charm and wit, Miss Danby had thus far managed to walk the fine line between scandal and social acceptability.

He didn't want to be the one to bring it all crashing down upon her head.

"I fear you'll regret your choice when you see the worst of it," he said. "I could ruin you, Miss Danby. I don't want to have that on my conscience as well."

"Ruin me...?" She arched an eyebrow and took a sip of her tea, though it must have been cold by now.

Incorrigible. Lyman's blood heated as he remembered all that had passed between them, which was no doubt her intent. He wanted to repeat their transgression. No, he *ached* for it. Not only for the meeting of desires, but to find the comfort she offered so freely. He could use some comfort today.

Instead, he said, "You should take this far more seriously."

"I am taking it seriously; I simply don't agree with your course of action." Miss Danby sighed and raised her hands in a gesture of surrender. "Shall we strike a compromise? Your case isn't being heard today, I trust. How much time do you have? If your chief concern is my reputation, we might keep things as they are until the story makes the papers."

Keep things as they are. Lyman wasn't sure what that meant, exactly. Sparring with Miss Danby in her drawing room while telling himself he wasn't enjoying her company too much, and sharing the occasional kiss after a night at a casino?

"They've set the hearing for February 17."

"So soon! That's less than three weeks away."

"You should try to finish your book as soon as possible," Lyman said, "so we have time to go over the manuscript first."

"Don't worry." Della smiled, her eyes betraying a trace of mischief. "I work best under a little pressure."

Della felt a good deal better after her talk with Lord Ashton. As uncomfortable as the revelation had been for both of them, it had finally helped her to understand the behavior she'd found so perplexing when they first met. His refusal to drink or gamble, his discomfort whenever the subject of his marriage came up, even the way he'd balked at the prospect of spending the night with her.

I must remind him of the worst period in his life.

If Della felt a measure of relief at finally having everything in the open between them, it was tempered by sadness. She didn't like to think of what was in store for him if his wife proceeded with her plans for divorce.

Besides which, he'd been right. There wasn't any hope for an amorous connection between them—not when she owned a gambling house and he had such a dreadful reason to avoid them. She would be more careful in what she said and did in his company now that she understood the whole story, but the damage was likely already done. He must see her as a threat to his efforts to live a better sort of life.

Is he right?

Della tried to focus on her work. She'd managed to start the chapter on parks, adding a few paragraphs on some locations she'd tested with Miss Chatterjee last week. After that, she'd paused to consider what she might tackle next and realized she hadn't included anything on gambling clubs, even though that had been the impetus for the whole project! She was sitting before a blank page of foolscap now, trying to land on the right words.

She didn't feel nearly as enthusiastic about the subject after her talk with Lord Ashton.

They would never have allowed such a thing to happen at Bishop's, of course. There were strict limits on how much the ladies could wager. But all the same, the prospect of such a terrible loss was enough to give her pause.

Were she and Jane wrong to carry on a business like this when it could cause such pain?

"Ahem."

Della jumped at the sound of another person nearby. Annabelle hovered in the doorway, like a spindly butterfly poised over a flower, all limbs. What nectar did she search for here?

"Are you going to come in?" Della asked, irritated. "It's very off-putting to lurk."

Annabelle shuffled into the room and shut the door behind her, but still didn't explain herself. After a moment, she inched close enough to spy Della's papers.

"Why have you crossed everything out?" she asked. "Don't you need to *keep* some of the words if you intend to write a book?"

"It's all part of my process." Della set both hands in the middle of her notes, shielding them from view. "What is it you want? I have heaps of work to do, and I'm meant to be at Bishop's in two hours." She shot a precautionary glance to the clock to make sure the hands were still moving.

Annabelle didn't walk across the room so much as slide, like a heavy, brooding mist. She slumped onto the little divan just past Della's desk. Her posture would have earned her a scolding from their old governess.

"Please just tell me," Della repeated tiredly.

She'd been expecting a scolding for banishing Annabelle from the drawing room and sitting alone with the viscount that morning, but her sister's deportment was far too glum for that. This must be something more personal to her.

She's gotten herself in some sort of trouble and needs me to free her from prison.

Della knew the lines to this play by heart. First, Annabelle would protest that it wasn't her fault. She would put on her doe eyes and plead innocence. Second, she would lay out the terrible fate that awaited her (or, very possibly, Miss Greenwood), to stir up sympathy. In the third and final act, she would appeal to Della's sisterly compassion, and they would strike some bargain for their mutual advantage, though Della often got the more miserly end of the deal.

What would she do without me?

"I've...gotten myself into a spot of trouble," Annabelle said, perfectly on cue. She rubbed her arms as if she were cold, though the room was comfortable enough. "It really isn't my fault. I was *so careful* to be discreet, but how could I have known her father was so overbearing?"

Oh dear. This already had the makings of a sticky problem.

Della put away her notes with a touch of regret. There was little chance she'd get to write any more today. Why couldn't she find a few hours of peace in this house?

"What have you done?"

"You remember Miss Greenwood?"

"Of course I do." Honestly, they'd been buying bonnets for the girl just last week.

"I may have...climbed through her bedroom window last night. Don't look at me that way. She was *very* inviting! Anyway, it seems that her father saw me when I snuck back out."

"Good Lord, Annabelle!" How were they going to explain things this time? The older her sister got, the more difficult it became to excuse her actions by pleading some childish lapse in judgment.

"How was I to know that he smokes outside?" Annabelle protested. "Who smokes outside? That's why they have *smoking* rooms!"

"All right." Della sighed. She held up a finger to signal silence as she contrived a plan. They were going to have to admit some measure of guilt on Annabelle's part, if she'd been caught fleeing the scene of her crime. The trick was to make it a socially acceptable measure of guilt. "Here's what we'll do. You'll make your apology to her father and say you wanted to invite Miss Greenwood to sneak out with you to attend a party without your chaperones, but she convinced you the idea was too improper and sent you straight home. That leaves her looking innocent, and we'll ask him not to speak of it to protect your reputation. If we're lucky, he'll agree."

That would serve. She was too good at this, really.

"No, you don't understand." Annabelle's voice shook as she continued. "It's much worse this time."

"Why? What is it?" Della was starting to feel uneasy. They would normally be at the bargaining stage by now. "He didn't catch you in a compromising state with her, did he?"

"No." The denial should have brought some measure of relief, but Annabelle still sat white-knuckled and bent under the weight of her distress. "It's a question of what I looked like when he saw me. Promise you won't be cross. I feel badly enough as it is."

"Annabelle, just tell me."

"I was wearing the suit I had made for when we went to Laurent's Casino the other night. He thinks he saw a *gentleman* leaving Eliza's room."

"What? Why would you—"

"I had to get over there *somehow*, didn't I?" Annabelle hissed, cutting her off. "I couldn't very well take the family carriage and be recognized. I needed to walk the streets to hail a hansom cab. I wouldn't have been safe doing that dressed as a lady. Besides, it looked very dashing on me, and I wanted Eliza to see."

Della felt as though she had a lead ball in her belly.

"Annabelle, this is bad."

"I know that!" Her eyes were bright, and it didn't look to be feigned. "Now her father won't let her out of the house, and he's looking to force the man who compromised his daughter to marry her immediately. Look here, she managed to smuggle me a note through her maid."

Annabelle produced a worn and folded paper from her fist. By the looks of it, torn from the flyleaf of a book. The hurried script read:

Papa says I must be married or sent to the continent! I'm not allowed out. You must save me!!

All my love,
—E.

"I didn't mean to get her in trouble." Annabelle had begun to cry a little by now, dabbing at her eyes with a handkerchief, so Della decided to forgo a scolding. It would serve no purpose at this stage.

"Did Mr. Greenwood see your face? Might he recognize you?"

Annabelle shook her head. "It was too dark, and he was across the garden. He just shouted after me, and I panicked and ran. All he could know is that he saw a man's figure running away from her window."

Until Eliza Greenwood confessed the rest of the story under familial pressure, which must be reaching considerable force. They would have to think of something before she cracked.

Owning the truth, in any form, was impossible. If it should be known that the girls were lovers, or that Annabelle had paraded around London after dark while dressed as a man, they would be cut from society forever.

"As I see it, there are only two choices, neither of which is ideal." Della left her desk to join Annabelle on the divan, reaching an arm around her narrow shoulders to bolster her courage. "Either you abandon poor Miss Greenwood to her fate and let her be exiled, or we find you an excuse to join her on the continent and try to set you up in a place where you can live together discreetly."

"Live together?" Annabelle jumped to her feet, withdrawing from Della's embrace so swiftly that she caused her to lose her balance and lurch forward on the cushions. "I'm *nineteen*, not ninety! I don't want to be banished to the ends of the earth."

"You'd have the chance to see the world! Don't you love this girl?" Della asked, incensed. She'd thought that's what the tears were for. "This might be the only way you can be with her now."

But Annabelle snapped back, "Of course I don't love her; I barely know her! This was a bit of harmless fun. I certainly didn't expect to be caught."

God help me. Why do I even try?

"Well, you've seduced her and ruined her," Della reminded her sister. "Now you intend to abandon her as well? Really, Annabelle."

"I wouldn't be asking for your help if I intended to abandon her, now would I?" It must be witchcraft that allowed the author of such a scandal to look so superior. "There is another choice that would allow us all to continue on with our lives and cover up this unfortunate misunderstanding."

She paused here while Della struggled to rein in her exasperation.

"Are you going to tell me what miracle you've contrived to save your skin?"

"Miss Greenwood must be married to the man who compromised her. It's the only way to avoid total ruin. All we need to do is find the man."

Della was so stunned she lost the power of speech for a full minute. This posed no hardship, for her sister kept right on talking.

"I was thinking of Peter. It's not as though he's likely to find himself a bride on the power of his own charm, and Miss Greenwood is terribly pretty. We'd be doing him a favor, really."

"Peter?" Della echoed helplessly.

"Someone needs to carry on the family name and produce a few children, don't they? We aren't likely to do it."

"I beg your pardon!"

"It's a compliment," Annabelle assured her. "You've always said you see no reason to marry too early, which I consider a rare showing of good sense."

"You should watch your tongue if you still want my help in this fiasco." Della might not have found the love of her life quite yet, but that didn't mean she was *firmly* on the shelf.

"Very well." Annabelle sighed, as though *she* were the one suffering ill-treatment. "But you must admit it's the best option we've got."

Della wasn't convinced of that in the least. It was on the tip of her tongue to retort that sending Annabelle to the continent was still the better plan.

Perhaps then I could finally make some progress on my manuscript!

"Why do you keep saying *we*?" Della asked. "Surely you can persuade Peter to marry your ruined lover without my involvement."

What a sentence.

"Alas, I cannot," Annabelle said, with a note of regret. "He'll refuse if I ask, but he always does favors for you."

"That's because I pay him for it." Honestly, did Annabelle think these things just fell into her lap? No one had any regard for her hard work. "Though I think the going rate for a forced marriage will be far higher than my standard bottle of top-shelf champagne."

"Oh." This revelation seemed to put a stumbling block in her sister's plans. "I didn't realize."

"You see? This is a ludicrous idea."

"Come now," Annabelle insisted. "I won't let Eliza be exiled forever. Then I'll have to feel awful about it. We must do something, and this is the only course that suits."

"Does Miss Greenwood think it suits? Does she even fancy men?"

"She fancies some men, although I can't say whether Peter will qualify. He is a *drastic* step down from me." Annabelle frowned into the distance for a moment, perhaps reflecting on their brother's faults. "I suppose she might prefer the continent. Let's focus on securing Peter's consent first, shall we? If we get that far, we'll smuggle Eliza a note to check her preference."

How do I always get roped into these things? It was unfair. She had more important matters to attend to than convincing Peter to marry Annabelle's lover. She had *two* separate business endeavors demanding her time. She should say no.

But without her expert touch, Annabelle would probably botch the whole thing and end up exposed to all of London, and then where would they be? As much as her sister might annoy her, Della didn't want to see her exiled from society. No, she would have to help. There was nothing else for it.

And if she was going to be put to work, she would take her cut.

"If we succeed in this absurd plan of yours, I want you to stop chaperoning my meetings with Lord Ashton. Only tell Mama and Papa you're still accompanying us and that nothing untoward has happened, should they ask."

Not that they will.

"Ha!" Annabelle clapped her hands with glee. "It's a deal. I knew you'd do it. But be careful what you wish for, dear sister." She held up a finger in poor imitation of their former governess. "Unlike Eliza and I, *you* have to worry about finding yourself in a family way for your indiscretions. And I'm not convinced we'll be able to find you a substitute husband when the viscount can't marry you."

"Be quiet before I change my mind," Della snapped, swatting at her arm. "You're so vexing!"

At least after this task was done, she'd be free of Annabelle's editorializing once and for all.

"Let me do the talking, and follow my lead," Della whispered. She and her sister huddled outside the door to Peter's study, listening for any sound within.

Though Annabelle nodded, her face solemn, there was no telling if she would stick to their plan. She had an irritating conviction that she knew best. *Ah well, too late to turn back now.* Della raised her fist and rapped lightly on the door.

"Come in." Peter was lounging on a chaise, flipping through a hunting journal. When he saw them, he set his reading to the side and propped himself into a more upright position, though his expression still implied a desire to nap. "What are you doing here?"

They didn't often pay him a visit together unless they were all attending the same event.

"We have a delicate matter to discuss with you," Della began. Behind her, Annabelle shut the door.

"Oh God, what now?"

"No, no," Della amended. Perhaps she should have opened differently, but why should Peter assume the worst from *her*? She normally solved her own problems. "I only mean that it's a matter of the heart."

"Is one of you in a certain way?"

"No!" Both girls chimed at once. It was hard to say who was more insulted.

"Why would you even think such a thing?" asked Annabelle.

"This is a matter of the heart for *you*, Peter," Della explained patiently. She would keep this conversation on course if it killed her. "We have an eligible friend and we thought you might suit, that's all."

But Peter only wrinkled his nose, plainly unimpressed. "For me? Why? What's wrong with her?"

Della would have liked to reply that there was nothing wrong, but it was quite impossible. If he was to present himself to Mr. Greenwood as the gentleman who'd run from his daughter's bedroom a few nights ago, Peter would have to know something of the story. Still, she wouldn't have chosen to get bogged down in the details before they could even sell him on the idea of a wedding. It was important to do things in the proper order.

"Why all the suspicion?" she protested. "We're trying to do you a service! At least let us tell you who, before you jump to conclusions."

"Very well then. Who?"

"Eliza Greenwood." It was Annabelle who spoke, and Della shot her a warning look. But she kept on talking. "You remember her, don't you? The fair-haired lady who was talking with me at the Pearsons' rout the other week. She's about so tall, stunning face, dazzling smile, *very* alluring figure. She has a mole on her right cheek, just here."

"Annabelle," Della said sharply. This was already getting out of hand.

But Peter must have known whom they meant, for he sat a bit taller. "Yes, I remember her."

That was a good sign.

"But why should you want to push your friend my way?" he soon continued, his eyes narrowing. "You've never shown any interest in my love life before."

"Do you have one?" Annabelle asked, with an arched brow.

"Annabelle!" They would've done better to shut her sister out of this conversation. She was utterly useless. "You were too young to settle down before," Della tried. "But four-and-twenty is a good age to begin planning for the future, wouldn't you say? Don't men want to carry on the family name and what not? Anyway, let's focus on what you think of her. You agree she's very fetching?"

"I'll agree to that much." He looked from Annabelle to Della, as if trying to identify the weak link. He finally settled on the younger sister. "But I don't believe for a minute that you'd be playing Cupid out of the goodness of your hearts. So what's the catch? Hereditary madness? She's penniless? Someone's compromised her already?"

"It seems you're too clever for us," Annabelle said. "You've guessed it in three. Miss Greenwood is indeed compromised, but only *very slightly*. Hardly worth counting, in my opinion. You'd be getting a bride of the highest caliber at a bargain rate."

Della whirled to face her sister. "Why did you ask for my help if you're just going to ruin things?"

"*You're* the one ruining things!" Annabelle snapped back. "He figured it out five minutes into your speech."

"Because you're both appallingly predictable," Peter said. He rose from the chaise and poured himself a brandy, then addressed them from behind the rim of his glass. "Anyway, your game is up. I'm not interested in helping you unload another man's castoffs, so you can tell your friend she'll have to find another mark."

"Peter, at least hear us out," Della pleaded. "Setting aside the matter of her minor ruination, you must acknowledge that Miss Greenwood would be an excellent match for you. She's beautiful, witty, well liked, and she comes from a good family with a bit of money. It would be difficult to find anyone better—"

"*Very* difficult," Annabelle added, with a speaking look to their brother's rumpled hair and uneven cravat.

Della continued, "Surely you must want to have children one day, to pass on your, er...your legacy?" At present, Peter's legacy was poor luck at cards and slightly better luck at hunting. Never mind. He still had decades to prove himself useful at something. Starting right now.

"You must intend to marry eventually. Don't dismiss a perfectly good option over a little misunderstanding."

"I don't see why I should marry soon," Peter retorted. "I might happily put it off for another decade, at least. And as for children, I have no desire to find a cuckoo's egg in my nest, which is what you're offering me."

"There is no chance whatsoever that she's expecting," Annabelle said. "I promise you."

Peter gave a snort. "So far as you know. Do you think she'd be honest about such a thing? I'm sure she told you it was only a few kisses, but her word won't be worth much with me, I'm afraid."

Oh dear. It was for Annabelle to handle this part. Della had done her best, but she couldn't say much to refute Peter's assumption without revealing everything.

The odds were against us from the start.

"We *must* find her a husband," Annabelle said. "If you won't do it, do you have any friends in need of a wife? Preferably an urgent need. To fulfill a dying mother's wish, or satisfy a condition in a will, or something along those lines."

"That doesn't happen as often as you think. And at any rate, I could hardly call them my friends if I recommend they wed a light-skirt."

"You are insufferable!" Annabelle snapped. "I never ask you for anything. Can't you just marry this one lady for me?"

"No." Peter glowered at his sister. "Why should I? It would bring me nothing but scandal and regret."

"I promise you, you'll have plenty of that if you refuse."

Annabelle's threat carried enough edge that Peter froze, his glass suspended halfway to his lips. "What do you mean?"

Annabelle strode over to the sideboard, poured her own drink, and took a long swallow before she replied, impervious to her brother's shock. "Because Miss Greenwood knows a very damaging secret about me. And if we don't rescue her from her current predicament, there's a good chance she'll reveal it."

"A blackmailer as well as a light-skirt. This gets better and better. What's the secret?"

"You're happier not knowing," Annabelle replied. "But believe me when I say it's such that I would have to retire from society, which is not something I plan to accept without a fight."

Peter hazarded a glance to Della, who gave a curt nod. He rubbed a hand over his brow, at last troubled. He hated their continual flirtation with scandal. "I'm sorry, but I still won't do it. You've told me next to nothing of your reasons for helping Miss Greenwood, what little I know of her character paints a damning portrait, and there's no advantage to me whatsoever. Whatever your secret is, you'll have to weather the gossip somehow."

"I'm the one who ruined her," Annabelle blurted out. She edged closer to Della's side, looking less like a demanding busybody and more like a lost youth.

"Pardon?" Peter squinted at Annabelle as if she'd grown a second head. "But...but you're a *woman*. How could you...?"

"Don't be obtuse, please."

As the silence that followed begged to be filled with a few details, Della took it upon herself to add the most essential ones. "Annabelle was seen sneaking out of their house by Miss Greenwood's father, but in the dark he mistook her for a man. If we don't find someone else to step forward, the truth might emerge."

Peter returned to his spot on the chaise and buried his face in his hands.

"Why can't you two be *normal*?" he moaned. "Gambling clubs, seducing other women. Do you know how many of my friends have to marry a ruined lady to save their sister's reputation? *None*. It would never happen."

"Does that mean you'll do it?" Annabelle asked, hope creeping into her voice.

"No," Peter repeated, although less forcefully than before. "You still haven't told me why it should be my burden to save you from your own mess."

"Because even if Annabelle is judgmental and annoying, she's family."

Annabelle elbowed Della sharply in the ribs. "I think you were meant to offer him something. We've reached the bargaining stage. Remember?"

"No, we haven't," said Peter. "I've said *no*."

"Oh, that's right." The situation had seemed so hopeless, Della had almost forgotten they still had a few uncashed chips. "Annabelle, please remind me what Miss Greenwood's dowry is worth?"

"Six thousand."

"My, my, such a sum!" Della placed a hand to her lips in exaggerated surprise. "But surely her parents will revoke it to punish her for her transgressions?"

"Impossible. This is a departed-mother's-estate-settled-on-an-only-child situation." Annabelle paused to skewer her brother with her look. "In fact, one might even speculate as to whether the amount has room to *increase* as a result of what's happened. I suppose it would depend on the groom's skills as a negotiator, but wouldn't you show some flexibility if you were desperate to cover up your daughter's indiscretion?"

"I certainly would!" Della replied without missing a beat.

Peter was definitely sitting taller now, his full attention fixed on their little show.

Della took the lead again. "By the way, Peter, what's your current debt at Brooks's?"

"I–I beg your pardon? That's none of your business."

"Something in the range of fourteen hundred, isn't it?"

"How—you—" Scarlet crept up Peter's neck.

"It's a small circle, London gambling clubs. I'm acquainted with their bookkeeper."

"Fourteen hundred!" Annabelle echoed. "A distressing sum. Why, it sounds like you could use a wealthy bride, dear brother. Miss Greenwood's dowry would wipe the slate clean with enough left over to fund your hunting parties for the rest of your life. I think she even likes the sport. You have so much in common, it must be fate."

"I don't need that money." Peter's protests were beginning to take on the air of a stubborn child who was not quite ready to accept the futility of his own position. "I'll just ask Father to cover it."

"Again?" Annabelle pulled a face. "Do you think he'll agree? I recall him warning you that last time was really the *last* time."

"That's between him and me."

"I wouldn't be surprised if he decides to cut off your funds once he hears about this," Della said. "You can hardly expect him to trust you when you keep going behind his back to incur more debt after promising you wouldn't. Think how much happier everyone would be if you simply married well and paid up without Papa ever learning of it."

They'd played their hands well, and Della was about as confident as she could be of victory—which was to say, it could still go either way. But Annabelle hadn't quite finished.

"He probably won't believe much of anything you say once he learns how much you've concealed from him." Annabelle inspected her fingernails with a casual air. "If someone were to let slip that it was *you* who compromised Miss Greenwood... Well, I don't think your protests would carry much weight."

Della could only stare, nearly as stunned as Peter by this turn. They hadn't discussed this beforehand! Still, she should have known Annabelle wouldn't hold back.

"You lying little cheat," Peter sputtered. "You villainess. Do you really think you can get away with this?"

"I told you I wouldn't go down without a fight." Annabelle shrugged her narrow shoulders. "It isn't *my* fault you gambled away all your money and hid it from Papa. I'm offering you the perfect solution. But if you'd rather take your chances..."

"For God's sake, I'll do it. On the condition you never speak to me again." Peter was turning green about the gills.

"You will?" Annabelle looked like a child who'd found the pea in her Twelfth Night cake, her eyes growing wide with joy. "I mean, of course you will. You won't regret it. She'll make you a wonderful bride, I'm sure."

"Won't things be terribly uncomfortable at family parties?"

"I promise you, it won't be uncomfortable for me in the slightest," Annabelle said. "In fact, I'd prefer we forget about my history with Miss Greenwood and pretend you found her first."

"None of us has asked whether *Miss Greenwood* will be uncomfortable," Della pointed out. She suffered a trace of pity for the girl, enduring a connection first with Annabelle, and now with Peter! She really could have aimed much higher in life had she not been found out. There was probably a lesson there, somewhere. "Do you suppose this means we're all selfish?"

"Probably," Peter agreed, mopping at his brow with a handkerchief. The stress of their conversation seemed to have overset him.

"Let's write her now and solicit her opinion." Annabelle crossed to Peter's desk to find a fountain pen and a sheet of paper. "I hardly know what to say."

Her long face always looked more serious than her actual mood, but this time the two seemed to match. After a minute spent staring at the page, she scratched a few short lines:

*Would you accept my brother? Forgive me, but there
aren't many options. He is harmless and you should be
able to manage him easily.*

"You do realize that I can read, don't you?" Peter asked. "I should take back my agreement, for that."

"Oh hush," chided Annabelle gently. "Enjoy your beautiful bride and your six thousand pounds. You're getting the best end of this deal."

Thirteen

THE NEXT WEEK SEEMED TO DRAG ON SO SLOWLY IT BECAME A torture. Lyman awoke each morning conscious that he had one day less before Ellen's suit reached Consistory Court. He informed Mr. Hirsch of his troubles (though he could ill afford to spend money on a solicitor these days, his landlord was good enough to offer occasional, friendly advice to the man paying him rent), and was advised that if he wanted the divorce to go through swiftly, the best thing he could do was to stay away from the hearing. The courts were suspicious of collusion, and he would only muddy the waters if he admitted any of the allegations against him. He needed to appear indifferent.

It would give credence to the claim that he'd abandoned his wife.

Lyman was on watch for any further news from Michael, but he, too, seemed to have decided that silence was best. When some mail finally did arrive over breakfast on Monday morning, it was nothing more foreboding than an invitation to the theater.

I was planning to attend Martin Chuzzlewit tonight
at the Lyceum with some friends. My parents were

supposed to join us, but they've just remembered another engagement. Would you like their tickets? You may safely consider this invitation to fall within the terms of your request that our meetings be strictly a business arrangement. I hear the theater is under new manage-ment, so this is essential research for my book!

—D.

P.S. We have more women than men in our number, so you may bring another gentleman along if he is not too dull.

Lyman smiled to himself. The tone was so much like Della that it was hard not to imagine her voice speaking the words as he read.

I should probably decline. Nothing had changed since they'd last spoken—his days of social acceptability were numbered. But wasn't that all the more reason to seize the occasion while he still could? And she'd been considerate enough to spell out plainly that she expected nothing more from him than the pleasure of his company (and possibly that of a not-too-dull friend). It seemed churlish to refuse.

He lowered the note and spoke to Clarkson, who was eating his eggs across the breakfast table. "How would you like to come and see a play tonight? It's a Dickens adaptation. *Martin Chuzzlewit.* There's a group going and they have extra tickets."

Clarkson took a moment to swallow his food before he replied. "I could probably ask Mr. Hirsch for the evening off. They won't mind the intrusion?"

Clarkson watched him with a cautious eye. Certainly there were some members of the ton too snobbish to mingle with anyone a touch lower down the social ladder, but Lyman didn't think Della fit that category.

"Not at all. They asked me to bring another gentleman to balance their numbers."

Clarkson inclined his head in agreement, and Lyman began penning an inquiry for the errand boy to send back in reply. As he wrote, Mr. Wood asked archly, "Who's the invitation from?"

"Just a friend," Lyman replied absently. A moment later, he thought to add, "A gentleman who enjoyed my books and wanted to introduce me to his set."

"Is he anyone I might have heard of?" Wood was trying very hard not to crane his neck, but his eyes kept darting down to the letter, no doubt wondering whether Lyman's friend was important enough to warrant his interest. He was a hopeless social climber. At least there was no risk that he might identify Della from a simple "D."

"I'd be happy to attend if there's an extra ticket," Wood continued hopefully, evidently having judged it likely that Lyman's friends would be worthy of his acquaintance. "I do love the theater."

Lyman raised his eyes to Wood while the ink on his message dried. "I'm terribly sorry, but there's only the pair. Perhaps another time."

Wood ground his teeth, but he and Clarkson left to attend their work shortly after, while Lyman dispatched his reply with an errand boy.

Later that evening, he and Clarkson found Della and her party waiting for them outside the theater. She introduced them to Mr. and Mrs. Williams, a dark-haired couple who seemed quite attentive to each other, and Miss Williams, who bore a strong resemblance to her older brother and said very little to Lyman beyond her initial "How do you do?" Once everyone had exchanged a few pleasantries, they went upstairs to find their box.

So this was the other co-owner of Bishop's that Della had mentioned. Lyman had been expecting someone older. None of them could be beyond their mid-twenties. It seemed their club had been founded by people without much experience in life. Perhaps this explained why they weren't yet doing well enough to hire more staff to lighten the burden on Della.

Mrs. Williams seemed to share his curiosity, for she fixed her attention on him immediately.

"Couldn't your wife join you this evening, Lord Ashton?" she asked him as they moved to take their seats.

Lyman struggled not to flinch. He hadn't been expecting that. "No," he replied carefully. "She's not in town at the moment. She prefers the country."

Once the words had left his mouth, he realized they were probably false. Ellen would need to come to London once the court proceedings began, if she hadn't already relocated before filing her suit. Was that why Mrs. Williams asked about her? Had they met somewhere? There was no way to discover what she already knew without ruining the evening.

Mrs. Williams turned to read her playbill and said no more about it, though the question didn't seem like an accident. Lyman shot a glance to Della, who had claimed the seat to his left. She looked as surprised as he felt, but helped him by turning the conversation elsewhere.

"I had a lovely idea I wanted to share with you," she said, addressing her friend. "What if we had musicians play at Bishop's in the evenings? They make everything so lively! Our members would love it."

Mrs. Williams looked up from her playbill. "That sounds rather expensive for something that won't bring in any extra profit."

"It will if it makes our guests want to stay longer," Della returned.

"I'd rather we didn't change too much at once." A small furrow had appeared between Mrs. Williams's eyebrows. She looked worried, though the suggestion had seemed harmless enough to Lyman. "We've just collected the art you wanted and we're about to add a new table and dealer. Let's take a month or two to see the effect of all that before we throw anything else into the mix."

Della looked downcast, her shoulders drooping slightly. Would it have killed Mrs. Williams to consider the proposal a little longer? Lyman had a hunch that the brief exchange he'd just witnessed was part of a larger pattern. Mrs. Williams looked to be an overly cautious sort of woman, while Della was practically allergic to caution. No doubt they balanced each other out when managing their business, but Lyman didn't like to think how it must feel for Della to be always on the receiving end of a swift no. She had such boundless energy. She needed room to explore her ideas.

"What if you tried it for an evening or two, just to see how your guests liked it?" Lyman suggested. "Then you wouldn't be under any obligation if it didn't work out."

"Oh, that's perfect!" Della exclaimed. "I've already made a few inquiries, Jane. You won't have to do a thing."

Mrs. Williams looked startled by Lyman's intervention. "I didn't think you took an interest in our club, my lord. Didn't you refuse to include it in your book because we cater to women?"

It was plain she'd dug up just enough information to form a damning portrait of his character.

I take no interest whatsoever in your club, he nearly retorted, put out by Mrs. Williams's arch tone. *But I take an interest in Della.*

No. That was no good. She could never be for him, and everyone here knew why.

Della came between them a second time, with a nervous laugh. "Lord Ashton didn't exactly refuse to include us because we cater to women. It was—" She broke off here, and Lyman could see the precise moment she realized that the repugnance of his past made any honest conversation impossible. If her friends weren't already aware that he'd gambled away his country house nine years ago, she wouldn't want to be the one to share the news. "It was a misunderstanding," she finished awkwardly. "Anyway, I'm happier including us in my own guide, and Lord Ashton has been more than helpful in achieving that end."

Clarkson, seated a little further down the row, shot Lyman a bemused look over the heads of the others. Lyman couldn't find any humor in it. He didn't like that Della should have to defend him to her friends, spinning half-truths to avoid embarrassing him.

By this time the footmen were extinguishing the gaslights that lined the walls and the audience took the signal to hush their chatter, putting an end to the conversation. Della cast a nervous glance between Lyman and her friends. He caught her eye and offered a faint smile to reassure her that she needn't worry. It was nothing he hadn't dealt with before.

The play began with the introduction of a great many characters— the Chuzzlewits and the Pecksniffs and the various people who had attached themselves to these families in the hopes of an income—and proceeded to lay out the quarrel of young Martin and his grandfather with an appropriate dose of humor. Della laughed easily at all the absurd characters. Lyman enjoyed the show well enough, but found that her exuberance did far more to draw his attention than the actors on stage. She had lost herself completely in that unselfconscious way of hers, fully immersed in the story before her.

Even as he liked to see her so happy, Lyman couldn't help but recall the last time they'd been seated together like this before a stage. The tableau vivant at Laurent's Casino. When Della had slid her palm over his thigh, beginning an affaire they'd never brought to its logical conclusion.

No. Not logical. There was nothing logical or reasoned about his desire for her.

Lyman stared shamelessly at Della from the safety of the darkened room. It was refreshing not to have to worry about schooling his face into a more impassive expression, as he usually did. No one was watching him now.

She was so lovely. In another life, one where he hadn't bowed to the pressure to marry too early and then ruined his good name, he might have accompanied her here tonight as a suitor. Might have held on to the memory of every precious smile to grace her lips as a promise of more to come, instead of a possibility that was lost to him.

She's for someone else, not you. Nothing so joyful could be for you now.

There was an intermission once Martin Chuzzlewit traveled to America (a horrid place, Dickens concluded), and Della accompanied Miss Williams downstairs to find the powder room, leaving Lyman and Clarkson alone with the rest of the party.

Mr. Williams was a gregarious fellow and soon drew Lyman into a conversation about the places they'd each traveled to. He was much warmer than his wife, who observed them without joining in.

"And what made you decide to write a guidebook?" Mr. Williams asked Lyman.

Conscious of Mrs. Williams's scrutiny, he adopted a self-effacing tone. "I suppose most people would consider such a thing a vanity project, but I simply wanted to accomplish something useful with my time. I considered myself competent to advise newcomers on places of interest, so I did. It was nothing more profound than that."

"And now Miss Danby has followed your example," Mrs. Williams interjected. Her expression gave no hint of her thoughts on the matter.

"That was entirely her idea," Lyman said.

"I know." Mr. Williams laughed. "I was there when it came to her. She was very enthusiastic."

"She often is." Mrs. Williams said gently. She seemed to want to say more, hesitated, then added in a low tone, "I mean no offense, my lord, but I do hope you're being careful with her. Miss Danby might give the impression of being very worldly, but she has a trusting heart."

Too trusting, her eyes added. Whatever she'd learned about him, it was enough to make her anxious for her friend's well-being.

Her husband seemed unprepared for this turn of conversation, watching Lyman cautiously.

"Don't worry," Lyman said with a nod. "I understand you perfectly."

There was no point in argument or regret. Mrs. Williams had only echoed the fears in his own mind. This outing had given him a glimpse of what it would mean for Della if he tried to go out with her in public—pointed questions about his wife's absence, flimsy excuses to paper over his past, fear and suspicion from anyone who truly cared about her. These were the troubles he would offer as a poor exchange for her company.

Della and Miss Williams returned at that moment, and everyone else looked away quickly, as if they'd been caught at some mischief.

"Oh good. We haven't missed it," Della said brightly, reclaiming her seat.

Lyman forced a smile that didn't reach his heart.

"You didn't miss a thing."

If Lord Ashton seemed a bit more distant than usual at their meeting the next morning, Della could only attribute it to the worry he must feel at the prospect of having his personal affairs dragged before Parliament soon. The only good thing was that Della could speak to him freely now. True to her word, Annabelle had relinquished her role as chaperone in exchange for the successful engagement of Peter to her ruined lover.

"How are you? Has there been any news?"

"Nothing yet," he replied. "I doubt I'll have anything to tell you until after the court date."

"When it is, exactly?" She'd known the date, but she hadn't written it down before it flitted from her memory. She only recalled that it was soon. Next week or the one after.

"Next Friday," he reminded her.

How had the time gone so quickly? They might only have one more meeting together, if he insisted on ending their connection if the story should make the papers.

Della pushed the unwelcome thought away. She wasn't ready to say her goodbyes yet.

Ashton must be thinking the same thing, for he wore a solemn expression as he took some papers from his leather satchel. "I reviewed your chapter on the shops and wrote some notes for you in the margins. You'll see there's nothing too significant I would change; it's quite good. Do you have anything else for me to look over?" He paused, then added, "We might want to work quickly."

She had nothing, of course. Nothing at all. She'd gotten home from the play too late last night to start writing the chapter on theaters. Besides which, she hadn't visited any place but the Lyceum recently. It was difficult to attend performances when she could only get away from Bishop's on Sundays and Mondays, and every place was closed on Sunday so it hardly even counted. She'd already shown Ashton the only chapter she'd managed to finish, and their time together was nearly done!

Why didn't I start on this sooner? Della lamented inwardly. She might have accomplished so much more if only she hadn't put it off.

"I, uh...need a touch more time to finish up the next few chapters before I can share them with you. I'll have them ready at our next meeting."

They spent the rest of their half hour discussing how long she expected the book to be, given that she kept adding new subjects. Della assured Ashton that she still intended the volume to be shorter than his original, owing to the omission of several establishments that only admitted men (though she was less certain of this plan than she might have been if she'd only managed to locate her missing outline, which still eluded her). Sooner than she would have liked, it was time for him to go, and there was nothing left in her drawing room but a faint sense of longing.

Della wanted to start directly on her next chapter, but before that, she was determined to pay a quick call on the musicians she'd been thinking of engaging to perform at the club, a quartet Reva had recommended. As it turned out, they would be traveling for another obligation soon but they were free to attend tonight. Though she hadn't planned on arranging the details on the spot, she didn't want to lose the opportunity.

And so went most of her afternoon.

When she arrived in her office at Bishop's—notebook in hand, lest she find a way to steal some time to write during a lull—she found Eli already waiting for her with a fair-haired man she'd never seen before.

"May I present Mr. Silas Corbyn?" They rose to their feet as she entered the room. "This is Miss Danby, the other co-owner of Bishop's."

Oh yes, she still had the new dealer to interview! So much for her writing.

"I'm so sorry, am I late?" She looked to Eli, who gave a sheepish sort of a look that indicated yes, she was. "I was held up meeting with some musicians to play here like we talked about. They're coming tonight, so we need to decide where we should put them."

Della wasn't about to confess that she'd completely forgotten that their meeting with the new dealer was today, despite the fact that Eli and Jane had reminded her twice *and* she'd written herself a note. (No doubt it was with her missing outline.)

Why can't I do anything right?

Della finally turned to assess him.

He was handsome enough, she supposed. Not to her personal taste, but she couldn't complain that Eli had thwarted her plan to find a dealer the other women would stay longer to see. His hair was somewhere between honey and brass where it caught the light, and he sported sideburns that were a little smaller than the standard muttonchop. His clean-shaven jaw had a nice firm line to it, which was further improved by a small scar that wrapped over his chin, stopping just short of his lower lip.

The ladies will love that.

She inclined her head. "A pleasure to make your acquaintance, Mr. Corbyn."

Eli hadn't called for any tea, she noticed, but she didn't like to interrupt the servants in their preparations for the evening at this late hour. Better to leave it.

"Please have a seat." She gestured to the chairs on the opposite side of her desk, while she herself took the large armchair behind it. Mr. Corbyn obeyed too quickly, without waiting for Della to sit first. *Rough around the edges.* Not the best trait for someone who would be surrounded by well-born ladies every evening. "Shall we begin with your telling me how your naval service ended, exactly?" Della suggested, recalling Eli's mention of a dishonorable discharge.

"I don't wish to pry, but I need to know if you pose any risk to our reputation."

"He doesn't." Eli said firmly. "It was all a misunderstanding. I can vouch for him."

Mr. Corbyn glanced around the room, which was still silent and peaceful save for the sound of the dealers setting up their tables and counting out chips beyond the large oak door. "You're a gaming hell. I wouldn't think you'd need to worry too much about a scandal."

Really?

Della shot an accusatory look at Eli, who shot an accusatory look at his friend.

"What Mr. Corbyn *means* to say is that he had a dispute with his commanding officer, but it wasn't due to any fault of his."

"What sort of dispute?"

"I broke his nose." Corbyn muttered through gritted teeth. "But he deserved it."

Good Lord. What did one say after an announcement like that? Should she continue interviewing him, as though breaking his superior's face weren't a fatal flaw?

She would be his superior soon, and she rather liked her face.

"Where is your family from?" Della tried, deciding that she didn't want to ask any more about the fight, lest his answers prove too terrifying.

Surely Eli wouldn't have brought him here if he posed a real danger.

Della hazarded a glance to the man's arms, noticing how muscular they looked even through the broadcloth of his shirt. He wasn't dressed like a gentleman, nor was his speech softened with the polish of an Eton boy. Eli had said he'd been a midshipmen, hadn't he? They were often drawn from the lower classes. It seemed likely that was this case here.

"Don't have any family," Mr. Corbyn said, his voice suddenly hard.

"Oh. You're an orphan? I'm so sorry." She should have thought to ask Eli about his background before this meeting, to avoid exactly this sort of blunder. Maybe the man had suffered a difficult life, and that explained his cold manner and the fighting. Eli was the sort who liked to help those in need.

"Not an orphan," Corbyn corrected. "Just no bloody family worth speaking of."

Oh goodness. She was trying her best, and he really wouldn't give her anything to work with.

"Do you, er, have much experience at card play?"

Mr. Corbyn shrugged, his expression bored. "When we can manage to get a few minutes of rest from our duties, we often play cards at sea. I'm sure I can handle this."

His "this" somehow managed to carry with it an unspoken disdain for everything she'd built over the course of the past three years.

That's quite enough.

Della could forgive him for wasting her time. After all, she wasted her own time in a multitude of ways each day. She could *even* forgive him for making no effort to please her. Not every employee needed to sparkle with enthusiasm. If they were competent, turned up on time, and didn't steal from the pot, she would dole out their pay with a smile.

But to show open *disdain* for Bishop's was unforgivable. She suffered enough of that attitude outside these walls; she wouldn't tolerate it within them.

"Eli, might I have a private word?" Della was using her most polite voice. The one that she only employed when she needed to keep herself from blurting out something truly inappropriate, like, *Eli, why have you brought a violent criminal into my club?* Or, *Eli, if you weren't married to my best friend, I'd demote you to floor-sweep for this.*

Mr. Corbyn rose to his feet and left the room without so much as a backwards glance.

"You can't expect me to take him on," she hissed, the moment the door had shut.

"He's making it sound worse than it is." Eli looked far more worried about earning Della's approval than his friend had been. "I know for a fact that his captain took advantage of a lady, and he was only trying to defend her honor. As for his family, they cut him off after he was discharged without even hearing his side of the story. I don't think he wants to say more because of his pride, but it hasn't been easy for him. He's a good man, Della."

"It doesn't make things any better if he was starting duels over some sort of love triangle! You see why it would be dangerous to put that kind of man into a club full of women, don't you?"

Why did she have to be the one to convince Eli this was a terrible idea? Normally other people tried to convince *her* that she was the one with a terrible idea, and she quite preferred it that way! She wasn't meant to be the voice of reason.

"If Jane were here, she would tell you Mr. Corbyn is entirely unsuitable."

Eli winced at the accusation, but clapped back. "You and I both know that Jane can be overly cautious sometimes." He seemed to regret the words only a second later, for he quickly amended, "And we love her for it, even if we don't always have to make the same choice she would."

Easy for him to say. Eli wasn't the one trying to fill Jane's shoes.

"Besides, it wasn't a love triangle," he added. "When I said 'took advantage,' I didn't mean that his captain simply violated propriety. I gather he was actually trying to harm her. Corbyn was very tight-lipped about it, but I understood that much."

"Oh."

That took the wind from Della's sails. If he was protecting a woman in need, he deserved her respect.

But, oh, it would be easier to bestow it if he hadn't been so rude!

"I still don't like him," she muttered. "He can't swear like that in front of the ladies. And he needs to learn to smile on occasion, or he'll scare them off."

She was speaking as if she was going to hire him. Why did she have such a hard time saying no to a sad story?

"Thank you." Eli recognized his victory for what it was, but he was graceful enough not to revel in it. "You won't regret this. I'll talk to him about his language."

Della heaved a sigh. "You're responsible for him if anything goes wrong. Keep an eye on him, won't you?"

"I'll go start training him for the extra vingt-et-un table right now, only I can't stay all night. I have to leave in about an hour."

"What?" This news transformed Della's voice into a high-pitched squeak. "You're leaving me alone? But we have the musicians coming any minute!"

"I'm sorry, but I didn't realize you'd planned that for tonight. I promised my mother I'd fetch her some things from the apothecary. She's been feeling poorly lately. I thought you wouldn't need me since we're slower on Tuesdays, but I can try to get back here afterward if you think it will be too much for you."

Della didn't like this one bit, but what was she supposed to do, beg Eli to stay? If his mother wasn't well, she could hardly hold it against him. And though he probably hadn't meant anything by it, she bristled at the suggestion that managing the club alone on a Tuesday might be too much for her.

"No, I can handle it," she said with a sigh. "But *promise me* you'll make sure Mr. Corbyn knows what he's doing before you go. I won't have time to check in on him if I'm all alone."

"I promise. Thank you, Della!"

Eli hurried out the door, no doubt eager to impart the good news to his friend. She wondered if Mr. Corbyn would be half so excited by it.

By this point it was ten minutes to opening and Della hadn't done anything she'd intended. She hurried to the kitchen to make sure everything was ready. Cook had fallen behind and was still scooping the filling into her lemon tarts, but there was nothing Della could do for this except urge her on and rush back out again. The musicians had arrived ages ago, and no one had told them where to set up their instruments while she'd been shut up in her office. Della would have liked to consult Eli, but there was no time. She frantically instructed the waitstaff to push the card tables in the largest room closer together to free up a patch of floor in the corner. Not very elegant, but it would have to do. Perhaps she should construct a little platform for next time. Get a carpenter in here and make an elevated area so the sound would carry better. She should ask Jane what she thought.

"I need to run," said Eli, appearing at her shoulder without any warning. "I explained everything to Corbyn, and he promises not to swear in front of the women. Are you all set here?"

Of course I'm not! Della wanted to say. A few early arrivals had already begun streaming in, and no one was ready to greet them except their doorman. They were still rearranging the furniture. Couldn't he see all the work to be done?

"Of course I am," she replied through clenched teeth. "You go on."

The moment he left, she turned to the musicians. "You can set up just that way, gentlemen. Please keep the music lively. Oh, and no polka!"

Lady Eleanor didn't care for it, and if she complained everyone else would follow suit.

"But that's what we'd prepared!" the clarinetist protested. It was too late. He was already speaking to her back as Della fled shamelessly from this problem.

She spent the next half hour welcoming Lady Eleanor and Mrs. Duff and several other of their loyal regulars, until a familiar voice interrupted her thoughts.

"Miss Danby?" It was Geórgios, an old friend of Eli's whose enormous physique made him a particularly imposing doorman. They operated on a system of subscription memberships, and it was his job to make sure no one got in unless they were on the list. "You asked me to tell you if Mrs. Muller came back." He motioned to the cluster of ladies who had just come through the cloakroom.

"Thank you, Geórgios. I'll keep an eye on her." Della had already warned all the dealers that she was only allowed to play at the penny table, and they had strict instructions to turn her away if she tried to place a wager anywhere else.

"And...Miss Williams is also here," Geórgios added. "Should I let her in?" His expression betrayed some doubt.

"I'll be right there," she replied. Della turned to Mrs. Duff, with whom she'd been speaking before Geórgios called her. "Please tell us how you enjoy the music tonight. We're trying something new."

Geórgios was already busy with the next batch of ladies while Hannah stood off to one side, fiddling with her hands. Her face lit up when she saw Della approach. "Jane and Eli said that I could come and help you tonight so you wouldn't be alone."

Thank you, Jane!

Della was so flooded with relief, she swept Hannah into her arms and hugged her tight. "That's wonderful. You have no idea how happy I am to see you. I'm so glad Jane changed her mind!"

She must have felt badly over how many evenings she'd missed lately, and this was her way of lightening the load.

"Er, yes. Me too." Hannah squirmed in Della's grasp, reminding her that she was probably making a spectacle of herself. Della released the younger girl and tried to assume a cool, collected air.

"Forgive me," Della said. "I'm just so glad you're here."

"What can I do?"

Mrs. Muller's name was on the tip of Della's tongue, but then she thought better of it. Hannah was barely twenty, and Mrs. Muller was old enough to be her mother. It wouldn't be kind to ask her to keep watch over the woman as if she were a naughty child. Besides, she wasn't much of a risk with all the dealers on watch for her.

Nor could Della ask Hannah to take charge of circling the crowd and making sure all the women were enjoying their evening. She lacked the confidence for it, and she hadn't been in London long enough to know half of these ladies and learn their little quirks. It would take more time than Della had available to explain everything. What could she do?

"Have you ever been in charge of instructing your housekeeper or your butler about the service of drinks and meals at home?"

"Mama handles all of that." Hannah seemed to shrink a bit as she admitted this. "But I could learn!"

Oh dear. They've sent me a greenhorn.

If only Hannah had come two hours earlier, there might have been time to explain all the workings of the club. As it was, Della was conscious that every tick of the clock took more time from her own duties. She hadn't been able to greet all the women who streamed in while she was chatting with Hannah, and she didn't hear any music yet, which meant she should check on the musicians and make sure nothing *else* was wrong. Monitoring the service of refreshments was the easiest thing Hannah could do that would still lighten Della's load. She would just have to learn as she went.

"Keep an eye on how much the ladies are drinking and whether anyone appears to have overindulged, or whether anyone is hungry and hasn't been offered enough food. Check on our cook and the wine cellar every so often to make sure we aren't running low on anything and send our errand boy over to the greengrocer's if we need it." Was that too much for her? Della felt a bit guilty, but she would be here if Hannah needed any advice. "Oh! And your brother hired a new dealer, Mr. Cooper? No, Corbyn! That was it. He's a bit rough around the edges. Could you keep an eye out that he doesn't offend any of our members and fetch me straight away if there's a problem? He's the blond one with a scar on his chin. You can't miss him."

"Right." If Hannah looked a bit intimidated by all of this, she was too stubborn to admit it. "You can count on me."

"*Thank you.*" Della clasped her friend's hands and gave them a reassuring squeeze. "Just fetch me if there's any problem you don't know how to solve. I'll be right here the whole night." Then she turned and hurried back to the musicians.

Everything seemed to happen so quickly that by the time Della next looked at the clock, hours had passed. The musicians were mostly a success, thank goodness, though they did run out of songs partway through and let a polka slip into their repertoire (which Lady Eleanor absolutely noticed). Della wasn't sure that Hannah was keeping track of the champagne quite as well as she should, for she noticed Mrs. Duff steadying herself on the wall as she made her way to the powder room, but she did spot the girl observing Mr. Corbyn's table, and their newest dealer didn't seem to have made any of the ladies slap him yet, so that was a good sign. Della lost track of them when she had to separate two women who'd begun insulting each other over baccarat. One of them was Mrs. Duff, who had apparently transferred her grudge against Reva to *another* young lady who'd caught her husband's attention.

I'm going to have to talk to Jane about revoking her membership if this keeps up, Della realized with a sinking feeling. But the woman was friends with Lady Eleanor, and it might cost them her patronage if they sparked a row. What were they to do?

And now she spotted Mrs. Muller at Parekh's table (which was *not* the penny table)! Della hurried over, but a discreet word with Parekh reassured her that the older woman was only watching a friend and hadn't placed any wagers. She breathed a sigh of relief.

Everything is fine. Della tried to calm her pattering heart. It felt as though she were juggling more balls than she could catch.

She went to check in on Hannah as soon as there was a lull in the pace of the evening. It was getting late, and a few of the less dedicated players had begun to peel off from the crowd and head home to their beds.

"How are you doing?" Della tried to catch her breath as she took in Hannah's appearance. The girl looked flushed and the wisps of hair around her temples were stuck to her face with perspiration, indicating she might have been run off her feet nearly as much as Della, but she seemed happy. *Wait, is that a glass of champagne in her hand?* "Have you been drinking?"

"Only a little!" Hannah said quickly. "I got so hot when I was in the kitchen checking on Cook."

"It's all right." She didn't look drunk, so Della was hardly about to lecture her. She must get enough of that at home. "I saw you at Mr. Corbyn's table earlier. How is he with the guests?"

"I see what you mean when you said he was rough." Hannah wrinkled her nose. "He swears like a sailor."

Oh goodness. Eli would be upset if they had to fire the man on his first evening.

"Were the ladies very offended?"

"Not really. I think that redhead has taken a fancy to him. The one in the green gown."

"Miss Berry," Della supplied, following her gaze. The lady in question was leaning forward to better expose her décolletage, though Mr. Corbyn kept his eyes on his deal. Would she have to intervene? "She'd best stay well enough away, before she ruins her prospects."

"Why?" Hannah dropped her voice to a conspiratorial whisper. "He's very low-class, then?"

"Not only that. He was dishonorably discharged for fighting with his superior. Your brother could probably tell you more about it than I could, but I certainly wouldn't be caught flirting with a man like that where everyone could see me."

The two of them watched the exchange playing out at Mr. Corbyn's table for another minute, but nothing untoward seemed to happen. Let Miss Berry handle herself then. Della was too exhausted to go looking for new tasks.

"By the way, how is your book coming?" Hannah asked. "Is the viscount being kind to you?"

"*Very* kind," Della agreed with a little wink, but instead of provoking a smile from Hannah, the gesture made her go completely still.

"What do you mean by that?" Her voice was suddenly cold. Sharp as a dagger.

Oh no. What on earth made me say that? She'd been talking with Hannah as though they were old friends. She hadn't thought about the dangers before she spoke.

"Nothing. I only meant—"

"Are you and he...?" The look of pure horror on Hannah's face made her views on the matter plain. "But he's *married*, isn't he?"

"No. *No.* You don't understand. There's nothing between us. It's just a harmless flirtation." Della's words came out in a frantic whisper. *Oh, what have I done?* "And he's been separated from his wife for years, and she plans to divorce him before Parliament, so she wouldn't be hurt by it even if there were any connection between us, which there *isn't*."

Instead of calming the girl, this speech only inflamed her temper.

"Not be hurt by it? Not be *hurt* by it?" Hannah was red in the face and had raised her voice. People were turning to stare. "You're carrying on with a *married man*, and you don't see anything wrong with that?"

"Shhh." Della grasped Hannah's hand, but she jerked out of reach. "What are you saying? Hannah, calm down!"

"Don't tell me to calm down," Hannah snapped. "What a joke marriage is. Don't you care that you're driving a couple apart?"

"It isn't like that. Hannah, please—"

"Get away from me!" Hannah turned on her heel and ran away, the crowd of onlookers parting before her.

How much did they hear? Della tried to draw a shaky breath, but it felt like the air had gone out of the room. Why on earth had Hannah reacted so violently? She might have been a bit emotional over her mother's efforts to marry her off earlier, but this was far beyond anything Della had seen before. In fact, she'd been behaving oddly since she got to London—quite changed from the way she'd been in her previous seasons.

Everyone was staring. Della had to say something.

"I–I'm so sorry about that, everyone. This was all just a misunderstanding." What would Jane think when she heard about this?

Della's hands were shaking, but she forced a smile. She had to act as if everything were fine. After all, an honest misunderstanding wouldn't bother her, and she'd just told her guests that's what this was. "Miss Berry, how are you enjoying your evening? Let's get you another glass of champagne, shall we? I—"

Oh no. Glancing over to Mr. Corbyn's table, she saw that the empty seat Miss Berry had left behind a moment ago had been taken up by Mrs. Muller, who had a heaping pile of chips before her. *No, no, no, no, no—*

Before she could open her mouth to protest, Corbyn was sweeping them toward his pot. All lost.

"Excuse me just a moment." Della was well past the point of being able to smile. She raced to the table, gripping their newest dealer by the arm. "What are you doing?" she hissed. "You weren't meant to let Mrs. Muller bet anything! She's been cut off, remember?"

Couldn't this idiot do anything right?

"You mean that tiny old lady?" Corbyn stared at her in unfeigned confusion. "You never said anything about that."

"Of course I—"

Della's voice died midsentence.

He's right. I didn't say anything. Her stomach threatened to eject the measly cucumber sandwich she'd managed to wolf down in lieu of supper a few hours ago. *I talked to the others before he was hired. I forgot to tell Eli to warn him.*

She was the idiot who couldn't do anything right. Not Mr. Corbyn. Her.

"I..." Della looked around, but Mrs. Muller must have turned tail as soon as she'd seen her coming. The wretched sneak! And after Della had given her another chance out of the goodness of her heart. "Find her. Escort her out of here."

"You want me to leave my table?" Corbyn jerked his scarred chin toward the three ladies who sat riveted to their exchange, each with a full hand of cards already in play.

"Yes. Wait, no." Della could feel something like hysteria bubbling up in her chest. "I–I don't know."

The man was giving her the most insufferable look. She knew the one. It said: *Who put this woman in charge?* and *You don't know what you're doing* and *What a joke* all at once.

"Stop staring at me and go look for her," she whispered. "You take the rooms toward the back and I'll take the entrance. Just don't make a scene." There had been enough scandal for one night. Turning to the ladies, she said, "I'm so sorry, we need to halt play for a few minutes, but Mr. Corbyn will be happy to complete the hand once he returns."

There were protests at this, but Della didn't have time to deal with them. She turned her back on the table and hurried toward the entrance. Sure enough, Mrs. Muller was there, doing up the clasp on her cloak and about to escape. She squeaked in surprise when she saw Della.

"You lied to me," Della said. "You *promised* you wouldn't bet anymore, and I trusted you."

"It was only one little wager!" Mrs. Muller protested. "I didn't bet a thing all night, but then I thought I only needed one lucky hand and I might repay my debt and put all of this behind us. I know I can make it back." She was crying now. A group of ladies beside them had stopped to stare, their cloaks forgotten. "You have to give me a chance, Miss Danby. I can't tell my husband about this. My luck is bound to turn around soon. Just let me make back what I owe."

"I can't do that."

"Miss Danby?" It was Geórgios calling her again from just beyond the front door.

What now?

"Just a moment," Della hollered back. Couldn't she have one minute to catch her breath? She lowered her tone again to finish addressing Mrs. Muller. "I'm sorry, but I have to insist you stop attending our club."

"You can't do this to me!" The older woman turned to the group of ladies watching her. "Do you see how they treat their members? So much for loyalty!"

"We'll refund your subscription fees and deduct the amount from what you owe us," Della said firmly. "Now please go."

"Miss Danby!" Geórgios's voice had grown more urgent.

Della walked a sobbing Mrs. Muller outside to see what the problem was. Geórgios stood barring the way while a gray-haired woman tried vainly to squeeze herself around him. It was Jane's mother-in-law.

"Mrs. Williams, what brings you here?" Della asked, praying it was nothing bad. But one look at the woman's face confirmed her fears.

"Where is my daughter?" she cried. "I know you're hiding her in there somewhere. I demand to speak with her."

Good Lord. How can this night possibly keep getting worse? Della was nearly at the point of following Mrs. Muller's example and bursting into tears. Instead, she forced herself to draw a deep breath. *I can still fix this.*

"Hannah was here earlier, but she told me she had permission from Jane and Eli. Was that...er, not the case?"

"*I* certainly didn't know anything about it. I would never give her permission to set foot in a...a *gambling* den!" She said the words with such horror that they might have been an insult instead of a perfectly factual description.

Hannah must have been lying. Jane wouldn't have given her permission to come without her mother-in-law's blessing. *Why must everyone try to trick me this evening?*

"I'm sorry about the mix-up, but I believe Hannah left some time ago." At least, her manner of stomping away from Della after their row had a sense of finality to it.

"I know she's hiding here somewhere, and I'm not leaving without her."

"Fine." Della was far too tired to endure another emotional

outburst. Two was more than enough. "If you *promise* not to disturb our guests, you can come inside and look through the rooms. If Hannah is still in here, you're welcome to take her home with you." This seemed to appease Mrs. Williams. She was silent, if stone-faced, as Della led her inside.

The club was still busy enough that the task of finding one girl wasn't simple, but things were starting to wind down. It took about ten minutes to confirm that Hannah was not in the three main gaming rooms, nor in the powder room. After a brief quarrel over whether it was necessary to search the kitchens (Della finally relented, and they did), they had made a full tour of the establishment and were back in the largest hall, where Mrs. Duff was complaining that Mr. Corbyn *still* hadn't resumed her game of vingt-et-un and Mr. Parekh was trying his best to smooth things over by persuading her to join his table instead.

"You see, Mrs. Williams? Your daughter isn't here."

"What about that door?" Mrs. Williams asked, motioning to the wall behind Della.

"That just leads to our office. There's nothing else there."

"I want to see it."

"Mrs. Williams, really." Della was fighting to retain her composure. It felt as though everyone had been staring at her since her quarrel with Hannah. "I think I've been more than patient. This is our private property."

"If you're not hiding her, you have no reason to refuse me entrance." Mrs. Williams thrust out her chin in challenge.

People *were* staring. Della wasn't just imagining it. What would they think if she refused, after all that they'd seen tonight? Better to prove that there was no one there before her guests started spreading rumors that they'd abducted a virtuous young girl from her mother to corrupt her with the wicked power of card play.

"Very well," she relented. "But you'll see that there's no one—"

A great many things all happened in the span of the next three seconds.

One: Della turned the knob and opened the door, fully expecting it to show nothing more interesting than the disordered papers she hadn't found time to tidy. Oh! Maybe her missing outline was there! She would give her desk a good search as soon as they closed up.

Two: Mrs. Williams screamed as though she were being murdered, which naturally made every remaining guest in the club rush to her side to see what was the matter.

Three: Della turned her head to find the source of this reaction, only to discover Hannah and Silas Corbyn inside the office. Alone. Together. Kissing passionately in full view of the forty- or fifty-odd women who were still in the club.

Not one soul had any comment on the music that evening.

Fourteen

"I DON'T UNDERSTAND HOW THIS HAPPENED," DELLA WAILED, dabbing wretchedly at her eyes with her handkerchief. "I just d-don't understand. She was scarcely out of my s-sight for ten minutes when her mother turned up! Why should she have th-thrown herself at Mr. Corbyn? She doesn't even know the man!"

Della was on the divan in Jane's sitting room, her friend pacing the floor in front of her. It had been too late to speak with her by the time she'd closed up Bishop's last night amid the murmurs and speculation of their guests. Mrs. Williams had dragged her daughter out by the elbow, too livid to speak, leaving Della to sack a tight-lipped Mr. Corbyn and deal with the aftermath of the most devastating scandal their club had ever witnessed.

The only scandal, really. Even if there were plenty of people who didn't like the idea of a ladies' gaming hell, they'd always managed to avoid any real problems.

Until I ruined everything.

Jane would never have let Hannah fool her. Nor would she have given Mrs. Muller a second chance, nor gotten herself involved with a married man. Della was the one who created trouble, the one who seemed to ruin everything, no matter how hard she tried.

She'd hoped things would look better in the light of day, but the minute she presented herself to face Jane's recriminations, Della had broken down in tears, unable to cope with the certainty that she'd destroyed everything they'd ever worked for.

"Why on earth did you let her in?" Jane asked. Though she looked nearly as upset as her mother-in-law had been last night, she kept her tone measured. It was probably hard to be cross with someone who couldn't stop crying. "You knew I forbid her to go."

"I'm s-sorry." Della couldn't stop hiccuping in between her words. "She said you'd ch-changed your mind and sent her to h-help me. I was so busy I didn't really have t-time to think it through."

"Della..." Jane trailed off, but her disappointment was written on her face. She probably wanted to tell Della what an idiot she was and was only holding herself back out of pity. Della couldn't say she blamed her. Why hadn't she thought to question Hannah's story? She should have known Jane would never have relented.

Della gathered up her courage to ask, "What's going to happen now?"

"That's for Mrs. Williams and Hannah to sort out." Jane shook her head sadly. "I doubt she'll force her daughter to marry a disgraced serviceman. It's more likely she'll be sent away somewhere."

For the rest of her life, or only until the ton forgets? Della wondered. Like as not, they were the same thing.

"And Bishop's?"

Jane finally stopped her pacing. When she spoke, she sounded as if she were weighing each word. "We'll stay open as usual and try to reassure our members that we're still running an establishment of quality."

Della winced at the word *still*.

Jane drew a long breath before she added, "You...might want to take a few nights off. Eli and I will ask his mother to watch Gloria in the evenings so we can handle things."

"What? No!" Della couldn't fight the panic that set her heart racing. "You need me. Jane, I know I made a hash of things, but I can fix this. Please don't cut me out."

Something about her own words triggered a sense of déjà vu. But that was ridiculous. She had never been excluded from her own club before. Then she realized what it was.

She sounded just like Mrs. Muller, pleading for another chance at cards despite the fact that it would only make things worse. Desperate and unlucky.

Is that what I look like to everyone?

"I'm not cutting you out," Jane assured her. "I know you didn't mean for any of this to happen. But you're tired and overwhelmed. I've probably been asking too much of you since Gloria—"

"You haven't." Della scrubbed the tears off her cheeks with the back of her hand and tried to force herself to stop crying. She wasn't entirely successful, as her breath kept coming in uneven gasps no matter what she did. It felt as though she were about to lose her dearest friend. "You can count on me. Y-yesterday evening was an exception, not—"

A knock on the door interrupted them.

"It's probably Eli," Jane explained. "He went out to find Mr. Corbyn before you arrived." Her tone grew flinty on the dealer's name. Della suspected Eli would be in nearly as much trouble as she was over his decision to recommend his friend for the post, but it was different for him. He was family and would always be forgiven.

Except it wasn't Jane's husband who joined them a moment later, but her cousin. Cecily's keen gaze took in Della's tearstained face before she hurried across the room and swept her into an embrace.

"So it's true, then? Hannah compromised herself at your club last night with one of your dealers? How dreadful! I can't *imagine* what you've suffered."

Della tried to slip free of this tangle of arms without appearing rude. "Who told you that?"

"Miss Berry," Cecily replied without missing a beat.

"Cecily, *please* don't repeat the tale," Jane said. "This has been hard enough on Hannah and her mother. We don't need the whole ton talking about it."

"Of course. You know I'm the soul of discretion. But I'd say the story is already out, at this point. Miss Berry made it sound like the most exciting thing to happen all season."

All because of me.

Della was in real danger of crying again, but she couldn't lose her head if she wanted to persuade Jane she was steady enough to return to the club.

Unfortunately, Cecily hadn't even finished yet. "She also told me Mrs. Muller made a scene about her gambling debts, and that Hannah accused you of carrying on with a married man! Whom did she mean?"

Oh no. Della buried her face in her hands. She'd hoped that part of the evening would have been forgotten in the face of the greater crisis that had followed.

"What?" Jane whirled on Della with horror in her eyes.

She couldn't explain herself. Despite Cecily's promise not to spread gossip, she was sure to repeat every word of this conversation to a half dozen intimate friends who would likewise be sworn to secrecy except for a half dozen of *their* intimate friends.

"I'm sorry about Mrs. Muller," Della began. "She wasn't supposed to be gambling but she got away from me in the crowd, and Mr. Corbyn didn't know he was supposed to turn her away because he was new." She drew a large breath. "As to the other matter, Hannah misunderstood me. She didn't know what she was saying."

She didn't like to shift the blame for her mistake, but there was no help for it. If anyone learned of her connection to Lord Ashton, Della would face the same fate as Hannah—a swift marriage being impossible, her only option would be exile.

Hannah hadn't actually mentioned Ashton by name when she lost her temper. As long as no one gave anything else away, the rumor was too vague to pose a serious threat.

Jane was back to pacing. This latest blow seemed too much for her.

"Let me come tonight and help you put things right again," Della pleaded. "You're going to be shorthanded without Mr. Corbyn to deal."

"No." Jane shook her head. "It's best you stay away for now and let things cool off. This is my responsibility. I shouldn't have taken so much time away."

I shouldn't have trusted you. The unspoken recrimination pierced Della's heart. If she couldn't attend the club, she would never have a chance to put things right. All of this was her mess, but Jane would be the one to clean it up.

"Go home and rest," Jane said gently. "You probably didn't get much sleep last night, and I'll have my hands full here sorting out what to do with Hannah. We can talk again later."

Della rose to her feet at this dismissal, weighed down by the knowledge that there would be no coming back from this, either for Hannah or herself.

Lyman was about to set out for the house of the young gentleman he tutored on Wednesday mornings when a cryptic note arrived.

*Come soon, please. There's been some trouble and my
sister needs you.*

—*A.D.*

Lyman would have said that he didn't know any A.D.s, but for the
reference to her sister. Hell must have frozen over if Miss Annabelle
was writing to him. Imagining an increasingly worrisome list of possibilities, he sent a message to his pupil's house to apologize for his
absence and hurried to the Danby residence.

Della might be terribly ill. No, they would send for a doctor, not a
disgraced viscount.

Our trip to Laurent's Casino has been discovered. This possibility was somewhat more likely, though once again, why would Miss
Annabelle send for him? Unless their father was waiting at home
with a dueling pistol and this was her way of luring him into the trap.

When Lyman arrived, the butler bade him wait a moment until
Miss Annabelle came downstairs to greet him.

"Where's Della?" he asked as she led him into the drawing room.

"Miss Danby," she corrected, "needs a minute to fix her face."

"What's happened to her face?" This got worse and worse.

"Oh no," Annabelle added quickly. "I only meant she's freshening
up. I don't think she slept a wink last night, and she'll want to look
pretty for you or some such nonsense."

"Is she all right?" Lyman was relieved both at the fact that Della
had apparently *not* suffered any disfiguring injury and that no one
had challenged him to a duel yet, but he wouldn't mind knowing
what was going on.

"I gather there was some trouble at her club and she's had a row
with her friend over it. She was in hysterics this morning. I thought
you might do a better job of calming her down than I could."

Lyman paused, letting the significance of this statement sink in. For all their bickering, the Danby sisters looked out for each other when it counted. He wasn't sure when he'd earned Annabelle's trust, but he appreciated it all the same.

"Thank you, Miss Annabelle."

Della came in just then, and Annabelle excused herself with a parting curtsy in his direction. Lyman rose to his feet to guide Della gently to the divan. It was obvious that she'd been crying, despite her efforts to hide the evidence. Her face had been scrubbed pink and clean, but her eyes were swollen and dull, with no sign of their usual sparkling mischief.

"What are you doing here?" she asked.

"Your sister summoned me."

"Really?" Della glanced toward the door where Annabelle had just made her exit. "I must be a sorry sight indeed."

"What happened?"

"I've ruined everything, that's what." Della brought a hand to her face as she recounted the tale. Her hands were bare—she must have forgotten to put on gloves in her distracted state. "Miss Williams lied to me about gaining her family's permission to attend Bishop's so that I'd let her in, and then she ruined herself by kissing one of our dealers in front of her mother and half our members."

Lyman had trouble digesting all of this. How did the girl's mother get there just in time to catch her with a dealer, and what had any of that to do with Della?

"I'm not sure I understand how her behavior is your fault. Surely you didn't force her to kiss this fellow?"

"But I was in charge!" Della replied, as if this were sufficient reason to spend the morning in utter misery. "I was supposed to watch out for her."

"It sounds as if Miss Williams did everything possible to prevent you from watching out for her," Lyman noted. "And I imagine you had other things to attend to. Were you all alone again?"

"I wish you wouldn't say it that way. You make it sound as though it's Mr. and Mrs. Williams's fault for not being there, when I really should have been able to handle things. They aren't neglecting the club, you know. They have a family to look after!"

Lyman wasn't entirely persuaded by this, but he wouldn't criticize her friends. It would only upset her further. Besides, he had some experience with the sting of self-recrimination.

"You're very understanding of your friends," he said gently. "Is it possible they might be equally understanding of you? Surely they must see that this girl set out to give you the slip so she could get herself into some trouble, whatever her reasons for it might be."

Della sniffed and dabbed at her eyes. "You don't understand. This is the worst thing that's *ever happened* to Bishop's. If we gain a reputation for ruining young ladies, we might lose all our members."

"In my experience, no gaming hell was ever harmed by a bit of scandal. Quite the opposite."

This seemed to mollify Della somewhat, though she still protested, "For gentlemen, perhaps. Society holds ladies to a different standard."

"Are the ladies who frequent Bishop's particularly rule-abiding, or do they tend to be a more rebellious lot?"

"Stop being so rational! You're starting to make me feel silly for crying so much." Della swatted his shoulder lightly. A second later, her expression transformed into one of mild horror. "Oh! I'm so sorry. I've been going on and on about my problems, and I didn't stop to think about how you must feel. I shouldn't be talking to you about my club, when it—I mean, you must not like to be reminded of all that..."

"It's all right," Lyman assured her. "I don't enjoy being invited to play cards at parties, but this isn't upsetting me."

He studied Della a moment. She looked so downcast that Lyman's instinct was to find a solution for her. Some way to save the young lady who'd been caught with their dealer or to suppress the rumors. But the truth was that there wasn't an easy solution to this problem, and barging in with his own ideas might make things worse. Della knew the situation better than he did.

Instead, he asked softly, "What do you need now?"

Della blinked. She looked startled by the question, as if this were the first time she'd considered it. "I'm not sure," she began. Then, tentatively, she added, "I need to do something to set things right again, but I don't know how I can. Mrs. Williams asked me to stay away from the club tonight."

She fell silent, dropping her gaze to her hands. This seemed to upset her more than anything else, though Lyman privately thought a little rest might do her good.

A moment later Della spoke again. Her voice was very quiet. "I think I'd like to finish up my guidebook so that I'd at least have done one thing right, but I'm afraid I haven't made as much progress as I hoped. I don't know if I'll be able to meet the deadline we agreed to."

She mumbled the words in the direction of her lap, as if ashamed of this confession.

I'm the one who should be ashamed. He'd imposed a two-month limit on their time together out of a selfish desire to get back to his own work, without any concern for how much pressure it might put on Della. He hadn't known her then. He hadn't been thinking of her well-being.

"It doesn't matter if you meet our deadline," he reassured her. "I shouldn't have been so demanding with you. You can take more time if you need it."

"But I don't *want* more time. You might not be there soon! I should have been able to finish this already, if only I hadn't been so distracted. I've had two months and I haven't done anything of any value."

"That's not true," he pointed out. "You saw the views with me, and you went to the shops and the theater. You were researching attractions so that you could write about them persuasively. I happen to think you could write a very engrossing section on the tableau vivant at Laurent's Casino, if you like."

Della smiled reluctantly. "It doesn't amount to anything if I can't finish the book and get more members for our club like I wanted."

"Very well. What would help you write?"

This time, there was no hesitation. "A quiet place where no one will disturb me."

"Shall I leave you to work now?" Lyman didn't like to walk out while she was suffering, but he would go if his presence was a burden. At least Della seemed in better spirits now than she had when he'd first arrived.

"No," she replied. "It's impossible to get a moment's peace here, with Annabelle and Peter bothering me all the time and guests popping by for morning calls. And I can't *bear* to face the visitors who will turn up to sniff for gossip once word gets out. I might ask Miss Chatterjee or one of my other friends if I can hole up in their house, but then I'll feel obliged to socialize instead of writing. What I really need is someone to keep me on task, without trying to talk to me for longer than five minutes at once."

Lyman mulled all of this over. "Would you like to come to my rooms and try to write there?"

It wasn't the most likely place to bring a woman of her status. She must be accustomed to the sprawling country houses of the landed gentry and town houses that made up for their constrained size with an abundance of decor.

"I'll warn you, it's not much," he added quickly. "And there are two other gentlemen who let rooms from my landlady, but they shouldn't be home at this hour of the day. They both have apprenticeships and don't usually return until late evening."

"I don't mind what it looks like," Della assured him. "Just so long as there's nothing to distract me and we can work in peace. But are you sure I wouldn't be a bother? I don't want to impose."

"Not at all. You can work on your book and I'll work on mine. I'm nearly finished my guide to Bath."

"That's perfect!" Finally, Della's smile had regained its usual spark.

Fifteen

Lord Ashton instructed Della to wait on the landing of the stairs that separated the rented rooms from the family's home while he went up first to check that no one else was there. She kept the hood of her cloak pulled low over her brow. Once he'd confirmed the coast was clear, she padded quietly upstairs, through a hall with faded wallpaper, and into a little room that was arranged as a study. It wasn't much, just as Ashton had said, but it was tidy and it carried subtle signs of his presence that Della enjoyed observing.

The walls were papered over in the same blue damask that the owner must have chosen for the hall some time ago. Over this, Lord Ashton had hung many decorative objects—maps from a variety of places, more than one portrait of individuals who seemed to share his eyes and firm jaw, and a series of watercolors that all looked to have been painted by the same hand (one of only middling talent). Della might have dismissed his artistic taste, but the obvious explanation was that he must have sold anything of real value to pay his debts and these remnants were all that he'd judged himself able or willing to keep. Rather than making her sad, Della found something

hopeful in the act of trying to improve one's surroundings in the face
of a setback.

The room had a little window overlooking the street, shrouded
by white curtains, with a writing desk set before it. Beside the desk
were two slender bookcases that housed an assortment of volumes.
At the end of the room, a door stood ajar. Through it, Della could
just see Lord Ashton's bed. She looked quickly away, her face heating.
Perhaps she shouldn't have come here.

Della had taken more than her fair share of risks in her life, but
this one made her unexpectedly nervous. Would Ashton think she
intended to proposition him, rather than work on her writing as she'd
claimed? She'd been too distressed to consider the appearances of
things when they'd left the house. All she knew was that she needed
one thing to go in her favor today, and he'd offered the means to
make that happen. But now that she was here, in a room that smelled
faintly of sandalwood just as he did, the gravity of Della's decision
hit her. She was in the place where Lord Ashton lived, wrote, and
slept, looking at all the things he'd collected and kept nearest him.
This was...*intimate.*

Lord Ashton didn't seem to have noticed her sudden shyness. He
moved quickly around the room, tucking away a few stray objects.

"Sorry about the mess."

"Mess?" Della looked about the room. It was spotless. She'd seen
him move nothing more significant than a notebook and a tie pin.
"I'm glad you never came to my bedroom. The sight would have
given you conniptions."

Why on earth did you say that?

If she'd resolved not to proposition Lord Ashton, reminding
him of her previous (and still recent) proposition wasn't the best
beginning.

He blinked, pressed his lips together for an instant, and then looked quickly to the desk, "Please, sit. Will this be enough space for you?"

Della obeyed, happy to have something else to focus on. "Yes, I should think so. But what about you?"

"I can sit there." He motioned to a little settee in the opposite corner. It was far from the light of the window and there would be no place to set down his pages or ink to write, unless he braced his work on his lap.

"You won't be comfortable. Do you have another chair? We can fit two at the desk."

"If you're sure…" Lord Ashton's doubtful gaze rested on her a moment, then he went out into the hall and returned with a dining chair that he set beside Della.

It was a bit cozy for two people, but they were able to fit both their notebooks side by side. She would just have to ignore the way every rustle of Lord Ashton's sleeve made her want to lean his way and trace the faint stubble on his jaw with her mouth.

The book. You asked him to come here to write your book. You need to finish this if you're ever going to get more members for Jane. Despite everything, she could still do one thing right.

Della sat a bit straighter in her chair and set to work. She'd brought all her notes with her, though now that it was time to assemble them into a coherent whole, she rather regretted her habit of jotting down ideas on whatever was handy when they came to her—the back of a letter, the borders of the morning post, and only very rarely in the notebook she'd purchased for precisely this purpose. She'd shoved it all haphazardly into a bundle when she'd left her house and had a devil of a time getting it back in the proper order now. Once she'd finished organizing her things and actually started writing, though, she found the words came quickly. The chapter on the views was easy. She recalled the way the city had stretched out before them and the pure delight she'd felt at the sight of so many steeples and rooftops bunched together, each hiding an entire world within. Not only for herself, but for Ashton too. The sight had brought a warmth to his eyes that she'd wanted to fix there forever. The lines of strain around his lips and eyes had softened, and she'd known it must be something worth writing about if it had impressed him.

Once she'd captured the feelings of that morning to her satisfaction, Della rounded out the chapter with some of the other vistas she'd explored since. Fleet Street, but also Primrose Hill, Parliament Hill, and the view of the city looking out from the upper stories of Saint Paul's Cathedral. Though none were as exceptional as the bridge, she searched for some pretty language to dress them up. When she'd finished, she set down her pencil and noticed that her hand was all cramped up. She flexed it for a moment, trying to ease the stiffness in her knuckles.

Lord Ashton looked up at the movement, watching her in silence.

"How long were we writing?" she asked. She hadn't thought to check the clock when they'd arrived, and she'd lost all sense of time this morning after being up most of the night.

"A little under two hours."

Most encouraging. She normally didn't get that far without an interruption at home. If only she hadn't been gripping her pencil quite so tight in her excitement.

Lord Ashton was either a mind reader, or he'd grown tired of watching her flex and unflex her fingers, for he took her hand in his and began to massage her palm.

"Oh." Heat flooded Della's whole body, but she didn't pull her hand back. She wasn't sure that she would be capable of it even if she'd wanted to. Neither of them wore gloves, and the rasp of his fingertips over her skin combined with the gentle pressure everywhere it hurt nearly made her moan. She bit her lip and kept her dignity, silently relishing every minute.

"How did it go?" Lord Ashton asked.

"Very well, I think. I've finished the chapter on views, and I plan to start on theaters and nightlife just as soon as I've had a little break."

But Lord Ashton only asked, "Do you need anything? Would you like to stretch your legs and walk for a while?"

You might kiss me, if you like, she nearly answered. That would be a lovely way to reward herself. But she managed to hold her tongue. It was only his kindness after the rotten day she'd had that made her thinking so muddled.

He was still massaging her palm.

"I suppose we can't exactly stroll around Pimlico together," Della said regretfully. She might have liked to explore his neighborhood if they'd been properly chaperoned. She'd never been to this part of town before. But it wouldn't be wise to be seen coming out of the same lodgings.

"No," Ashton confirmed. He finally released her hand, and Della clutched it to her chest with a faint sense of loss. "I can offer you a turn about the room. If you go slowly, you may stretch it out for two or three whole minutes."

Della laughed at the jest, but decided to take him up on the offer. She rose to her feet and wandered to the bookshelves, peering at the titles. She was curious to see what they told him about his character and interests.

Mostly reference materials and scientific journals. Languages, histories, and a touch of economics. *Ugh, how boring.* But wait! Here were a few lonely novels: Dickens, Balzac, and most encouragingly, George Sand, whom Della admired. So there was hope for Lord Ashton yet.

He watched her investigation from the writing desk, unperturbed.

Della returned to her place beside him and wrote for another hour or so, a sense of urgency driving her onward despite the fatigue that dulled her brain. She had returned to the passage on gambling clubs, determined to secure the reputation of Bishop's and make all of this worthwhile. Ashton was so silent, she could almost forget he was there, but for the soft rise and fall of his breath and the occasional brush of his knee against hers when Della shifted positions. It was her stomach that finally made her stop. Though she hadn't even noticed that she was hungry while she was immersed in her text, an embarrassing gurgle from her midsection reminded her that between her distress this morning and her flight to Ashton's residence, she hadn't eaten all day.

"I'm rather hungry," Ashton announced, gallantly pretending not to hear her. "Shall I go fetch us something to eat down the road? I won't be more than a quarter hour."

"Thank you so much," she said. The stress of the day was catching up with her all at once, and she felt pitifully grateful for his kindness. "No one has ever..." She broke off, not sure what she'd intended to say. Della had plenty of people in her life who'd given her presents before, or helped her with something. Plenty of people who loved her, even. She had her parents, Annabelle, Peter, Jane, Reva, Eli, and countless other friends.

But until today, she couldn't say that anyone had looked at her with so much patience, asked her, "What do you need?" and listened to her reply with total sincerity.

He'd given her exactly what she asked for. Not what he thought would be best or what she was supposed to want instead.

"Anyway, thank you," Della finished awkwardly.

He held her gaze for a short moment, his eyes darkening to the hue of an ancient forest, then gathered his hat to leave.

Once Ashton had gone, she was forced to acknowledge that she was simply too tired to work anymore without sustenance. Della rose from the desk and crossed the room to collapse on the little settee in the corner. It immediately let out a groan and sank eight inches beneath her weight.

Goodness. And Ashton was planning to write on this thing? It must be as old as the house itself. She hopped back to her feet and paced the room instead, trying to stretch her legs. They felt like lead. It would have been so nice to rest for a moment until he returned with something to eat...

As she circled the room, Della's gaze slid to the crack in the open door leading to the bedroom. There was nothing spectacular inside; no four-poster with velvet curtains. But the plain wooden frame and thick mattress perched atop it looked like heaven right now. She couldn't, could she?

It would be inappropriate. That was the viscount's bed, where he spent each night. (*Naked, perhaps? Oh dear.*) Della had absolutely no business slipping off her shoes and padding softly into the room, running a finger along the soft linen sheets, and finally resting her head upon his pillow.

Oh, but it *was* heaven!

She inhaled deeply, imagining Lord Ashton beside her. With his scent all around her and the brush of his sheets against her skin, it wasn't too difficult. All she wanted was to bury herself in a comforting embrace and pretend yesterday was a bad dream.

Lyman returned only five minutes later than promised with two roast beef sandwiches wrapped in a parcel of brown paper, but found the room empty.

His heart skipped a beat. Had someone come home and found Della here? But there was no sign of anyone.

"Della?" he called softly. No answer. Wait, there were her shoes on the floor. He set their collation down on the desk and nudged the door to his bedroom open. Della was sprawled diagonally across the bed, snoring softly.

Lyman crossed the room and sat gingerly in the space behind the bend of her knees. Half of her skirts were trailing off the side of the bed, but her legs were firmly on the mattress, her stockings exposed where the fabric had twisted up a little way. He didn't know whether he should wake her or let her sleep, or perhaps try to reposition her in a more comfortable manner. Then again, if she'd managed to fall asleep in her stays, comfort must not have been her primary concern.

Miss Annabelle had said she didn't think her sister had slept all night. Rest was probably more important than food now. Better not to disturb her.

The gentlemanly thing to do would be to put a blanket over her and go wait in the next room until she wakes up.

But Lyman drank in the sight for another moment. He didn't have the right words to say what he felt now. If Della were awake and asked him to ravish her, he would have been hard-pressed to refuse. But the feeling swirling in his chest was about more than desire.

He'd never had a woman sleep in his bed before.

He and Ellen had kept separate bedrooms when they'd lived together. Later, his lovers were ladies in charge of their own households. He'd slipped in at their invitation, then slipped out again before any curious neighbors could spy him in the light of day.

This was something new. Lyman wasn't sure he knew what to do with it—how to fit this development into their agreement to keep a distance between them.

Slowly, he lay down in the empty space around Della's body (a difficult feat, as she'd flung her limbs out in every direction). If he'd been married to a woman he'd loved, might they have passed the night this way instead of retiring to separate rooms each evening? It felt strange to have another person so close.

"Di' you find sumthig to eat?"

"*Christ!*" Lyman nearly jumped out of his skin. "I thought you were asleep!"

"Mmph." Della's voice was slurred and thick. "Awake th' whole time."

"You weren't," he insisted, sitting back up. "You were—" He'd been about to say, snoring, but thought better of it at the last minute. Never mind. Perhaps she was too tired to even realize she'd been insensible in the short time he'd been away. "I'm sorry I disturbed you. I wasn't going to take advantage," he assured her quickly. "I was just—"

What *had* he been doing? Pretending he knew what it felt like to share a true union with someone, instead of a cold parody of it? He couldn't settle on an explanation that didn't sound ridiculous.

"I know." Della had opened her eyes by now and turned to watch him through heavy lids, though she made no move to rise. "I'm sorry I came in without asking. I only wanted to rest my head a minute. I hope you don't mind."

"I don't mind," he said softly.

For a moment, there was a charged silence. Until Della broke it with a whisper. "You could join me if you like."

Lyman could scarcely breathe. He must have fallen asleep beside Della and slipped into a dream.

You shouldn't. It will only make things harder when you part ways.

But Lyman didn't want to stop and consider all the reasons he should refuse. He didn't want to be rational. What he wanted was to forget himself for long enough to be with Della—to drink up every drop of pleasure she offered and damn the consequences. Lyman lowered himself back upon the bed. Not as he had a minute ago, when he'd taken care not to touch her. This time he would touch her everywhere.

He settled his weight on top of Della as he claimed her lips. Lyman was already growing hard, and pressed his hips into hers, but was frustrated to find only infinite layers of fabric to meet him. She winced slightly.

"Forgive me. Am I too heavy?" Lyman withdrew, propping himself on his elbows.

"It's not that," she assured him. "Just that this gown isn't meant for lying down in." With a wicked smile, she added, "Could you help me?" and rolled onto her stomach, exposing a long line of buttons to his reach. Lyman set to work on them at once, but the blasted things were so small that it was hard to push them through the delicate fabric loops on the other side. It was rather like trying to unwrap a long-awaited present, only to discover that the giver had seen fit to bury it beneath five layers of paper and twelve types of ribbon.

"I'm going to need your help getting back into all this again," Della pointed out, once they had finally succeeded in wrestling her free of her gown and Lyman was growling his frustration at the laces on her corset. "Try not to rip anything."

"Might we not burn it instead?"

Ladies' maids were criminally underpaid, if they had to do this twice a day.

But when the task was finally done, the sight of Della naked was worth it. *Holy hell.*

Lyman groaned, falling upon her like a starving man before a feast, running his hands over every inch of her generous curves. Her full, round breasts and the gentle slope of her belly before it reached the spread of her hips. She was so soft. Like silk everywhere.

Della had already removed several of his layers while he'd still been undressing her, and Lyman's clothes quickly joined her gown on the floorboards.

"We have to be careful," she warned him. "I don't want any accidents."

"Don't worry," he whispered. "There's plenty we can do together without any risk."

※

Della considered this pronouncement, though it was quite difficult to concentrate while Ashton was running his lips down the sensitive skin of her throat and his hand was toying with her breasts. She shivered.

She wanted to undo him completely. To drive him wild with desire and smash his typical restraint into pieces. But he was the one driving *her* self-control away.

He has an unfair advantage, really, as my self-control isn't much to start with.

Della ran her hands down the firm planes of Ashton's body, over the scruff of hair on his chest, down his waist, until she landed on his cock and gripped it firmly. His answering groan was delicious. She began to stroke, relishing the heat of his skin in her palm and the urgent pace of his breath. Ashton copied her example, slipping his fingers inside her. He didn't ask for any guidance this time, falling expertly into the rhythm she'd shown him before. Della was truly lost now.

They pleasured each other this way for a few minutes, until Ashton caught her wrist and pulled her hand away.

"No more," he rasped, his face tight. "I want you to finish first."

"I don't mind," Della reassured him. "I'd like to see you come apart."

"*I mind.*" He was using his Stern Viscount Voice, the one she hadn't heard much of since they'd grown more friendly. She might have missed it, at least a little. "I intend to ravish you completely. You may only touch me again once the job is done."

Della couldn't very well argue with that. In fact, the command in his voice was doing just as much for her as his touch. "Very well," she replied breathlessly. "How do you plan to begin?"

"Tell me what you want."

"No, no," Della insisted. "I like it better when you take charge with that scolding tone of yours."

"I don't scold." Ashton drew back, affronted.

"You do, but it's enjoyable in the proper setting."

He scoffed but seemed to consider this. When he looked at Della again, his face had grown more serious.

"Spread your legs for me." His voice was low and clipped. Like a determined schoolmaster.

Della was quick to obey, sucking in a breath at his boldness. *This* was the side of Lord Ashton she'd hoped to uncover.

Ashton positioned himself on his knees at the foot of the bed, watching her for a long moment. His face remained impassive, as if the sight of Della's sex didn't move him, but his cock still stood at attention.

He raised his eyes to meet Della's where she lay. They shone with anticipation. "I'm going to pleasure you now, but I don't want you to climax too quickly. Only when I say it's time."

That would be difficult, if he kept talking to her this way. She was so eager she could scarcely keep herself from leaping on him. Ashton gripped her thigh, his hand hot and rough against her skin. He cocked one eyebrow, as if testing the waters, but the only thing to escape Della's mouth was a desperate whimper.

Now. Please.

He bent his head over her sex, his tongue flitting over the sensitive flesh so quickly she dug her nails into his arms to anchor herself. After so much anticipation, the sudden contact sent a wash of sensation over her body. When he thrust his tongue inside her, she cried out.

Ashton withdrew immediately. "I said *slow*."

"Please," Della begged. "Slow might kill me."

A self-satisfied smile flitted over Ashton's face, but he suppressed it quickly.

When he spoke again, he enunciated each word. "If you can't control yourself, perhaps we should do something less stimulating."

The groan that escaped Della's lips was an explosive mix of arousal and frustration. "I can control myself," she ground out. "Try again. *Please*."

He made a liar out of her within a minute. Though Della bit her lip to keep from crying out the second his tongue reached her, she couldn't fight the pressure that had been building inside her. She squirmed beneath him, her body responding faster than her mind could seize control. Ashton was spreading pure ecstasy between her legs. How was she supposed to resist this onslaught?

I can't. He was simply too good at this, and she'd been waiting too long. Della grasped his shoulders and clung for dear life as her climax shuddered through her, sharp and inevitable.

Ashton raised his head to frown at her. "That *still* wasn't slow."

"I couldn't help it," she murmured weakly. The rush of her own heartbeat was still sounding in her ears. "I was too excited. Let me do the same for you now."

"No. I'm not finished with you yet."

Really?

"This might be a bit much."

"Is it?" Ashton asked mildly, creeping back up the bed until their faces were level once more. "I said I planned to ravish you completely and you agreed. It seems you underestimated my thoroughness." Though he was still attempting to look stern, a giddy laugh escaped Della's lips. She wasn't sure what was in store for her, but it promised to be enjoyable.

Ashton leaned over her and kissed her deeply. His hand traced the contours of her breast. His touch was lighter, more patient than it had been a moment ago. But the firm reminder of his own need pressed into her thigh. How could he stand to wait so long for his own pleasure?

Della slid her hands down to cup his rear and pull him closer, until his arousal came to rest against her sex. A low rumble in Ashton's chest signaled his approval. She loved the weight of his body atop her own; the insistent reminder of his need.

"I want you inside of me," she pleaded. Anything less wasn't enough. She wanted to know she'd had everything Ashton could give her, even if it couldn't last forever. "If you think you'll be able to withdraw in time?"

"I'll be careful," he promised her, his face suddenly serious. "But there's always some risk, and you know I won't be able to offer you any security if there's an accident." He paused, appearing hesitant. "I have French letters if you don't object to my using one. They prevent conception and I could withdraw as well."

Della wouldn't have expected Lord Ashton to have such a thing at hand, as they were generally looked upon with disdain. But she supposed a man in his position needed to be sure. She appreciated the extra measure of care he offered, at any rate.

"All right."

Ashton rose to open the drawer by his bedside, found it empty, and was obliged to spend a moment trying to locate the condoms before he found them in the commode against the opposite wall.

He returned to the bed with a sheepish look that made him seem younger. Once he slid the condom over his length, he paused to look at Della, his eyes darkening. "Are you sure?"

"Yes," she replied without hesitation. She was probably *too* sure— not only about bedding Lord Ashton, but about most everything in her life. Della knew that she leapt into things without thinking them through. Her friends and family would be the first to point it out.

But she didn't think this was a mistake. It wasn't only that she'd found Ashton attractive from the first moment of their acquaintance, nor that she wanted to claim the victory of seducing a man who'd been so aloof at first. Somewhere along the way, it had become far more than that. She'd come to respect Ashton. To trust him as well as her dearest friends. There was something about his patience, his steadfast forbearance in the face of any setback, that Della found enormously comforting. She might once have considered such dependability to be only a step above boredom, but now she saw things very differently. It was a rare and amazing quality, to offer someone else what they needed.

She wanted to give Ashton what he needed too.

He eased himself inside her, breath hitching. Della still felt warm and loose-limbed from her climax, and she took him with ease. A low groan escaped her lips at the sensation it produced. Ashton captured the sound with a kiss, his tongue exploring hers.

He rocked his hips in a slow, deep rhythm. Too slow, she might have said an hour earlier. But now that she was thoroughly relaxed, Della found that she could better appreciate Ashton's insistence on thoroughness. She kissed him back, burying one hand in his hair while the other one gripped his back, pulling him close. She loved the feeling of his firm chest pressing down on her softness. He seemed to savor her body as well, running his hands eagerly over every curve. But best of all was the tension that hummed in his every movement.

Ashton was like a rope pulled so taut it seemed destined to snap, yet still he held firm.

"Please," she murmured. "Let go. I want you to lose control."

Ashton gave a strangled groan as he thrust a bit deeper. "I'm supposed to pull out, remember?"

I don't care, she nearly said. *This feels too good to stop.* But she caught herself in time. That was her reckless side again. She would regret it if she found herself in a family way.

"I need *you* to let go," he commanded, with none of the cool assurance he'd shown before. This sounded more like a plea. "And quickly."

Ashton slid his free hand down from her breast to find the place where they joined, and wedged his fingers between them, pressing down. Della whimpered. He increased his pace, driving her mercilessly toward climax again.

"That's it," he ground out. "I told you I wasn't finished with you yet."

"Ashton," she gasped. "Please."

"Please what?" He seemed to be fighting to keep his voice steady. "Don't stop. Don't—*Oh!*"

Della gasped as pleasure overtook her yet again. A wave of heat seemed to wash over her entire body, radiating outward to her limbs. Ashton rode it with her for only an instant before he pulled out and spent himself against her belly, his face contorting. She drank in the sight. When his own climax had passed, he bent his forehead down to rest against her shoulder, struggling to catch his breath.

They were both silent for a long time. Della didn't think she would be capable of speech for some time yet. Whether it was Ashton's skill as a lover or the effect of too little sleep, the room was still spinning.

He was the one who finally spoke, murmuring the words into her skin in the form of a kiss. "Thank you. I haven't enjoyed myself this much in…" He paused. "Well, I don't know how long."

He rose to the basin to clean himself up. Once he'd put his trousers back on, he turned back to Della with an appreciative glance.

"There are still sandwiches if you want one."

Food! Della felt far too lazy to put all her clothes on quite yet, but she managed to tug her shift over her shoulders and drag her feet to the writing desk where Ashton had set their meal. She sighed with contentment as she finally tucked in. The first bite was heaven.

"May I ask you something personal?" Della said, once she'd had the chance to get a few mouthfuls into her stomach.

"I could hardly object at this point."

Della liked the easy way in which Ashton acknowledged what they'd shared. She'd half feared he would suffer regrets once they left the bedroom.

"Why do you always postpone your own pleasure? You were the same way after the casino. You scarcely let me touch you." She'd never met a man quite *this* patient.

Ashton's face fell. He seemed a bit uncomfortable as he answered. "When I still lived with my wife, we weren't…" He broke off here, searching for his words. "Let's just say there wasn't much passion between us. She thought it unseemly to discuss what happened in the bedroom, and I never knew what she wanted. I always felt that I'd failed her, even before I lost the house." He drew a long breath. "It's important for me not to feel that way again. I want to know that the woman I'm with is satisfied."

"Well, I most definitely am," Della said with a gentle laugh. She took another bite of her sandwich and swallowed before she spoke again. "But I hope you don't put *too* much pressure on yourself. It's normal for things not to be perfect every time, you know. I would have been content just to be close to you."

Ashton appeared surprised by this, but took a bite of his sandwich and said nothing.

"May I ask…" Della hesitated, not wanting to intrude, but letting her curiosity guide her anyway. "If you and Lady Ashton weren't in love, why did you marry in the first place?"

"The same reason most people with a title marry," he said ruefully. "Our families pressured us into it. My father was on his deathbed and wanted to see his legacy carried on before he passed. Hers was eager to consolidate the family fortunes and see her children styled as lord and lady one day. Everyone seemed to want the match except me, and I didn't have the heart to fight it.

"I was very angry with my father after he died. I blamed him for my situation. He'd left me without any other family, and things with Ellen were already starting to fall apart. I began to spend all my time carousing with friends instead of at home. A self-indulgent sort of rebellion that didn't help anyone." Ashton offered Della a bleak smile. "You already know the rest."

"How awful." Della took his hand in hers and gave it a small squeeze.

"I don't want you feeling sorry for me. My present circumstances are entirely of my own making."

"Even so, I'm sorry you were put into that situation in the first place. It makes me very glad my own parents don't care one fig if I marry."

"They may care if you don't return home all night," Ashton countered, with a glance to the clock on his mantel. "It's getting late."

"I doubt they'll notice that either," she replied with a laugh. But he looked at her oddly, as if she'd said something wrong. "What's the matter?"

Ashton seemed to struggle for a moment, then said, "Nothing. It's not my place."

"I don't mean that they don't care about me," Della added quickly, guessing the source of his concern. "They're very kind."

He looked her square in the eye as he spoke. "If I had a daughter—or a son for that matter—I would make it my business to know if they were safe."

"But I'm perfectly safe here. Would you rather they locked me up in a tower, and I never had the chance to sneak into your bed?"

He raised his hands in surrender. "That's why I told you it wasn't my place. I can hardly criticize when *I'm* the person they should be protecting you from."

"Nonsense," Della said heartily. "They trust me to make my own decisions, and I think I've made an excellent decision in coming here."

She rose to her feet and kissed Lord Ashton to underscore her point. "I regret nothing, and neither should you."

At that moment, heavy footfalls sounded on the stairs outside.

I may have spoken too soon.

"Are they on their way up here?" Della asked, worry creeping into her voice.

"Shh!" Ashton looked frantic. He motioned for her to hide in the bedroom (she took the last half of her sandwich with her; she was *not* dealing with whatever this was on an empty stomach), before he slipped out the door. A pair of masculine voices filled the hall a moment later, though Della couldn't make out their words. Whoever it was, he was definitely nearby. *Oh, goodness.*

How was she to get back home?

Sixteen

"YOU'RE BACK EARLY." LYMAN WAS TRYING FOR A NONCHALANT tone, but feared he hadn't managed it. He cleared his throat and tried again. "Is something the matter?"

James Wood stood before him, still in his hat and coat. Lyman, in contrast, wore only his trousers and shirt. This was a marked departure from his usual attire, as he never ventured into the common areas where Mrs. Hirsch or the other lodgers might see him unless he was fully dressed. Wood's expression signaled that he'd noticed.

"Not at all. Clarkson said he would finish up the work that was left," he explained, still eyeing Lyman suspiciously. "Is everything all right?"

"Of course. I was just working on my book. Are you, er, back for the evening, then?" *Please say no.* Wood might take an early supper at the public house down the road or have an errand to run. Anything to take him away long enough for Della to slip back out.

"I suppose so." Wood looked him over. "Why?"

Blast my luck.

"I was just making conversation," Lyman replied coolly. "I'd best get back to my work."

"Did you move that table?" Wood craned his neck to look into the dining room just as Lyman was about to walk away. He crossed through the doorway to inspect things more closely. "And what happened to the other chair?"

"I borrowed it," Lyman replied, thinking quickly. "The one at my desk has a loose leg."

Wood frowned at this. "Of course I don't mind, but I wonder if Mrs. Hirsch might object to you taking things from the common space and rearranging the furniture..."

There were four chairs at the dining table and only three lodgers. The man was insufferable.

"I'll be sure to put it back just as soon as I've had mine repaired." Lyman spoke through gritted teeth. "Good day."

He hurried back into his rooms, careful not to open the door beyond the absolute minimum required to get himself inside. Della had concealed herself in the bedroom, but peered around the doorframe at his entrance. He brought a finger to his lips to signal silence until he came close enough to whisper in her ear. "One of the other lodgers is back early. Whatever you do, don't make a sound."

Her dark eyes grew round at this. She stood on tiptoes to reach his ear and whisper back, "How do we get out?"

I have no idea. If it had been Clarkson that came home early, Lyman could have asked him to wait in his room a moment to avoid embarrassing Della as she left. But Wood would be sure to poke his nose in and run straight to Mrs. Hirsch to complain about the indecency of Lyman having a woman in his rooms. He would get Lyman turned out of the house, not to mention the consequences for Della if anyone learned who she was.

"I'll think of something," he promised. "Let's finish getting dressed." It was the only thing they could do for the moment.

From somewhere outside his rooms came the sound of Wood dragging the table across the floorboards.

Lyman tugged his waistcoat and day coat on quickly, then redid his cravat. In the same period of time, Della started the laborious process of relacing her corset extremely loosely and tugging it back over her shift, so that all that remained was to pull the laces tight again. Unable to progress any further without Lyman's help, she motioned to her back and turned away to let him finish the job.

He shouldn't have been able to appreciate the intimacy of the situation. Not when they were in danger of being exposed any minute. But the heat of Della's skin teased his fingertips through the thin shift; reminding him that he hadn't quite had his fill. Lyman leaned in close to her ear to whisper, "Tell me if it's too tight," as a chestnut curl brushed his cheek.

He could have taken her again right there, if not for their unwelcome intruder.

Della nodded, which he took to mean that he hadn't botched the laces too badly. He had no idea how women got in and out of all these contrivances; it seemed to involve some form of sorcery.

Her gown was next, with its multitude of buttons, and then her gloves. Finally they were both nearly as presentable as they had been several hours ago, except for Della's hair, which he judged beyond his power to repair.

There's only so much I can do.

Once they were both ready, they stared at each other expectantly. Lyman had hoped something would have come to him by now.

With an apologetic look, Della returned to the desk and picked up her pencil.

"How can you write at a time like this?" he hissed, following her.

"He has to leave eventually, doesn't he? And I still have work to do. I may as well accomplish something while we wait."

She didn't even look worried, though she had far more to lose than Lyman did.

"What if he stays for the rest of the evening? You can't intend to wait until he's sleeping."

"I could." Della bit her lip. "I'm sorry to impose on your hospitality, but I don't see what choice I have."

She must have meant it when she said her parents wouldn't notice her absence, but Lyman didn't think Annabelle would be quite so understanding.

"I could distract him somehow while you slip out." It sounded too risky even to his own ears. How could he keep Wood trapped in his room? He might go downstairs and ask Mr. Hirsch to summon his apprentice to complete some task, but then he would have to explain *why*. He didn't want to incur his landlord's suspicion. "Oh! I could find an errand boy to come back here and call him away for some emergency. By the time he realizes it's a hoax, you'll be long gone."

"I'm impressed to see you have a knack for scheming, my lord," Della whispered with a smile. "I wouldn't have thought it. But won't he suspect you?"

Probably. Lyman didn't have a history of playing pranks, but there was no one else around to take the blame, and he'd already made Wood suspicious. "I'll handle it."

Della bit her bottom lip. "Are you sure it's quite safe to leave me alone here when you go out to find a messenger? There's no chance the other lodger or your landlady would try to come into your rooms while you're gone, is there? I'm not dressed for a climb out the window."

"They shouldn't." Lyman frowned. Now he was doubting himself. There was no logical reason Mrs. Hirsch should pry into his rooms, but she *did* have the keys. And while it would be a gross intrusion on his privacy for Mr. Wood to attempt such a thing, Lyman couldn't rule it out completely. If the man suspected him of doing something improper, might he not poke around in search of proof the minute Lyman left? "Never mind," he finally said. "Let's wait a while and see if he goes out on his own before we run the risk."

Della nodded. "Anyway, it will be harder for anyone to see our faces if it's dark out when we leave."

She went directly back to her work, while Lyman found it impossible to focus now. He listened to every creak of the floorboards, trying to pinpoint Mr. Wood's location from moment to moment. Every so often, Della would set down her pencil to ask Lyman's opinion on a subject or to reread a passage she'd written. It was a novel experience to collaborate this way. He might have enjoyed it if he weren't so preoccupied.

When at last they heard footsteps on the stairs, they were coming up, not down.

"That will be Mr. Clarkson, whom you met the other night at the theater. I can ask him to help us. I won't mention your name, of course."

"I trust you," said Della easily. It was hard to believe this was the same woman who'd wept this morning over her club's reputation. Lyman couldn't for the life of him understand why a business should mean more to her than her own well-being, particularly when her family didn't seem to need the money.

Her friends had something to do with it, no doubt. Della was too loyal for her own good.

Stop thinking of that. Lyman didn't want to start regretting what they'd shared so quickly, and dwelling on her club was the surest way to do it. Besides, they had more immediate problems to worry about.

"Wait here," he whispered. He crept into the hall with a light step, meeting his friend in the entryway where he was still hanging his hat.

"Good evening." Clarkson nodded in greeting. His voice was deep and clear, with a tendency to carry too easily.

"Shhh." Lyman motioned for silence as he whispered. "I need you to distract Mr. Wood for me. Can you find a way to keep him in his room for five minutes?"

Clarkson's eyebrows shot up, a smile playing at the corner of his lips. "Dare I ask why?"

"Better not to," Lyman replied with a rueful sigh. Though Clarkson was intelligent enough to guess, he'd rather not recount the specifics of his predicament while Wood was just in the next room. "Will you do it?"

"Of course." Clarkson stopped to think for a moment, his rich brown eyes narrowing in concentration. "Though the surest way to keep him talking is to pretend I'm too ignorant to understand something without his help, which I shall *never* live down. I hope you appreciate what a sacrifice this is for me."

"I'll buy all your tobacco for a year," Lyman promised.

With a look of great forbearance, Clarkson turned himself toward Wood's room. He hadn't yet drawn close enough to knock when the door opened and its occupant stepped out. He looked startled to find both men watching him.

"I thought I heard you come in." Wood nodded toward Clarkson. "Did you finish reviewing the jurisprudence for Mr. Hirsch?"

"Yes, but I'm not sure how to interpret an older case I found. Would you have time to go over it with me before I turn in my notes? You might spot something I've missed." Clarkson was doing a convincing imitation of someone who looked up to Mr. Wood, which couldn't be easy. But just as Lyman had started to slip away, confident that all was in hand, his friend's tone changed. "Wait a minute. Is that my cravat?" He pointed at the blue silk encircling Mr. Wood's collar.

"What?" Wood glanced down. "No, I don't believe so. I have one in this color, you know."

"It's been missing for weeks. Did you borrow it without asking?"

"What an accusation!" Wood turned to Lyman for assistance, forcing him to halt his retreat. "Are you hearing this?"

"Mr. Clarkson, didn't you have something you wanted Mr. Wood to look at?" Lyman tried hopefully. But the subterfuge was forgotten.

"Let me see it," Clarkson insisted. "Mine has my initials sewn in at the back. Then we'll know."

"This is absurd!" Wood huffed with indignation. "I won't be treated like a common thief in my own home."

"I never said you were a thief," Clarkson replied, his voice tight. "I said that it looks exactly like the cravat I've been missing and I want to check for my initials. Perhaps the washerwoman mixed it up."

This didn't sound like an explanation that anyone believed for an instant, but it would have allowed Wood to save face, if only he would take the opportunity. "I can't believe your insolence! If you keep this up, I'll have words with Mr. Hirsch."

Clarkson snorted. "You're going to ask him to preside as judge in a dispute over a cravat?"

Wood grew red in the face. "I'll tell him you've been harassing me with unfounded accusations!"

"Fine," Clarkson said. "Keep my cravat. I'll buy another." He didn't sound happy about it, but the embarrassment of taking the quarrel to Mr. Hirsch must have outweighed the value of the patch of silk in his estimation.

"It isn't yours," Wood returned peevishly.

"Which you could easily prove by letting me have a look."

"You've no right to look! My word as a gentleman should be

enough." Wood stamped his foot on the floor. "That's it. I *am* going
to tell Mr. Hirsch about this. He should know what sort of man he's
opened his house to." Wood strode toward the door.

"You can't be serious," Clarkson called after him, hurrying to
catch up. "I said you could keep the bloody thing."

Lyman didn't waste a minute. This wasn't the method he would
have chosen to empty the second floor, but empty it was, and who
knew for how long. He raced back to his room and motioned to Della.
"Hurry, they've gone downstairs for a minute. If we're quick, we can
have you out of here before they return."

Della didn't need a second warning. She snatched up her things
and scurried to the door, holding the hood of her cloak up to hide
her face as she went. They paused at the top of the stairs to listen.
They could hear knocking on the first floor below and a flurry of
voices as the argument was recounted. A click of the latch signaled
that they'd gone inside.

Lyman went first, motioning Della to follow as he confirmed the
landing was safe. They fled the street as soon as they could to find
a hansom cab on the corner. He didn't feel right sending Della off
alone with an unknown man as her driver, so Lyman accompanied
her to Mayfair and said his goodbyes there.

"I'm terribly sorry about all of that," he began. "I should have
known it was too risky to bring you to my lodgings."

"Don't be sorry," she said quickly. "I don't regret a thing."

She was daring enough to risk a kiss, her mouth brushing over his
so quickly that Lyman scarcely had time to reach out to touch her
before she pulled away, and then he was watching the sway of Della's
skirts as she rushed back to the safety of her front door.

By the time Lyman had made his way back to the Hirsch residence, the quarrel was long over. Wood was barricaded in his room,
though Clarkson came out to greet him at the sound of the door.

"It *was* my cravat," he announced with grim satisfaction. "The initials were right where I said."

"Where on earth have you *been*?" Annabelle was waiting to confront her as soon as Della arrived home. "You've been gone all day, and without a chaperone. I hope you weren't with Lord Ashton all this time."

"You're the one who sent for him in the first place," Della reminded her. "What did you think would happen?" But the reminder of her sister's role in starting the whole evening had her feeling charitable enough not to start a quarrel. "Don't worry. I only wanted to work on my book without any disturbances, that's all."

"You've been gone nearly ten hours!"

"Another of the lodgers came home earlier than expected and I had to wait him out. The important thing is that I'm back safe and sound, and I finished two whole chapters plus my introduction."

"That doesn't sound like very much for all the time you were there," Annabelle observed wryly. "How did you and your viscount pass the rest of the day, I wonder?"

"I won't listen to such wild accusations," Della replied. It was all she could do not to squeal with glee at the memory. She judged it best to change the subject before she gave herself away. "You just don't have any proper conception of how long writing takes. Anyway, did I miss anything here while I was out?"

"Supper. Also, several of your friends came to call, including Jane. She left a note."

"Thank you."

Once her sister had accepted that no further information would be forthcoming and given up trying to learn more, Della went to retrieve her messages and asked a footman if Cook would be kind enough to prepare her a plate of leftovers she might take in her room. While at Ashton's lodgings, she'd succeeded in forgetting the catastrophe at Bishop's for a short time, but now it all came rushing back.

She flipped through the calling cards, casting aside all those that weren't Jane's.

Della,

> *All is in hand. Eli and I will handle the club tonight while his mother watches Gloria. I have persuaded Cecily to help us counter the rumors. (I know, not the most likely solution but she is good with people.) Get some rest. I'll try you again when I have more time.*

> *—Jane*

Cecily? *Cecily?* It should be Della's job to quell the rumors and smooth over ruffled feathers, not hers! Della had years of practice keeping their members happy. She was *good* at it. Why should Jane suddenly trust her cousin, when the pair had been rivals more often than friends?

Della set the note down and began flipping through the other cards she'd tossed aside. Miss Berry, Lady Eleanor, Miss Anwar... It seemed many of her regular attendees had stopped by the house this morning to discuss what they'd seen or heard last night. And now Della couldn't return their calls unless she consulted Jane or Cecily first, lest she say something that contradicted their story.

As she picked at her meal, Della wondered what type of reception she would receive at the Williamses' town house when she next called. What if she arrived to find Hannah in the middle of packing her bags for an extended voyage to the continent? Her mother probably wouldn't be too happy to see Della again, assuming the poor woman hadn't keeled over from apoplexy yet.

It's too late to call anyway. They'll have left for Bishop's hours ago.

The doors would already be open by now. Would there be more members than usual, drawn by the scent of gossip, or less, as women sought to avoid being tainted by association? She wasn't sure what news would be harder to receive—that Jane hadn't been able to solve everything without her, or that she had, proving once and for all that Della was entirely superfluous in this operation.

It was too maddening to think of it, so Della resolved to stop. She was exhausted, and her bed was right here. Although it had the disadvantage of not having the Viscount Ashton inside of it, it was otherwise quite comfortable. Besides which, she had the memory of their recent lovemaking to warm her as she slept.

Seventeen

LYMAN DIDN'T SEE DELLA AGAIN UNTIL THE EVENING OF HER family's ball. Peter Danby's invitation seemed so long ago that he'd nearly forgotten about it. But even his usual worries over the threat of discovery and his imminent hearing before the Consistory Court couldn't provide an excuse to keep him away. From their first meeting, he'd been curious to see what sort of people had produced a woman as singular as Cordelia Danby. Now he would finally know.

Mr. and Mrs. Danby proved to be surprisingly ordinary. He was a polished gentleman somewhere in his mid-fifties, with muttonchop sideburns and a trimmed mustache framing his smooth-shaven chin. She looked to be about a decade younger than her husband, with rich chestnut hair going toward gray and a plump, smiling face that reminded Lyman of her daughter. They greeted Lyman warmly and asked him a few polite questions—what part of the country he'd grown up in, whether he were already acquainted with the other guests in attendance, and lastly, how he'd met Peter. If Lyman betrayed any surprise over this assumption, the Danbys didn't notice. He'd barely had time to explain that their son was an admirer of his guidebooks before they turned their attention to the next arrival and repeated a similar welcome. The questions seemed automatic, though the Danbys were charming enough and gave each guest their full attention for the brief minutes they spent with them. Lyman found Della and her brother beneath a large oil painting of a coastline in a brewing storm. "I thought you said that your parents knew you'd been meeting with me to work on your manuscript," he said, once he'd greeted them.

"They do." A small worry line appeared in the middle of Della's brow. "Why, what's the matter?"

"They didn't seem to realize we knew one another when I met them just now."

"Oh, they probably just forgot." Della gave a light laugh, her brow growing smooth once more. "That's just their way. I wouldn't think anything of it."

"I'm so glad you could join us," Peter cut in before Lyman could respond. He had a fair-haired woman on his arm. "May I present Miss Greenwood?"

"How do you do?" Lyman was obliged to give the young lady a few moments of his attention, and the opportunity to say anything further on the subject of Della's parents slipped away.

Though no one else thought anything of it, the encounter troubled him. Was writing a lady's guidebook really such a mundane occurrence that it hadn't warranted the notice of anyone in her family? Except for Annabelle, they never seemed to wonder how she spent her time.

Lyman found the echo of his concerns later that evening, when they sat down to supper. They were an intimate number around the table, perhaps thirty people all told, as most of the guests would be arriving after the meal. For now there was only the Danbys, the Greenwoods, and four or five other families with children old enough to be out. Among them, Lyman recognized the St. Claires, a couple that he had a passing acquaintance with from before his disgrace. He hadn't seen them in over a decade, but the husband had obviously recognized him. They'd spent enough evenings gambling together at White's.

Would they recount his past to the others as the night wore on? *Perhaps this will finally be the thing to provoke some concern from the Danbys for their daughter's welfare,* Lyman thought grimly.

There was nothing he could do about it. He tried to steer clear of their side of the table.

Peter Danby was seated across from him and kept peppering Lyman with questions about the upcoming season at the Lyceum, so that he scarcely had a chance to speak to Della until the main courses arrived. She'd been lost in conversation with a gentleman to her right, but in a brief lull she turned toward Lyman and spoke in a low voice.

"What do you think of the idea of including a chapter on all the hospitals in town?"

He blinked at the abrupt shift in topic. Peter, who'd overheard them while his attention was fixed on Lyman, used this hesitation to put forward his own opinion. "I thought it was a guide for sightseeing. Who on earth would want to tour a hospital for fun?"

"Women, of course." Della gave an exasperated sigh. "For *charity*, Peter. You remember, it's the thing you're always saying I should do more of."

"So you're really going to write up a chapter on Bethlem?"

"Yes." Della sat very stiffly in her chair. Though she kept her voice light, it was apparent he was embarrassing her. "And the Royal Hospital Chelsea and Christ's Hospital, and whichever others I'm forgetting now."

Peter caught Lyman's gaze, then rolled his eyes as if to say *Can you believe it?*

Lyman paused halfway through the act of cutting his lamb. Had he done something to give this man the impression that he was eager to look down on Della? He was behaving as if they were old friends, snickering at an outsider. It wasn't just this evening either. He'd been much the same when they'd signed the contract.

Lyman understood his error now. He'd been reluctant to speak up in front of Mr. Armstrong, unsure how it might be received, but his silence had only encouraged whatever this was. He should never have let it go on.

"I think it's an excellent idea, Miss Danby," Lyman said pointedly. "I wish I'd thought to include hospitals in my guide. I'll be glad to see you correct the omission."

Lyman put on his best viscount face—the one his father had used on underlings he wanted to frighten—turned to Peter, and said nothing for a full five seconds without breaking eye contact.

"Well, I suppose... Of course, if you think it best—" Peter coughed and reached for his drink.

"Don't forget Greenwich Hospital," Miss Annabelle added from across the table, breaking the tension. "They have a chapel and dining hall with all sorts of paintings you can visit, though there's an admission fee for those."

Suddenly Lyman recalled something Clarkson had told him once. "I believe that Guy's Hospital will even allow interested members of the public to request tickets to view some of their surgical operations being performed. That might be worthy of a mention as well."

"My!" Della's cheeks had turned pink. She smiled as she turned from Annabelle to Lyman. "Thank you for all these suggestions. Though I don't know if the prospect of viewing an operation might be too gruesome for a ladies' guide?"

Lyman raised an eyebrow. He hadn't been expecting that. Della must have read his mind, for she laughed and colored more deeply.

"You're quite right. If it's likely to be of interest to at least a portion of my readers, I must include it. Who am I to say there are no aspiring lady surgeons who might thank me?"

It surprised him how quickly they'd learned to read each other. Della was easy enough, for she wore her thoughts openly on her face, but people didn't normally find him quite so easy to pin down unless he spoke his mind. Yet she'd known what he was thinking instinctively.

Peter held his tongue and asked Lyman nothing more about theaters or hospitals or anything else for the rest of the meal.

Della had rarely seen her brother so uncomfortable, and she was quite delighted by the sight. It did him a world of good to be put down by a gentleman he respected from time to time.

"Thank you," she whispered to Ashton, once Peter was distracted by a conversation with Miss Greenwood.

He didn't need to ask what for. His jaw was tight as he murmured, "They shouldn't talk to you that way."

"It's only Peter. He's always been a bit smug, but he means well."

"It isn't only Peter," Ashton insisted. "And I wish you wouldn't pretend it doesn't matter how other people treat you."

Della found herself momentarily unable to reply to this. Her throat was suddenly tight, though she hardly knew what they were talking about. "I don't—"

She couldn't finish, so Ashton went on. "You've worked hard and you've accomplished a great deal in your life. Your family should be proud of you. Just because your achievements aren't conventional doesn't make them any less important."

Oh goodness. She was getting far too emotional over the praise he offered; any more might be dangerous. They were at her parents' supper party, for pity's sake. What was she to do if she started tearing up?

She took a long swallow of her wine.

Why should Ashton be so good to her when they were destined to part ways? His court hearing was only a few days away. This might be the last time they saw each other, if he stuck to his foolish resolution to put distance between them once his name was in the papers.

I don't want to say goodbye. She was about to take another drink, but thought better of it and set the glass down. She was going to make herself weepy.

She would far rather make the evening memorable.

"I have a painting I'd like to show you in the study," she said abruptly. "If you can spare a little time when the men go out to smoke. It won't take a minute."

"You—" Ashton bit his tongue as he understood.

"It's just down the hall to your right, second door you see."

"Here," he murmured the word so softly Della could scarcely hear him. "You can't mean it."

"I'm only showing you a painting."

But Della did not show him a painting.

Instead, when the men retired to smoke and they'd slipped away to find one another in the study, she pressed herself into Ashton and kissed him with all the urgency of someone who only has a few minutes of freedom. She tugged her hand free of its glove to run her fingers over the stubble on his cheek, savoring the rough scrape of it against her skin.

"I can't believe this." He broke off their embrace to hiss at her furiously. "What if we're caught?"

"You shouldn't have come if you're so worried," Della retorted. "Now be quiet and let me do something nice for you."

She showed him exactly what she meant by reaching for the falls of his trousers. His swift intake of breath marked the fate of the first button.

"Della..." Ashton's voice had grown thick. He did nothing to stop her as she pulled his member free and began to caress him. A soft moan escaped his lips. She kissed him once more, then lowered herself to her knees. "Wait," he said. "I can't touch you like this."

"I told you, I want to do something nice for you," she repeated. "Why don't you let yourself enjoy it?" It wasn't as though he hadn't been generous with her the other night. Now she would return the favor.

Ashton gripped her shoulder as she took him into her mouth, his fingers pressing into her as if to steady himself. His cock was harder than it had been only a moment before, as his breath came in a faster rhythm. He relaxed his grip and slid his hands over her gently. At least, the parts of her he could reach. He caressed her hair, then the back of her neck.

Della raised her head to scold him. "You're holding back."

"I am not."

"We don't have much time," she reasoned. "I want you to let go completely." While their circumstances provided a handy excuse, Della was honest enough to admit (at least to herself) that this was exactly what she'd wanted from the start. A reason for Ashton to surrender.

He held her gaze for a second. There was a hint of uncertainty there, but finally he nodded. She bent her head once more, pleasuring him at a more urgent pace. She spared nothing, and Ashton was soon gasping for breath. His reserve didn't break away in an instant with his promise. Rather, it crumpled in little starts and shudders, until he'd given himself over entirely to Della's seduction. She slipped a hand up to pull him closer, urging him on.

The fact that they were risking discovery at any moment only added to the thrill of having Ashton exactly where she wanted him. Della wouldn't have traded this moment for anything, not even the pleasure she'd found in his bed. She could tell when she'd brought him close, and savored the play of tension in his body. She would have liked to hold him there on the edge for a little longer, but that game would have to wait for another day. Besides, Ashton wasn't holding back any longer. He jerked his hips and groaned as he found release, his grip biting into her shoulders. When he'd finished, he swayed on his feet.

Della arose victorious. She couldn't keep a smug little grin from her face, which called an answering warmth to Ashton's eyes when he saw it.

Yet the satisfaction was fleeting. It wasn't enough to know that she'd brought Ashton to the edge. She wanted to *keep* doing it. She wanted him to look at her that way again and again, instead of only once.

She hadn't quite figured out how she could achieve that part.

Lyman scarcely knew how he found his way back to the smoking room. He couldn't think straight after what Della had done. But even though his pulse was still crashing in his ears, no one spared him a second glance as he slipped in the door. The men were all occupied with their own conversations, exchanging ideas in between whisps of smoke that filled the room with notes of spice and oak.

A footman offered him a brandy, which Lyman declined with a word of thanks.

He didn't miss drinking, except for the social aspect of it. It didn't call to him the way the cards did. But the two things had always gone hand in hand when he was still living recklessly, and if he permitted himself a glass or two, it would only be a matter of time before he ventured to play.

He couldn't diminish his good judgment that way.

He did, however, accept one of Mr. Danby's Havana cigars. "An excellent batch," the man said as he offered Lyman the matchbox. "Worthy of a celebration." He winked toward his son, but had moved on to tend to the next guest before Lyman could ask what he'd meant.

There must have been a question in his eyes, for Peter answered it. "We're meant to announce my engagement to Miss Greenwood later, once all the guests arrive."

"Oh." Lyman tried not to let his surprise show. He hadn't realized that there was any attachment between them. Though he'd noticed Miss Greenwood often seemed to be at Peter's side, she'd never looked particularly enthusiastic about her position. He'd assumed there was only some family obligation linking them, the way the children of intimate friends were often pressed into the same circles. "Congratulations."

"Thank you." Peter took a little puff of his cigar through thin lips. Without the women around, he'd lost some of his bluster, appearing more sheepish than arrogant. Or perhaps that was simply the after-effect of Lyman having undermined him earlier. In any event, he kept his gaze downcast as he added, "I wouldn't mind a spot of advice, actually. If you have a moment."

"Of course."

Peter cast a nervous glance around the room before he made his confession in a low whisper. "I'm not sure I'm ready to marry yet. Everything happened so fast that I hardly had time to think it over."

Lyman immediately regretted having offered his ear. He was the last person who should give Peter advice on something like this.

But even if the young man could be a bit much at times, he was still Della's brother.

"I'm probably not the best one to advise you," he warned. Della must not have told her brother how Lyman had ruined his own marriage, or Peter wouldn't have come to him with this. "Perhaps your parents might be a better choice?"

"Hmm." Peter gave a humorless smile. "They just said they were sure it would all turn out well."

"What made you decide to propose to Miss Greenwood?" Lyman tried. Maybe if he reminded Peter what he loved about the young lady, it would help to restore his confidence. Remind him of what they had in common, or why he wanted to—

"My family pressured me into it."

A sinking feeling congealed in Lyman's gut, and he didn't think his supper was to blame. Peter only looked to be twenty-one or twenty-two, at a guess. About the same age Lyman had been when he'd married Ellen. But the Danbys didn't have a title to pass on. Why were his parents in such a hurry to shackle the boy into an arrangement if there was no affection between the couple? Maybe passing on the family name and fortune was enough incentive, even without a title.

"I was an only son as well," Lyman confided. "My father took ill when I was about your age and wanted me to marry quickly so he could see his line carried on before he passed."

"Were you happy with the woman your family chose for you?"

Here we come to it. Peter looked at him so earnestly, it reminded Lyman of Della. Their eyes were the same: a warm brown framed by thick lashes. They both trusted him without a second thought, though he'd never done anything to deserve it.

He couldn't lie, even where manners demanded it.

"No," Lyman admitted. "We were ill-matched, and we hurt each other often, though neither of us meant to." Since he was being honest tonight, he felt compelled to add, "The fault was mine."

"I expect it will be my fault too, if things go poorly." Peter took a large swallow of his brandy, staring darkly into the glass. "But what am I supposed to do, break my word? I can't say I've changed my mind *now*."

What was he supposed to tell the boy? It was true—he was already trapped.

"Why don't you plan a long engagement? Give yourselves some time to get to know one another. If you're ill-suited, perhaps she'll release you."

Peter took another drink, draining his glass. "Impossible. They want us married by special license."

Another similarity between them, though Lyman had no reason to think Peter's parents were trying to outrace death. Like as not, they only wanted to be fashionable. But whatever their reasons, it didn't lessen the pressure they were putting on their son.

Everyone wanted to see their children settled, their legacy secure, but they never stopped to think about the harm they might do. Peter and Miss Greenwood were the ones who would have to live with the consequences if they were wrong. He couldn't let the error pass while he might do something to stop it.

"Tell your families you need more time," he suggested. "You're the one who'll be bound to Miss Greenwood for the rest of your life. They have no business pushing you into something you might regret."

It might not be his place, but if he could save Della's brother from a life of misery, it was the right thing to do.

"What on earth did you say to my brother?" Della hissed, the minute she could contrive to get Lord Ashton alone in a darkened corner of the room. The men had rejoined the ladies a half hour ago. Peter had wasted no time informing his sisters that their deal was off before he went to impart this news to Miss Greenwood's father, who looked as though he was only holding on to his composure due to the presence of so many other people.

"Pardon?" Ashton had the nerve to blink at her in confusion, as if he had no idea what she meant.

"His *engagement*. The one that my parents were planning to announce tonight," Della explained. "He's just told Mr. Greenwood that he needs more time to think things over, and now half the people in this room are trying not to let the other half see that we're at each other's throats."

"Oh." Now Ashton understood her. The expression on his face was a blend of guilt and defiance, which didn't bode well for the rest of the evening.

Peter had been infuriatingly vague about his reasons, but whatever had possessed him to do such a thing, it had come about while he'd been away with the men. "He was fine at supper," Della continued. "Something must have happened while you were in the smoking room. And my father told me that he was speaking to you practically the whole time."

Ashton cast a glance around the room, but with the additional guests filtering in for dancing after their meal, most of the household was occupied with greeting the new arrivals. They had as much privacy as they could hope for.

"I only told him that he should delay things until he was sure." His green eyes flashed with resolve as he spoke. "I don't see what's wrong with that."

Why should it be any of his business what Peter does? Ashton was hardly the sort to meddle in someone else's romantic dilemmas.

"If he jilts her now, both their reputations will be ruined. Go and tell him to stop this foolishness before it's too late. He has to marry Miss Greenwood."

"Why? Because your parents say so? He deserves some control over his own life."

"Our parents have nothing to do with it," Della retorted in an urgent whisper. "Annabelle and I are the ones who arranged the match."

Ashton drew back at this, surprised. "But why would you do that to your own brother? He doesn't love this girl. They'll be miserable together."

Miserable? Miss Greenwood was pretty and wealthy—nearly the only two traits that everyone looked for in a spouse. Were it not for her indiscretion, she would have had her pick of suitors.

"Why would you assume they'll be unhappy together? She has plenty of good qualities. Peter isn't charming enough to find himself a better bride, but he's harmless and won't mistreat her. Happy marriages have been built on far less."

"I can't believe this." Ashton was staring at Della as if she were a stranger.

Her heart began hammering. She hated when people were cross with her. If only she could make him understand that this was in everyone's best interest! But how could she explain herself without giving away Annabelle's secret?

"I know it might look like it from where you stand, but my sister and I had good reasons for proposing this match. It wasn't done on a whim." Everything would be ruined if the engagement fell apart now. Even if Della was starting to doubt her choices in the face of Ashton's criticism, it was still the lesser of two evils.

Besides which, it was too late for Peter to back out. He'd already let Mr. Greenwood believe that he was the one who'd snuck from his daughter's bedroom. The time for second thoughts has passed.

"What about Peter's wishes? Doesn't anyone care how he spends the rest of his life?"

"Of course we do," Della protested. "But you're presuming Peter will hate being married to Miss Greenwood, when we know nothing of the sort. Or that he would make a better choice for himself if left to his own devices, when the truth is that he spends most of his days in total idleness. A little responsibility might do him good!"

Ashton's face was hard and unrelenting. He was plainly unwilling to even consider the possibility that Della might know more about the situation than he did.

"I know this must bring up unpleasant memories," Della continued, "but Peter isn't you. Your past isn't his future."

This had been the wrong thing to say. Ashton's face closed off completely, the hard planes of his jaw tightening into stone.

"You'll forgive me," he said coolly. "I have somewhere else to be this evening."

"Ashton!" Della must have spoken his name a touch too loudly in her shock, for he shot her a warning look. She lowered her voice again as she continued. "Trust me when I say that if you rush off now and Peter jilts his bride, the consequences for everyone involved will be dire."

What if Mr. Greenwood challenged Peter to a duel? He would be well within his rights to do so, unless they could prove that Peter hadn't really compromised his daughter. But there was no way to do that without throwing Annabelle to the wolves.

I can't let that happen to her. As annoying as her little sister could be, Della would never want her to suffer.

But Ashton was unmoved. "I have no intention of persuading your brother to trap himself in a match he doesn't want against the dictates of my conscience. Good evening, Miss Danby." With a look of disdain that cut more deeply than his words, he turned and strode from the room.

Eighteen

THEY DID *NOT* ANNOUNCE PETER'S ENGAGEMENT TO MISS Greenwood that evening. And while Mr. Greenwood hadn't yet challenged Peter to a duel, Della suspected this was only because he didn't wish to raise any suspicions concerning his daughter. At present, only the two families knew that she'd been compromised.

In any event, Mr. Greenwood had some harsh words (exchanged in the safety of the family study) for Peter, the Danbys as a whole, and the state of society when a young man's word was worth so little. Della attempted to placate him with the observation that perhaps the happy couple only needed more time in each other's company to realize how happy they were.

She hoped it would prove true.

Annabelle, for her part, was less concerned with their brother's happiness than with her own.

"What are we to do if he can't be made to see reason?" she lamented over a late breakfast the next morning. The sisters had come down to the sitting room to take their meal together and confer while their parents still slept and Peter hid upstairs. "Why did I let you talk me into choosing *him* as Eliza's bridegroom?"

"*Me?*" Della set down her teacup so hard she might have chipped the saucer. "This whole thing was your idea! I was only trying to help you, and now you've made me quarrel with Lord Ashton over it."

She'd been so upset about their row that she'd tossed and turned all night.

As frustrated as she was by the trouble Ashton had caused them, once Della's temper had cooled she had to contend with the uncomfortable possibility that he might have a point. Peter had every reason to be happy with the beautiful Miss Greenwood. But if he weren't—if he should prove just as miserable as Lord Ashton had been in his own marriage—what then?

"Do you think there's any risk that we're"—Della had to pause to find the right words before she finally settled on her honest fear—"well, ruining Peter's life?"

"Nonsense!" Annabelle countered. "*He's* ruining *my* life. If he was going to refuse us, the time to do it was before he spoke to Mr. Greenwood. Now it's too late to get someone else to take his place."

"At least Miss Greenwood's father has let her out of the house again," Della pointed out. "Have you asked her if she has any ideas?"

"She's not exactly speaking to me at the moment." Annabelle paused to take a bite of her biscuit and dab her napkin to her lips. "She's still cross that I put Peter's name forward instead of running away with her."

"Oh."

This got better and better. But Della had no further time to ponder Annabelle's dilemma, for the butler announced that Miss Chatterjee had come to call. Della hurried to finish the last few bites of her breakfast, instructed her sister to think of a solution that didn't involve threatening Peter with defenestration, and went out to meet her friend in the drawing room.

Reva rushed to her side as soon as she entered.

"Is everything all right? I heard..." She trailed off here, looking uncomfortable.

Della shut the door firmly behind her. "It's all right; you may speak plainly."

"Miss Berry has been telling people that one of the dealers at your club seduced a girl in full view of all the guests a few days ago. It isn't true, is it?"

"As far as I know it was only a kiss," Della admitted with a sigh. "But everyone saw them, yes. I'd rather not relive the details, if it's all the same to you. I feel just awful about it. I sacked the dealer immediately, and neither of them will be allowed back to the club. That's all we can do for now."

"How dreadful." Reva's eyes widened in sympathy. "I'm sure it wasn't your fault."

"I wish Jane felt the same," Della said. "She's asked me to take some time away."

Though she'd done her best to put the matter out of her mind, remembering it now made her throat go tight. Everything she'd worked for had gone up in smoke so quickly.

Remembering what else had transpired that night, Della asked, "Did Miss Berry say anything else?"

Reva didn't meet her eye. *That's a yes.*

"I'd rather hear it from you than from a stranger," Della encouraged.

"She said that there was a rumor that you were involved with a married man." Reva looked apologetic for repeating it. "I told her that was nonsense, of course."

"Did she have any guesses as to who this man might be?"

"No." *That's one good thing.* Reva gave her hand a reassuring squeeze as she continued. "I'm sure this will pass. We all know you would never do such a thing. It's just like when Mrs. Duff was gossiping about me."

Except that you were innocent.

Della felt quite wretched. Even if Lord Ashton's marriage were destined to end, it changed everything. It was the reason Della had to hide the truth from her friends.

"What's the matter?" Reva asked, studying her with concern.

Della didn't want to lie anymore. It only made her feel worse about all of it.

"Promise me you'll keep a secret." At Reva's nod, she continued, "The truth is, I did harbor some feelings toward Lord Ashton."

"I knew it." Reva couldn't suppress a little smile. "Are you worried this story will reach his ears? I'm sure if you explain—"

"*He's* the married man, Reva. He has a wife, though they've been separated for many years, and she's planning to seek an act of divorce from Parliament."

Reva's smile faded quickly, her warm brown skin turning slightly ashy at this revelation. She managed to squeak out a soft "Oh."

"I know," Della said. "But we aren't... That is, I'm not chasing a thrill or stirring up trouble. I truly care about him."

More than she liked to admit.

Reva was silent for a long time. When she spoke, her voice was gentle. "Does he intend to marry you, once his divorce is taken care of?"

"I don't know. We've never talked about it." There was a queer feeling in Della's stomach. She'd never expected marriage from Lord Ashton. After all, he was a far cry from the man she'd always imagined for herself—the dashing poet or diplomat. She hadn't thought she'd wanted more than a brief tryst, but the idea that *he* might not want anything more suddenly stung. "I suppose that's my answer, isn't it?"

What did I expect? Their quarrel last night likely hadn't raised her in his esteem, but even if Ashton weren't soured on the prospect of marriage forever, he could never take a woman who ran a gambling club for a wife. She would be a constant source of pain.

Reva sighed. "If he plans to go before Parliament, you don't want to be mixed up in it. The story is sure to be in the papers, and you know how they love to make everything seem sordid."

"He said much the same thing to me," Della agreed sadly. "That we should take care to keep our meetings strictly to the business of writing my book, and that I should break ties with him before there's a public reckoning."

Reva nodded in grim approval.

It had all seemed very abstract when Ashton had warned her about it. She'd wanted so badly to comfort him that she hadn't really let herself contemplate the extent of the damage the press might wreak. But hearing Reva echo his fears made everything feel real.

"The important thing is that no one knows," her friend advised her in a hushed voice. "Don't be seen with him again and don't let Miss Berry add any more fuel to these rumors. Carry on as if everything is normal, and soon enough it will be."

"Nothing is normal," Della murmured. "Not while I'm banned from Bishop's."

"Are you banned? I thought you said Jane asked you to take some time away."

"It amounts to the same thing."

"Not quite," Reva insisted. She bore a striking resemblance to Lord Ashton right now, with her unwelcome rationality. "Besides which, would it really be so bad to take a short break from your work? Don't be angry with me for saying this, but you always seem so harried lately."

"Of course I'm not angry." This was a lie. Della was struggling not to tell Reva how obviously wrong she was (Della wasn't the *least* bit harried!), but managed to formulate a kinder reply. "I love the club. I *can't* give it up. I'd be letting Jane down."

Reva's deep brown eyes were studying her carefully. "What do you love most about it?"

"Well..." Della had to think about this for a moment. She didn't particularly love having more things to manage than she had time for. Nor did she have the skills to handle the financial side of things, which were entirely Jane's domain. "The social aspect, I suppose. Seeing all our guests and making sure they're comfortable." Although she didn't like having to turn out Mrs. Muller or defuse Mrs. Duff's temper. She liked the nicer bits very well, though! Visiting with everyone and sharing a sense of triumph when their night went well.

"Couldn't you get that from events outside the club? Or even attend the club a few nights a week instead of every night? There must be someone else who could split the task with you."

"Why should Jane want to replace me?" Della protested. "We built Bishop's *together*. If I stepped back now, how could I still call myself her friend?"

"*I* used to help with your club when you were first starting out and then I stepped back, but we're still friends, aren't we?"

"Of course. But it wasn't the same with you, Reva. The club is Jane's whole *life*. If I'm not part of that, then..." Della shrugged helplessly, reluctant to finish the thought.

Reva seemed to realize that she'd touched on a sore spot. "It's up to you what to do. I just hope that if you're going to dedicate *your* whole life to the club, it's because that's what you really want and not because you feel obligated."

"It *is* what I want," Della replied. But she felt as though she were reassuring herself more than Reva. This visit had become so confusing.

"I should go." Reva rose slowly to her feet. "I promised my mother I'd be home soon. I just wanted to check in on you and make sure you were well."

"Thank you, but you needn't worry." Della gave her friend a

warm smile, grateful for her concern. "You know I always manage to come through trouble unscathed."

$\mathcal{J}\!\!\sim$

Della had never possessed the talent that some ladies had for appearing effortlessly serene when something was bothering her. It was doubly upsetting when there were two things bothering her: her quarrel with Lord Ashton and her quarrel with Jane.

She didn't even *like* quarrels! She was always the first one to smooth over a minor disagreement with a kind word or a joke. How had she managed to arrive at an impasse with two of the people she cared about most?

Given that Della was too cowardly to venture into Jane's house and risk a scolding from the elder Mrs. Williams, she would have liked to deal with Lord Ashton first. Whether to apologize to him or demand that he apologize to her, she couldn't say. If only Peter would simply decide of his own accord that he was passionately in love with Miss Greenwood, it might have made matters a good deal easier for everyone. But only two days after their argument at the dinner party, a letter arrived that dashed all her hopes of setting things right.

> *Dear Miss Danby,*
>
> *As we agreed, in light of my current situation I regret to say that I won't be able to call on your family again. I remain available to answer your questions by correspondence if you need my assistance. You may send me your latest chapters and I should be happy to read them.*
>
> *—Ashton*

"He doesn't even say if he's still cross with me!" Della exclaimed, crumpling the useless note into a ball in her fist. He must be, if he'd decided not to come back. His hearing was today, and he hadn't even told her what happened.

"Hmm?" Annabelle looked up from her book.

"Nothing," Della muttered. "Never mind."

Della wished that Ashton were before her, so she might gauge his feelings on the matter. How could he send such an empty letter? Swallowing a frustrated noise, she went upstairs to her writing desk and pulled out her stationery. It took her several tries, but she finally arrived on a conciliatory paragraph.

Lord Ashton,

You cannot expect me to say goodbye to you this way, when our last meeting ended on such a disagreeable note. Please come by the house, or I shall be forced to visit yours. I'm sorry for what I said to you after supper. I can't explain here, but I truly did have a good reason to suggest the match. I don't see why Peter should be unhappy, but I wouldn't like to be the source of his troubles if you're right. I expect we might never agree. I only hope you won't let those be our parting words to one another.

—D.

There. That was the best she could do to mend things for the moment. Now it would be for Ashton to decide whether to accept her olive branch. After considerable thought, she added:

P.S. Thank you again for all your help. I am attaching
my draft chapter on charitable endeavors if you have
time to look it over, but the entry on Guy's Hospital
isn't complete yet so just ignore that one. I'm trying to
persuade Annabelle to go and view a surgery for me to
verify the facts, as I'm far too cowardly to do it.

She packed up everything into a large envelope, sealed it with wax, and gave her footman instructions for its delivery. This business attended to, she had nothing left to do but go and face Jane.

Della greeted the maid with a smile when she opened the door. "I'm here to see Mrs. Williams. Er, the *younger* Mrs. Williams, that is."

Why did I say that? The woman saw her often enough to know whom she was here to call on, but Della was so nervous that she hadn't been able to stop the words from spilling out.

"Is...the elder Mrs. Williams at home, by any chance?" she added as she was led into the pale-green sitting room.

"No, miss," the maid, Molly, replied. She had a perfect servant's voice—carefully scrubbed of any opinion on the chaos that must undoubtedly have ruled this house over the past few days. "She's out at the moment. I'll tell my mistress you're here."

Della heaved an enormous breath of relief at this news. Now she needn't jump at every creaking floorboard, certain that a mother's vengeance was coming for her.

When Jane came in, she offered Della a sad smile and sat on the divan beside her.

"How is everything?" Della asked. She had no idea which problem to address first, so she would let Jane pick for her.

"The club is doing well," her friend replied earnestly. "There was some talk, of course, but it seems that most of the women who've heard about the fuss with Hannah place the blame on the individuals involved rather than the establishment." A mixed blessing, if their gain was her downfall. "And Hannah?" "I hardly know what to tell you." Jane massaged her temple, appearing fatigued. "She's insisting that she's in love with Mr. Corbyn and won't accept anyone else for a husband, which is an *obvious* lie seeing as she barely knows the man. Her mother is desperately trying to foist her off on an elderly baronet who's too disconnected from the ton gossip to have heard of her indiscretion, and none of us can talk her out of it. They've been fighting like cats and dogs, and of course poor Eli is caught in the middle."

"Can't you send them back to Devon?" It would be the easiest solution for everyone.

Jane heaved a great sigh. "Mrs. Williams won't allow it. Hannah's already snubbed every potential suitor she knows there. Besides, it *is* helpful to have her here to watch Gloria in the evenings so we can attend Bishop's, and Hannah has been learning how to help me with the bookkeeping."

"I beg your pardon?" Surely Della had misheard her. "You mean to tell me that Hannah is allowed to come back to the club after what she did?"

"Not during opening hours," Jane replied swiftly. "Just in the mornings to help take care of some of the work we don't have time to get to."

"But she kissed a midshipman in front of everyone! She's the reason there was a scandal in the first place."

"Which is exactly why she should make it up to us by pitching in."

"*You* were the one who didn't want her there," Della blurted out, exasperated. She felt as though she were losing her mind. Had she hallucinated Jane's opposition?

"I didn't want to upset her mother," Jane corrected. "But as that

ship has sailed, the best thing I can do now is to try to keep the two
of them apart when I'm able and put Hannah in a place where one
of us can keep close watch over her." Jane paused for a moment,
then added as an afterthought, "*And* try to save her from marrying
a baronet who's somewhere in the tail end of his fifties, I suppose."

"I can't believe this!"

"Why are you angry?" Jane's voice rose slightly to match Della's
pitch. "I thought you were trying to help Hannah get some distance
from her mother."

"But it's not fair." Della was aware that this was something a pet-
ulant child would say, which only served to make her more annoyed.
"Why am I forbidden to come to my own club because I let Hannah
in, while Hannah gets to take my place even though *she* caused all
the trouble? And Cecily, I might add, whom you've always said was
awful until now."

Jane blinked, pulling back slightly. "Della, no one is replacing
you. Hannah's only helping to keep track of our accounts, which
you never did anyway. And as for Cecily, of course I don't like her
better than you. But she's proven far more useful than I expected. I
wouldn't trust her with anything too delicate, but she *does* know how
to make sure everyone is enjoying themselves."

"So do I."

"I never said you didn't!" Jane drew a long breath and tried again.
"I'm not trying to punish you for what happened, I only thought you
might need some time to rest. I know you've been working yourself to
the bone since I had Gloria, and I feel badly I haven't done something
about it sooner." Her blue-gray eyes softened as she added, "It was
my fault. I've been so busy that I didn't see how you were struggling."

Della cast her eyes downward, somewhat mollified by this. Her
voice came out too small when she asked, "You really aren't disappointed in me?"

"Of course not." Jane took Della's hand and gave it a little squeeze. "You can come back if you're ready, but I don't want us to fall into the same habits. You always try so hard not to let anyone down that you end up taking too much on yourself. I think we should consider keeping Cecily on permanently, at least for a few nights each week."

"Would she become a co-owner as well?"

Jane frowned. "Let's not get ahead of ourselves. Why don't we consider this to be a sort of trial period? If things go well and she wants more responsibility, we could consider offering her the chance to make an investment once we're sure she's truly committed. It would certainly be nice to have some more funds in the bank."

Della let this sink in. What would it mean if Bishop's didn't belong to her and Jane alone anymore? As much as she knew they needed more help, she didn't love all this uncertainty.

"Would that be all right with you?" Jane prodded, when Della didn't speak up.

"I *do* think we could stand to have another hostess in the evenings," she admitted. "But...it just feels as though so much is changing. The club started out as just the two of us, and we never had any problems. What if adding more people ruins everything?"

What if you don't need me anymore?

She left this last fear unspoken.

"Things *do* change," Jane said gently. "My life is different now than it was before I became a mother. There's less of me left for the club, but it will always be a part of my life. If Cecily or anyone else becomes a co-owner one day, she wouldn't be replacing you *or* me. I'll still be here when you need me."

"What if..." Della bit her tongue, afraid of what she'd caught herself thinking. It felt like a betrayal.

"Go on," Jane encouraged.

She'd never imagined herself saying these words, but she

remembered her conversation with Reva the other day. It bolstered her courage to know that someone she trusted felt the same way.

"What if one day *I'm* not there? What if things don't work out for some reason, and I had to step back?" It felt as though the ground might split apart beneath her feet as she finished. "What if I weren't a co-owner anymore?"

Jane couldn't conceal her surprise. Her lips parted, formed the beginning of words she didn't say, then closed again. Finally, she said, "Do you want to leave?"

I don't know, Della nearly wailed. It felt wrong to even be thinking about this. It had always been her and Jane together, as a team. What sort of friend would she be if she abandoned her now?

"You know I love how much we've accomplished," she began, "and I don't want to leave you shorthanded. But I feel as if I've lost my spark lately. I don't know if I'm up to the task. Look at how I botched everything with Mrs. Muller."

"I told you, I don't blame you for that. You had too much work to handle everything."

"It isn't only that," Della protested, before Jane could go any further. "I'm not good at being strict with people. I hate it, to be quite honest. It makes me feel like I'm the most heartless person in the whole world and that everyone despises me. But one *must* be strict when it comes to enforcing debts, so where does that leave me?" Della twisted her hands in her lap as she poured out her fears. "I don't even know how I feel about the whole idea anymore. Our club made Mrs. Muller so miserable! Is it our fault that she feels that way? Mine, mostly, since I didn't have the courage to cut her off sooner."

"But we limit the bets. We don't let women ruin their families the way they do at White's or Brooks's. Do you mean to say that you've discovered you object to gambling?"

"No," Della replied quickly. "I don't have any problem with it

for *myself*. Nor for those who are careful with their fortunes. I just...
have doubts as to whether I can be the one to let someone else cause
themself such grief in our establishment."

Jane took a moment to absorb this before she replied in a cautious
tone, "Is this change of heart because of Lord Ashton?"

Della wanted to refute the suggestion immediately. If he took the
blame for her decision, Jane might hate him. But the truth was far
more complicated.

Ashton *did* have something to do with it. Not because he'd persuaded her to adopt his own views on gambling; rather, it was because
she couldn't help but think of his example alongside ladies like Mrs.
Muller, and it had put a sharp sense of regret in her heart where
once there had only been a very thoughtless sort of joy. She hadn't
understood there was a darker side to their club—either because the
example hadn't been held up before her nose until now, or because
she hadn't wanted to see it.

"I've heard about what he did," Jane continued when Della didn't
reply. "Surely you don't think anything like that could happen at
Bishop's. We would never allow it. Just because he made a poor decision doesn't mean we should—"

"I know that," Della said. "It isn't because of Lord Ashton. But
my own feelings on the matter have changed. When we were first
starting out, I was so excited to build something with you and there
was so much work to do that I never really stopped to consider any
of the unpleasant bits. And now that I have, I just—" She broke
off, not sure how to finish. The words made her feel like such a
failure. "I'm not sure I have what it takes to run the club the way
we should."

Jane's distress was written plainly on her face. "Are you saying
you want to sell your portion? I–I don't think I can come up with the
funds to buy out your initial investment."

"No!" Della reassured her. "You don't need to repay me anything. You know I can spare the money. And I'm not saying I wouldn't help at all. But maybe...maybe we could try something like you talked about for Cecily? A trial period, where I reduce my responsibilities a little."

Jane appeared shaken, but she took a deep breath to steady herself. "If you're *sure* that's really what you want and not just an idea that Lord Ashton has put in your head."

"It isn't!" she protested.

"I know you've been spending a lot of time together recently. And you know how you tend to get carried away with new things. I don't want to meddle, but I do worry about you. He isn't safe, Della."

"You don't know him," she replied. "He's very kind and proper. You actually have that in common with him. If only you could have a bit more time to become acquainted, I'm sure you'd like him very much."

Jane appeared to be holding her tongue with considerable effort. "If he's important to you, I shall try to respect your choice," she said evenly, "but I'm sorry to say I don't think he's the sort of person I *could* get to know better. He's an adulterer. He *abandoned* his poor wife—"

"Have you been talking to Cecily?" Della interrupted. "She doesn't know the full story."

"I don't need to talk to Cecily. It's in the papers. Haven't you seen it? His wife has sued him in Consistory Court."

It's already in the news? But of course it would be. She should have thought to check for herself.

"Do you have a copy?"

"Yes, of course." Jane rang for her Molly and asked her to fetch the paper for them from Eli's study. A moment later, she'd found the law report section and set it before Della.

CONSISTORY COURT—

Lady Ashton v. Lord Ashton

Lady Ashton brings a suit for divorce a mensa et thoro against his lordship by reason of adultery and intolerable cruelty. Mr. Clinton appeared as counsel for the lady. No counsel appeared for Lord Ashton, who was absent. Proof that a citation had been duly served upon his lordship was provided by Lord de Villiers, brother to Lady Ashton. A libel had been brought in containing twenty articles and evidence from three witnesses who establish full proof of the offense. The marriage was celebrated on April 3, 1830. The parties lived most happily together near Whitchurch, in the county of Bucks, for three years. There was nothing to create the smallest suspicion in the mind of Lady Ashton that her husband's conduct was anything less than becoming of a gentleman of his rank and status in society until the spring of 1833, when the lady was shocked to discover that he had accumulated gambling debts in such an excess as to bring about his utter ruin and the loss of his estate. Lord Ashton then abandoned his wife and took up residence in London to pursue his vices, leaving the lady to seek refuge in her father's house. Lord Ashton did not perform any of the usual duties of a husband or see to his wife's comfort. Testimonies were provided from an acquaintance of Lord Ashton and a former maid of his house who had witnessed such indiscretions between his lordship and other women as to conclude that he had committed adultery. As there was no opposition to the suit, the court agreed that in light of the proof of adultery, abandonment, and gross financial profligacy of Lord Ashton, the lady should have the relief sought and therefore pronounced for the divorce.

So it was already over. At least this stage. Della returned to the start of the story and read it a second time, lingering on the part where it said that Lord Ashton hadn't attended the hearing to make any defense to the claims against him. How could he bear to let everyone think him a villain without even attempting to explain? It made her quite indignant on his behalf.

When Della finally set the paper aside, she found Jane watching her with an expression caught halfway between sympathy and conviction. The very gentlest form of I told you so, which was just as aggravating as any other kind.

She had been influenced against him, just as anyone reading the story must be.

Jane spoke slowly, as if afraid that the words might hurt more if she delivered them at a normal pace. "I know this must come as quite a shock..."

"It doesn't," Della cut in. "He warned me this would happen."

"All of it? You knew what he'd done and it didn't matter to you?"

"He and his wife were very unhappy, and they parted ways years ago. I don't understand why we're pretending we don't know dozens of people like that. The only difference is that Lady Ashton wants her freedom back, so the story has reached the courts instead of remaining a subject of whispers. That hardly makes him a villain. Would you judge Mrs. Duff if she decided to live apart from her husband, when we all know how he behaves?"

"Mrs. Duff didn't gamble away her house," Jane returned.

"Nine years ago! He hasn't gambled since then. He regrets it deeply."

"Fine." Jane raised her hands in surrender. "Let's say you're right. There are plenty of people who are unlucky in their choice of a spouse. Perhaps Lord Ashton has truly reformed, whatever might have happened in the past. You know him better than I do, to be able to judge."

"I *do*," Della agreed emphatically.

"But that doesn't change the fact that you could never have a respectable future with him. Even with this divorce, they can't remarry unless Parliament allows it."

"Which it may," Della couldn't stop herself from pointing out, before she thought to add, "But whether or not he can remarry is none of my business. Lord Ashton is a *friend*."

At least, I hope he's still my friend. Now didn't seem the best time to solicit Jane's opinion on their recent quarrel.

"I saw the way you two looked at one another at the Lyceum." Jane was altogether too observant for her own good.

"There was an attachment," Della admitted somewhat reluctantly. "But he hasn't made me an offer, nor would I expect him to in the circumstances. He's been honest with me about his situation from the start."

Would things be different now that the court had granted Lady Ashton her ruling?

"I just can't see why you would give up our club for a man who can't marry you. What if you regret it later?"

It was hard to find an answer for Jane. These were the same questions she'd been asking herself. Though Della wouldn't have said she was giving up the club for Lord Ashton when she didn't even know what his intentions might be, she had to admit that a part of her did hope it would change things between them. That if Bishop's no longer posed an obstacle, he might decide that he wanted more than a brief tryst from her.

But Jane was right. The decision had to be her own, or she might come to regret it.

"I'm not giving it up for a man," she said firmly. "I told you, my own feelings are...conflicted. What meant so much to me was never the club; it was about us building something together. I wanted to be there for you when you needed help. I didn't want to let you down."

"Are you saying I pushed you into it?" Jane looked truly stricken. "I never meant to make you feel like you couldn't say no to me. I thought we were equal partners."

"We were," Della assured her. "I was happy there at first. I'm still happy in many ways. It's only that I'm not sure if it's something I'm meant to do for the rest of my life, that's all. And it isn't your fault I didn't have the courage to tell you so sooner. I was just worried that if I left we might not...well, see each other anymore," she finished awkwardly.

"Of course we would. You're my dearest friend. Why would you think that could ever change?"

Della only looked at her lap, her face hot. Her fears felt silly now.

After a moment, Jane amended, "I know things haven't been the same since Gloria was born. If I'm being quite honest, I think I've been afraid to let anyone help me. She just seems to need me so much, it felt like I couldn't trust her to anyone but Eli or something might go wrong." She offered a shaky smile. "But since our little crisis I've had to ask Eli's mother to watch her so that we could both attend Bishop's in the evenings. After the first night they seem to have figured things out. I think it will do me some good to have a bit more time away. I'll try to make more time for you from now on, whatever you decide about the club."

"Thank you," Della said, meaning it. "I'm only suggesting we reduce my commitment a bit, as we discussed. Nothing drastic. And as for Lord Ashton, please don't blame him for my decisions. I care about him and I hope you can try not to judge him too harshly without having the occasion to know him better."

"I'll try," Jane promised, which was probably the best Della could hope for in the circumstances.

Nineteen

LYMAN RETURNED FROM THE HOUSE OF LORDS THAT EVENING feeling exhausted. Though he'd been trying to lie low until talk about the court proceedings had blown over, he still took his seat for important matters, and the Mines and Collieries Bill was up for debate. It had been damnably awkward, though. Men he'd known for years eyed him warily instead of greeting him with warmth. One or two had offered their support, but it was of a repugnant flavor and brought him no comfort.

"You can never trust a woman," Lord Esterhazy had told him, with a grave shake of his head. "Doesn't she have any shame, dragging such business up in public for the whole world to see? It's a wife's role to stand by her husband through a few hardships."

"I wouldn't expect her to," Lyman had replied coolly. "The fault was mine, not hers."

This had provoked some awkward blustering and driven away the only sympathetic ear in the House that evening.

If that weren't bad enough, Mr. Wood had seen the story in the paper earlier and offered him unsolicited advice about the conduct of the case for the duration of their breakfast. Even Lyman's pointed reminder that Wood was training to be a *solicitor* rather than a proctor, and had thus never set foot in the ecclesiastical courts, failed to silence the man. The prospect of watching his fellow lodger endure real legal proceedings was simply too much for Wood to resist. He'd insisted on dissecting every detail he'd seen in the papers with Lyman, telling him where his proctor should have done more to defend his good name and what *he* would have done differently if it had been his case, until Mr. Hirsch had rapped his broom on the ceiling to signal that he'd been waiting on his apprentice downstairs.

When Lyman returned home, he tried not to let his steps make a sound on the creaking floorboards, lest the noise summon Wood once more, but he was relieved to discover the man was absent. Only Clarkson was at home, though he didn't come out from his room to greet him. He must be busy with his own work.

Lyman set the kettle on to boil, seeking distraction in the familiar routine. Though the first step was over, the hardest part was still before them. The Consistory Court of London was less reticent to grant decrees of divorce a mensa et thoro in recent years than it once had been, largely because the parties remained bound not to remarry and the church didn't have to worry about any new unions complicating things. Parliament would be another matter entirely.

A soft rap on the door interrupted his thoughts.

Please not Wood, he prayed. Lyman knew his absence had been too good to be true.

But when he opened the door, it was Della who stood on the landing. Though she'd wrapped herself in a cloak with a deep hood, Lyman recognized her short, plump figure even before she pulled it back to reveal her face.

"What are you doing here?" he hissed. "I told you not to come!"

"And I told *you* that I wanted a chance to explain myself. Why wouldn't you just call on me like I asked? It would have been easier than making me ride all the way out to Pimlico unseen."

"I didn't make you do anything," he pointed out, irritated at this intrusion. Hadn't she learned anything from their near miss the last time? "It's too dangerous for you to be here."

Luckily for her, Clarkson was discreet enough not to come out to inspect the voices in the hall, but there was nothing to stop Wood from returning to find them at any moment.

"*Please,* Ashton." Della rested a gloved hand upon his forearm. "I won't stay long. Only I can't bear the idea that I'll never see you again, and the last time we spoke ended in a quarrel. I hate making people angry with me."

There was genuine remorse in her voice. Her wide brown eyes were liquid in the darkening room. It was well past sundown already.

Lyman felt his resolve waver. He hadn't felt easy with the way they'd parted either, though he wouldn't apologize for trying to spare Peter the same fate he'd endured. But being right wasn't as much comfort as he'd hoped.

"Very well," he relented. "But only a minute. I don't know when Mr. Wood might return. He's probably only stopped for supper somewhere."

"Thank you," Della said softly. She slipped inside and shut the door, bringing a faint hint of her lemon-tart scent with her. She didn't remove her cloak or gloves, but drew a long breath and looked around the entryway, as if unsure how to begin. Lyman didn't invite her to come to his rooms. Better to avoid the temptation.

"I do feel badly about Peter," she began, her eyes downcast. "Maybe you're right about him, and we shouldn't have meddled. But I promise you, we were only trying to find a solution to a larger problem."

Lyman must have looked skeptical, for she flushed pink as she added, "We *were*."

"I don't see what problem could be worth trading your brother's future."

Della sighed. "Can you promise never to breathe a word of this to a soul?"

"Very well," Lyman replied, a little uneasily. He would have preferred it if the explanation didn't involve dire secrets.

"I can't go into all the details without betraying a confidence, but Miss Greenwood *needs* to marry."

There were only a few reasons that could provoke that particular sense of urgency, and he didn't think poverty was the cause, given how finely dressed the woman had been the other night.

"So she's in a family way," he guessed. That *did* change things. If Peter had been careless enough to ruin the girl, he owed it to her to provide for their child.

"No, no, no!" Della clapped a hand over her mouth, as if she wished she could seal the words back inside. "That's not what I meant to say at all. Oh dear, this is so difficult. Let's just say that her father believes Peter compromised her, even though the truth is a bit more complicated than that. Regardless, you see why he can't just walk away from the engagement now, don't you?" Her warm brown eyes pleaded with him for understanding, but Lyman couldn't grant it.

"What do you mean, 'he *believes* Peter compromised her'? Did he, or didn't he?"

Della looked as if this were the last question she wanted to answer. "He didn't, but he's already confessed to the deed, so it's as good as if he had."

"Why would he confess to something he didn't do?"

"Please, let's not go into all that. I've already told you more than I should have."

Very well. Maybe he didn't need to know all of the details. Peter Danby's engagement would have been of no concern to him if the young man hadn't pulled him into his confidence. He rather wished he could turn back time and never have been drawn into a conflict that would sour his last days with Della.

"I'll take you at your word that the situation is quite desperate for Miss Greenwood," he conceded. "But I still don't see why your brother should have to sacrifice himself over it. If he isn't responsible for her current situation, then it isn't for him to set things right."

"I wish it were so simple." Della bit her lower lip. "We thought he would come out well by it. He could have used the dowry money to settle up some debts, and she'd be a perfectly good match for any man."

"It takes more than that to ensure a happy union." Ellen had been a "perfectly good match" by any objective standard. They should have been happy together. But even knowing what she did about his experience, Della didn't see the danger that awaited her brother. How could she be so naive as to think that she could simply push two near-strangers together and expect the rest to work itself out?

Lyman's thoughts must have shown plainly on his face, for Della spoke in a careful tone. "I know that your marriage caused you a great deal of suffering, but surely you can't think that it will end that way for everyone?" Her voice rose with doubt on the last words.

Lyman held his tongue, unable to find an answer that would satisfy Della. He suspected she wasn't only asking for her brother's sake.

"The first time we met, you joked that no sane person should ever seek to marry," Della continued. "At least, I'd assumed that it was a joke. But now I wonder, did you really mean it?" She seemed suddenly vulnerable as she looked up at him, and Lyman suffered that familiar, maddening fear that he might hurt her with his answer.

Surely she couldn't hold out any hope for him in that respect. Why couldn't she have a care to guard her own heart?

Lyman's throat was dry. He couldn't find the right words to walk the line between honesty and kindness.

"I wouldn't presume to judge that for anyone else," he finally said. "But it seemed to me that in your brother's case, the match would be a mistake."

Della winced. "There's no chance of persuading you to talk to him then. Even if it were the only way to help Miss Greenwood."

"I'm sorry, but no."

He *was* sorry. Not for following his conscience, of course, but for the pain it caused Della. He'd wanted to part on good terms. To preserve what they'd shared as a bright memory to look back on when he needed it. Now he would always remember that he'd hurt her at the end, just as he'd known he would.

Della nodded sadly. She seemed resigned to his decision—an unexpected blessing, given how headstrong she could be. He'd half expected her to argue with him. But she only said in a soft voice, "And for yourself?"

"Pardon?"

"If Lady Ashton gets her bill through Parliament, would you ever wish to remarry one day, or have you concluded that it's out of the question?"

Lyman sucked in a swift breath. He hadn't expected her to come at him so directly. Surely she could never have imagined that they might have a real future together, with his circumstances being what they were?

"I wouldn't have anything to offer a wife," he said. "I have a title, but no country house, a meager income, and if my reputation isn't already in shambles by now, it will be by the time Parliament is done with me." He paused, wanting to be sure Della understood him.

When she met his gaze, he added deliberately, "Any woman I might admire enough to contemplate marriage with, I wouldn't insult with such an offer."

A pucker appeared between Della's brows to mark her disapproval. "If you truly care for someone, their character matters far more than any of those things. And plenty of ladies have wealth of their own to support—"

"Della," he interrupted, not wanting to hear her reasons. It was plain that they weren't speaking in hypotheticals. "You know why I can't offer you more."

Her cheeks grew very red. Any other lady would have been too embarrassed to press the matter further, but Della, with all her stubborn courage, was undeterred. "No, I *don't* know," she said, her voice trembling. "Because we haven't had a conversation about it. Not really. I don't want to be presumptuous if you simply don't feel that strongly about me. But I—" She broke off here, twisting her hands nervously. "Well, I suppose I have come to feel rather strongly about *you*. Far more than I intended at the outset. And I know that my club must pose an obstacle, but I've been thinking about it and I've decided not to be quite so involved now as I was before..." She let her voice trail off, appearing unsure.

Had she done that for him?

Something twisted in Lyman's chest. How had they come to this point? He should never have let things go so far. He should have ended their connection ages ago, before he could get close enough to break Della's heart. But he'd been selfish and weak, as usual, and now she would pay the price for it.

Lyman took her hands into his, stilling their nervous movements. Della looked up at him with eyes that were far too bright. "It isn't only your club," he said slowly. "And it isn't you. You are everything that's bright and wonderful, Della. Any man would be lucky to have you."

She blinked, not fooled by this opening.

Lyman pressed on. "You know what's coming next for me. Even if you didn't read what they printed in the papers—"

"I did." At his wince, she added, "I'm sorry, but I couldn't do otherwise."

He wished she hadn't seen all that. He hated to imagine Della poring over all the sordid details, trying to separate truth from fiction. But at least she should understand why he had to reject her.

"Then you must realize that things will only get worse from here on out. Don't you see how uncomfortable your friends are around me? They all think I'm a danger to your reputation—"

"They don't know you yet. Jane is just a bit slow to warm up, that's all. Once she has a bit more time—"

"*They're right.*" Lyman's voice was sharp enough to cut through Della's excuses. She stiffened at his tone, but he pressed onward. Better to hurt her now if it meant that she finally understood. "I'm poison to you. To anyone who intends to maintain their good name. If they had reason to worry when my transgressions were a decade behind me, how much more so now that everything is being aired out in public?"

But Della hadn't understood anything, it seemed. "I don't care what they think of us," she protested, her jaw jutting out in defiance. "I've never worried about public opinion before. What kind of life is it when you let fear dictate your choices?"

"You think everything is a grand adventure." Lyman sighed. "I don't want to be the one to make you realize how painful it can be to become an outcast."

"Why should you decide what's best for me? Just because you're older and more worldly doesn't mean you know better than I do. If your biggest concern is truly my reputation, then it should be for *me* to decide what risks to run."

Lyman bit back a strangled noise of frustration. Couldn't she see that he was only trying to protect her?

"It's for me to decide because I can't bear to see you hurt on my behalf. I can't destroy another woman's life."

They were both silent for a long time. Lyman had spoken the words without thinking, fueled more by emotion than reason for once, but he felt their truth in his bones.

If he stayed with Della, he *would* destroy her. It was only a question of time.

"I'm not your first wife," she finally ventured. "I'm made of sterner stuff than that, I daresay. And you aren't the same man you were back then either."

"Aren't I?" he retorted. "All of London thinks me a monster, after what they've read. You're the only one who insists on believing otherwise." This wasn't technically true, but Lyman refused to count Lord Esterhazy. He had some standards.

"But they haven't printed the full story! It's unfair to you."

"Of course they have," he snapped. Why wouldn't she see what was right in front of her? "I did everything Lady Ashton accuses me of. I gambled away our home, I left her destitute, and I haven't been able to provide for her properly since that day. I *did* commit adultery, even if we'd already separated by then. I can hardly use that as my excuse when my own conduct is the reason she couldn't stand to live with me."

"You know my feelings on that already. I wouldn't fault you for it while you and your wife were living separately. And as for the house, that was nine years ago." Della's voice had taken on a pleading note. "You make it sound as if you're an awful person, when you're not. I *know* you're not. You made a terrible mistake, but you've tried your best to set things right since then. That counts for something."

"Not enough," he said softly. "I'm still the man who did those things."

Della shook her head, her chestnut curls bouncing out an echo of the movement after it was done. "No. You're a man who's decided to remain trapped in the past instead of letting himself move forward."

Anger flared hot in his chest, threatening to spill out from his lips. How would she know what it felt like to live with that responsibility? It wasn't just something you could walk away from. But Lyman bit his tongue, not wanting to lash out at her.

Della might have sensed some of his turmoil, for she reached out a hand to touch his forearm. "I should go," she said softly. "I promised you I wouldn't stay long."

She looked at him with a question in her eyes, as if she hoped he might say something more. Ask her to stay, perhaps. For the night, or forever.

Both options were impossible.

Instead, Lyman nodded curtly. "You can still write if you need any help for the book, though I'll understand if you decide not to."

Della slid her hand up his shoulder to find purchase upon the back of Lyman's neck and pull him down for a long kiss. He didn't hold back, tasting her too deeply for his own good. If this was to be the last time, he would make it count.

But another moment revealed his mistake, for Della had no intention of holding back either. She molded herself against his body, pulling him close. A little whimper escaped her mouth. *Always so eager.*

Lyman devoured it.

Someone has to stop, he reminded himself. Someone had to break this moment of pleasure so that it could turn into longing, regret, and then one day, into nothing but a memory.

It would be him, of course. Lyman pulled back, tilting his face upward and beyond reach. He listened to the sound of Della's breath as it slowed back to a normal pace.

"Please take care of yourself," she whispered. "Whatever happens, I'm glad that I met you."

Then she tiptoed away, leaving nothing but a faint trace of her bright scent behind to fill the empty room.

Della didn't see Lord Ashton again for two months. Apart from a package that came for her a week after their last meeting with some comments on the draft chapter she'd sent him on charities, there was no word from him again. Nor did she take advantage of his offer to provide further advice. Though she'd started more than one letter, she couldn't seem to get past her salutation. It was too painful.

She attended the club three nights a week to carry out her duties as hostess, a role that was now divided between herself and Cecily, who took on the remaining evenings. Much as she hated to think that it might be this easy to replace her, Della was forced to acknowledge that Cecily did a more-than-adequate job of keeping everyone happy, well fed, and supplied with champagne. Besides which, she seemed utterly thrilled with her new role and loved to recount every detail of gossip from her evenings, so that Della never really felt that she was missing anything.

Even if she hadn't quite decided what the future would hold, it *was* nice to have room to breathe again. She spent her newly discovered free time focused on her writing and visiting friends that she'd neglected over the past three years. It felt a bit like emerging from a long dream. Without the club taking up nearly every evening, Della was able to make swift progress on her manuscript. Every time she thought of Lord Ashton and felt the melancholy creeping up on her, she threw herself into her work. Before she knew it, she'd finished.

It was a bittersweet moment. She would have liked to share it with someone, but the only person who could truly appreciate what she'd accomplished was gone.

"Do you think I should send Lord Ashton a copy?" she asked Annabelle one morning. She was loath to turn to her sister for advice, but there was really no one else who understood the complexities of her situation.

"Of course you should! He's to be your co-author, isn't he? Doesn't that mean he needs to agree to the text before you can print it?"

"He's already seen most of the chapters back when he was still calling on us to help me," Della explained. That might be an exaggeration, but never mind. He'd seen enough to have a general idea what the rest would look like. "And I hate to write him now if it might be a bother."

She'd been reduced to scouring the papers every day for news of his divorce (another good distraction from tragic feelings), but the months that had followed the Consistory Court's decision had been largely silent. Until last week, that is. There had been a prominent headline and a much smaller text beneath proclaiming the arrival of Lady Ashton's divorce bill before the House of Lords, who were to hear the evidence next Tuesday.

Della suffered a nervous flutter in her stomach just thinking about it.

"You're being silly," Annabelle scolded. "Are you afraid that he won't want to hear from you just because you got angry at him for scaring Peter off of marriage and ruining Miss Greenwood's life forever?"

"Something like that." Della sighed. "How is she faring, anyway?"

"She's to be shipped off to an aunt in Paris, last I heard." Though Annabelle had the decency to look regretful as she imparted this news, they both knew it could have been far worse. Although Peter had stubbornly maintained his refusal to go through with the marriage, Miss Greenwood must not have confessed the truth to her family, for no one had come to lay any accusations at Annabelle's feet.

"That's not so bad, is it?" Della could think of worse places to spend one's life, at any rate. "I wouldn't mind seeing Paris." There would be art galleries, all the latest fashions, and high society in abundance. What more could anyone want?

"Her French is atrocious."

An awkward silence descended over the room at this assessment.

"Do you suppose there's anything we can do for her?" Della asked. There was really no reason to send the girl away when no one else knew of her indiscretion and it must be obvious to her father by now that she wasn't in a family way. If only the man were more forgiving, he might have chosen to forget the whole incident and let Miss Greenwood go on with her life.

"Not unless you can find her a replacement husband before then," Annabelle replied in a grim tone.

Della was halfway through drafting a mental list of potential candidates before she stopped herself. Had she learned nothing from the disaster of Peter's engagement? Better not to meddle any further.

"To return to our earlier conversation," Annabelle said briskly, eager to turn the subject away from her ruined lover. "Yes, I think you need to write your viscount to share a copy of your book, and no, I don't think you'll be bothering him. Isn't he divorcing his wife? I would've thought you'd have secured yourself a place as the next Lady Ashton by now."

"Don't tease me," Della replied glumly. "We haven't spoken in months and I miss him."

Every time a caller came to the door, she knew a foolish hope that it would be Ashton, come to say that he couldn't do without her another day.

But of course he could. Of course she could too. They'd led

separate lives before they'd met and now they would do so again, only a little lonelier for the experience.

She missed talking to him. She missed his gorgeous, understated green eyes and those adorable wire spectacles. She missed his scolding tone, and the fun she'd had trying to persuade him when he was wrong about something.

"Why can't you be together once he's free?" Annabelle asked, while gazing back down to a book she'd had in her lap, as if she hadn't yet decided whether it might prove more interesting than their conversation. "What did he say about it?"

Della scoured her memory to produce a faithful transcription of the essentials: "Something, something, he made a terrible mistake nine years ago. Something, something, something, he's determined to be miserable forever now. I believe that's more or less how it went."

Annabelle buried a laugh in her palm. "You're exaggerating."

"I'm really not! I've never met a man more averse to joy in my entire life."

"He wasn't averse to *you*, though," Annabelle observed, "and you tend to make other people joyful, so he can't have been quite as austere as he seems."

Of course now that Lord Ashton was no longer a regular fixture at their town house Annabelle would decide she liked him. The contrary little imp only wanted to disagree with whatever view Della expressed.

But the truth was plain enough. Ashton wasn't here. He'd chosen to go through his present troubles alone, believing it to be some sort of noble sacrifice rather than a disguised cowardice. However much he might have cared for Della, it hadn't been enough to make him stay.

"Did you see his new book yet?" Annabelle was still talking, though Della had been too lost in her own thoughts to follow.

"Hmm?"

Her sister had already left the room. A moment later, she returned with a small volume in hand. It wasn't a *new* book at all, but rather, the second edition of his guide to London.

"When did you get this?" Della snatched the guide and began flipping through it, her face turning hot. She'd meant to keep better track of the date, but it had entirely slipped her mind. How embarrassing that Annabelle should have to remind her.

"Only two days ago," she replied. That wasn't so long. "I tried to tell you, but you were at Bishop's when—"

But Della's relief was short-lived, chased swiftly by a new worry.

"Don't you think that if Lord Ashton wanted to hear from me again he would have sent me a copy himself?"

"You're so rude! You don't even let me get a word out before you're off on whatever *you're* thinking of." With a fierce glare, Annabelle plucked the book from Della's hands and began turning to the page she wanted before handing it back. "I was *trying* to show you this, before you interrupted me."

Della glanced down. It was the chapter on night life and gambling clubs. There was the text on White's and Brooks's that she'd read often enough to have nearly memorized. And beneath it, in little black letters, was something unexpected.

Our readers will be surprised to learn of a new addition on Piccadilly, which caters to ladies. Bishop's Chocolate Emporium is open from Tuesday to Saturday evenings, and promises to offer its members an incomparable experience.

He's added us.

Della placed a hand to her breast, unsure whether the feeling in her heart was joy or pain.

"Why should he have done it, after he swore he wouldn't?"

"Because he loves you, probably." Annabelle snorted, making the pronouncement seem more like an annoyance than a blessing.

You're wrong there. Or rather, if she was right, it wasn't the sort of love that was strong enough to act on. What good did it do either of them?

"I feel guilty," Della confessed. "I'd already accepted that he wouldn't include us. I hate to think I made him compromise his principles for me."

"Oh, don't get so worked up. He kept the men's clubs in, didn't he? It's only fair to have yours alongside them, if you ask me."

This made Della smile to herself. Perhaps it *was* only fair. And think how happy Jane would be when she saw it! *An incomparable experience.* It was everything they could have asked for.

"You're right," she conceded, turning back to Annabelle. "It was kind of him to include us. I'll send him a copy of my manuscript before I turn it in."

It would take her ages to write it all out again, but it probably wasn't a bad idea. She could check for any last errors while transcribing the text.

"There's one more thing," Annabelle said. She'd suddenly lost her teasing tone. "I wondered if you might let me add a few lines of my own to your book."

"You?" Della frowned. Except for the occasional love sonnet to a hapless debutant, Annabelle had never written anything in her life. She had no business cluttering up the guidebook with her own comments now that it was finally finished. "Why should you want to write anything?"

"It isn't for myself," Annabelle explained. "It's for others like me. I just thought...if your book is a guide for ladies, it should include all of us."

Oh. Perhaps she shouldn't be quite so quick to dismiss her sister's request. After all, Della *had* just included an entry on a place where one could watch surgeries performed on the principle that if even a handful of readers might be interested in it, then it belonged there.

"What would you put in?" Della asked.

"Just places where we could find one another. That sort of thing. Don't worry, I'd be careful to use language that wouldn't be too obvious to anyone who wasn't looking for it."

"Very well." Della agreed. "But you have to get it to me soon. I don't want to delay things."

"Thank you." Annabelle clapped her hands, looking thoroughly pleased with herself. "It won't take me more than a day or two. I already know just what to write."

Della wished she knew just what to write to Lord Ashton.

Twenty

THE TIMES, WEDNESDAY, APRIL 6, 1842

Lady Ashton's Divorce

The House of Lords assembled on Tuesday afternoon to hear counsel and evidence in support of Lady Ashton's divorce bill. Mr. Willis said that he had the honor of appearing at their lordships' bar on the present occasion as counsel to support the petition of Lady Mary Ellen Ashton, and promised his statement should not occupy the attention of their lordships for too great a time. Lady Ashton accused her husband of adultery, abandonment, gross negligence of her morals and comforts, and gross profligacy.

The petitioner was born to a most distinguished family as Lady Mary Ellen de Villiers, daughter to the Earl of Eastmeath, a member of this House. She became acquainted with Lord Ashton in 1830, and the parties were married that same year. Of this marriage, Mr. Willis was happy to say there was no issue.

He would prove that the parties had lived affectionately together until about April 1833, at which evil hour the lady was shocked to discover that her husband had gambled away his entire fortune and country estate. Following the reception of this calamity, Lord Ashton abandoned his wife, who returned to live in her father's house in Leicester. Lord Ashton did not perform any of the usual duties of a husband or reside with her again. In 1841, Lady Ashton was informed of acts of adultery on the part of Lord Ashton. Mr. Willis should prove all these statements by evidence at their lordships' bar and should submit that the case would entitle the petitioner to the relief she sought, namely, that their lordships would pass a bill bestowing a divorce a vinculo matriomii.

Witnesses were then called who proved the marriage and that the behavior of Lady Ashton toward her husband had been in all respects affectionate and proper and that she had not invited such cruel abandonment through any fault of her own.

Mr. Thomas Clinton, of Paul's Bakehouse Court, Doctors' Commons, proctor, was called to prove the instructions he had received to bring proceedings before the London Consistory Court in February last to obtain a decree a mensa et thoro. A copy of these proceedings was presented at the bar of the House.

Miss Susan O'Driscoll stated that she was a maid in the house of Lord Ashton from about 1828 to 1833. While in his employ, she discovered letters to his lordship detailing indecencies that had taken place with another woman, without his wife's knowledge.

Lord Esterhazy—But it is scarcely possible that these letters could have stated that a criminal intercourse was going on between the correspondents.

The witness replied that such was her impression.

Lord Esterhazy—Can you provide these letters to the House? Who was the lady who wrote them? .

The witness said she had not taken them from her master's possession but left them where she found them. She no longer recollected the lady's name.

Mr. Henry Wilkinson, a gentleman from Leicester, was then called. He was a friend of the parties and had seen Lord Ashton in London following his separation from his wife, in about 1838 or 1839. He had on several occasions witnessed Lord Ashton in the company of other women and had seen many improper liberties pass between them. On one occasion he had seen a lady sitting upon Lord Ashton's knee and kissing him.

The Lord Chancellor—Who were these women?

The witness replied that he could not recollect their names.

Mr. Willis thereupon said that this was all the evidence he proposed to offer, but that the petitioner was in attendance to answer any questions that their lordships might think proper to put to her.

A consultation then took place between their lordships, resulting in Lady Ashton being required to offer certain explanations.

Lady Ashton was unable to say whether she had written to her husband to entreat him to reconcile with her. She was in a state of great distress following the loss of Lord Ashton's country house and had difficulty recalling the details of her conduct whilst under the influence of this shock. In response to questions from the Lord Chancellor seeking to ascertain why she did not bring proceedings before Consistory Court before this year, the lady replied that she at first wished to spare her family the embarrassment of disclosing the circumstances of her case publicly and that she had only learned of Lord Ashton's adultery in 1841, upon speaking to Mr. Wilkinson.

The Lord Chancellor moved that the evidence be printed and in the meantime said it would be well if the learned counsel could procure some additional evidence to show, firstly, clear proof of adultery as no witness had provided a satisfactory account on that point, and, secondly, that Lady Ashton had been sufficiently diligent in her conduct as a wife. The second reading of the bill was then adjourned to May 2nd.

THE TIMES, TUESDAY, APRIL 19, 1842

Lady Ashton's Divorce

Mr. Willis stated that their lordships would bear in mind that this matter had been adjourned on the former occasion for the purpose of enabling the petitioner to produce further evidence. He now proposed to call Mr. John Wood, an apprentice solicitor who shared lodgings with Lord Ashton in London. He has known Lord Ashton for two years and was well acquainted with him.

Mr. Wood stated that on or about February 9 of this year, he had returned to his lodgings at about four in the afternoon to find that Lord Ashton had brought a woman to his rooms. His lordship appeared surprised to see him when he came out and was in a state of undress, with his shirt half-buttoned and without any coat or cravat on.

Lord Esterhazy—Was the woman in a likewise state?

The witness replied that he had not seen her undressed, but had heard her voice inside his lordship's rooms with the door shut. They both were whispering as if they did not wish to be discovered, and he considered their behavior quite improper.

Lord Esterhazy—Could it have been a maid inside?

The witness said he knew the maid's voice well, as well as the voice of the landlady, and that he was quite sure it was neither of them. There were no other women who would have any cause to be in the house. Lord Ashton remained in his bedroom with this woman for another three or four hours, and they had not yet emerged when Mr. Wood was called downstairs to attend some business. He then looked through the window and observed the lady outside, departing the house. He believed her to be Miss Cordelia Danby, whom he had seen once before in attendance at the theater. Miss Danby had also been writing letters to Lord Ashton for some time before this event.

This concluded the petitioner's evidence.

The Lord Chancellor, in moving the bill be read a second time, adverted to the want of sufficient diligence on the part of the petitioner. However, the fact of Lord Ashton's gross profligacy and neglect, abandonment of his wife, and of the subsequent adultery has been clearly established and their lordships held the petitioner entitled to relief. The bill was accordingly read a second time and ordered to be committed.

"I simply don't understand what would possess you to do such a thing," Mrs. Danby said. It occurred to Della that she'd uttered similar words on the divan in Jane's sitting room about Hannah Williams not too long ago. Of course, she'd been in tears, while her mother was not. "What will my friends say when they see this? How could you embarrass us this way?"

They were in Della's bedroom, where she'd been eating breakfast before her mother interrupted her, her hair still tied up in paper for curling and a copy of the *Times* in her hand.

"I'm sorry," Della replied numbly. "I never meant to..." She wasn't sure how to finish that sentence. *Cause trouble?* She *had* meant to do that, she just hadn't meant to be caught. Nor to make anyone cross with her. She'd imagined that the worst thing that might happen if she were seen leaving Ashton's lodgings was a stern talking-to, or the creation of a troublesome rumor, not *this*. Not her name printed in the papers, staining the fingertips of every person she'd ever known.

Perhaps she deserved it. Hadn't Ashton told her a hundred times how reckless she'd been?

But why should this Mr. Wood wish to destroy my life? That was the part she couldn't wrap her head around. It wasn't as though Della had ever done anything to hurt him; she didn't even know the man! Why mention her name, when he could just as easily have kept it to himself?

"We'll have to send you away, I suppose." Her mother paced the floor, oblivious to Della's musings. She hadn't asked for them. "Would you prefer France or Belgium? We'll have to hire a companion, unless your aunt Caroline would be willing to take you."

"What are you talking about?" Annabelle's face popped round the doorframe. "Why is Della going away?"

"There's a story about me in the papers." Della motioned to the copy that still lay on the foot of her bed. She felt too tired to explain. Once she'd given her sister a moment to read it and watched her expression wilt in horror, she put on a brave face. "If I pick France, I might become friends with Miss Greenwood in exile. At least I would know someone."

"But that's nonsense!" Annabelle looked from Della to their

mother. "We're not going to abandon Della just because of some... some *busybody* with nothing better to do than print gossip about people with more interesting lives than he has. You can't!"

"Annabelle, this doesn't concern you." Mrs. Danby spoke through tight lips. "If your sister didn't want this to happen, then she should've thought of that before she snuck off to a strange man's house in the middle of the night."

"It wasn't the middle of the night," Della couldn't stop herself from pointing out. "I was there all day and evening; it's only that no one noticed I was gone except for Annabelle."

And Ashton. He'd worried over how long she'd been away, while she'd laughed it off. How different everything looked now.

"What are you saying?" Mrs. Danby drew up in offense. She certainly hadn't been happy at the outset of this conversation, but there hadn't been any real anger in her voice either. Until now. "That this is somehow *my* fault? For heaven's sake, Della, you're six-and-twenty. I thought you had enough sense to keep yourself out of trouble."

"You're right," Della conceded. "I'm sorry I've embarrassed you. But I do wish you'd asked about me once in a while."

Her mother's face went pink and splotchy. "Of course I ask about you! I'm right here anytime you want to talk to me. Why do you make it sound as though I've done something wrong?"

How can I answer that? There was no point in upsetting her mother any further, especially when she'd already caused so much grief. But it hurt all the same, to think of all the times she'd been left to handle things on her own even when she might still have needed a little help. And when she'd gotten it wrong, she was to be sent away.

For you to manage your own lives. Well, she hadn't managed her own life very well, now had she? And soon she would be utterly alone.

A knocking and the sound of footfalls downstairs told Della that someone was on their doorstep. A moment later, their butler stood respectfully in the hall outside her room and announced that Miss Chatterjee and Mrs. Williams were downstairs asking for Della.

"Why should they call at this hour?" Mrs. Danby asked, indignant. "It's far too early. Tell them we're still having breakfast."

"No," Della cut in. "Please let me see them, Mama. I only need a minute to get dressed."

Mrs. Danby shook her head and sighed, looking exasperated. "I suppose it can't make things any worse. We'll finish talking about this after my hair is curled."

Once their mother had gone, Della rang for her maid and got dressed as quickly as she could manage. Her sister stayed by her side even once she'd gone downstairs to meet her guests. Della didn't have the heart to send her away. Annabelle seemed more upset about her fate than she did.

As it turned out, Reva and Jane were equally distraught. They both looked as if they'd been crying. *Don't worry*, Della wanted to say. *I'm fine. See?*

But she couldn't bring herself to do it. They might think her delusional.

"We saw what they've written about you." Jane swept her into a tight hug. "You mustn't panic. We'll find a way to sort this out."

"I'm not panicking," Della assured her, the words muffled by Jane's shoulder.

Her friend released her and gave her a once-over. "No, I suppose you aren't. How are you so calm?"

"I'm not sure," Della admitted. "I suppose it doesn't feel quite real yet." The fact that she'd only had ten minutes to contemplate her fate since her mother stormed in with the *Times* this morning probably had something to do with it. No doubt she would fall apart later.

"You should sue the papers for defamation," Reva suggested. "Make them print a retraction."

"Oh, *there's* an idea," said Annabelle excitedly. "That's just the thing. Mount a counterattack."

"Do we know any barristers?"

"Maybe Mr. Bhattacharya could help..."

Watching them, Della was overcome by a wistful regret. *Look at them all.* Their plan was doomed, of course—she'd done everything Mr. Wood had claimed, and no amount of strategizing could erase that—but she loved them for trying. Had Della believed that she was alone a moment ago? How maudlin she'd been. She wasn't alone. Everyone she loved most was right here with her.

All except one.

"Della?" Jane was watching her hesitantly. "I wish you would say something. You're making me nervous."

"Don't be. I'm happy you both came." Della smiled gently. In the days ahead, there wouldn't be many who stood by her side. She drew a long breath. "It's kind of you to want to help, but I'm not going to sue the papers."

"But—"

"It's all true," she said firmly. This produced an uncomfortable silence, which Della moved to fill before anyone could come up with another misguided idea for her salvation. "I'd like for us to talk about the club for a moment, if you please. This isn't how I would have chosen to leave, but you must see that I won't help business by staying on. Can you and Cecily manage without me? Do you need help finding a replacement?"

Jane bit her lip. Though she couldn't bring herself to agree with Della's frank assessment, she must not have another solution at ready.

"I could help?" Annabelle's voice crept up at the end, more of a question than an offer.

She'd made that proposal months ago on the Waterloo Bridge

and Della had scoffed, but a great deal had changed since then. She wouldn't be so quick to dismiss a helping hand now.

"That's perfect," Della assured her. "I don't want Jane to have to worry about buying out my share right now, and you could exercise my powers as co-owner in my place, at least for the time being. If that's all right with you, Jane?"

"I—" Jane swallowed, looking uncharacteristically lost. "Of course I'm grateful to you." She nodded toward Annabelle before turning back to Della. "But what do you plan to *do*?"

It wasn't easy to say the words that would hurt them. Della took a moment to enjoy the sight first. Her sister and her two dearest friends, all together with her.

She was going to miss them.

"Mama wants to send me to the continent for a little while—"

"Which is *completely* unfair," Anabelle interrupted.

"And I've decided to agree."

"What?" Her sister whirled on her. "You can't mean it!"

"It will give things time to blow over. For people to forget." She took Annabelle by the shoulders and gave her a squeeze. "I know you shall be utterly lost without me, but you must be strong. At least Bishop's will keep you busy."

Annabelle rolled her eyes. A small victory.

"But you *will* come back?" Jane asked, biting her lip.

"Eventually." How long would it take before her name wasn't a blight? Before she might hope to be accepted in polite company again? A year or two, at the least. But no, she wouldn't dwell on the things she had no power to change. Della clapped her hands briskly. "There's no need for such long faces! I'm not going to Siberia. I expect you'll change your tunes when I send you copies of all the latest fashion plates from Paris. Now that I'm publicly ruined, I've decided to spend my dowry on clothes."

No one laughed at her joke, which was really quite rude of them. She deserved some credit for her efforts to keep up good cheer.

"I know you'll miss me," Della conceded. "But you can always visit if the need arises. For right now, I need you to try not to be too upset. I'm trying to make the best of a bad situation, and it would help me enormously to know that all of you will be all right."

Reva was the first to respond. She held Della's gaze as she offered a smile. Slightly strained, perhaps, but the affection in it was real. "You will write to us often, I trust. I might take you up on the invitation to visit if I can arrange for a honeymoon in France."

"Good." Della nodded approvingly.

Annabelle was next. "It's just like you to run off to the other side of the channel the minute you put me in charge of your share of the club. Don't be cross with me if I do everything differently than you would have."

"I'll let Jane be cross with you for both of us. But I'm not leaving tomorrow, you know. I'll have time to give you advice before I go."

"Who's to say I need your advice?" Annabelle retorted, prompting Della to elbow her in the ribs.

Only Jane stood silent. Her lower lip quivered dangerously. "I don't much like the thought of you going off all on your own."

"I won't be alone," Della assured her. "I've decided that Lord Ashton should accompany me, if he'll agree to it."

Three pairs of eyes widened. Reva gave a little gasp.

"After all this?" Jane asked.

"Everyone already thinks I'm his mistress," Della pointed out. "The damage is done. I may as well enjoy some benefit from it."

"But—"

"I love him," Della said firmly. "And I've spent every day since I met him trying to fight any attachment and keep my feelings a secret and worrying about what other people might suspect. Now that everything is out in the open, it would be so lovely to just...stop. To enjoy each other's company in a place where no one knows us and we don't have to worry about any of that."

Now Della understood why she wasn't in more of a panic over the news this morning. Despite the fact that her good name was ruined, she felt *free*. There would be no more lies. No more wondering what might have been if only things were different. If Ashton truly wanted to be with her, there would be nothing to hold him back. And if he didn't...well, it would break her heart, but at least she would know that she'd tried.

What must he be feeling now? He wouldn't see things the same way; that much was certain. He'd always been so worried that this would happen—that she would be hurt by his past. For him, it must be a nightmare come to life.

She had to go to him. To show him that she was safe and whole and didn't blame him for what had happened. He must be in so much pain.

"I need to see him," Della explained. "You must excuse me. Thank you again for coming. And don't worry, I'll come to see you again before I leave London."

She was halfway to the door when Jane's voice stopped her. "Della."

She turned around, expecting that her friend might try to reason with her. After all, that was what they did. Della came up with reckless ideas, and Jane brought her back down to earth. And this was a reckless idea if ever there was one. But Jane merely smiled. Her eyes were soft with unshed tears as she said, "Good luck."

"*Wood!* Are you in there?" Lyman pounded on the door to the little snake's room, but there was no answer. "You can't hide forever."

He was going to murder the bastard once he got his hands on him. What the hell was he playing at, mentioning Della's name? Lyman hadn't attended the proceedings before the House, but he read the summaries in the papers every day. Nothing could have prepared him for the words that had greeted him this morning.

"Wood!" he called again, trying the knob this time. It was unlocked. Lyman pushed it open to reveal an empty room. It wasn't only its occupant that was missing, but all of his things. The bookcase stood empty; the wardrobe gaped open, the hangers inside bare and tinkling against each other in the gust of air he'd stirred up when he flung open the door.

What the hell?

The coward must have made his escape in the night, before Lyman could learn what he'd done. Where had he gone? There must be some clue.

He stalked inside and began rifling through the desk drawers, looking for anything that Wood had left behind.

"He isn't here." Lyman jumped at the sound of Clarkson's baritone. He stood in the doorframe, observing the scene with an expression of mild concern. "He informed Mr. Hirsch yesterday that he was terminating his apprenticeship. Said he'd found a new benefactor and an opportunity more in keeping with his skill." Clarkson placed a dry emphasis on this last word, his thoughts on the subject clear.

"Michael." That made *two* people who needed to answer for this. "Where did he say he was going?"

"He didn't. He just paid up his last month's rent and left."

Lyman muttered an oath. It made perfect sense. Ellen and Michael had needed more evidence to get their bill through the House, and Wood had no doubt enjoyed the banknotes they'd lined his pockets with, plus whatever position they'd secured him with someone higher up the social ladder than Mr. Hirsch.

If he tore up every town house in Mayfair, he would find his brother-in-law soon enough, but Wood could be anywhere by now. Still, Michael must have some idea where his newest lackey had gone.

"I saw the story in the papers," Clarkson continued. "I'm sorry."

"I need to find him," Lyman ground out, shoving the desk drawer closed with a rough motion. There was nothing useful here. He was wasting precious time.

"And do what?" Clarkson asked carefully. "Rip his skin from his bones?"

"It would be a start."

The man had trampled Della's good name in the mud, had dragged her into this for no better reason than to earn a few pounds and advance his own station, if Lyman's suspicions were correct. He'd *ruined* her. He had to answer for it.

Lyman stalked past Clarkson and down the hall to his own rooms, where he fetched his gloves and coat.

"Might we take a moment to talk this over before you rush off?" his friend called after his receding back.

"There's nothing to talk about. He can't get away with this."

"Wood is a worthless little shit," Clarkson conceded. "But what do you plan to do, murder him? Then you'll be thrown in jail, which isn't likely to improve anything."

Lyman crammed his hat atop his head, pausing a moment to think this over.

A gentleman doesn't resort to his fists, he could hear his father say. *He solves his problems with civility.* He'd tried to obey this advice all his life, but he'd never been tested like this before. His blood was pounding in his ears. The familiar sight of his lodgings receded in a red haze. The only thing he understood was that he *had* to fix this before it was too late.

"I'll make him recant his testimony," Lyman said, seizing hold of the idea with a grim sense of triumph. That was it. There was no way to make the public unsee the story, but he could still discredit its source. Make it clear that James Wood was a bitter, petty little man willing to do anything to advance his station.

"How are you going to do that?"

"I'm confident that I can find the means to persuade him." Thus far, Lyman hadn't pushed back. He'd let them say whatever they wanted, do whatever they wanted, all while telling himself that it was the only form of atonement he could offer. But this crossed a line.

If he threatened to fight the divorce, to thwart their efforts before Parliament, he might persuade Michael to withdraw whatever patronage he'd offered Wood in exchange for his testimony. Once the man found himself without protection, he wouldn't be so brave. Exert a little pressure and he would bend like the coward he was.

"But the hearings are already over," Clarkson pointed out. "It's too late for him to recant."

"Before the House of Lords, maybe. But the bill still has to pass through the Lower House and get royal assent before it's final. It's not too late to change things."

It *couldn't* be too late. He couldn't let himself think about what it would mean if this was final. If Della's name was forever linked with his in a sordid scandal.

What would become of her then?

Lyman gulped in a large breath. There didn't seem to be enough air in the room.

"Ashton…" The pity in Clarkson's voice was like a vise squeezing his skull. "You know as well as I do the House of Commons isn't going to oppose the bill now that it's passed the House of Lords. The matter is done."

"It's *not* done." Lyman caught himself shouting at Clarkson. "I have to do something. Otherwise—"

He couldn't bring himself to finish the thought. Otherwise what? He would have ruined Della. Not Wood, *him*. If he hadn't invited her back to his lodgings that day, if he hadn't been so swept up in his own selfish desire that he'd abandoned all the rules that held him in check, she would never have been exposed.

Lyman sat down with a heavy thud and buried his face in his hands, the little settee in his room giving a creak of protest that echoed his misery. There had to be something else he could do. If he could only think straight, he would see it. This couldn't be how things ended.

A knock at the door made him jump to his feet, but Clarkson pressed a firm hand on his shoulder. "I'll get it. Wood's not likely to come back here. Take a minute to cool your head."

Impossible. Lyman's thoughts wouldn't stop spinning. He heard murmured voices at the door, but he couldn't understand any of the words, either because they were too far from him or because he was too far from his senses. All he could think about was that there must be some way to make all of this a dream, to turn back time and do things differently. When Clarkson's footsteps came back toward him, alone, he couldn't summon the energy to look up.

"Ashton." The gentle voice that called his name wasn't Clarkson, but Della. Lyman whipped his head up. He must be hallucinating. Why would she come now?

She should hate him, after what had happened. He tried to say as much, but his tongue stubbornly refused to obey.

"I—" That was as far as he could get. Nothing more would follow.

"I know." Della crossed the room and took him into her arms. She felt reassuringly steady, though she only came up to his shoulder. "It's all right. I know."

"I'm so sorry. I never meant for—"

"I know," she repeated. "It isn't your fault. Let's not do any of the part where you blame yourself or tell me I need to go or any of that, all right? We're past it now. Let's just talk a while."

"How can you say it isn't my fault?"

"Because it *isn't*." Della released him only long enough to set him at arm's length and meet his eye, her gaze firm. "I made my own decisions, and I'm responsible for them. Besides which, *you* weren't the one who went spreading my name around. Mr. Wood bears the blame for that part."

"He's run off to hide somewhere, but I'll find him," Lyman promised. It was important that she know he wouldn't let this pass.

But Della brushed off his vow even more easily than she had his guilt. "There's no need for that. What's done is done. I wouldn't want you to get yourself in any trouble on my account."

How could she be so nonchalant? Hadn't she read what the papers had written about her? "I'm surprised you're so calm," he said warily.

"Why, because you expected me to fall apart?" Della cocked her head to one side, her tone somewhere between sadness and teasing. "I was meant to come around to your way of thinking and conclude that I should have lived my life following the rules and be overcome with regret. Is that it?"

"But don't you regret it? You must. This will ruin your life, Della."

"It won't ruin anything unless I let it," she shot back fiercely. "What can they do to me, decide I'm not welcome at their parties anymore? Fine. I'll be cut. My real friends will stand by me. I don't much care if my circle becomes smaller, so long as the people who matter are still there."

This was so unexpected that Lyman could scarcely wrap his head around it. "But your friends will be cut too, if they continue to associate with you—"

"Hush," she interrupted. "I'm not ignorant of the dangers. That's why I've decided to go away for a little while to let the talk die down.

I can come back in a year or two, once the ton has turned its attention to other things. I've always wanted to see the continent, so it won't be a true hardship for me."

She said it so matter-of-factly, she might have been discussing plans for a holiday rather than an exile.

Della slipped her hand into Lyman's palm as she added shyly, "I was hoping you might come with me."

"Pardon?" He must have misheard her. They'd been publicly accused of adultery. If they ran away together now, they would be acknowledging the truth of the story for the whole world to see.

But Della continued, "I'd much rather travel with a companion than travel alone, and I don't want to have to hire some strange woman for it. You'd be doing me a favor." She flashed her mischievous smile, bringing an ache to Lyman's heart. How long had it been since he'd seen it? He hadn't expected it to survive this disaster. "If you insist on blaming yourself for what's happened even though I've told you there's no need, you could even consider this your atonement."

"But—" Lyman let his thought die unfinished. None of this was supposed to happen. Della was supposed to hate him. She was supposed to cut ties with him forever, not shrug her shoulders and invite him on a holiday. That was what happened when you did something this terrible.

Could he really accept? It must be wrong, to benefit from such a mistake.

"I was thinking of Paris," she babbled on happily, growing animated at her plan. It was just like the early days of their acquaintance, watching her follow the spark of a new idea. The sight was a familiar comfort. "But we could travel around if you'd like to see other places. Think how nice it would be, not to have anyone know us. There wouldn't be any gossip to worry about. We could even use other names, if you like."

The portrait she painted was seductive. Attending the theater or strolling down a busy street with Della on his arm, never worrying who might see them or what they might think.

"What about your club?"

"I've already stepped back in the last few months. Annabelle will exercise my rights as co-owner while I'm away."

"And after that?" Lyman couldn't help but ask. He didn't want to dictate what Della did with her time, but he needed to know what he was risking if they took up with each other again. As much as he'd missed her company, there were some things he couldn't do.

She seemed to understand his fear, for she was solemn as she answered. "I understand why it's a problem for you, but you don't need to worry. I don't plan to come back to Bishop's. Even aside from this"—Della made a vague gesture with her palm that encompassed everything from the story in the paper to their too-brief affaire—"my feelings about what we do have changed. I'd like to give it some time to see how Annabelle and Cecily fare without me, but I intend to transfer my ownership once it can be done without causing Jane too much hardship."

"You won't regret it later?" He didn't want to entwine their futures, only to discover Della wanted to return to her old endeavors in a year or two.

"No." She spoke with conviction. "What I loved was building something with Jane. Helping her to make a place in the world. But Bishop's isn't *for* me, not really. It's time to move on."

It was as if a weight had been lifted from Lyman's chest. He'd grown so used to thinking of Della as impossible and beyond his reach, it was hard to imagine that might not be so. That they might really have a chance for a future together. His wife's bill wouldn't receive royal assent for some time yet, but it would come. And most of Europe had a more tolerant attitude toward divorce than England.

Once he was free, he might marry her, if they wished it. The possibility was dizzying. He hadn't thought he would ever be in this position again. Truth be told, he was more than a little frightened by it.

But she isn't asking me for that. Della was a different woman than Ellen, and he was a different man than he'd once been. Perhaps they would find the time to discover whether they might fit together, once they had the freedom to explore.

"I can't afford to travel in luxury anymore," he warned her, well aware that he'd begun to think about her invitation in terms of *when* and *how* instead of *if.*

"Oh, don't worry about that." Della laughed. "I have my own money. I'd be paying for my accommodations anyway, and if you refuse me, then I'll have to pay for a companion, as I said, so it really wouldn't be any imposition to put you up."

"Am I to be your kept man?" He raised an eyebrow. "I'm not sure how I feel about that."

"Well..." A faint blush of pink dusted her cheeks. "It wouldn't need to be that way. I was thinking, what if we wrote a guidebook to Paris, or wherever else we might choose to go? We made an excellent team. And then you'd still have an income. I finished my book, by the way. I meant to give you a copy to look over before I turn it in to Mr. Armstrong, but with all the excitement this morning, I forgot it at home. You don't suppose he'll want to renege on our agreement now that my name's been tarnished, do you? It was supposed to be anonymously published anyway." Della bit her lip.

"I doubt it," he reassured her. "What Armstrong cares most about is whether the book will turn a profit. We'll go see him together to talk it over."

"Does this mean I've convinced you?" A bright smile broke through Della's worry. "Are you really coming with me?"

The emotion that surged in his chest was sharp and poignant.

Something very near to heartbreak—that familiar sense that he might shatter her smile if he got too close. But it was tempered by something else now: an understanding that Della was a good deal stronger than he'd given her credit for. After all, hadn't the worst thing he'd imagined already happened? And they were still here.

He wasn't sure the fear would ever vanish completely, but for the first time, it seemed possible that it might not dictate his every choice. Not this choice, at least.

"I suppose." Lyman cleared his throat, for it was suddenly tight. "I can't very well let you roam through France on your own, can I? Who would keep you out of trouble?"

Della gave a little shriek, throwing her arms around Lyman's neck. "You're going to love it! You'll see. We'll have so much fun together. I can't wait."

When she pressed his lips to his, he tasted hope.

One

1839

LIEUTENANT ELEAZAR WILLIAMS WAS RESURRECTED ON A Sunday—which, though fitting, proved terribly inconvenient for his family.

The Williamses were just getting ready to attend church (where, it so happened, they intended to light a candle for their departed son, now some two years in his watery grave), when their butler announced a visitor.

"It's the young Mister Williams!" he gasped, his face white. "Returned to us!"

This statement produced some confusion, for Eli's younger brother was away on his grand tour, and therefore a more likely candidate for an unexpected return.

"But he's just reached Rome," protested Mrs. Williams. "Why should he have come home now?"

"Not Jacob, ma'am," the servant amended. "Eleazar."

At that moment, Eli himself walked into the room, looking nothing like a man long-drowned. He was breathing, his flesh was a healthy tan, and he wasn't even wet.

"Hello," said Eli.

Mrs. Williams screamed and fell into a dead faint. Her daughter barely managed to catch her before she hit the ground. With a stagger and a grunt, she tipped her mother toward the settee. Hannah was a sturdy girl.

"Good God!" cried Mr. Williams. "We thought you had drowned."

"No," replied Eli. "Terribly sorry to have frightened you."

Needless to say, no one made it to church that morning.

"The most important thing," Jane Bishop began, with an earnest look to the pair of ladies before her, "is never to wager more than you're prepared to lose. Both in life and in card play."

It might seem self-evident, but a remarkable number of people couldn't grasp this principle. They left more than they could afford on the table, or took risks with their hearts or their reputations that no sensible person would counsel. Not Jane, though. She knew exactly what her odds in life were (poor, especially in the financial sense), and how to best safeguard against future risk (don't play a losing game). It had served her well thus far.

"Wait a minute." Miss Reva Chatterjee frowned and tilted her head, her long lashes shadowing her dark eyes. She was several years younger than Jane, and spoke with the sort of innocence only a debutant could muster. "I thought you said the most important thing was to always hold if you reach seventeen."

"No, no, I said you must always hold if you reach *nineteen*. If you have seventeen, it depends on the other players and whether you have an ace or not. If you memorize my chart, you'll see how it all works."

Another thing most people didn't seem to understand was that gambling wasn't actually a risk if you understood maths. At least, not for the house.

Miss Chatterjee shot an uneasy look to the large piece of foolscap on the table between them. Jane had written out every possible combination the dealer might draw relative to the players and indicated where one should hold or seek another card to maximize the chances of winning, shrinking her neat script to the most miniscule proportions to fit everything in. What better way could there be to show their newest helper the ropes? All she needed to do was to follow it perfectly, and profits were guaranteed.

Cordelia Danby—Della to her friends—cleared her throat delicately. "Jane, dear, I thought we agreed that the chart was a bit much to start with and we were just going to focus on the other rules for now." It had been Della's idea to invite Miss Chatterjee to join them this morning.

They'd agreed that they needed to train a third dealer if they were to have any hope of expanding their card club, and Miss Chatterjee was the logical choice. She was a regular member and a trusted friend of Della's, but she was already starting to look a bit overwhelmed by the vast array of possibilities listed on the page. Jane loved the numbers best, but not everyone shared her enthusiasm. *Oh dear.* Della was going to be cross with her if she scared the poor girl off. They'd managed well enough on their own thus far, but they were starting to have too many guests to continue without help. They needed this to work.

"You're quite right," Jane conceded with a last, regretful glance at her chart. "We can cover that next week. Let's get back to not wagering too much. That was the part I wanted to tell you about. It isn't just yourself you need to keep in check, it's the guests as well. You'll need to step in if they're being too extravagant."

"But isn't it good if the ladies wager a lot?" Miss Chatterjee shot a hesitant look to Della. "Then we'll win more."

"That's what I've been saying," Della agreed. She had a cherubic face and laughing brown eyes that lit up when she was excited. That, combined with her short, plump figure and high-pitched voice, gave her an almost childlike appearance, though her character was anything but innocent.

"*No.*" Jane pressed her palms to the table. They'd been over this a hundred times. Della might be her dearest friend, but they held opposite views on what constituted an acceptable level of risk. It probably came from being born to such different circumstances. Della had never needed to worry much about how her life would turn out, with her parents as wealthy as they were. "The goal of our card club is to make a steady profit, not a quick one. If we have to explain to an angry father how his daughter came to lose the family rubies over a game of vingt-et-un, we'll be shut down within a week."

Miss Chatterjee considered this a moment before she nodded, and Della wilted a bit at the loss of her ally.

Before Jane could savor the victory, a rap on the door interrupted them.

Drat, not Edmund! I told him I was using the study this morning.

But it wasn't Jane's brother who entered the room a moment later; it was her uncle.

"Good morning." He nodded to their guests. "Jane, darling, I'm so sorry to interrupt your callers, but I'm going out and I simply *must* know what sort of fabric you'd like me to order or we won't have time to make you a new gown for Cecily's rout. You've been putting me off all week."

Jane suppressed a sigh. *Not this again.*

Some people suffered the trials of the matchmaking mamas of the ton, those tenacious, indefatigable creatures who flitted from one ballroom to the next, ensuring the reproduction of the upper classes with only marginal inbreeding. Jane had no such figure in her life. Instead, she was blessed with a matchmaking uncle. Though he might not have seemed the most likely choice for the role, Uncle Bertie had risen to the challenge of conquering the London season with remarkable enthusiasm. Almost—dare one say it—*too* much enthusiasm.

"Thank you, Uncle, but I really don't need anything new." They couldn't afford anything new, truth be told. But Bertie believed that Jane's wardrobe expenses should be dictated by his affection rather than his finances. "I was planning to wear that cream gown with the gold flowers on it."

"*Jane.*" He stomped one foot so sharply it made her jump. "You've worn it twice already. How shall we ever find you a husband if you won't make an effort to look your best?"

Jane risked a glance at Della, who understood her anguish and was trying valiantly not to laugh.

Uncle Bertie followed her gaze, adopting his most inviting tone as he addressed their guests. "Girls, you'd love to go to the modiste together, wouldn't you? Talk some sense into my niece. Wouldn't she look lovely in a new gown?"

"Um." A look of mild panic flitted across Miss Chatterjee's face. She obviously hadn't counted on being thrust into a family squabble when she'd called this morning.

Indeed, Jane had been quite safe from this sort of thing only last year when Cecily was still at home to serve as the center of Bertie's universe. But now that his own daughter was happily married, he had fixed his sights squarely upon his niece.

She loved Uncle Bertie, but being the sole object of his enthusiasm could be a bit exhausting.

"What is it you girls are doing in here, anyway?" Bertie had finally noticed the chart of all the vingt-et-un hands stretched out on the table between them. Jane might have shoved it out of view, had she been a bit quicker, but she couldn't bear to crease the page. She'd worked so hard on it.

"Nothing," she blurted out. "We were just..."

Oh goodness. What feminine pursuit could this giant list of numbers possibly resemble? Calligraphy practice? Dance steps, perhaps?

"It's a ranking system for eligible gentlemen," Della supplied without missing a beat.

How does she come up with these ideas of hers?

Unlike Jane, who never had a fib ready when she needed one, Della's silver tongue was the solution to (or the cause of) many a scrape.

"Beg pardon?" Uncle Bertie drew his graying brows together in confusion. "How would one rank gentlemen?"

"Yes, Della. How *would* one rank gentlemen?" What a thing to choose!

"It's simple, really. You just assign a value for attributes such as income, good manners, temperament, and so forth, and then you add up the total to see if the gentleman in question would be a good match."

Bertie stared at the paper for so long that Jane began to worry he'd seen through their trick. When he finally spoke, there was a hint of disappointment in his tone. "I know one must consider practicalities, but in my day, young people used to hope for a *love* match. Ah, well. I suppose I should be happy you're taking an interest in your future." His index finger traced the first column on the page. "Tell me, which gentleman does this one represent? Who's your best match?"

Oh Lord.

With three seasons behind her already and nothing to show for it but a split sole on her favorite dancing slippers, Jane had all but given up on attracting a husband. Only Bertie's steadfast faith kept her from voicing her thoughts aloud. He'd been so good to her and Edmund after their parents died; surely she could muster a better effort for his sake. But no matter how Jane tried to follow the path that was expected of her, the task proved impossible.

No one wanted an orphaned lady without any dowry for a wife. Much less one who aspired to run a clandestine gambling club.

Even if she could find a gentleman willing to overlook her poverty, marriage would be nothing but a losing game for her—the sort of risk she couldn't afford to take. Without any funds to settle on herself or her future children, she would be entirely dependent on her husband. If he mismanaged his fortune or died unexpectedly, she would be left with nothing all over again, a poor relation shuffled from house to house, forever unwanted.

She couldn't endure that.

Far better to make her own way in life, if Jane could manage it. Once she and Della had earned enough money to prove their club could work, she would explain everything to Bertie and make him understand.

"Er...that's—that's Mr. MacPherson," her friend offered when Jane hesitated too long.

Mr. MacPherson had spoken to Jane for ten minutes after the opera last month, and then danced with her exactly twice the following evening. That had propelled him to the status of her most promising suitor, at least in Uncle Bertie's estimation.

"How lovely!" His mood brightened once more at this news. The prospect of a match always had this effect, no matter how unlikely. "I *did* think he took a particular interest in—Jane, you're frowning. We've talked about this, darling. You cannot afford to wrinkle your brow at three-and-twenty."

"I'm not frowning, that's just my face." Jane sighed, though she endeavored to turn the corners of her mouth upward instead of down. It cost her some effort, given that she was fairly certain her uncle would be on the subject of her future marriage to Mr. MacPherson for the rest of the day, all thanks to Della. There was no chance they would finish preparing Miss Chatterjee now. "Do you know something, Uncle? I've had a change of heart. I believe we *shall* go to the shops this morning."

Acknowledgments

The experience of writing the second book in a series is very different from writing a debut, because you have a deadline and about a hundred extra things to juggle. First and foremost, thank you to my husband and children for their patience and understanding when I needed time to myself to write. I could not have done any of this without you.

Thank you to my wonderful agent Rebecca Strauss for her patience and support in answering my questions as I tried to balance promotion for book one with drafting and editing for books two and three.

As always, I am grateful to the community of writers who have supported me as I navigated the sometimes difficult ups and downs of publishing, especially Liana De la Rosa, Bethany Bennett, and the loon slack. It means so much to me to have your encouragement.

Thank you to everyone at Sourcebooks Casablanca for your work to bring this book to life: my editor Deb Werksman; assistant editor Jocelyn Travis; art director Sarah Brody; design lead Stephanie Rocha; production designer Rosie Gaynor; manufacturing lead Emma Grant; production editor India Hunter; managing editor Heather Hall; and marketing lead Alyssa Garcia. I also consider myself very fortunate to be able to thank the incredibly talented and experienced Alan Ayers for this book's cover, and to have received the most careful and thoughtful edits from Diane Dannenfeldt.

Finally, I'd like to thank you for reading, whether you supported this book by buying a copy or by borrowing it from your local library. I hope you enjoyed it and that you'll come back for book three in this series!

About the Author

Faye Delacour was raised in the Canadian prairies before deciding that she needed a challenge and should move to a place where everybody spoke French. She now lives and works in Montreal with her partner and children, a reformed street cat, and an Australian shepherd who hasn't yet accepted that he can't herd the cat.

Faye writes historical romance featuring strong, feminist heroines and enthusiastic consent.

Website: fayedelacour.com
Instagram: @fayedelacour